TO LUKE, FOR SAVING THIS NOVEL!

Xiene is a work of fiction. Names, characters, places, and incidents are the product of the author's imagination or are used fictitiously. Any resemblance to actual events, locales, or persons, living or dead is entirely coincidental.

2025 Rabbooks Publishing First Edition

ISBN-13: 978-0-9982474-5-8

Book Design and Illustrations by Alex James. © 2025

XIENE!

Alexander G. J.!

ACKNOWLEDGMENTS!

Special thanks to all the people who helped in one way or another, either by inspiration or perspiration, to place this book in your hands.

A special thanks to Luke Neher for his tireless editing and support and for whom this novel would not exist.

CONTENTS!

IN THE BEGINNING!

Atlanta, GA
Friday, November 13, 1992

Allen got off at Five Points Station. Monroe waited on the opposite platform, spacing out. Allen walked casually to the stairs, ran as soon as he was out of view to the other side, and crept up behind his friend.

"Death by mugumba!' he yelled, grabbing Monroe's shoulders.

Monroe pushed backward, away from the train tracks, flailing his arms. When he turned and saw Allen, he burst out laughing.

"You're on the wrong side," Allen said. I told you to be over there."

Monroe's face broadcast he had thought he was on the correct side. "Oh."

Allen had called Monroe Friday night, and they'd decided to spend Saturday taking pictures at Oakland Cemetery, a gothic landscape of giant monuments, stone lions, angel statues, and masterpieces of tombstone architecture covering five blocks of land. Set aside for war heroes, the place felt more ceremonial than scary.

Monroe posed on the head of a statue of a giant lion sleeping with Confederate flags under its paws. Like Allen, Monroe wore black so the two could get better contrast with the black-and-white film. After Allen snapped the shot, they started up the hill where a woman appeared to be breaking into a mausoleum with a crowbar.

"Gee, should we stop her?" Allen asked.

"Why?" Monroe asked.

Good point," *What's she gonna steal?* Allen thought.

The woman opened the door and entered. Monroe and Allen slowly made their way to the entrance and peeked in. Her hands and white hair were all they could make out in the dark room.

"Hello?" Allen said quietly.

She quickly turned around.

"Hi," Monroe said. "Getting close-ups?"

"Oh, shit!" She grabbed her heart. "You assholes scared the fuck out of me!"

"Sorry," Allen added, trying to get a good look at her face.

She held up a camera. "I'm setting up a shot of the stained glass figure in the back window. Keep an eye out for me."

Monroe and Allen stepped outside. *The security guard at the front gate warned us to not take pictures of the insides of mausoleums, now, here we are, acting watchdog to a woman who just broke into one.* Someone grabbed their butts. He and Monroe shrieked and jumped away from the mausoleum. Giggling, the woman came through the door, allowing Allen to get a good look at her: hair completely white and cut in a Prince Valiant bob, a nose ring, crucifix earrings with Jesus miniatures, and black lipstick. Like them, she wore all black and had a trench coat,

"Hi, I'm Xiene."

Allen shook her hand. She was wearing fishnet gloves with finger holes. Her nails were painted black and the index finger had a blue eyeball ring. "Allen, and this is my friend Monroe."

"You guys taking pictures too?"

"Yes," Allen said. *Please let me take your picture.*

"Good. You can help with my next shot." Xiene lead them to a statue of a headless angel. "Here, help me up."

Allen boosted her onto the statue. Her legs dangled off its shoulder and her feet rested on its stomach. She grabbed the headless neck.

"Quick! Take my picture! My camera's ready to go!"

Allen picked up her camera. As he took the picture, the statue's arm fell off, causing her to slip and fall on the ground. Monroe and Allen ran over.

"You all right?" asked Monroe, helping her up.

She was laughing. "Did you get it when the arm fell off?'

"The arm will probably look like it's just floating in midair," Allen answered.

"Yeah! Fucking great!" She brushed herself off.

"Can I get a shot of you?" Allen asked.

"Sure. You gonna pose for me?"

"Sure."

"Nude?"

Is she serious? "Nude?"

"Yeah. You know, butt naked?"

"Er, ah, no."

"Oh well, I'll just have to pose for you fully clothed, then."

Would she really pose nude for me?

At some metal park benches near an old oak tree, she lay down in a dead-person pose. "How's this?"

"Man, I'm not into necrophilia." *Why did I say that?* She laughed and sat up in a very normal position, hands in her lap. Allen framed the shot, but when he clicked, she gave an Elvis sneer. "Could—" He stopped himself from asking to take the shot over. Somehow, he knew she would do something worse the second time.

"Okay, my turn, Alex."

"Allen!"

"Oh, sorry. Sit down."

He sat on the bench in a regular pose, like Xiene's.

"Boring!" she yelled. "Do something interesting!"

He smiled and put his arms in the air.

"Don't smile, you asshole! This is a cemetery!"

He stopped smiling. She took his picture, and made a goofy expression on her face, causing him to smile. She took a second shot. "Great! You know, you have pretty eyes."

What? *Was she being sarcastic, but her face was dead serious.* In that one second, he wanted to know more about this woman, he wanted to peer into her mind and read every thought she was having, and he sensed she was actually a good person, just with a weird sense of humor and a lack of material respect. She looked at him. Her staring without saying a word confirmed his suspicions; they wanted to be in each other's lives and had fallen in love.

"Allen!" Monroe called, breaking up the two's daydreaming.

"What?"

"We better get going. I have to help do inventory at work…" Allen looked at Monroe and without a word, conveyed the message 'I'd rather eat a bowl of maggots than leave right now'. "…But I guess you don't have to come with me," Monroe added. "I'll meet you back at your place."

"Okay. Later, Monroe." Allen waved to Monroe and turned back to Xiene, still staring at him. "What's wrong?" He checked his mouth. "Do I have spinach on my teeth?"

She laughed. "You're funny. You want to go to Peto's Pizza with me?"

"Huh? Sure." *Like I've got better things to do!*

The music at Peto's Pizza was loud, and the rats were bold—Allen watched one scurry from the men's room to the back door. The walls were graffiti-covered, and patrons were more than welcome to add their own. He hadn't heard what Xiene had just said about the graffiti she had added so he gave an 'uh-huh', hoping it would fool her. She continued speaking, indicating it had.

"…and this is my friend, Charles." She pointed to the crude cartoon drawing of a guy with hair in his face like Cousin It.

"He really has hair in his face?"

"No, silly. He's a hippie." Xiene lit up what must have been her third cigarette since sitting down.

An hour ago, Allen could have sworn they'd experienced love at first sight, but now, hearing her talk about her other friends, a strange feeling had crept in that he was just intended as an addition to her extensive collection.

When Xiene waved to someone two booths behind her, Allen snuck a peek at her breast, housed in a lacy black silk top. *What are my odds?* He started estimating: *She has one million friends, it seems. That gives me a 20% chance of getting intimate. She hasn't asked me about myself. That drops it to 10%. No physical contact of any kind, such as hand touching. 5%.*

Xiene tapped his hand. "That's my ex-roommate, Jennifer."

Okay, 10%. "Really? Why did she move out?"

"To live with her boyfriend."

"So you live alone?"

"Yeah."

15%.

"What do you do, Alex?"

"Allen."

"Oh, shit! I'm sorry!"

"I just started working at a T-shirt shop."

She took a drag on her cigarette. "Doing what?".

"I'm an artist."

"Oh, wow. Really? Could you draw my picture?"

Like most artists, Allen hated hearing this question when meeting people, as if he were a walking photocopier. "Now?"

"Sure." She reached into her backpack and pulled out a pen. "Here."

"Ah, there's nothing to draw on."

She yanked a napkin out of the dispenser. "Here. Draw on this."

"Er, I really wish I could do this in the right way."

"That's okay. I'm not expecting a Renoir."

He started sketching. "You like Renoir?"

"I like all artists, even Christo."

"Yeah, I don't know if I can find anything artistic about Saran-draping anything."

"Art is where you look for it." She snuffed out her cigarette.

Allen had got as far as the head shape and hair when a White guy sporting a mohawk and a thin Black woman butted in. While Xiene talked with them, he preoccupied himself by looking around. People at some booths were staring. He wasn't sure if it was at Xiene, in her all-black vampire-looking outfit and her Prince Valiant white hair, or that this popular girl was with Allen. *Sort of like spotting Queen Elizabeth and Benny Hill at a grimy pub.*

Allen's pizza slice—as hard and crusty as always—and Xiene's spinach calzone arrived. Are you a vegetarian? he asked.

"No, I just eat meat every other day, for health reasons."

"You eat it on Fridays?"

"Sure. It's easier when my friends and I get pizza on video night."

"You have a video night?"

"Hell, yeah. You can come if you want."

"Alright." *Just another friend for her collection.* "Who was that guy?"

"Why? Are you jealous?"

He laughed nervously. "No."

"Bummer."

"Why?"

"That was Mark. We used to go out," she answered, avoiding Allen's why question. "It didn't work."

"Why not?"

"Let's just say I'm a little hard to be friends with."

"You don't seem like it," he lied.

"Bullshit. You don't know me very well, do you?"

'I just met you."

"Oh, where's my picture?"

Allen looked around. Xiene was wiping her mouth and hands with it. "Er, right there."

She slowly unwrapped the sauce-stained, more mess than a masterpiece. "Oh shit! Oh, god I'm sorry, Alex."

"Allen!" *Now I'm getting pissed.*

"Allen, Allen, Allen! I can't help it. You remind me of my best friend in college, Alex."

"You went to school? Where?"

"GSU."

Allen's opinion of her rose a little. He had been sure she was a high school dropout, ex-Hell's Angel mama.

"Here." She took out another pen and started writing on her left forearm. He recognized it as a Sharpie, a permanent marker that would take a lot of scrubbing to remove. "A-L-L-E-N There, now I won't ever forget. Now you."

"What?"

"Give me your arm."

Reluctantly, he stretched out his left hand. Xiene grabbed it and started writing up his forearm. Normally, knowing about the permanent pen, Allen would not let anyone do this, but she was holding his hand, and as little skin contact as there was, due to her fishnet gloves and eyeball rings, it still caused his heart to race. *I wonderer what color her hair used to be? What would happen if she kissed me wearing that black lipstick? What does 'Xiene' mean?*

She finished writing. "Ooh, what a big heart line you have." She bent his fingers back a little. "See?" she fingered his top palm. "Not a bad head line, either. Hmm. You have a big break in your lifeline."

"Really? Something bad's gonna happen?"

"That's okay, it gets stronger after that."

"Great. I die a happy old man."

She let go and he read what she wrote: 'Without pain, without doubt, without emotions, who are the humans?' Not what he'd expected. "Rather esoteric, isn't it?"

She lit a cigarette.

"So, why do I remind you of this Alex guy?"

"You both try to hide your true feelings." She exhaled some smoke.

"I do not. I'm quite up front."

"Naw. You have a wall six feet high between us."

"I don't know you. I'm not going to completely open up, no more than I expect you to."

"I hate the bullshit games you have to play when you meet new friends. 'Do they like me?', 'Are they crazy?', 'Am I gonna get laid?'." She sipped her soda.

"I usually base friends on their mistakes,"

"That's terrible."

"Not really. It's like this: If they do three major things to me and I can still be friends with them, then I'll probably be friends with them forever. If not, then I drop them down to acquaintance level."

"What am I?"

"You? You're a girl I just met and have no idea about."

"What do you think so far?"

Allen grew nervous. *This girl is extremely confrontational.* "Er, ah, a little upfront, aren't you? I haven't known you that long."

"Doesn't matter. When you meet someone, it takes five seconds to make an impression and six months to change it."

"No way."

"I was studying sociology. I should know."

"That your major?"

"That, and photography."

Allen's eyes lit up. She had just gained 25 points for being creative.

After an hour of discussing art, photography, and related school stories, Xiene held up her hand. "Okay, you've had plenty of time, so I'll ask you again: what do you think of me?"

"Um, check, please."

"Oh, that bad, huh?"

"No. I'm just kidding. I don't like being put on the spot."

"Hey, if you don't like me, just go ahead and tell me so I can stop whatever we're trying to start."

This statement shot anxiety to Allen's stomach. He took it apart. *Is she trying to start a friendship or a relationship? If it's a friendship, why didn't she say so?*

"Dude?" she said, stopping his daydreaming.

"I don't know. I'd rather not discuss these things when I first meet people."

"All right. I'll tell you what I think of you."

"I'd rather not know, thank you."

She stared, tapping a finger on the tabletop. "You can always leave."

Allen remained seated. She smiled, then lit another cigarette. "You're conservative."

"No, I'm—"

"In your lifestyle. Politically, you're more left. You're a Catholic, aren't you?"

"Yes. How did you know?"

"You seem like you'd be better at discussing your problems over the phone than in person."

"So, what does that have to do with anything?"

"Confessionals. You know, the priest behind the wall and shit."

"Shit is right."

"You're also very skeptical. I bet someone needs to put things in writing for you to believe them. Words mean nothing to you, which suggests you've never heard 'I love you' in a relationship." *Dead on!* "This means you've never had a long-lasting relationship, or if you did, you haven't gotten over it. Underneath, you're a very passionate person. You probably like sex, a lot. I guess that also comes from being Catholic. You like art, probably because you use it as a pacifier."

"What?"

"You know, something that gives you security, that you can predict the outcome of, that won't break your heart. You're looking to change your drab lifestyle and spark things up. You probably find me exciting, and that's why you're here with me, but you can't figure out what I want."

"What do you want?"

"I want to finish my calzone and go home." Half of her calzone was finished already.

"I'm sorry if I'm keeping you here."

"You're not. The calzone is."

Allen felt insulted. It was as though, having gotten categorized, he had no other use. He was nothing but a dinner date or another tack on her friendship wall. Again and again, while they ate in silence, Allen's mind went over what she'd said. She had seemed quite accurate, but first impressions couldn't all be true. If someone kissed you on a first meeting, and then the next day punched you in the face, your five-second impression would change instantly, not over six months. *Why am I so angry at her?* As he stewed, he remembered what his roommate Brandon once told him: 'We always dislike the most in other people what we don't like in ourselves.' *What nerves is she hitting?*

A girl wearing a torn-up jean outfit with various patches asked Xiene for a cigarette. Yet another conversation started and, of course, before it was over, the girl had been invited to video night.

"All right. Later, Xiene," the girl said, departing.

"Who was she?"

"That's C.J." Xiene put her keys in her purse, offering no other information. She checked her watch less arm, "Allen, I'm heading out. I got about a million things to do, so I guess I'll see you around." She smiled and headed off.

He felt like a cheap whore. *Goddamnit! What happened? Just because I won't open up, she thinks I hate her or something. What does she want? What a waste of time. I'm pissed!* He refused to let it end there. If he got anything out of this meeting, it would be to tell her off.

He ran outside. Xiene had already made it across the street. Her trench coat was flapping behind her like a cape, her boots clopped on the parking lot.

"Xiene!" he yelled.

She turned. "What?"

Think, man, think. You need an excuse to chase her down. He rolled up his coat sleeve. "Did you write this poem?"

"Yeah."

He looked at her. Dead silence. She was waiting for him to say something. "It's very good."

"Thanks."

Allen shuffled around. "So, when is your video night?"

"Friday."

"Can I come?"

"If you want."

He looked up from his shoes. "I would really like to."

The wind blew her hair into her face. She brushed it away. "I would like to see you there."

"Okay. What's your phone number?"

She pulled out her Sharpie. "Stick out your arm."

"Tell you what." He took his business card out of his wallet. "Just write it on the back of this."

She studied it. "Allen J. Montgomery. Illustrations, cartoons, airbrush, graphics. Cool. What's the rabbit logo for?"

"It's a long story." She looked up at him as if he had refused to open up again. "I'll tell you later."

"Okay." She wrote her number down and handed the card back.

"Great. I'll call you and get instructions."

"Sounds fine. I'll see you, Allen. Bye."

Allen reached out his hand. She looked at it and stuck out hers. *Take a chance,* something told him. He moved in and gave her a quick, polite hug. When he pulled away she was smiling. "I'll see you," he said, proud of his accomplishment.

"Okay. Hey! You need a ride anywhere?"

"I live kind of far away."

"That's okay. I can get you to a MARTA station. Will that help?"

"Sure! Great!"

"Hop in."

Xiene got into the driver's side of the VW van. She unlocked the door and tossed various items from the passenger seat into the back. Allen got in, knowing this really was the beginning of the ride.

DAMNED CELEBRITY!

1994

Before it closed and moved to Neopolitan in 1997, the Acid Pit was inside an old warehouse located on Moreland Avenue in Atlanta, Georgia. When it first became the Acid Pit, they put in a bar, lights, props, and speakers. Everything else remained the same. Allen liked going there on Industrial Music Night when they would play everything from Euro Dance, to some guy screaming onstage, accompanied by a slide show of pigs fucking.

They were going to Punk Night. He hated Punk Night almost as much as Mohawk Night.

"You know, no one gets in without a mohawk," said the guy at the entrance. Allen, because of his friendship with Xiene, usually got into a lot of clubs for free. 'The little darling of the clubs,' he called her. The crowd outside the warehouse indicated the place was still in its zenith. All of the other clubs suffered from yuppie disease. It worked in cycles: First, the punks, bikers, and scum show up, then the artist, and homosexuals, the punk fashion plates, and then the frat types, signaling the end is starting. When you find a newspaper with William F. Buckley, Jr. on the cover, you might as well burn the place down and collect the insurance money.

Xiene and Allen waited in line behind a large blonde girl in a farm dress and leather jacket. The girl took a puff on her cigarette and looked at Allen. *Yes, I know it's Punk Night,* thought Allen. *I don't have a mohawk, a skinhead, an earring, makeup, or a bad disposition. Cut me some slack. At least I'm wearing black. Hey! That rhymes!*

The girl with half-open black mascaraed eyes turned back around. Allen looked at Xiene. She had on long black Spandex, no socks, black ballet shoes, a black T-shirt with the word Ministry in white letters, and her thick, black leather jacket with a painting of James Dean on the back. She finished her cigarette, threw it down, and snuffed it out.

"Oh, just throw your trash on the ground," Allen said in a snippy voice.

"Fuck you," she said, turning to see the people behind them.

"Hey!" a guy behind them said.

He looks like Elvis on crack, Allen thought.

Xiene turned around and hugged the guy..

"Hi, howya been?" she said. Turning to his companion, she recognized her. "Hi. How ya been?" she turned to hug the girl dressed like Xiene.

Somebody behind them looked around Elvis On Crack. "Hey, Xienna!"

"Buddy!" she walked around the precious couple and hugged the chubby guy with thick glasses and a Mellow Mushroom T-shirt.

This went on for the entire time it took to get to the entrance of the Acid Pit. Allen counted. She must have known ten people in the line. Bored without Xiene standing next to him, Allen picked a flyer off the ground to see the group list for the night. The blue flyer had a shot of an elephant skeleton saying, with a word balloon, 'I fell in the Acid Pit, and I feel much better!' The groups, except for one, were unknown to Allen. Uncle Fester, he remembered, was Kail's group. Someone grabbed Allen's butt. Quickly turning, he saw Xiene with a grin on her face.

"Where's your friend?" Allen said, noticing they were very close to the door and would have to pay soon.

"There he is." Xiene pointed.

Kail came from the bar. Studying him, Allen finally figured out who he looked like: a young Warren Beatty with spiky bangs. He walked up to Xiene. She hugged him and kissed him on the cheek.

Grrrr, Allen said inside.

"Kail, you remember Allen." Xiene gestured to Allen.

"Hey," he said, sticking out his hand in a leather glove. Allen shook it and put his hands back in his denim jacket. "Sorry, I'm late. I had to work late at the restaurant," Kail explained to Xiene.

"Are you a waiter?" Allen asked, picturing this punky, stocky Warren Beatty saying, 'Give me your order or die!'

"No, I'm a chef."

"He's been one for years. He's very good," Xiene added.

As they walked under the wrecked 1957 Chevrolet over the entrance, Xiene and Kail talked about subjects and people Allen had no idea about. Now and then, Kail would make a joke, causing Xiene to grab his arm and laugh.

Grrrr!

They walked past the bouncers at the front after Kail nodded to them. The one who looked like Santa Clause with muscles and a greying mohawk smirked at Allen as he passed.

Yes, I know. I don't look radical enough. So sue me!

They walked down the hallway, which must have been designed by 'Alien' artist H.R. Giger. Intestines, faces, wires, machinery, and scenes of Hell filled the walls.

Xiene and Kail walked in front of Allen into the strobe light and fog coming from the second entrance. The music formed a wall of sound. Heads—bald ones, spiky ones, warped ones—blocked Allen's view of the stage. A picture of three rabid dogs hung over the stage. Near the disco lights, A banner like the Russians hung behind their leader when they addressed the people read: 'Abandon all hope ye who enter here.' The large windows on each side had been covered up, and inserted in them were anything from crucifixes, mannequins, or twelve working television sets. Allen looked at the planks high above them, accessible only by the cargo elevator on the right. People hung over the edge, danced, and increased the insurance rates.

A girl passed Allen. She looked no older than thirteen. *How'd she get in here?*

The bar ran the entire length of the right wall and ran behind the stage. On the left wall were stacks of old wrecked cars, all with working headlights. Some girls danced on the Ford Mercury, denting its roof even more.

Xiene, Kail, and Allen shoved past the crowd, making their way to the far right corner. A light showing through the fog indicated it had to be an exit or a bathroom of some sort. Allen spotted two frat types. *Oh, no, it's the end!*

"This place sucks. Let's go to Hooters," he heard the one in the white shirt said.

Whew! That was close!

Xiene and Kail almost lost Allen two times. When he caught up, Xiene grabbed his hand. He felt like a kid at K-Mart being dragged by his mom. They entered the light. Bathrooms were on the left and right. Three pay telephones, one with a guy covering his left ear and trying to listen with his right. *Why have pay phones in this place? You can't even hear yourself.* They went down a wooden stairwell into an employee break area. The sight of a soda and snack machine made Allen hungry. Two women were sitting. One had slick blonde hair and a nose ring. The other had very long, straight black hair and red lipstick, which, against her pale white skin, made her look like a vampire. The vampire stared at Allen and took a drag on her cigarette. With her eyes half-closed, she raised one eyebrow.

Leave me alone! I don't own a leather jacket!

The guys were talking in what must have been the manager's office on the left. Looking in, Allen noticed four video monitors viewing the entire scene upstairs. As Kail and Xiene walked into the manager's office, the three men stopped talking.

"Hey, Xiene!", "Hey, girl!", "Hey, Xienna," each man said, talking over themselves. While they hugged her the manager left.

"What's your name?" Kail said, pointing to Allen.

"Allen."

"Okay, Allen, this is Mark." The one who looked like a brunette Billy Idol nodded. "And this is C.J." The one who looked like a young Robert Duvall nodded.

Gee, shit, Warren Beatty, Billy Idol, and Robert Duvall in one room.

The vampire made her way into the little office. Turning, Kail introduced her. "Oh, and this is Caro—"

Before he could finish pronouncing 'Carol' or 'Caroline', she interrupted with "Milaria!" tapping the ashes off her cigarette. Allen coughed from her smoke. She turned and looked at him while the others talked about the gig.

"Smoke bother you?" she asked in a low, sexy voice.

"Sometimes."

She took the cigarette out of her mouth and extinguished it on her left thigh.

The crowd was stomping in unison for the next band. Xiene and Allen were near the front, behind the slam dance pit, where those with knives, guns, and football gear wouldn't even think of going into. The packed crowd kept pushing Xiene and Allen against the rail, so Allen put himself behind Xiene.

What a gentleman—what an idiot! Again a Sid Vicious clone shoved his spiked leather jacket into Allen's ribs. Turning around, Allen noticed the guy had been talking to a long-haired hippie, maybe twenty years old. He picked up the conversation.

"Yeah, I hear Milaria's pissed as shit, man!" said the hippie.

"I think she's going to quit," said Sid.

The house music playing 70's disco hits stopped, causing some sarcastic mumbles from the audience, and some to stop singing along.

Why were they playing that here?

The lights dimmed. "And now, you shitheads, here they are—Uncle Fester!" said what Allen referred to as the voice of god. Out came the group members. Some of the crowd cheered as they took to the stage.

Xiene reached her hands behind her back and grabbed Allen's hands. The band started into a very loud set. Allen wished they weren't so close to the speakers. Xiene started dancing.

Where's Milaria? She hadn't come out on stage. The band members kept looking offstage for her. After a minute or so, they stopped playing, looking like chickens with their heads cut off.

"Where's Milaria?" Allen asked Xiene, who appeared to be asking Kail the same thing. Kail mouthed something to her.

Xiene turned around. "That bitch just packed up and left!"

Ha, ha, ha, Allen thought, feeling even for Kail making him jealous.

The audience's rumbling got noisier as the band waited for Milaria. Kail kept talking to Xiene. They had to yell at each other to be heard.

"Why don't you do it?" You know all of the songs!" Kail yelled.

"I should, I wrote half of them!" Xiene yelled back.

"You never told me you wrote songs," Allen said, looking over Xiene's shoulder.

"Yes, I did. You weren't listening, as usual."

Kail talked to the bearded bouncer near the stage. The bouncer pushed through the mosh pit to Xiene. Xiene held out her hands like a baby. The bouncer picked her up and carried her to the stage. Some people in the crowd cheered. Allen felt very uncomfortable and alone at the moment.

Sid Vicious turned to the hippie. "Who's she?"

"Her name's Xiene. I see her at the health food store sometimes."

Jesus, I should take a poll: hands up who knows Xiene?

"Hey, everybody, we lost our lead singer," said Kail. The crowd rumbled.

"Let's go home," someone said.

"But we have a substitute for tonight—Xiene!"

Everyone in the crowd roared with approval. Allen thought again about 'hands up who knows Xiene'.

"Thanks," Xiene said, sounding kind of nervous and shy. "Okay, I'd like to start with a song I wrote about my boyfriend. It's called 'Climb On Top'.

"What?" Allen yelled.

The music started, with Kail playing wailing guitar, Mark on bass, and C.J. on drums. Xiene moved around conservatively, still shy and nervous. She started singing very low, gradually became more confident, and started moving more. Allen caught some of the song lyrics in between loud guitars blaring over the 10-foot speakers.

"I want to live! I want to breathe! I want to love!" Xiene sang.

The crowd shoved and spiked Allen against the rail. A fight broke out in the dance pit. The bearded bounder broke it up. Sid turned to the hippie and yelled, "She's better than Milaria, man!"

"Yeah, she dances around more!"

Looking back at the stage, Allen saw Xiene doing what he called 'fuck art, let's dance'—arms out, stomping feet, and her blonde and black hair swinging around like a duster.

Two skinheads kept stage diving. Allen worried one would hurt Xiene while next to her. Xiene grabbed one around the neck in a headlock and started pulling him around the stage. With every chorus of the song, she hit his head. He seemed to enjoy the abuse, not realizing Xiene hated skinheads and was actually trying to hurt him. At the end of the song, she threw him off the stage into a Black guy with an 'Afrika Rules' T-shirt.

As the bouncers broke up the fight, the crowd roared and cheered "Uncle Fester!" Kail leaned over and hugged Xiene. Every song they played outdid the last one. Allen couldn't hate them, he'd never seen Xiene put this much energy into something non-sexual. By the end of their performance, the whole place became a mosh pit. Even the railing up above where the elite punk snobs hung out, danced.

They played three encores. The next band, off to the side, kept checking their watches. *I wonder if they don't outdo Uncle Fester, they'll be killed and used as more window decorations.*

"Thanks," Xiene said, raising the mike.

The band went offstage. Allen pushed through the crowd to get back to the manager's office. Even though he said "Excuse me", no one would get out of his way. Two Black guys in leather jackets and bandanas walked through the crowd like it was made of paper. *Maybe that's it—if you say 'excuse me', they think you're weak and won't move. So I'll just walk straight through without saying a word.*

"Hey, man!" yelled the first guy Allen walked into.

"Sorry."

"You will be sorry!" yelled the Charles Manson lookalike. His friends held his arms back as Allen made a hasty retreat.

Allen made his way to the manager's office. The Charles Manson lookalike yelled at him. Due to the house music, he couldn't hear a thing.

Laughing, drinking, and hugging went on in the employee break room. Xiene was behaving like a kid on sugar, going from group member to employee saying how much she loved the gig.

Allen stood in the wings with no idea what the group and her were talking about. The girl with slick blonde hair came up to Allen.

"She your girlfriend?"

"Yeah, I guess."

"You guess? You're not sure?"

"Yes, I'm sure!" Allen said, wondering what she wanted. Reaching into her black shirt with cut-off sleeves, she handed Allen a slip of paper. She then walked up the stairs. He opened the note. It read: "Milaria 555-2890."

Oh, shit! A come-on!

Trying to hide the note as much as possible, he quickly stuck it in his back jeans pocket.

Xiene walked up to him. "What's that?"

"Oh, ah, a flyer for here."

"Oh, okay." She grabbed Allen and gave him a big kiss with an extra loud smack at the end.

"I'm so happy," she said, showing her pearly whites.

"Hey! Party at Kail and C.J.'s house! Be there," said Mark.

"Or be square," added C.J. in a mock nerd voice.

Allen looked at his watch. 4:45. "Jesus Christ, I told Monroe, Brandon, and Oswald we would have breakfast tomorrow."

The crowd in the break room grew bigger and louder. Xiene moved from person to person. Allen, feeling like a third thumb, sat down next to the soda machine and simmered in squareness.

"You ready to go?" Xiene finally asked after hugging a few people.

"You going to the party?"

"Oh, of course. Aren't you?"

"No, I got to get up at nine. We're supposed to have breakfast with the gang. Remember?"

Xiene fumbled with her keys as they climbed the stairs.

"Can't you just stay up all night, go to breakfast, and go home and sleep?"

That's logical, but I don't want to hang around these people anymore! I want to go home with Xiene! No Kail! "I'm about to die. I have to sleep, now."

"How are you getting home?"

What? She's going anyway? "You mean you're going?"

"Of course. I haven't seen a lot of these people for eons. Plus, I'm not tired," she said, dancing out into the main area.

Whistles and cheers and 'Xiene' yells greeted her.

Damn celebrity!

They slowly made it to the exit. The bouncer who looked like Santa Claus called out, "Hey, you were fucking wonderful!"

"Thanks," she said, dancing out the front door.

More claps and cheers from people leaving the Acid Pit. Xiene twirled around a light pole and grabbed Allen's arm.

"My public. How I love them."

Betty Davis impersonation, Allen guessed.

"You still not going?" she asked.

"No."

"I can get you to a MARTA station. The trains will run again at five."

"Okay."

Allen fumed inside. *You bitch! Go on to the party without me! See if I care!*

Xiene and Allen hopped in her VW van. It sped down the street to the Inman Park station, Xiene singing and banging the steering wheel in rhythm. They pulled into the Kiss Ride.

"Ohh, Kiss Ride," Xiene said, raising her eyebrows. She leaned over to Allen, eyes closed, ready to kiss.

I wish I had a big dead fish right now with huge lips! Reaching over, he gave her a peck, the kind you give your lost aunt on her deathbed.

"Ehwww, that sucked! I want a refund!"

"Nope, that's all you get," he said, trying to open the door.

"Okay," she said, her expression changing from ecstatic to manically depressed.

Allen headed into the station. Xiene paused to watch Allen enter the station. Before she pulled off, she blew her horn three times—one for love, one for lust, and one for us. Allen headed up the escalator feeling like the world's biggest asshole.

Shoney's on Piedmont Avenue had a breakfast buffet til 2 pm. Oswald, Brandon, and Allen sat in the front on the sun deck. The sun shining through the roof acted as a spotlight on Oswald as he finished his story of Tennessee living. Allen had his head on his hands, resting on the table, extremely tired because he never went to sleep once he got home.

"How did it go at the Acid Pit last night?" asked Monroe, his blond hair glowing in the sunlight.

Allen looked up. "What?"

"I said, how did it go last night?"

"Oh, wonderful. The lead singer of the group quit, so Xiene went on stage and gave them the best show they ever did."

"Wow!" Brandon said with a boyish smile on his chubby face. "That's great."

"Where is she?" Oswald asked, cleaning his thick-frame glasses.

"She's not coming," Allen said, sinking lower into his hands.

"Why not?" asked Monroe.

"She's too famous to hang out with us now," joked Oswald.

"No, she's too tired I guess."

"I have her number. Maybe one of us should call her," Brandon suggested.

Before Allen said, 'You do and I'll kill you,' the waitress came by for their orders.

Back at home, the pancakes kicked in by 2:00, and Allen fell asleep during Kung Fu Action Theater. Brandon's vacuuming woke him up at 5:00. He crawled upstairs and continued sleeping. A knock on his door at 8:15 woke him. The door opened and there stood Brandon's silhouette.

"Allen, telephone. Xiene."

Groggy as hell, Allen picked up the phone. "Hello?"

"Hi, babe. What's happening?"

"Nothing much. Just sleeping."

"You been asleep all day?"

"Yep," he said, getting the gunk out of his eyes.

"Why didn't you call me after you had breakfast?"

"I didn't think you'd be home."

"What?" Xiene said, confused. "Why wouldn't I be?"

"The big party?" Allen said sarcastically.

"I can go to parties til five, sleep until two, get up, and go do things. You know that."

"Yeah, whatever," Allen said, not admitting he should have called her instead of sleeping all day.

"Whatever?" Xiene questioned.

"Yes, whatever, how did it go?" Allen asked, not caring but looking for Kail alerts.

"Great. Guess what?"

"What?"

"They asked me to be their new lead singer. Isn't that great?"

"Hmm." Allen had nothing to say.

"Well? What do you think?"

Allen wasn't thinking. He was tired from sleeping too long. "I don't care," he said, actually meaning to say she can do what she wants, it's okay with him.

"Fuck you, too!" she said.

"We'll, fuck you!" he said, still not awake.

A click and a dial tone signaled the end of that phone conversation.

The world's shittiest weekend finally ended. Brandon and Allen drove home from work. Brandon told Allen about gas stations he can't stop at because of unfair practices, South African investment, or ugly logos.

Brandon finally asked what he had waited a week to ask Allen. "Xiene called you yet?"

"No, Xiene hasn't called me yet!" he said, jaw down, brows raised, voice very sarcastic.

"You call her?" Brandon asked while avoiding the brown Fairmont cutting him off on the 285.

"No. Why should I? I'm not the one going on the road with my old boyfriend."

"She leaving?" Brandon said with worry.

"No, she's not leaving. I don't care what she does! I don't give a shit!"

Brandon dropped the subject.

Blockbuster videos were packed with people and empty with tapes. They had one copy (rented) of the animated 'Speed Racer Volume 1', and thirty copies of 'Coming to America (two rented). Allen walked over to Oswald reading a label with Mi Cha, his Korean girlfriend. Brandon walked around the corner with two black-and-white classics.

If they had rented a video with twelve topless beautiful women running in place for two hours, Allen would have hated it.

While they all sat on the couch watching a movie Oswald rented for the soundtrack, the phone rang. Brandon picked it up. "Hello? Oh, hi!" he said happily. "Yeah, hold on."

He looked over at Allen. "Allen, Xiene."

Allen walked over to the phone wondering what to say. "Hello?"

"Hi, what's up?"

"Nothing much."

"You in a better mood yet?"

"No."

"Okay, bye." A click and a dial tone.

Allen went upstairs to bed without saying a word to the others.

The next day Allen received a phone call at work from Oswald. "Hi, Allen. Have you read the latest issue of Creative Loafing?"

"No, why?"

"Just get one."

At lunchtime, Allen went to the record store and picked up a copy of the alternative newspaper, Creative Loafing, along with another free newspaper that reviewed CDs. Searching through, he found nothing odd until he got to a Danny D. article. Music critic,

Danny D., in short, was infamous for trashing rock groups, famous or just starting out. Unless the group sweated, suffered, or had a cute lead female singer, he hated them. Underneath his trashing of a group called Big Black Cock-a-Doodle Doo was a review of Uncle Fester. Allen read:

"I don't usually see many groups that go from stink-a-roo to good, but that's Uncle Fester. I caught them at the Little Five Points Pub last week and realized how much I hated Milaria, their old lead singer.

Xiene, not to be confused with Exene Cervenka of the rock group, X, is a jumping bean of kick-ass enthusiasm!

"Egads! Allen said putting the paper down. "Danny D. likes them!' Allen had hoped the band would fail and Xiene would come crawling back. He realized he was going to be doing the crawling.

Oswald, Jojo, and Kathy almost had to drag Allen into Oswald's brown Oldsmobile.

"I want to see them," said Oswald.

"Me, too," added Jojo, a short curly-haired girl.

"I don't know," said Allen.

"Hey, I haven't seen them yet, and if Danny D. likes 'em, they must be good!" said Oswald, pulling the car into The Mask parking lot. The marquee on the black building lists the groups: 'Disillusions of Grandeur', 'Big Black Cock-a-Doodle-Doo', and, finally, 'Uncle Fester'

They entered the old mill, now turned into a disco. The usuals were there: a few punks, lots of frat types, and yuppies. The Mask was broken into three sections: Heaven, Hell, and Purgatory. Each provided you with three distinctly decorated places to go. Because Oswald and Kathy got sick of coaxing Allen off walls and staircases, they went into purgatory so he could get a Long Island iced tea to loosen him up. They cut through Hell to see if anyone was in there. The chainlink fence separating the under-21 set had three dancers on each side. They climbed the back entrance stairs to Heaven. The three Long Island iced teas Allen sucked down took effect and Jojo started pushing him up the last flight of wooden steps.

"Hey! I know what youuu guysss are doing," Allen said in a slur. "You're trying to get Xien-Xie-Xi." Allen couldn't pronounce her name, so he gave up.

"I haven't seen this many people since Butthole Surfers," said Kathy, blowing her long blonde hair away from her face.

Even the real Heaven was never meant to hold this many people.

Jojo and Oswald took Allen around the chain link fence separating minors from the bars. They sat up in front of the minor section.

"Gee, whiz, if you drink, you can't see the show through that fucking fence," Allen said, gesturing behind them. Allen told everyone what a lightweight drinker he was while Oswald stared at a cute Asian girl and didn't hear a word.

The first band came on—they were bad. The three guitars and drums drowned out the lead singer so much that you were not able to tell if it was the voice of a woman or a man in drag. The Afro-punk Big Black Cock-a-Doodle-Doo got a good review from the foursome. Jojo liked the Black drummer with the dreadlocks. The audience grew even more, so bad the foursome had to get away from their table or not see anything due to the wall of people. Allen spotted Milaria. She had sunglasses on, but it was no doubt her. She made her way to the group, pushing some yuppie ex-football player out of her way.

"You never called me!" She said.

"My roommate washed my pants with your number." *Crazy as it sounded, that part was true.*

"Oh. Okay," she said. She reached into her bag, pulled out a gold, $25 ink pen, and proceeded to write her number on Allen's palm.

Kathy, Jojo, and Oswald, who witnessed the whole thing, were speechless. After giving Allen the palm tattoo, Milaria stood next to him. Kathy whispered to Jojo. Milaria grabbed Allen around the arm. Allen, too woozy to pull away, leaned on her for support.

The band came on. Cheers all around. No Xiene in sight. They started playing. After five minutes the crowd roared again as Xiene came up from behind the crowd, being carried from person to person, like riding a human wave to the front.

How many guys in the audience are feeling her butt as she's passed?

Making it to the front, Xiene grabbed the mike and started to sing. She looked like a 20th Century goth punk—the makeup on her eyes appeared to have been caked on then smeared back; her lips, black, matched her vinyl gloves; her hair, now white and pink; her wedding dress had 34 plastic baby heads running around the edge; her feet, bare beneath five or six ankle bracelets, some with fake barbwire designs. She crawled, rolled, jumped, and screamed. Even if you didn't like her punk opera voice you still had the dress to look at. Milaria started rubbing her hand on Allen's chest. Allen, too freaked by Xiene's performance, ignored her.

"We got to do something!" Kathy yelled at Oswald.

"What?" yelled Oswald, covering his ears.

Maria stuck her tongue in Allen's ear. He noticed this.

"Hey!" Allen said turning his head almost breaking his neck. When he did, Milaria kissed him.

Jojo ran between the two and started pushing Allen away from her. Allen backed into the Charles Manson lookalike.

"Hey, man!" he said, pushing Allen over Jojo. As they both lay on the ground and tried to keep people from stepping on them, Milaria pushed through the crowd towards them. Oswald and Kathy looked around for Jojo and Allen, who were crawling in the crowd. A girl kicked Allen in the mouth with her cowboy boots. Allen grabbed her and used her as a ladder to get off the ground. The girl slapped him, sending a stinging pain on his face, preventing him from seeing the bra he ripped off of her. Milaria grabbed Allen before the girl slapped him again.

Kathy and Oswald helped Jojo up. Kathy pointed to Milaria helping Allen out of the club. As they left Heaven and headed down the stairs, Uncle Fester finished their song. The crowd roared its approval.

"Th-thank you," stuttered Xiene, wiping her eyes.

Where are we going?" Allen asked Milaria, pulling him through the parking lot.

"My place. Where else?" she said, unlocking the door on her red Mustang.

"No, this isn't right." Allen held his head, feeling his senses coming back. He turned around and started walking back.

"Allen!" yelled Milaria, "Xiene and Kail are sleeping together."

Allen stopped.

"That's right."

Allen turned around and looked at Malaria. She lifted her leg onto the front left tire, showing a well-defined thigh in black, fishnet hose—fishnet, Allen's kryptonite.

He heard a roar from inside Mask. He turned back around and saw Xiene coming out, followed by Kail. Xiene sat down on the curb and started putting on a pair of black high-top tennis shoes.

Allen started walking towards the two.

"That's it, Kail, my last performance! I can't take this shit anymore!" Xiene said.

"Hey, all the proof is there! Allen and Milaria are an item! There's nothing to keep us here! That guy from Red Records said this is the perfect time to tour!

Kail noticed Allen and Milaria.

"I'm tired, man, I haven't slept for—"

Xiene turned and saw Allen standing over her. She quickly jumped up.

"You fucker!" she yelled, pushing and punching Allen into the chainlink fence. Allen then fell to the ground, the alcohol still effectively preventing him from getting up.

"Me? What about you? You and Kail are sleeping together!"

"What?" Xiene looked at Milaria, who had her arms folded and stared at Kail.

"Kail told me you and Milaria are riding the hobby horse!"

"Bullshit! Why would I sleep—"

"Yes, it's true." Milaria reached down and grabbed Allen. "We've been humping for two weeks now," she said.

"What the hell are you talking about?" Allen said, pulling away from Malaria.

"Xiene, let's go." Kail grabbed Xiene by the arm.

"Let me go!" She shook him off and started walking up the street. "You're all driving me fucking crazy!" she yelled.

Allen stood up.

"You're so stupid!" Kail said to Milaria. "One day! You couldn't wait one day!"

"Don't call me stupid! You asshole! Why did you bring her out here?"

"I didn't! She started crying—said 'It's over, folks', and walked out in the middle of our set!"

Allen stood up and looked at them. "You bastards! You're working together! You're trying to get Xiene to help your fucking group!"

Oswald, Kathy, and Jojo came out of Mask.

"You want her to go on your tour! And you…" Allen pointed to Milaria, "…you never left the group! You just stepped out of the spotlight so Xiene would fall in love with Kail! Then she wouldn't leave the group! You bastards!" Allen yelled, looking on the ground for a weapon to throw.

"Yeah, right, like Xiene can have a better life with you!" Kail yelled. "At least with me, she'll be famous! We packed every club since we got her!"

"You're using her popularity, dickhead!" Jojo yelled.

"Let's go, Kail!" Maria grabbed his arm and they walked away.

"I'm stupid. I'm stupid. I'm stupid," Allen kept saying, walking up the hill where Xiene had disappeared.

"Allen! Get in the car, we'll take you!" said Jojo.

Allen waved no and kept walking.

6:45 am

The sun rose. After Allen searched the House of Pancakes again, he walked down North Avenue to Argonne and checked the Krispy Kreme one more time. There she was, inside, her back to him, sipping a coffee and smoking a cigarette.

He walked into the doughnut shop. The cold, pure smell of sugar made his stomach upset. He saw Xiene staring into her cup. *How do I handle this? I hope she doesn't throw coffee on me.* He waited until she put it down before stepping closer.

He sat in the opposite chair of her.

"Please don't throw coffee on me. Or hit me," he pleaded.

She hazily looked at him, almost as if she looked through him.

"I'm sorry I'm a jealous asshole. I should always support you, no matter what, and I'm just sorry. If you never talk to me again, I'll understand. But believe me, Milaria was just working with Kail to get you to tour with them."

"So?" she said.

"What?"

"So? That has nothing to do with the fact you never came to see me perform, or thought I would go off with Kail."

"You're right. But Xiene, it's just you're so popular that sometimes I feel you'll get bored with me."

"You asshole!" Xiene hissed. "You think I like you because you're exciting? Ha! You, exciting?"

Allen felt insulted.

"I like you for you, stupid! If I want a roller coaster ride, I go to Six Flags. If I want love and understanding, I come to you, dumbass!

Drained, Allen placed his left cheek on the sticky table. After a minute, he raised his head. A napkin stuck to his ear. "I am a dumbass."

Xiene laughed and covered her mouth. Her eyes squinting, she coughed up her coffee.

Allen peeled off the napkin, stared at it, then at Xiene, and broke into a laugh attack.

"Don't let coffee come out your nose," Allen said as tears came out of his eyes from laughing so hard, or was it from something else?

Xiene threw her coffee onto his face and fell out of her chair laughing.

THE MONKEY CLUB!

"Toot, toot," Xiene said, pushing the toy battleship towards Allen's chest.

"Godzilla!" Allen yelled, bringing his hand down on the ship. The ship sank for a second, then floated back to the top, near the rubber duck. Xiene submerged her mouth into the water and started blowing air bubbles with a motorboat sound. Allen picked up the yellow water gun and shot her in the forehead. She lifted her head, reached over the edge of the tub, and came back with a Uzi squirt gun. The battle didn't last long. Allen rubbed his eyes. Victorious in the Uzi assault, Xiene moved her foot up and down Allen's chest while blowing soap bubbles through some scissor handles.

"Put that down, young lady."

"Okay," she said, positioning the scissors over Allen's crotch. "Bomb's away!"

"No!" yelled Allen as Xiene almost dropped the scissors.

"You know I wouldn't do that to you."

"Yeah, right!" Allen put his hands in between his legs to protect himself from future assault.

Xiene looked down at her breasts, then started to rise and sink in and out of the water over and over again. Her breasts would form two islands that disappeared a second later. Allen stared at her doing this for three minutes.

Xiene stood up in the tub, startling Allen, who had been hypnotized by the breast islands. She reached for her jeans hanging over the sink and pulled out her cigarettes and lighter.

"No, not in here!" Allen whined.

Sticking out her tongue and blowing a raspberry, she sat back down with the cigarette and lighter. Allen grabbed her hand with the lighter and submerged it in the water.

"You asshole!" Xiene said, splashing his face.

Allen picked up the bar of soap on the left, held it over her head, and dropped it.

When the bar of soap bounced off her head into the water, she picked it up and threw it at Allen, hitting his right eye.

"Ow! Shit!" Allen splashed water in his eye, washing the soap out.

Xiene leaned over and checked for damage. After moving his hand and examining his face with her right hand, she kissed his cheek. "Ah, you're alright, you baby."

"Yeah, right. Thanks, doc." Allen said sarcastically.

Xiene put the ruined lighter and cigarette into the toilet and flushed. Allen leaned over to see if they went down. Xiene had pretended to flush the items so she could push his head down, causing his mouth to kiss the toilet seat. Allen began dry spitting and throwing water in his mouth. Xiene laughed.

"You are dead meat!" Allen said, splashing his entire face.

Xiene hopped out of the tub and ran out. Allen followed. She ran downstairs as Allen grabbed a towel from the closet. By the time he started downstairs, he heard "Oh, shit!", and then Xiene ran back upstairs with a distressed expression on her face. Allen watched her push past him, enter his bedroom, and slam the door. Looking down, he saw Brandon coming around the corner very slowly, followed by Monroe. Both had freaked expressions on their faces.

"Oops," Allen said, looking down.

"When's the second show?" Monroe asked.

Allen entered the bedroom. Xiene sat on his bed, in the center, completely covered except for her face by a white bedspread. Allen laughed at her appearance.

"I'm so embarrassed!"

Allen laughed more.

"It's not funny, you asshole!" She picked up a pillow and hit him in the face.

Allen stopped laughing. "Gee, whiz, what's with you and my face? Is this something Freudian?"

"Shut up!" Xiene said with her Elvis sneer.

Allen walked over to the dresser to look at the dust covering his Japanese robot models.

"Did they see anything? Oh, god, what did they say?" She put her forehead on her kneecaps.

"They said, 'My, what tiny breasts Xiene has'."

Xiene lifted her head, believing Allen for a second. "No! bullshit!"

"Yeah," Allen returned to lying, "Monroe said, 'If I had a butt like that, I would sell tickets'."

"No way!" Xiene said in a voice that let Allen know she halfway believed him.

"Yeah, don't you think if you were a guy with a woman's butt, you'd sell tickets?"

Xiene laughed. As Allen walked over to the bed, she lay down on her back, feet still upright. Xiene pulled the spread down until her breasts showed. Looking down, forming a double chin, she began examining her breasts with her hands.

"Do you really think I have small breasts?"

Allen laughed. "What? Don't be ridiculous. You know I like your breasts."

"Hmm," she said. "Maybe I should have breast surgery. She put her hands under them and lifted them.

"What? Don't you dare!"

"Hey, I could perform at the Monkey Club then."

"They have small-breasted women at the Monkey Club." *Oops. I just let her know I've been there!*

"You've been to the Monkey Club?"

Let's see, do I lie or come clean? Either way, she'll raz me! "Yeah, once."

"Really? What's it like?" she sat upright and grabbed her knees.] She seemed enthusiastic.

"It's just your regular old strip joint," Allen lied.

"Really? I've always wanted to go to one of those places."

"Why?"

"I don't know. Just to see what it's like." Allen felt it coming. "Hey, let's go to one, Xiene said, eyes almost childlike.

"Why?"

"Why not? It will be fun."

"For me, but not for you," Why would she want to look at naked women?"

"Hey, maybe the strippers can teach me a thing or two."

"Yeah, how to degrade yourself," Allen said. *I sound like Brandon.*

"Okay, let's go to a male strip joint!"

"No way!" Allen pictured Xiene looking at some bohunk and stuffing dollars into his g-string.

"Oh well, I guess I'll go alone," she said, looking up.

Allen knew she would go alone, so he had to decide: male strip joint or female strip joint. "Okay, Monkey Club, here we come."

✖

"How's this?" Xiene held out her arms and turned around.

"No," Allen said, looking at her in the extra-large black Cramps T-shirt and blue jeans. She walked back to her bedroom. Ten minutes later, she came back in wearing white painter's overalls spattered with different colors. Underneath she wore a long-sleeved black shirt. On her head, a white painter's cap turned backward.

"How's this?"

"Nope. Men will still undress you with their eyes."

She raised one eyebrow, turned, and walked back into her bedroom. Allen resumed reading Creative Loafing. Eight minutes later Xiene walked out wearing a black slip, lace top, a black leather mini skirt, black fishnets, and a pair of red spiked heeled shoes. She put on her leather jacket, grabbed her leopard purse, and headed for the door, leaving Allen on her couch with his mouth agape.

"Come on, let's go," she said, opening the door.

By the time they made it to the Monkey Club, Xiene felt like smacking Allen, who kept trying to wrap newspaper around her, saying 'Come on, it will be a new fashion statement'." Xiene snatched the newspaper and threw it in the back of her VW van, then blew smoke in his face. Allen, almost gagging, opened the window and stuck his head out for air.

They drove down Piedmont until they spotted the Monkey Club. Its infamous logo could be seen by anyone passing by on the MARTA train, the moving neon ape handing the neon big-breasted jungle girl a banana over and over.

How Freudian. Allen thought.

Xiene paid the parking attendant. The VW Wagon parked next to a white Mercedes with a 'No fat chicks!' bumper sticker. Xiene walked around the back of the Mercedes. Squatting, she took a red marker out of her purse and wrote 'would be seen with this impotent asshole!' on the sticker. Allen looked around for the parking attendant, ready to make a run for it.

Xiene grabbed his left arm and they walked to the entrance. They passed potted palm trees and entered the double doors. An usher watched Xiene's butt go past. The disco music blaring forced the receptionist with a Marilyn Monroe mole to raise her voice. "ten dollars, please."

"For two?" asked Xiene.

"No, each!" she yelled.

"Shit! that expensive? Men pay this much for tits and ass?" Xiene protested. Allen only picked up the word 'shit' in between the music's drum beats.

They walked along the red carpet to the second entrance. Allen studied the pictures of famous people who had been there. He only recognized a local weatherman.

"Gee, if I were them, I would have a black bar across my face," he said.

Xiene laughed, then pushed the red and gold doors with two Art Deco female figures on them.

"And now, level two!" said the voice of god.

The strippers on the stage started taking their tops off. The white stage in the center had over fifty men around the edges, some holding up dollar bills. On the very high ceiling, hung a large spiky structure embedded with hundreds of tiny lights. Potted palm trees adorned each corner of the room. Now and then the white stage would light up under different dancers. Off to the right were twenty round tables, some with women on them doing table dances.

A balding, overweight Burt Reynolds type on the right stared at Xiene. Two Japanese businessmen at the bottom of the stairs looked at Xiene. Another overweight Burt Reynolds with a toupee stared at Xiene. At this point, Allen felt it impossible to keep track of the sea of horny men. He felt like Xiene was a steak in a lion's den.

She held his left hand so tight her red nails dug into his knuckles. Through his vision, Allen saw a woman shaking her tits two feet away from his face on the right. Turning, he noticed she had been doing a table dance for some blond frat type and his two buddies."Let's sit here." Xiene pointed to a spot next to the stage.

Oh, great, front-row butts!

As she moved her head with the disco beat, a waitress in a furry bathing suit complete with a monkey tail and ears leaned over the table.

"Can I get you anything?"

"Just a diet soda," Xiene replied, wanting to be in full control at this time.

"Same for me," Allen said, noticing the stripper moving near them.

"And now, level three!" said the voice of god, who Allen spotted in a windowed booth near the ceiling.

The woman, a 38-26-38-bodied brunette removed her bottom showing a crop of pubic hair cut so she obviously could wear French-cut bathing suits. Xiene smiled at the woman, who began grinding like a water snake. Xiene reached into her purse and pulled out a dollar bill. She handed it to Allen.

"Here, give it to her!"

"What?"

Xiene gestured for Allen to give it to her. Allen hated looking at other women while dating, but sticking bills in their garter belts was too much.

"Go on!" Xiene nudged.

Allen quickly grabbed her garter belt, slipped in the bill, and slapped it against the stripper's skin, at no point touching her skin.

"Ouch!" she said before moving away.

"Satisfied?" Allen said, turning to Xiene, who had already started laughing.

The waitress came by with their drinks. Allen paid the waitress.

"Look, a mohawk," said Xiene, pointing.

Sure enough, an Asian stripper with small breasts and very long straight black hair had her pubic hair in a straight landing strip. Allen looked around the room, picturing pig heads on all of the men, and a jackass head for himself. Xiene started clapping her hands with the music.

Thank god she's not drinking, Allen pictured Xiene getting up on the stage and stripping.

A girl on center stage caught Allen's attention—a blonde doing handstands and other acrobatic feats.

"Now, see, she works for her tips." Allen gestured.

"Hey, over here!" Xiene yelled at the woman. She cartwheeled over. "How much for a table dance?"

"Ten dollars," the blonde said, pulling her hair back.

"Allen…Allen," Xiene repeated. Allen wasn't listening because he was too busy looking at the blonde. She was very pretty, with green eyes and dimples. She smiled down at Allen who, she noticed, wasn't staring at her body. "Hey!" Xiene yelled lightly slapping Allen's left cheek.

"What?" Allen, startled, asked.

"You want a table dance?"

"Yeah, I guess so." After all, I'm just helping the stripper with her career. Right?

Reaching into her purse, Xiene looked for a ten-spot. Allen had already paid the girl by the time Xiene found one.

The girl, instead of just jiggling like a water snake, did splits—'ouch!' Xiene said—moved her hair around like a duster, stood on her hands with legs parting and coming together over and over, then, finally, lying on her chest, she brought her left foot over backward, touching her head with her silver heel.

"Wow." Allen reached in and gave her another five.

"Thanks," she said, getting back on stage.

Xiene was silent. She took a chug of her soda and lit up a cigarette. The music ended and the strippers departed the stage and began mingling with the audience. Allen watched the blonde make her way to their table.

"Hi, I'm Candy," she introduced herself, briefly putting her left hand on Allen's shoulder.

"I'm Allen, and this is Xiene."

"Hi, Xiene." She reached out her hand for Xiene.

Caught off-guard, Xiene put her cigarette down and shook hands.

"This your first time here?"

"Not me, but Xiene's." Allen gestured at Xiene.

"Really? How do you like it?"

"Oh, I don't know. Kind of reminds me of a slave tent and all of the men around here are holding chains," Xiene said, taking a drag on her cigarette.

"We'll, no one's holding my chain. I come and go as I please around here."

"Yeah, I guess it's better than hitting the streets," Xiene kidded.

Ouch!

"Pardon?" Candy asked.

"Well, you know, I guess this job's better than hooking."

"No one's forcing me to do this. I do this because I want to! I make $500 a night. How much do you earn?"

"Oh, I think I would go down to $18 per day not to degrade myself."

Ouch!

"I'm not degrading myself!" Kathy's voice got louder.

"Yeah, right. You just give horny businessmen hard-ons for cash."

"Hey, look at that painting!" Allen interrupted, trying to break up the argument.

"Hey, what people think is up to them! I'm a dancer and a performer. Men get hard-ons looking at Madonna! Does that make her a slut?"

Bad example.

"Hey, most people I know call her that," Xiene hissed.

At this point, Candy was leaning over Xiene, hands in a fist, Xiene gripping her soda as if she wanted to splash Kathy's face.

"If what I'm doing is so bad, what are you and your boyfriend doing here?" screamed Candy, now getting the attention of people around the bar.

"Oh, now and then I like to see how the sleazy half lives."

"Sleazy?" screamed Candy. "At least I don't dress like a whore!"

The soda spattered off Kathy's face and chest and sent droplets into Allen's face.

A second before he said, "That's it, let's go," Candy grabbed Xiene's white-and-pink hair. Xiene grabbed Kathy's blonde hair. Screaming, they both held on. Xiene lifted her foot and kicked Kathy away, against the stage edge.

Some men in the corner cheered. Candy came back and slapped Xiene's left ear. Xiene slapped Candy's face, making her scream. Random slapping sounds and hair-grabbing caused the whole place to start cheering like they were watching a cockfight.

Two big Arab-looking bouncers in Monkey Club T-shirts pushed their way through the crowd of men now surrounding the fighting femmes. Allen looked for an opening in the crowd of fists so he could grab Xiene and get out.

Xiene slapped Candy, sending her into the arms of a Japanese businessman, who, when helping her up, grabbed her breast.

Candy shoved the man into his associates while the crowd cheered on. A college frat-type tried to grab Xiene the same way. She turned around and gave a perfect left hook to the eye.

A bouncer grabbed Kathy, who started kicking at Xiene. Xiene picked up a bowl of nachos and flung them at Kathy. The nachos hit Kathy and the bowl hit a bald guy with glasses. A bouncer grabbed Xiene on the left. She kicked his shin. One on the right grabbed her in a headlock. She grabbed his balls, causing him to scream and let go.

Two cops came pushing through the crowd. *No, don't hit them, please!* One policeman grabbed Xiene on her right. She brought her left arm back for a haymaker to his jaw.

Allen grabbed her arm. "No! Stop!"

She turned and looked at him, teeth gritted, hair a mess. She struggled to break free for a second, then stopped.

Allen grabbed her other arm away from the policeman and they started to leave while the audience hooted 'More! More. *Sons of bitches!*

Outside the club, Xiene continued arguing with the policeman who wanted to jail her.

"No, listen, young lady! I can send you up the river for public fighting! You know that!"

"Yes, sir," Xiene said. Allen knew her logic had finally kicked in.

The owner talked to the other cop off to the left.

"You got to learn to control yourself," the cop continued to lecture Xiene in a country accent.

Candy came out in a coat, holding an ice pack on her face. She walked over to the manager, looked at Xiene, and then started to run over, holding the ice pack like a baseball. Allen got in between them, causing the ice pack to hit the right side of his head. Xiene tried to attack Candy, but Allen held out his left arm and grabbed her left shoulder. The other cop ran over and grabbed Candy.

"Bitch!" Candy yelled.

"Slut!" yelled Xiene.

"Cunt!" yelled Candy.

"You filthy cocksucker!" Xiene yelled, struggling to free herself from Allen and the cop, who held them from behind.

"Okay, that's it!" the other cop walked over to Xiene. "Leave, and I don't want to see you, or you!" he gestured at Allen, "around her anymore, or I'll personally throw your asses in jail!"

The country-accented cop let go of Xiene. She spat at Kathy. Allen grabbed Xiene before the country cop could, and headed for her van. Allen grabbed her purse, pulled out her keys, and handed it back to her. Xiene got in with a slam of the door, Allen looked over at her and then started the engine. As they pulled out of the parking lot, Xiene hit the dashboard with her fist.

"Where do you want to go?"

She was silent, simmering in anger and biting her nails on her right hand.

Heading down Piedmont, Allen took her to Jake's, an ice cream dessert place near Piedmont Park. As Allen got out of the van, Xiene took her heels off. She then turned around and flung them towards a football field across the street. With Allen in the back, she then walked over to the patio, and pulled back one of the metal chairs, causing a shrieking noise. She sat down and propped her legs up, crossed them, onto the table, and folded her arms. Blowing her hair out of her face, she noticed the two Black guys watching the whole thing.

"What are you looking at, asshole?"

Allen quickly ran over holding his hands up. "She's had a bad night. Ignore her."

They turned and resumed eating their sundaes. Allen sat in the opposite chair. He looked at her. She was breathing anger in and out, toes tightening, and looking at the ground. Allen looked over at the football stadium, wondering who would find her shoes.

"Goddamnit!" Xiene said before biting the nails on her right hand.

"What?" asked Allen.

"Places like that shouldn't exist!"

"What?" Egads, before, you loved the idea of going there!

"That place is degrading to women and is nothing more than legal prostitution!"

"Well, actually—" Allen said.

"That's it! Tomorrow I'm going to file a complaint!" she interrupted.

Okay. I'll let her ride this out, Allen got up. "What do you want?"

"Just coffee," Xiene said, flexing her toes.

By the time Allen came out with Xiene's coffee and his cappuccino, she had uncrossed her legs and lit up a cigarette. Allen sat down next to her, put the drinks down, grabbed her feet, put them in his lap, and massaged her tense muscles.

Xiene stared into space, holding her cigarette without smoking. She seemed to be deep in thought. Now and then, she would lay her head back and close her eyes, which meant the foot massage was working, and then she would lift her head and open her eyes as if she'd thought of something. She removed her legs from his lap.

"I'm sorry, baby. I don't feel like a massage right now." She extinguished her cigarette in the ashtray.

"You need to relax. You have too much anger in you."

"I'm alright now," she said, lying back and propping her feet on the sides of Allen's chair. He noticed the run in her right stocking leg.

"You have a run," he said, pointing.

Xiene fingered the hold. "Oh, shit! And I just bought these!"

Allen picked her pack of cigarettes off the metal table and began playing with them. Xiene crossed her arms, put her head down, and closed her eyes for ten minutes. *Is she sleeping?* He figured a quick nap would calm her down, so he let her rest. Looking across the street, he watched a bag lady pick up Xiene's shoes, which instead of making it inside, hit the fence in front of the football field.

A male employee from Jake's made his way over to them, stacking the chairs. Allen tapped Xiene's feet.

"Hi, Xiene," said the guy, lifting a chair.

"Hi, Charles," she said to the employee while stretching. "You guys closing?"

"Yeah. What you been up to?"

"Nothing much," Xiene lied while looking around on the ground. "Where are my shoes?"

"You threw them across the street," Allen informed.

"Oh, yeah," she giggled, looking at the football field, then at a confused Charles.

"I saw a bag lady pick them up. If we hurry, we could catch her," Allen said, standing up.

"Naw. Let her keep 'em. She needs them more than me," Xiene said, waving her hand.

They said goodbye to Charles and headed for Xiene's van.

12:18 am

Xiene hawked her throat and spat near an instant banking machine on the right.

"I'll drive." Xiene reached her hands out for the car keys.

"You sure you're up to it?" Allen said while digging in his pocket.

"Sure." She smiled.

The van traveled down the street.

"You want to be alone tonight?" Allen asked

She paused. "Yeah. I think that's a good idea. I need to think."

She dropped Allen off at the Midtown station. He gave her a quick kiss, knowing she wasn't in the mood for necking. Xiene's lack of protesting let him know he was right.

Allen made it home at 1:30, went to sleep, and got up at 6:50 for work. As Allen passed Brandon in the hallway heading to the bathroom, Brandon made the mistake of speaking to the zombie Allen after four hours of sleep.

"How did it go at the strip joint?" he asked, smiling.

Allen reached up with a choking gesture, growled, and continued heading toward the bathroom.

Work was hell. Allen was a week late on a T-shirt design. As he worked on the rabbit in the leather jacket and the words 'Raising Hair', Deborah knocked on the window separating the main office from the break room, where his drawing desk is located. He walked into the office.

"Allen, telephone." she said.

He picked up the phone. "Hello?"

"Hi. This is Don King. I'd like to have a rematch!" Xiene said in a deep voice."

Allen laughed. "Hi, how are you doing?"

"Great. I just got off the phone with my friend Beverly. You remember her."

Searching his Friends of Xiene file, Allen remembered Beverly. "Ultra-liberal, ultra-feminist, ultra-lesbian, ultra-everything. Yeah."

"She invited me to one of her meetings tomorrow. I can't wait to tell them about the Monkey Club."

"Why? So they can protest for you?" Allen asked, looking at Deborah eavesdropping.

"Yeah! I think they should close that place down! It's degrading to women!"

"Actually I kind of think like most jobs, they're voluntarily degrading themselves for a lot of money," Allen said, contradicting his earlier beliefs.

"What? No! They aren't! Jeez! I can't believe you said that! Those places cause men to rape women because they think of us as sex objects!"

"I don't think so. I think rape has more to do with violence than sex," Allen said, hoping Xiene won't yell in his ear again.

"Oh, Allen, you have such a sexist attitude, just like all men!".

"No, I don't! I treat everyone equally rotten," Allen joked. Xiene didn't laugh.

"I think I may have to take you along with me for an education."

"What? No. I don't want a bunch of lesbians castrating me."

"Oooh! Just because you're a feminist doesn't mean you're a lesbian or hate men," Xiene educated.

"Are you a feminist now? Does this mean you're going to wear pants from now on and throw away your makeup and pantyhose?"

"Maybe."

"Will you stop dating me, then?"

"Of course not. I'll still love you. Even if you have, and act like a dick."

"Ahh, I love you, too."

Allen looked over at Pat, who came in holding some T-shirts.

"The meeting's at 8:30 at Beverly's apartment. You coming?"

Okay, should I or shouldn't I? Maybe I can get another man to come with me, in case they run over me. But, I wouldn't put my worst enemy through this!

"Allen?" asked Xiene.

"Oh, okay. I'll be there."

"Great. Love you. Bye." Xiene hung up.

"Right on, sister!" said the Black woman with the afro."

Egads! I haven't heard that since the '70s! Allen winced.

The others applauded the speech made by Beverly about women's roles in today's society. Allen looked away from the circle of people sitting on the carpet and stared at Beverly's poster of Molly Yard. Underneath, a sculpture of two women embracing each other made of dark mahogany.

"Allen." He heard his name called and turned around. All eyes were on him.

"Yeah?" he asked nervously.

"I was just telling everyone about the Monkey Club," said Xiene, wearing a 'Women NOW!' T-shirt and jeans.

"Oh. Oh, yeah," said Allen, looking at Tawana Brown, the Black woman with the afro and African dashiki.

Xiene continued her story of the Monkey Club

Allen looked at the other women in the group. Most looked like your typical school teacher/nurse/older woman-sick-of-taking-shit-from-men types. A lesbian couple held hands next to a mousy woman with thick glasses. Xiene and Allen were the youngest in the circle. Looking back at Xiene, he noticed Tawana Brown looking at him like she hated him. Allen smiled. She turned her head away. When Xiene finished her story, Beverly spoke.

"Okay, everybody, now we have to decide what to do about the Monkey Club and other meat factories."

"Let's write our congressmen," said the mousy woman, followed by groans.

"Let's call N.O.W.," said a woman in a cutoff jean jacket and hair almost as short as Allen's.

"No," Beverly stated, "we have to do this ourselves."

"Let's bomb the fuckers!" yelled Tawana, followed by a scary silence.

"Er, I don't think so," said the Black intellectual with Black framed glasses.

"Yeah, that's too drastic," Beverly added. "I think we should protest. Let the people become aware of the problem. Therefore, even if they won't change the club, at least we'll get our message out to the people," Beverly suggested.

"Bullshit! That won't work! Protest never works!" Tawana yelled.

"It worked for Civil Rights in the 60s," Allen said, feeling like smacking the shit out of himself for disagreeing with the militant Tawana.

Tawana glared at him with pure disgust. "I don't know what the hell you're doing here, but—"

Xiene interrupted. "A protest! Yeah! I'll make the signs. Allen and his friends are all artists—they can help, too!"

"Great!" added Beverly. "We'll do it this Saturday when they're open."

"I'll call the news," said the Black intellectual.

"Okay." The meeting of Women for Women adjourned.

They all got off the ground and headed out the door. As she left, Tawana glared at Allen. Behind her back, he crossed his eyes and stuck out his tongue. He felt a smack on the back of his head. Turning around, he saw Xiene. She hit him with a copy of 'Men Aren't Pigs, Pigs Are Smart' by Tawana Brown.

"Ouch! Why did you hit me?"

I saw what you did."

"What do you expect? 'I think we should bomb the fucker?'" Allen said in a goofy voice.

"Now, now," Beverly said coming out of her kitchen with three cups of tea. Two cats moved around her feet. "You'll have to excuse Tawana. She can be a little headstrong sometimes,". She navigated around the cats. "She grew up during those Watts riots and I think they affected her." She served the tea.

Allen pictured a little Tawana throwing a Molotov cocktail through a cop's window. "She seems to think violence is the answer to everything."

Beverly took a sip of her tea.

Allen looked over at Xiene reading Tawana's book. "I know someone else who thinks violence is the only answer."

Xiene smiled. "So, Allen, are you going to help us protest?"

"Hmm..." Allen thought about a bunch of men pointing at him as he carried a sign, yelling sexist, or racist insults. He looked at Beverly, her overweight body sitting on the carpet, legs crossed, her smile causing her dimples to show on her chubby cheeks. He started to like this person, even though they had just met. "Sure, why not?"

"Pass me the red," asked Brandon, who had just finished painting an upraised fist. Oswald stood up on the hardwood floor and changed the CD on his stereo. Xiene, wearing her white painter's outfit, lay on her stomach painting the word 'sexist' in green, the bottom of her bare feet up in the air, covered in dirt from Oswald's floor. Oswald sat back down.

"How do you spell 'castrating?'" Allen joked.

They all looked up to see if he was serious, then continued working. While the Cocteau Twins CD played over Oswald's 4-foot speakers, Xiene put her head down onto her hands, exhausted. Oswald reached over and started rubbing her neck with his right hand.

Allen finished painting the ocean on his Earth. Underneath read: 'Women of the World, Unite and Fight!' "I wonder what Tawana's sign will say."

"Who's Tawana?" asked Brandon.

"It will probably be some guy's penis being cut off with 'Bomb the Fucker!' underneath," Allen said while dipping his brush.

Xiene raised her head. "That's not fair. You shouldn't talk about someone who's not here to defend themselves."

"Who's Tawana?" Brandon asked again.

"Yeah, well I can't picture her protesting peacefully."

"She's a neat person. You should read her book. She reminds me of a feminist Malcolm X."

"Bullshit!" Allen said silently while putting the exclamation point on the sign.

"Who's Tawana?" Brandon asked for the third time.

Xiene explained about Tawana. Allen stood to get a soda out of the fridge. Walking through the dialogue exchange to the kitchen he noticed a cartoon on Oswald's drawing table on the left. Leaning over, he read the cartoon. It had Humpty Dumpty in a courtroom, suing the king's horses and men for malpractice.

Allen got his soda and resumed sitting on the floor just when Xiene finished her Tawana explanation.

"Sounds like a weird woman," Brandon said, smiling.

"She is not!"

"See, I'm not the only one," Allen said, mumbling.

"You guys!" Xiene stood up.

Allen looked up. "Where are you going?"

"I need some cigarettes." Xiene reached for her Guatemalan handbag and walked out the door.

"What's with her?" Oswald said after sipping his soda.

"I don't know, she's been acting weird…or weirder than usual ever since the Monkey Club. I notice she hasn't worn high heels, earrings, or a dress in two weeks."

Nothing wrong with that," said Brandon.

"Yeah, it's fine if that's what you want to do, but I think Tawana person is telling her what to do. She's starting to think I'm the biggest male chauvinist in town."

"You are!" Oswald joked.

"Ha-ha, very funny," Allen said, mixing the paint. "Xiene said she likes earrings and heels and dresses, so I think she's being influenced."

That night, after driving Allen home, Allen leaned over and kissed her. She cut the kiss short with a bye-bye and a smile. Allen, feeling cheated, slammed the door to her car and headed for the apartment. *I can hear her now, 'Men are dogs, don't let them control you, Xiene!'*

Saturday came. Allen woke at 10:35 am, and called Xiene to invite her to breakfast. No answer. Later, at 12:30 pm, he called again. No answer. He tried until 4:20 pm. He gave up and went to Lennox Mall for a late lunch. At the magazine rack in the bookstore, while looking through a Comic Scene magazine, reading an article about Robotech, someone bumped into him. Turning around, he saw Beverly.

"Hi, Allen," she said hugging him.

"You hanging around here until the protest tonight?"

"Actually, I'm here with my girlfriend Maggie."

Maggie, a woman in her late thirties was not only Beverly's partner but also a divorcée and mother, which she explained to Allen as the threesome sat down to chat in the food court.

"So, Allen, where is Xiene?" Beverly asked between curlycue fries from Gyro Wrap.

"I thought you would know. I tried to reach her all day."

Hasn't Xiene been hanging around Tawana?" asked Maggie.

"Yes," Beverly said, almost as if Allen wasn't meant to hear it.

"You have her number?" Allen asked, standing up.

Beverly reached into her jeans and pulled out her address book. She handed Tawana's business card to Allen. It was very plain. Allen expected a castrated penis logo with 'Bomb the Fucker'.

He called home first to see if Xiene had called yet. Brandon answered and told him no. He checked his watch. 8:30. *Jeez, where is she? Is she mad at me?* Allen called Tawana's number. An answering machine was activated.

"This is Tawana Brown. Leave a message if you're a woman. Go fuck yourself if you're a man!"…Beep!

"What if you're gay?" was Allen's message before hanging up. He walked back to the table and sat down in silence.

"Something wrong, Allen?" asked Maggie.

"Xiene's not there, and hasn't called me all day."

"Are you guys having problems?" asked Beverly, her eyes showing sincere concern.

"Yeah, and her name's Tawana."

"What does she have to do with you two?" asked Maggie.

"She's coming between us. She's turning Xiene into a lesbian." First Maggie, then Beverly burst into hysterical laughter. "What?" Allen said, looking confused.

Beverly explained while wiping tears from her eyes from laughing so hard. "Allen, you don't just turn gay overnight. You're born that way. If Xiene were a lesbian you would know by now. I think she just sees Tawana as a hero figure. You know how Xiene likes radical thought and rebels."

"Yeah, but Xiene and me haven't…you know, in two weeks. Even her long kisses are becoming extinct," Allen explained.

"Sometimes people get in moods where they don't want to fool around. It's quite normal, even for someone like Xiene," Beverly educated.

"Hmm." Allen thought about it for a while. "I'll be back," he said, jumping up. He ran upstairs to the Dungeons & Dragons shop and bought a figure of Merlin holding a plastic red ruby, one Xiene had admired the last time they were in there.

Beverly and Maggie gave Allen a lift to the Monkey Club in Maggie's Volvo. As they pulled up, they saw the rest of the group crowding near the fence surrounding the parking lot, raising signs, some designed by him, and shouting at the horny businessmen pulling in. Some men covered their faces as if on TV, while others yelled anti-woman, anti-lesbian slurs. One man even got out of his Trans Am and got into an argument with the Black intellectual.

Allen held up a banner with 'Ladies First!' on it. After a while and a couple of anti-Black slurs aimed at him, he relaxed and started enjoying yelling back at the passing cars. After thirty minutes of no Xiene or Tawana, Allen walked over to Beverly holding a sign with 'Women Against Worldwide Oppression Unite!' on it.

"You're hurting women around the world!" she yelled at a passing white Toyota.

Allen tapped her shoulder. "Where's Xiene?

"What?" she turned around.

"Where's Xiene? She's thirty minutes late."

"I don't know." Tawana's not here, either."

"Oh, shit," Allen said silently. He looked around for a pay phone. He found one across the street next to a Mini-Mart. He called home, no messages. He called Xiene's. He got the answering machine. He called Tawana. This time, after her 'If you're a man, go fuck yourself' message, he said, "What about hermaphrodites?" He hung up the phone and looked across the street, at all of the cars blowing, yelling action. *Xiene wouldn't miss this for the world. Something's wrong!*

Allen ran across the street to Beverly. "Beverly, I got to get going! I think Xiene's in trouble! I'm going to check her place out!"

"You didn't get an answer?" Beverly asked putting her sign down.

"No!"

"How are you going to get there?"

"I'm going to take MARTA," Allen said, starting to leave. Before he could, Beverly reached into her pocket. "No, here, take Maggie's Volvo!" She handed the keys to Allen.

"No, I don't think—"

"Go ahead and take it, Allen!" Maggie yelled from the picket line.

"Thanks!" Allen ran to the parking lot of the closed Woolworths and hopped in the 1982 Volvo. Driving very carefully yet fast he headed down Piedmont Road to Xiene's apartment.

He noticed that all of the lights were on. After looking for a parking space he found one under a pine tree next to a Ford Bronco. He ran up the two flights of stairs and arrived at her door. He knocked a couple of times, then pulled out his keychain with a green change purse on the end. Picking out Xiene's key, he opened the door.

"Xiene?" he called, looking around the lit apartment. He opened the bedroom door. With no sign of her, he quickly checked the kitchen. He heard the water pipes being used. He ran to the bathroom. The door was locked.

Allen banged on it. 'Xiene?"

He heard the shower running.

"I'm going to knock this door down!"*Yeah, right!*

Another bang on the door. A wet-haired Xiene opened the door, completely nude. He grabbed her and pulled her into the hallway.

"Allen? What's wrong?" she asked.

"I was worried. You were late."

"Late for what?"

"The protest? Hello?"

"That doesn't start until midnight."

"It started like an hour ago! Are you insane?"

"No, Tawana told me it started at midnight. She just left so she should know."

Well, either she's lying or you both have the world's worst sense of time! We've been trying to call you all day!"

"Nobody has been trying to call me."

"Have you checked your answering machine?"

Xiene walked over to her phone and picked it up. She looked surprised. "Huh…no dial tone."

Alan walked over and took the phone from her. After listening to silence, he searched around the phone and pulled the loose cord. "No wonder, your phone is unplugged."

Xiene plugged the phone back in and listened to a long string of messages.

"See, I told—"

Xiene raised her hand, and cut Allen off, and listened intensely to one of the messages. "This one is from Tawana…She's apologized for unplugging my phone…she said she did it because she didn't want me to get arrested with everybody else …Holy shit!"

" What? Is it?"

"When she drops a bomb on the club at midnight!"

"What? She's going to bomb the Monkey Club!" Allen looked at her Micky Mouse clock on the dresser.

11:20 pm

"Shit! We have forty minutes!" He ran to the phone.

"Who are you gonna call?"

"The cops, of course!" Xiene grabbed the phone and slammed it down.

"What, are you nuts?"

"No police!"

"Why not? People are gonna be hurt!"

"It will ruin the Women for Women movement if they find out one of us is a terrorist! We have to stop her ourselves!"

"Ha-ha," Allen laughed insanely, "do you have a cape?"

"What?" Xiene didn't get the joke.

"A cape," he repeated. How are we gonna stop a militant terrorist with dynamite?"

"By trying!" Xiene said, heading into the bedroom to dress.

"Can't you go any faster?" Xiene bitched.

"Not with that cop beside us." The two policemen looked over at Allen and Xiene in the Volvo: Xiene in a black beret and sunglasses grinned nervously at them. They turned off at Piedmont and headed away. Allen floored the Volvo and ran through a red light, and a yellow two seconds before. A pickup truck screeched behind them and ran over the median.

Looking behind for damage, Xiene lowered her glasses, turned back around, and continued searching through her bag. "No damage done," she said, pulling out some mace.

"Thank god, Maggie's gonna kill me if I damage this car. Allen pulled into the Woolworth's parking lot.

They jumped out of the car and waited to cross the street. Traffic suddenly became so busy they were trapped.

"I don't think we'll make it," Allen said, checking his watch. "It's…

11:30 pm

He looked over at Xiene. She had made it between the first and second cars. A car screeched around her and hit a red truck from behind. All traffic on their side of the street came to a halt due to the accident. Xiene moved over the median to take the other three lanes. Allen walked across the first three lanes stepping on broken glass. Xiene stuck her combat boot off the median, causing a Volkswagen to screech on its brakes and a black Datsun 2802X to hit it from behind, followed by a white taxicab. Xiene waved to the Volkswagen driver yelling at her. Allen walked and chased Xiene.

"Allen! What the hell? Where's Xiene going?" asked a friend of Beverly who watched the whole car crash scene.

Allen tossed Maggie's keys to Beverly.

"It's Tawana! She's gonna bomb this place!"

Allen continued running.

"Holy shit!" Beverly said, dropping her sign.

"Wait up!" Allen called to Xiene.

"Run faster!" Xiene yelled, avoiding a large limo headed for the entrance. The usher grabbed Xiene before she made it inside.

"Hey! Where do you think you're going?"

"Inside! Is there a law?"

"It is if you're dressed like GI Joe!"

"Shouldn't we just tell him about Tawana?" Allen asked.

"No!" Xiene yelled, "I told you, they'll end up arresting everybody! We have to handle this!" Xiene took out her mace.

Allen jumped over the body of the screaming usher.

"Hey!" yelled the girl with the Marilyn Monroe mole as Xiene and Allen rushed past her.

Where is she?

Xiene disappeared into the golden doors. A second later she was being carried out by the two Arab bouncers, her camouflage pants kicking in every direction.

Allen, not seen by the bouncers, got pushed behind the door as they opened it, whacking his shoulder and sending him flying against the left wall of the hallway, as the bouncers continued carrying Xiene.

"You assholes let me go! This is a matter of life and death!" she yelled. Allen went in front of the doors

"Yoo-hoo! Hey, knuckleheads, you forgot me!" he yelled.

The right bouncer let go of Xiene.

"I'll get him! You get her out of here!"

Xiene kicked the other one in the balls. He backed against the wall in pain and let her go. As she maced the bouncer meant for Allen, Beverly and the wimpy-looking woman came in.

"Can't talk, gotta go!" Xiene said, grabbing Allen and running through the doors.

11:40 pm

They entered the club. The place was more packed than before. All twenty dancers were onstage, fully unclothed. A song by New Order played over the speakers. Xiene shoved past some businessmen, looking for Tawana. Allen split off and went right. Shouts and lots of 'Hey, asshole!' greeted him with every push. Meanwhile, some screams greeted Xiene on the other side of the room.

11:45 pm

Not enough time! Allen ran to the stairwell leading to the Voice of God booth. *Maybe I can get the announcer to evacuate the place!* A blond redneck grabbed Allen.

"Hey, boy! You just stepped on my boot!" He took a swing at Allen but being so drunk missed his face and hit his sore shoulder. Allen fell against a table, causing the naked redhead to fall off onto some Japanese businessmen, who weren't completely upset about it.

Xiene started pogoing, trying to look over the crowd off in the distance. The two bouncers burst into the hall, being beaten by Maggie and Beverly with picket signs.

11:50 pm

Not enough time!

Xiene jumped on the stage, pushing a stripper with 38-inch breasts out of her way, she fell into the crowd below.

Allen Jumped onto another part of the stage.

"Fire!" yelled Xiene. "Fire! Fire! Fire!" she repeated.

Fire will evacuate the place faster than a bomb will. Allen started yelling "Fire!" also, followed by Beverly and Maggie. The crowd rushed out the door, nude women and Japanese businessmen crawling over each other, screaming. There was the sound of glass breaking. The music scratched and shut off.

Allen looked for Xiene. She was in the back of the crowd. He ran over and helped her back onto the stage.

"We can go out the back exit!"

An explosion went off. *Oh shit! Oh, god! It went off a minute early!* Allen thought of the lost time he wouldn't have with Xiene—their kids, their house, their dog named Divine. Allen turned around and saw Tawana holding a smoking revolver.

"Nobody move!"

The crowd froze. Total silence. Xiene on the far right of Tawana, Allen on the left.

Xiene slowly walked towards Allen. Allen started walking towards Xiene. Both looked at Tawana holding a brown duffle bag.

"That's far enough, you two!" she yelled, pointing the revolver between them.

"Tawana, you don't have to do this!" pleased Xiene.

"The hell I don't! Look, look around you!"

Allen looked to his right, down at the terrorized businessmen and their strippers. Even the redneck who punched him had his eyes and mouth wide open.

"You see what it takes? Do you see what it takes to get the attention of people nowadays? Simple protests don't work! You got to make some noise!" She fired the gun, sending a bullet between Allen and Xiene, smashing a mirror behind them.

The audience screamed.

"Everybody shut the fuck up!" Tawana yelled. They did. She started walking around the stage. "Nowadays, the only way to get people's attention is by drastic measures, and that's why I got this!" She patted the duffle bag.

"Tawana, please don't! We don't have much time! Throw the bomb…" the audience rumbled, some saying 'bomb'. "Throw the bomb away and let's get out here!"

"Shut up, you bitch!" Tawana pointed the gun at Xiene.

Too far away to take her bullet!

"You're just like all the rest! You don't know shit about the movement! You let men use you like all the other guys in here!"

Xiene's face was frozen in fear. "Tawana, I don't let men use me!"

"We'll! What do you call him?" Tawana pointed the gun at Allen. *Should I close my eyes?*

"He's my boyfriend!"

"He's your enslaver!" Tawana yelled, "And he uses this to enslave you!" She pointed the gun at Allen's crotch.

Oh, god, not there! My kneecaps, my head, anywhere but there!

"Nobody's telling me what to do!" yelled Xiene. "I'm the master of my own body, I go and come as I please! Being a woman is more than just being equal to men! It means being better! Tawana, I'm not a man! Neither are you! Men are warlike, selfish bastards! Don't give up your womanhood to be like—"

Beep…beep…beep—Tawana's watch went off, signaling…

12:00 midnight

Allen looked at Xiene. "I love you!" he called.

"I love you, too!" Tears flowed out of her eyes.

Tawana's watch beeped for a minute in total silence. When it stopped, she reached into her duffle bag and pulled out a book.

"Boom!" she said, then dropping the book on the stage. She then turned on her heel and walked towards the back exit.

Allen and Xiene slowly walked over to the book. Xiene reached down and flipped the white jacket over. On the front, a picture of Tawana Brown and the words 'Time Bomb by Tawana Brown'. Xiene looked at Allen, tears still in her eyes. She laughed nervously and grabbed him. He held her as her laughter turned to sobbing. Maggie and Beverly came onto the stage and put their arms around the two.

Allen squinted from the sea of blue police lights. Two TV stations blinded them with more lights. A news reporter Allen recognized stuck a mike in front of Xiene.

"Tell me, is it true you are friends with the suspect?"

Xiene grabbed the mike and started singing Brown Sugar.

The reporter grabbed the mike. "We can cut that, right Bill?" she asked the cameraman.

Off to the side, the bouncers pointed to Xiene and complained about being assaulted. The club owner cut them off.

"You mean to tell me that little lady over there was able to beat up you two?" The club owner asked. "Do I need to hire someone else?"

"Er-ah, no." they rescinded.

Xiene and Allen squeezed through the wall of people blocking the exit. In the back of one of the police cars, Tawana looked down in defiance. She made eye contact with Xiene and turned her head away. Xiene sighed sadly.

"Everybody Just go home," said the same country-accented cop who had been at the Xiene versus Candy fight. "We've already got your statements. Just leave the premises."

That cop is really phoning it in.

Xiene and Allen squeezed through the wall of people blocking the exit. They spotted Maggie and Beverly in the Volvo parked next to the curb. Maggie leaned out of the passenger side and waved to them. They climbed in the back. As soon as Allen got in, Xiene grabbed him around the torso and put her head on his chest. The car pulled off, heading towards Beverly's house on Lavista. Allen took the beret off Xiene's head and put it on.

He reached into his back pocket and handed the Merlin figure to her. "Marry me."

"You bought it! Wait—marry what?" she said, lifting her head.

"You heard me. Marry me. After coming that close to death, you start thinking about all the things you're going to miss, so marry me."

"No."

"What?"

"No way, man! The only reason you want to marry me is because you thought we were going to die. If we get married I want it to be under better terms." She put her head back on Allen's chest and admired the Merlin figure. "Thank you, I love it!"

The car traveled down the avenue. Allen thought about the future of the Women's group. "Hey Beverly, I guess Tawana's actions are gonna hurt your cause."

"Not really," Beverly said while turning onto Lindberg Avenue.

"What?"

"Yeah, you think anybody's going to go into a club that gets bomb threats? That place is history."

"I wish she could have plugged her new book more quietly," kidded Maggie, playing with Beverly's hair.

Allen kissed Xiene's forehead.

"You know…"Xiene said. "…None of this insanity would have ever happened if you had just taken me to a male strip club in the first place."

Allen thought about it for a moment. "Still worth it."

THE THEORY OF RELATIVES!

Xiene came by to pick Allen up from work that Friday. As she walked in, Pat almost dropped the stack of envelopes she was holding. Xiene had gone out of her way appearance-wise. Using some mousse, she had spiked her white and pink hair on one side. The other side lay flat. Her eyeshadow could have been compared to that of a raccoon. She wore a tight black leather outfit from shoulder down, complete with spikes, studs, chains, and a tiny whip on her left. Her high spiked-heeled boots had silver toes and ran all the way to her thigh. Her nails, black, matched the voodoo chicken claw hanging around her neck.

"Hi, is Allen here?" she asked through black lips with a dash of red paint on the corner, giving the appearance of blood coming out of her mouth.

Pat nervously shuffled the envelopes and got up. "I'll see." She rushed out to find Allen.

Allen had just finished draining the photo chemicals into the plastic carton. It gave off the sound of someone peeing. Pat peeked in.

"Er ah, Allen, someone is here to see you."

Allen looked out of the stat room and knew why Pat had such a distressed look on her face. After washing his hands in the bathroom, he walked into the office. No one was there. Xiene grabbed his butt. He quickly turned around. She embraced him and stuck her tongue down his throat. When she finished, Allen looked over at Don and Pat on the left, mouths and eyes wide open.

"Er, ah, this is my girlfriend," Allen said through black-smeared lips.

"So, this is the T-shirt shop," Xiene stated while Allen packed his bag. Xiene walked around the break room beside Allen's office. Picking up the coffee pot, she looked over at Allen.

"Is this the coffee machine they keep coming in here to use?"

"Yeah. I never get any privacy, thanks to that damn coffee pot."

Xiene walked out of the break room with the coffee pot while Allen put the last bit of art supplies in his tackle box. He heard heard the sound of running water. *Is she making coffee?*

A few minutes later she came back with the pot half-full of water. She walked over to the coffee maker and started pouring the water onto the heating pad.

"What are you doing?"

"Watch," she said, cutting on the machine. After a few seconds, Allen heard popping noises and then an electrical fire smell.

"What did you do?"

"I shorted it out. Now they can't make coffee."

"That won't work. Don will just buy a new coffeemaker."

"Your cheap-ass boss buy something new? Ha!" laughed Xiene.

Allen was too tired to debate.

They headed out the front door, being watched by Don and Pat. Before she went out the door, Xiene turned and looked at them.

"Nice meeting you. Which one of you is Pat?"

"I am," Pat said, pointing to herself, not getting the insult.

"Okay," Xiene said, leaving with a smirk.

They got in Xiene's van. Allen leaned his head on Xiene's shoulder, avoiding the studs near his cheek.

Xiene put her arms around him.

"Tough day, babe?" she asked while pulling out of the parking lot.

"I don't even want to think about it."

By the time they made it to 285, heading home, Xiene put a Ministry tape in the player. The jangly, heavy punk-thrash music rattled Allen's nerves, so he sat upright the rest of the trip. By the time they made it to his home, he had a headache. Walking up to his apartment, one of his next-door neighbors came out. Allen wondered if they were drug dealer murderers because they never made any noise, they kept to themselves, they always had the lights off except for the glow of their TV set through the curtains in their living room, and they had visitors at odd hours.

The mustached man passed Xiene. "Hi, how ya doing? he asked.

"Oh, I don't know. My arm really hurts and I went to the doctor to get it fixed. My doctor's name is Paul Windal. You know the Windals, they're from New Jersey. They moved here for the hot weather, because their son, Bobby, got sick sitting in their black Cadillac one time at K-Mart—maybe it was an Eckerd drug's—Anyway…"

Xiene continued rambling for five more minutes before the man interrupted. "Listen, I gotta go. Nice to meet you." He lumbered down the concrete steps holding his head and mumbling.

Xiene walked into the apartment. Allen had lain down on the big couch with a wet towel on his head.

"You got a headache?"

"Yep." With every heartbeat, Allen's head throbbed.

"I know the cure for that." Xiene ran up the stairs. She returned ten minutes later. She had taken her boots off and carried a box of pins and some matches.

Allen turned and looked at her. "What the hell are you gonna do with that?"

"Acupuncture."

"Hell, no, not on me!"

"Ah, come on, you baby. I know how to do this."

"Bullshit!" Allen hopped up and ran across the living room. Xiene reached into the box and pulled out a pin two inches long. "I think this will do it."

"Hell, no! You keep that away from me!" Allen said, running into the kitchen.

Xiene took out a match, lit it, and heated the end of the pin while walking towards him.

"What are you doing?"

"I'm sterilizing it."

"More like the red-hot poker treatment!" Allen backed against the cabinet.

She chased him out of the kitchen and into the living room, laughing insanely. He ran to the front door and picked up the metal baseball bat in the corner.

"Get back!" he yelled, holding the bat in the air.

"Ah, you're no fun," she said, putting the pin back in the box.

He put the bat down, went back to the couch against the window, and lay down. Xiene went into the kitchen. As Allen rested, he heard her moving dishes around and running water. "What are you doing?"

"Washing your dishes."

"Why?"

"Why not?"

Allen turned over and went to sleep. The dream probably lasted ten seconds. In his head, it lasted an hour. He held Xiene's hand as she hung out the window of a burning building. Allen was losing his grip. As the heat singed his arm the sweat from their hands made her slip more and more. She let go and turned into a blackbird. But instead of flying away, she died and spiraled to the ground below.

Allen's scream caused Xiene to drop a dish and run from the kitchen. "What's wrong?"

Covered in sweat, he looked around the room, tightly gripping the cushions of the couch.

"You alright?" Xiene walked over, still holding a wet rag.

Allen looked around the room: house, *Xiene, street, Atlanta, USA, Earth,* trying to decide if the dream had ended.

"Honey?" Xiene said, walking up to wipe his head.

He grabbed the rag. Realizing he was awake, he grabbed her hand and pulled her on top of him. He moved his hands through her hair.

"What's wrong?"

"Nothing. Just a bad dream."

Xiene lifted her head off of his chest. "It must have been a doozy."

"Yep," Allen said, holding her face in his hands. She reached over and kissed him and resumed hugging him. Allen heard water running in the kitchen.

Xiene hopped up. "Oh, shit, I left the water running." She ran to the kitchen.

Allen lay on the couch, trying to figure the dream out. The front door opened and Brandon came in holding a bag of groceries.

"Hi!" Brandon said, headed for the kitchen.

When Allen heard Brandon scream he knew he had seen Xiene in her new makeup job. Brandon and Xiene passed Allen and walked out the door.

"Come on and help with the groceries," Xiene said.

Allen got off the couch and followed the other two. While getting the groceries out of Brandon's grey Chevrolet 510 truck, Allen noticed some little girls across the street playing jump rope. He stared at them for a few minutes until Xiene grabbed him under the armpits, causing him to shriek and drop his sack. As red liquid oozed from the bottom of the paper bag, searching through revealed the fall had broken a bottle of spaghetti sauce.

"Shit. Thanks a lot."

"I'm sorry. I didn't think that was in there," explained Xiene.

"You never think. That's your problem.

"Fuck you!" Xiene said with arms akimbo.

"I'm sorry. It's just that nightmare." Allen grabbed Xiene's shoulders. "I'm sorry," he said again.

"No problem." She hugged him.

Allen finished eating his spaghetti minus meat sauce. He sat on the left side of the small couch facing the television, Xiene in the middle, legs up, and Brandon on the right. Harpo confused Groucho on the TV. Xiene and Brandon laughed, Allen didn't, still thinking of the weird dream, trying to figure it out.

Xiene laughed then nudged Allen in the right ribs. "Waka waka! Don't you get it, Allen?" she asked. "Why are you so quiet?"

The movie ended. Brandon went upstairs to bed. Xiene lay down and put her feet on Allen's lap.

"Can I have a foot massage?"

Allen began massaging her small feet, causing her to occasionally moan. After a while he noticed she had fallen asleep, so he got a blanket out of the upstairs closet, put it on her, and went upstairs to bed.

At two in the morning, someone opened his door. Xiene's silhouette, lit by the hall light, entered his room and closed the door. He heard zippers and buckles being undone, followed by the sound of clothes hitting the floor. She slipped into bed with him. He felt her topless chest against his. He reached down and slid her underwear down. Just then a fire broke out. The ceiling caved in. Xiene jumped out of bed and ran to the window. She looked down, then at Allen. A beam swung down and hit her shoulder, causing her to tumble out of the window. Allen ran over and grabbed her hand before she fell. Her hand slowly slipped from his and she fell, turning into a dead blackbird.

Allen woke up in a sweat again. He hopped out of bed and ran downstairs. Xiene lay on the little couch snoring. He went over and squatted next to the couch and watched her sleep for an hour.

"Were you there all night?" Xiene asked.

Allen woke up sitting on the floor next to her. "What?" he asked, adjusting his eyes to the sunlight.

"I said, were you sitting there all night?"

He rubbed his eyes. "Yeah, I guess so."

"Ahh! Why didn't you go up to bed?"

"I did. I…" he began to tell her about the nightmare but decided not to. "I couldn't sleep up there without you."

"Ah, you baby," Xiene said while grabbing him. She kissed his head.

Allen got up and cut the TV on. They watched a couple of stupid Saturday morning cartoons, Xiene insulting every action the animated figures made.

Later, Brandon came downstairs and joined them. They decided to go to the park. Allen went upstairs to shower.

"You want company?" Xiene asked, raising her eyebrows up and down.

"Nah, I won't be long," Allen said, climbing the stairs.

A bird flew onto the Free Nelson Mandela statue. It looked at Xiene and Allen lying on the grass, then flew over their heads. Allen covered his face in case the bird crapped on him. Xiene rolled over, lay on her stomach, and moaned due to the coolness of the clover against her bare legs. Staring at Xiene's legs, Allen scanned his way up to her head, studying every part of her: Her black jogging shorts with white stripes, her grey T-shirt with her name on the back in black letters, her white and pink hair, her nose ring, the little hairs on her arms, the freckles on her smooth skin, her delicate fingers with two eyeball rings on the left hand, and her long purple painted fingernails.

She opened her eyes and looked at him. "What?" she asked.. "Allen, what are you looking at?" she reached her hand back and checked her pants. "Is the crack of my butt showing or something?"

Allen laughed. "No, I was just noticing how much I love you."

"Ah, come here." She reached out her left arm. Allen moved over and kissed her. A football hit him on the head. Behind him, he heard, "Oh, I'm sorry!" and another person laughing.

Turning around he saw Beverly and Maggie. Maggie, in front, had obviously thrown the ball.

"Sorry, I tried to make it land between you guys, but you moved."

"How dare I move when people throw things at me?" Allen said sarcastically while rubbing his head.

"Hey, let me see if he's alright. I'm a doctor." Beverly kneeled.

"You're a psychologist," protested Maggie.

"They both work with head injuries," added Xiene.

"I thought you were an anthropologist?" Allen asked.

"I am now. Maggie meant to say I used to be a psychology major back in college. I changed majors halfway."

"You remember any of it?"

"Sure," said Beverly.

I wonder if she could help me find the meaning of the dream?

Looking near the pond, Allen saw Brandon and Kathy walking near the dock. Brandon and Kathy spotted the group and walked over. Brandon, who had become friends with Beverly due to their discussions on liberal politics, hugged her. Allen stood up and looked away from the park at the football field across the street. Xiene's arm grabbed him around the neck, then her legs jumped onto his hips. Allen grabbed her legs, guessing she wanted a piggyback ride.

"Let's go to Frank and Ales," she said.

✖

While the others marveled at its 50s theme, complete with waitresses in roller skates, Allen walked over to the jukebox to find a song he liked. Xiene came by barefoot, arms out like a bird, dancing to Walk Like a Man.

"Good choice," she said, grabbing Allen and then twirling him around.

They started slow dancing. As Xiene ran her hands up and down his back, Allen stared at the airbrush painting of famous rock stars—Elvis, Little Richard, and Aretha Franklin all looked accurate, John Lennon wasn't so hot.

"Did I tell you where I ate yesterday?" Xiene asked.

"What?" Allen didn't hear.

"Where I ate yesterday for breakfast."

"Where?"

That new Mexican restaurant off Piedmont, Sin Amigos."

"Really, how was it?"

"Oh, awful. The meat was terrible, the tacos were hard as a rock.

"Sounds dreadful."

"Oh, it was."

They danced around some more.

"Are you ready to see my mom and dad?"

"Wait! That's today?"

"They fly in tonight but we are meeting them for breakfast at IHOP. So, you still have time to clean yourself up."

"Me? I'm not the one with two-tone hair."

Xiene coughed. "They know what to expect from me." They continued slow dancing. Xiene coughed again and again. Allen patted her back. She continued coughing. The others in the group looked over. She continued coughing. Allen patted her back.

"You alright?"

More coughing. She pushed away from him and then hung onto the jukebox. Allen walked over to her.

"She alright?" someone at their table asked.

More coughing, then vomiting.

"Oh, god! Xiene!"

Allen turned around, looking for something to catch the vomit. More vomiting, coughing, and more vomiting. Allen rubbed her back. The others ran over, some holding napkins. When they made it to her, she fell and grabbed her stomach.

"Oh, god, call an ambulance!" Allen yelled.

An employee roller-skated to the phone behind the counter. Allen put his arms on Xiene's shoulder, comforting her as she coughed more. More vomiting.

Beverly lifted Xiene's hair to keep it from getting wet. Brandon turned his head and seemed to be getting sick. Kathy had a frozen expression on her face.

"Here, drink this." The girl behind the counter handed a glass of water to Xiene.

"No!" Brandon said. "It will make her throw up more."

Xiene dry heaved, then coughed some more. They helped her up. She began crying.

Maggie wiped her mouth and tears. "It's alright, honey, the ambulance is coming!"

"I don't want a fu—" she started vomiting on the tile floor.

"Jesus, what's wrong with her?" Maggie asked.

Beverly wiped Xiene's mouth. Allen held her head to his chest, ready to jump back if she started up again. She held her stomach and continued moaning and crying.

The other patrons left. The employees watched Xiene's coughing and crying.

"God, what's wrong?" Allen said, wiping the vomit out of her hair. She started coughing. Allen pulled away. She continued moaning and crying. "The ambulance is gonna take forever! We have to get her to the hospital now!" yelled Allen.

"But none of our cars are here! The closest one is at my place!" said Kathy, referring to the fact she lived a few blocks away.

"I'll take her." The manager walked from behind the counter. They helped Xiene up. She ripped the neck on Allen's shirt. They carried her out of the restaurant and into a white Suzuki Samurai. The manager called back to the employees. "Call the ambulance off, if you can. I'm gonna take her Grady!"

Allen got in the back with Xiene. Beverly went up front.

"Brandon, call her sister!" Allen yelled. "Their number is on the refrigerator! Tell them to come to Grady!"

"Okay!"

The Samurai ran a red light, almost getting hit on Ponce de Leon. It screeched onto North Avenue and headed towards Grady. Xiene moaned and grabbed onto Allen's shirt.

Beverly reached back and stroked her hair. "It's alright, honey, almost there!."

A traffic jam near State University caused them to drive up on the sidewalk, the manager blowing his horn, causing two students to drop their books and run back into the parking garage.

They arrived at the Grady emergency entrance. Allen used to work at Grady back in '85 as a clerk in the student work-study program. He knew exactly which entrance they should go in.

They helped Xiene out of the car. Two policemen held the door for them. Beverly turned to the manager.

"We can handle it from here! Thanks for your help!"

"No problem! You tell me how she turns out."

"Sure thing!"

They entered the emergency exit and turned left to enter the surgical emergency reception area. Ten people looked up at Xiene. All seemed to be vagrants, poor people, convicts, or anyone who couldn't afford the overpriced private hospitals. The receptionist looked at the threesome, Xiene moaning and crying, Allen and Beverly on her sides holding her up.

"Dr. Chandler, upfront, please," the receptionist announced over the intercom.

A few seconds later a Black female came in wearing red scrubs. "What do we have here?" she put her glasses on, and a surgical mask.

"We don't know. She's been coughing and vomiting a lot. Allen said.

"My stomach! My god, I'm dying!" Xiene interrupted.

"Okay, any fever or pain in the right side of your belly?"

"No!" Xiene moaned.

"Vomiting blood?"

"Gross! No!"

"Did you eat any bad food?"

"Y-Yeah."

"Could be food poisoning. But I want to rule out anything else," The female doctor swung the door open. "Bill, can you take her to room 4 and give her a wash basin."

"Wash basin?" Allen asked.

"Puke bucket."

"Oh."

An intern ran to the back.

"I'm going to separate her into her own room in case it's a norovirus. You, give her…" she pointed to the receptionist, "all of the information."

The doctor grabbed Xiene and started helping her into the clinic. Xiene ripped Allen's shirt collar. Allen grabbed her hand.

"Come on, sweetheart, it's alright. We got you." The doctor said. She grabbed Xiene's arm and pulled. Her hand slipped out of Allen's hands and she was led inside.

"Allen?" she called from inside.

Allen turned around and Beverly hugged him, her tears causing him to tear up.

✖

Allen sat in the reception area filling out as much information about Xiene as possible on a form. He stopped on the insurance question. Allen wondered if she had any. Her parents used to cover her, but when she moved from Virginia dyed her hair, and changed her name to just Xiene they may have cut her off completely, being the Bible-thumping conservatives they are. On the other hand, Allen has seen her dad change his attitude. He still can't figure out why. He treats Allen nicer than the time they first met. Xiene's mother still calls Allen 'Mr. Montgomery to this day, probably so they won't get too close, he figured.

Allen looked over at the older woman and her two out-of-control sons, six and seven years old. They kept crawling on two of the chairs, playing with Mutant Turtle action figures.

"Look! I'm Leonardo," the blond-haired one said before whacking his doll onto the other kid's doll.

"Okay, then I'm Raphael."

Allen wondered if these kids knew what those artist names meant, or would they care?

The mother grabbed the boys by their arms. "Shut up and sit down!" They continued playing. She dragged them out of the office, both screaming at the top of their lungs.

Beverly came back into the reception area holding another clipboard. "Trivia time, Allen. What is Xiene's real hair color?"

"She's a redhead," Allen answered, thinking of her pubic hair.

Beverly wrote the information down. "You know, I never knew that. Her hair has always been dyed since I knew her. Her height?"

"I think she's five-foot-four."

"You know, for a short girl, she sure can fight."

"I think she uses her appearance to psych people out, then she beats them up."

Beverly laughed.

A woman came into the reception area wearing a white Emory University T-shirt. Allen knew her. "Mary!" he called.

Mary turned and walked over to Beverly and Allen. "Hi, Allen, Beverly. How is she?"

"They took her in. They think it's food poisoning.

"Shit, I told her to watch her diet," Mary said, jingling her car keys in her left hand. "My mom and dad here yet?"

"No."

"I left a message with their hotel to come here."

I'm glad Brandon reached you."

"Who's Brandon?"

"My roommate. He's the one that called…You met him at Christmas time."

"Oh, yeah, the fat guy."

"Yeah…sure…the fat guy." *Rude!*

Mary started going through her purse. "Okay, I'm going to try my brother again. I'll be down the hallway." Mary walked out, bumping into a homeless guy in a trench coat.

"Excuse you," he said to her as she continued walking.

"God, I hate her," Allen confessed.

"Yeah, if you look at Mary, Richard, and their parents, you can see why Xiene acts so wild," Beverly said, reaching for a brochure on the rack next to her.

"I never met Richard. What's he like?"

"Oh, just your typical Air Force fanboy. He's nice enough, I guess, just acts too much like his dad."

"'Their' dad has been nice to me lately. I can't figure out why."

"Strange. He treats me and Maggie the same way. Even though he did send a Christmas card to us this year." Beverly started thinking.

Allen grabbed the brochure from her and read Breast Cancer for You. He found the title almost as strange as the illustrations inside. Cartoons of women checking their breasts. He wondered how the brochure would look with traditional cartoon characters instead of the generic ones: *Lucy, Cathy, Blondie, and Nancy rubbing their breasts.*

Allen checked the clock.

9:30 pm

Mary came back in, holding coffee. She sat on the opposite side of the room and crossed her legs. Beverly stood up.

"I'm gonna get some coffee. You want some, pumpkin?"

"Naw, I'm okay, thanks."

Beverly patted him on the shoulder and left the room. Allen looked at the receptionist holding a conversation with a young nurse. They were joking around and laughing.

How can they joke in this place? Looking next to him he noticed the man with the broken arm.

"What are you in here for?" he asked Allen in a country accent.

"Food poisoning."

"Really? You look okay to me."

Allen resisted the temptation to say, "How's this?" and then make vomiting gestures at the guy. Instead, he said, "Not me, a friend has food poisoning."

The stranger then went into his story of the broken arm. It seems he had been working on his pickup truck. He reached under the back tire to pick something up when his hunting dog inside released the emergency brake, causing the truck to run over his arm.

Allen pictured the dog looking over its shoulder and steering with its paws, going for a joyride.

Beverly came back with a coffee and a magazine. The man next to Allen started telling Allen how, when he was a kid living in a one-room house in Conyers, all they had to eat were roots, berries, and dirt.

"Dirt?" Allen interrupted.

"Yeah, there's a certain kind of dirt you eat. It's sort of a white clay."

Allen pictured a family on their hands and knees making bulldozer noises.

A nurse came in and called the stranger into the clinic.

"I hope your friend pulls through," he said to Allen.

"Thanks. I hope you do, too."

"Oh, I will. This ain't nothing." Before leaving he told Allen how when he was a boy he had jumped off a barn into a pile of hay onto the head of his cousin Jethro.

"Ouch. Did he live?" Allen asked.

"Yeah, he's okay. He's an evangelist preacher up in Knoxville.

So that's how they're born.

Brandon and Monroe came in. Allen hugged them both and filled Monroe in.

"Have you seen her?" Monroe asked.

"Nope. We haven't got word yet," Allen answered, sitting back down.

Brandon noticed Mary but forgot her name."

"Hi."

She put her coffee down and cracked a smile. "Hi, Barry."

"It's Brandon," he answered, remembering her calling him that at Christmas.

Monroe sat down and hugged Beverly. They began discussing Xiene.

12:55 am

A policeman escorted a handcuffed man into the room. The man was bleeding from his head and yelling, "Motherfucker, next time you won't get so lucky!"

Allen moved his legs before the man kicked them out of his path.

The cop pushed him into the clinic. Allen looked at the trail of blood leading out the door. Because of AIDS, everyone checked themselves to see if they had any drops on them. A janitor came in wearing a mask and gloves and cleaned up the blood.

1:30 am

Allen had watched maybe three horrible accidents walk by. One had a father holding a cloth to his kids' bleeding nose, another a woman with an ice pack on her head and blood trickling from her ear, and the third Allen didn't look up at, because he heard 'Try and stop the swelling! Don't touch it!'

"I got to get a soda," Allen said, standing up.

"Get me one, too," Brandon said, reaching into his pocket.

"Me, too," said Monroe.

"Could you get me a candy bar, Allen?" asked Beverly.

"Gee, whiz, why don't you all come with me instead?"

"Good idea," said Brandon.

They left the reception area and walked towards the snack shop. People in white outfits walked in all directions. An old lady walked down the hallway pulling her IV drugs around and wearing a breezy hospital gown. They rounded the corner and went into the snack shop. Behind the counter, the store seemed to be run by a blind man. Every dollar bill he would get he would ask what it was.

How honest are people with him? 'Yeah, that's a $208 bill!' He pictured someone saying as they handed him a buck. Maybe he listens to your voice to tell if you're lying.

They got their snacks (which were very overpriced) and headed out. Allen stopped Beverly. She turned around.

"Yes?"

"I need to talk to you."

"Okay guys, Allen, and I will be back in a few minutes."

"Okay," Brandon said as he and Monroe went around the corner.

"Okay, what's up?"

"Not here."

The red neon soda advertisement sign outside could be seen a mile away by anyone driving on I-20. Allen studied the sign walked away from the window and sat down on the couch next to Beverly. They were in an empty waiting area on the 8th floor. Beverly waited for Allen to speak. She smiled at him, then put on her glasses on the top of her head.

Allen sighed. "Okay, you took psychology, right?"

"Yes, a little."

"Can you analyze dreams?"

"Oh, sure. I loved that part of school. I specialized in dreams."

"Great, because I have a doozy for you," Allen told her about the Xiene falling out of his hands from a burning building dream. "…and the blackbird dies," he concluded. "So, what does it mean?"

Beverly crossed her legs on the couch and began thinking. 5 minutes of silence passed. Allen looked out of the window at the glowing soda sign.

"Okay, Allen, I got it."

Allen ran over to the couch. The fire represented a change in your personality or viewpoint. The blackbird, I think that's a sign of dreariness or an indication of coming worries. As for watching someone fall, that's a sign you fear losing someone." Beverly finished and put her glasses on.

Allen laid his head back on the armrest. "Shit."

"Allen, how is your relationship with Xiene?"

"You know how many times I've asked that question?"

"Yeah. I know. I wish you two would work your problems out."

"That's what I'm asking you to do."

"So far your dream reads like an open book."

"Not really. I mean Xiene and I haven't even argued in a month. Things are great. I mean, she's been so nice lately. She even washed my dishes Friday." Allen paused. "A week ago she even let me open the door for her." Allen paused again. "And Friday was the first time in months I've seen her dress wild…" Allen paused for the last time. "Oh, shit."

Allen held his hands on the sides of his head. "Oh, shit. Do you see what's going on?"

"Exactly," Beverly answered. "You feel like you're killing Xiene. You think that your relationship with her is turning her soft and you are letting her down or changing her to normal."

"Oh, shit, I never noticed, but you're right. This is awful."

"Allen you have to remember Xiene does what she wants, and if she wants to act nice it's because she chooses to do so. Xiene wasn't as wild when she moved here at eighteen, but, let's face it, as you grow older you do mature a little."

"Are you saying she's immature?"

"Allen, I love her like a sister, but face it, anyone who puts french fries up their nose and makes walrus sounds can't be too mature."

Allen laughed.

Beverly put her hand on Allen's. "Tell you what. When you visit her, I want you to discuss this with her, and I'll bet she'll tell you the same thing I told you. She's a free spirit, Allen. Even when she's seventy-two she'll still act just as crazy."

✖

When Allen and Beverly walked into the surgical clinic they spotted Xiene's parents telling Mary about their plane trip. Xiene's father walked up and shook Allen's hand.

"Allen, nice to see you again. Hi, Beverly." He hugged Beverly. The expression on her face was almost as shocked as Allen's.

"How is she?" asked Beverly.

"The doctor said it was probably food poisoning. They want to watch her for a while longer to make sure."

"Can we visit?" Allen asked, looking at Xiene's mother, who ignored him.

"No, not yet. She's resting. We won't be able to visit until morning."

"It is morning," Monroe said.

They checked the clock—4:20 am.

"Golly, that's late. Has Maggie come by yet?" asked Allen.

"Maggie has to work at the crisis center 'til six. That reminds me, I'll go tell her about Xiene." Beverly walked out of the room to the phones.

"'Xiene'…I still can't get used to you guys calling Christine that name," Mr. Richards replied, smiling.

Allen walked over to Xiene's mom. "Hi, Mrs. Richards." He stuck out his hand.

She looked at it and then gave him a weak handshake. "How are you, Allen Montgomery?"

"Fine, ma'am, considering."

"Tell me, where did you take Christine to make her sick?"

"Nowhere. She went there on her own."

"Sometimes I wish she would move back to Virginia. Then we could keep a better eye on her."

"Well…"She moved to Atlanta to get out from under your wing.… How was your trip?"

"Awful. The plane was an hour late. I think our son, Richard wastes his money on those military discount tickets he gets for us —Tell me. What color is her hair, nowadays?"

"White and pink."

"Why?"

"It's a long story."

"Well, we have plenty of time."

Allen told Mrs. Richards of Xiene's new hair color. By the time he finished everyone but Mr. Richards, Mrs. Richards and himself lay asleep in the reception area.

"Six o'clock. The sun should be coming up soon. Don't you have to go to work, Allen?"

"Not on a Sunday."

"Oh, golly, I'm going to miss church," she said, looking at her reflection in the mirror.

Mr. Richards sat next to her, reading a sports magazine.

"I saw a chapel down the hall if you need it," Allen said.

"No. Thank you. We prefer our own church. God Knows what's been praying in there," she said. "Golly, you don't even know if the pastor is Baptist or not. You're a Catholic, right?"

"I used to be. I'm more of an…independent right now."

"An atheist?"

"No, not really. More agnostic."

"An atheist," she said, closing her compact. "I'm hungry. Is there anyplace around here open at this time?"

Allen thought for a while. "There's a Burger King at the bus station, just down the street."

"I meant a good place to eat. I don't feel like hanging around with vagrants and prostitutes."

"There's the House of Pancakes on North Avenue. It's a little better and has 10% less vagrants and prostitutes."

Allen was being sarcastic, but she didn't catch on. "Fine. Marty," she elbowed her husband, who had fallen asleep. "Marty, I'm going to breakfast with Allen Montgomery."

He nodded then fell asleep.

The taxi dropped them off at the House of Pancakes. Mrs. Richards and Allen went inside and sat down behind two gay intellectual types discussing John Waters' movies. The place was quite empty, so their orders were filled in no time at all. Allen started putting syrup on his strawberry pancakes. Mrs. Richards started on her cheese blintzes.

"So, tell me what is the name of the restaurant that made Christine sick?"

Allen put the syrup down. "Sin Amigos. It's a new place on Piedmont. The food's pretty awful."

"Well, you won't have to worry about them serving horrible food anymore." She took out a notepad and wrote the name of the restaurant. "I'm going to call my lawyer this afternoon and see if we can't get those people out of business."

"Have you done this before?"

"Oh, yes. We sued a gas station and a convenience store. Both had really bad service. The money from the convenience store was used to send Xiene to the State. Too bad she never finished. What a waste of lawyer fees."

"I think she'll go back one day. We talk about it sometimes."

"Really?" she picked up her coffee and blew on it. "I always thought you were the reason she quit school in the first place."

"Me? No, she just couldn't find time to work and go to school at the same time."

"I told her we would support her and she wouldn't have to work."

Allen started playing with his pancakes. "She wants to be independent. That's why she moved here in the first place."

"A lot of good it's doing. She's poor, has no education, and works as a—where is she working?"

Allen didn't want to tell her Xiene lost her job at the record store, so he lied. "She's doing freelance photography." *Xiene hasn't taken pictures in a month.*

"Oh. That must pay enough," Mrs. Richards said sarcastically.

Allen looked out of the window at the sunrise. Mrs. Richards turned her head.

"Looks like it's going to be a beautiful day," he said.

She nodded. "Yes."

I wish Xie—Christine could see this. She loves sunrises."

"Oh? And what are you usually doing with her this early in the morning, on Sunday?"

Allen thought about telling her Xiene and he liked to have Sunday Sex, but he guessed she didn't want to hear that so he lied again. "We have breakfast here after we go dancing at The Mask down the street. Allen pointed in the direction of the club.

"My god, you two shouldn't be out that late. No wonder you never go to church. You're probably too tired." She sipped her coffee and stared at the gay intellectuals behind Allen. "My god, would you look at that. It's just not natural."

Allen was becoming very irritated.

"Allen, where are you working?"

"I'm a T-shirt designer."

"Hmm. You design those awful rock T-shirts Christine wears."

"No, ma'am. Where I work we do mostly cute animals and company logos."

"Pay well?"

"No."

"Hmm." She reached into her purse and pulled out her compact. "Would you look at my hair? It's a mess." Allen stared at her graying red curly hair. "I guess it's still better than that rainbow mess Christine wears."

"I like her hair," Allen replied.

She looked up. "I guess you have to; otherwise you wouldn't date her."

"I like her for other reasons, not just her hair."

"Oh, really? Like what?"

"Her honesty, her sense of humor, her giving nature, her sensitivity."

"Are we talking about the same Christine?"

"Yes."

"Goodness, you must know a side of her we haven't seen yet."

Allen was officially irritated.

"You know, she used to be so pretty before she started dying her hair and wearing earrings in weird places." Mrs. Richards reached into her purse and pulled out a 4x5 photo album. She flipped past some pictures, then stopped on one. She showed it to Allen. "This is Christine before she left Virginia."

Allen was shocked. There stood Xiene next to a brown horse. It had been taken at the Richard's summer ranch home. Her hair down to her shoulders was a beautiful red color. She wore no makeup no earrings or nose rings. She was quite beautiful.

"She's so pretty in that shot, don't you think?"

Allen ignored her.

"Allen?"

"What? Huh?"

"Don't you think she's pretty back then?'

I'm trying to turn Xiene back into the Christine in the photo. I'm just as bad as her mom. "I think she's pretty now." Allen was getting tired of playing defense to Mrs. Richard's Xiene offensive. The waitress came by and gave them coffee refills. "Mrs. Richards, did Xiene smoke back then?"

"Christine is smoking?"

Oh, shit! Maybe she never smoked in front of them and I let the cat out of the bag. "Er, yes. Every now and then," he replied hesitantly.

"Oh, god, she told me she stopped."

Relieved, a little, Allen added, "She's cut down drastically. She's down to two per week."

"As long as it's not crack drugs. You aren't into crack drugs, are you Allen Montgomery?"

"Never touched the stuff."

"Good. At least we can feel safe Christine's not into crack drugs."

I wonder if Xiene uses drugs when she hangs out with her other friends?

"Allen, you know you and Xiene are an odd pair. How did you two meet?"

Allen thought about telling her the whole truth but gave her the short version. "We met at Oakland Cemetery. She was taking pictures and I was there with my friend Monroe walking around and we met her."

"A graveyard? How morbid

They got their check. Mrs Richards searched in her purse for money.

"Don't worry, I'll get it," Allen said, grabbing his wallet.

"My, how kind of you. You know, none of Christine's old boyfriends would ever pick up a tab." Allen felt a compliment coming. "Then again, there was that nice boy, Michael Landers. He was so polite, sometimes I wished she would have married him."

By the time they made it back to the hospital, it was visiting hours. Allen chose to go last so he could talk to Xiene alone while Monroe, Brandon, and Beverly visited. Allen wandered the hallway looking for a phone to call Kathy and tell them of Xiene's progress. The doctor told them she would return to normal within a couple of days after being on a really wimpy diet of toast, bananas, and apple sauce. Allen spotted a row of phones separated by tiny walls between each one. He called Kathy and related the good news. He hung up and began searching for the number to Frank and Ales to tell the manager everything was going to be alright. By the time he figured out he would be calling too early, he heard Mr. Richards on the phone next to his.

"Yes…she's okay now. Yes, I miss you, too. Oh, sweetheart, this weekend was pure hell…No, we didn't sleep together. Don't act so jealous. Yes, you know I love you…"

Allen sneaked down the hall. *So that's why he's been so nice! Mr. Richards is getting it on with another woman! Should I tell anyone? If I tell Mrs. Richards, she won't believe me, and what good would it do? If I tell Xiene, she would start throwing up again. He pushed the whole thing out of his head.*

Allen spotted Maggie coming out of Xiene's room. Maggie walked over and hugged Allen. "Sorry I'm late, sweetie, but I had this one lady on the phone. It took me three hours to talk her out of suicide."

"How is she?"

"Fine. She doesn't want to kill herself anymore."

"I mean Xiene?"

Maggie laughed. "Oh! Xiene's fine. I meant my lady."

"Oh, okay. I guess I'm next."

Maggie hugged Allen again and kissed his cheek.

Allen slowly opened the door. Xiene sat upright in the bed and was reading a Heavy Metal comic bought in by Brandon for her.

"You know, in your condition, you shouldn't be reading that stuff, with all the gore in there."

Xiene laughed.

He walked over sat on the bed, and put his right hand on her left cheek. She moved her head and kissed his palm. He leaned forward and kissed her forehead. Allen felt her stomach. "How ya doing?"

"I'm okay, now. But I bet they don't let me in Frank and Ales again."

Allen laughed. "I was so worried about you."

She held out her hands and he moved over and hugged her. After a while, Allen pulled back.

"Xiene, can I ask you something?"

"Sure," she said, stroking his head.

"In the time I've known you, do you think I've been softening you up?"

"What?"

"Well, you know. Am I turning you soft?"

"I don't understand."

"I'll give you a perfect example. When I first met you, you knocked the arm off a statue, and now you're in the kitchen washing dishes."

"Oh. Do you think I'm becoming domesticated?"

"Yeah."

"Bullshit! If I wash your dishes, it's because I want to do it. I have a dishwasher and I kind of missed doing dishes the old-fashioned way."

"What about your wild appearance? You haven't dressed wild for a month until Friday."

Xiene put her hands on her hair and lifted somewhat and pink strands. "Do you see any red roots in my hair?"

"No."

"Then I'm still doing whacky stuff to myself. When I get out, I'm going to get a mohawk."

"What about that time you let me open the door for you?"

"I was tired as shit. I didn't feel like arguing."

"I haven't seen you do anything bizarre lately."

"Okay, really? How's this?" She picked up a clean specimen cup and then poured her can of apple juice into it. She turned around and buzzed the nurse.

The nurse came in a minute later. "Yes?"

"I'm finished with my specimen."

"Oh, good. Let me take it for you."

The nurse walked over to get the cup.

"No, I'll get it," Xiene said before swallowing the contents. The nurse backed out of the room and ran to the bathroom. Allen was laughing himself to stitches. "You see, same nutcase." She smiled.

Allen reached over and she hugged him.

✖

The Richards were going to their hotel. They spotted Allen in the hospital lobby looking for something else for Xiene to read.

"Allen Montgomery." Mrs. Richards called.

He turned and walked over to her.

"Allen Montgomery," she said, "we're going to our hotel. Are you staying?"

"Yes. I figured I'd keep an eye on her. You know how crazy she is. She might try having wheelchair races down the hall.

Mr. and Mrs. Richards laughed. Mary cracked a smile.

"We want you to have dinner with us tomorrow.

"I'd love to." Allen looked at Mrs. Richards. They all seem so happy, they have no idea he's having an affair.

"Okay, I'll see you Thursday."

"Alright."

Allen shook Mr. Richard's hand and waved to Mary. Mary walked back to him and gave him a card.

"This is my dorm phone. Easier to reach me. If Christine does anything stupid, call me."

Allen pictured calling Mary every day, saying, 'Mary, Xiene is acting stupid again!'

Allen reached his hand out for Mrs. Richards. She leaned over and gave him a polite hug.

"You know, Allen, you're a very good friend to Xiene."

She called me Allen! "I'll try and keep that between us," he whispered.

She pulled back. "Thank you. Okay, I'll see you." She walked out the automatic doors to catch up with the other two.

That night Allen had a dream. The house caught on fire. Xiene fell out of a burning building. He held onto her hand that slipped from his fingers. She turned into a black bird that died and fell to the ground Allen watched as the blackbird, now on the ground, turned back into Xiene, and she stood up.

"Hey, Allen! That was fun! You should try it!"

Allen's laughing in his sleep woke Xiene up.

OUT-XIENED!

Xiene changed the disk of her CD player. She got off the floor, climbed back into bed, and straddled him. A second later, the album by the Cramps started up, blaring so loud Xiene couldn't hear what Allen was saying. She reached for the remote control on her dresser and turned the volume down.

"What did you say?"

"I said: Turn it down! You have neighbors, remember?"

"Hey, if anyone is asleep at two on a Sunday, they deserve to be woken up."

Allen started rubbing Xiene's thighs. "How much do weigh?" he asked.

"I don't know. Am I heavy?" She lifted herself and came down hard on Allen's thighs.

"Ouch! Watch it, Bolo!"

"Bolo?" she yelled. She reached over and pulled something out of her dresser.

What horrible weapon would she use on me? She threw a handful of plastic cockroaches onto his chest.

He almost threw her off the bed as he squirmed, screamed, and struggled to get what he thought were real roaches off. By the time he figured it was a prank, she was laughing hysterically. He reached up, grabbed her shoulders, pulled her down, pinned her down, and straddled her.

"You think it's funny, huh?" He started ticking her.

Xiene laughed to the point no sound came out, then to the point where you laughed so hard it hurt.

Allen stopped tickling. "Had enough?"

"Yes," Xiene said, gasping for air.

He reached down and kissed her she moved her head up and bit him on the nose. When he pulled back she still held on while giggling. Allen reached for her chest and grabbed her nipples.

"Okay, let go or these are history."

Xiene reached down and grabbed his genitals. Allen instantly let go.

"You were saying?" She still held on.

Allen whimpered. "Please let go slowly."

"Why should I? This is fun! I've never had this much power in my hands." She laughed.

"Please let go," Allen begged as he felt her nails.

"Oh, okay." She let go.

Allen lay back and checked for permanent damage.

"I'm sorry. You want me to massage it for you?" She moved her eyebrows up and down.

Three hours later, they lay down, cuddled, and watched Xiene's wind chimes of zodiac figures spin over their heads. Allen reached up and tried to touch the chimes, but they were too far. Xiene grabbed a pillow from behind her head and swung it in the air, hitting the chimes. She lay back down, put her head on Allen's chest, and began playing with his chest hair. He ran his fingers through her white and pink hair.

The phone rang. Xiene hopped out of bed and ran over to it. "Hello? Oh, hi, mom."

As Xiene talked to her mother, Allen looked around the room to find something to preoccupy himself with. He grabbed her crystal ball off the dresser on the right. As far as he could tell, the unflawed sphere was the size of a softball.

"Oh, Allen? He's fine," Xiene said, looking over at him. He put the crystal ball on his stomach and began moving it around by contracting his muscles. Xiene turned around, causing the long phone cord to wrap around her like a snake. "She's what?" she asked. "Ahh, Mom, I don't want her down here! Come on! Gee! Can't she stay with Mary instead?" Xiene seemed upset. Allen picked up the crystal ball and looked at her through it. Her image warped and twisted every time she moved. "Okay, but she better not expect me to entertain her while she's here!"

Who was coming to visit? He remembered Xiene explaining that the other side of the family were pure hicks/white trash whose idea of excitement was to watch the trucks pass by in front of their houses.

"Okay, love you, too. Bye." Xiene hung up and screamed.

"What? What's wrong?" Allen asked, putting the sphere back.

"My cousin Verna is coming to spend the next weekend with me. She's going to be going to that fucking tractor pull show at the Omni."

"Why can't she stay with Mary?"

"Mary has to study for midterms," Xiene said in a snippy voice.

"So what are you gonna do?"

"I tell you one thing I'm not: entertaining or going out of my way for her, that's for sure. God, I hate them!"

"Really? Why?" Allen reached out his hand for Xiene. She made her way over to the bed.

"They're just so county with a backwards 'k'. I mean, they all live in one house, grandkids and all, only half of them are working, and they spend all of their money on cars, satellite dishes, and guns."

"Guns?" Allen yelled.

"Yeah, you know the type—'They'll take my gun away when they kill my zombie ass!'"

Allen laughed. Xiene sat on the bed, put her head on his stomach, and acted as if she were crying.

"Why, why does she have to visit me?"

"Come on, Xiene, it's not that bad. I mean, she'll come, go to the tractor pull and leave. You hardly won't have to see her."

She lifted her head. "The worst part is, I haven't seen this girl in four years, and the last time she saw me, I had normal hair and no nose ring. I can hear her now: 'Momma, you should see Christine. She has a ring in her nose and hair like a circus clown!"

Allen laughed again. "You're nuts. Why don't you just be yourself? Better yet, freak her out. Then no one will want to visit you ever again."

Xiene thought for a few seconds. "Yeah, that's it. I'll freak her out, act extra weird, introduce her to the big city!" Xiene got up and ran to her desk, got a pad and pen out of the drawer, and ran back to the bed. "Okay, let's see, where are the worst places to take your relatives?"

"To the Acid Pit," Allen suggested.

"No, it's too mild on the weekends. They have the most fights on Wednesday's Mohawk Skinhead Night. Techwood Homes? Yeah." She wrote it down. "The Majestic Diner at 3 am. No, that's more interesting than dangerous. I need places that get named in the police blotter…"

"Well…" Allen started stroking her hair, "…anything on Stewart Avenue."

"Yeah. Wait," she thought for a few seconds. "I know—the GGG Club.

Allen could have sworn he heard thunder when Xiene said that. "Where?"

"The GGG Club."

Allen heard a car outside slam on its brakes and smash into another car. Xiene got up and looked out of the window to see if her van was hit.

"Any damage?"

"No. He hit somebody else. Anyway, the—"

"Don't say that word!"

"What, GGG Club?"

A car alarm went off from the damaged car downstairs.

"Wait, how old is this girl?"

Xiene started counting to herself. "Oh, shit!"

"What?"

"She's seventeen! They won't let her in anywhere. Damn it!" Xiene sat back down and put her head on her knees. Allen reached over and started giving her a back massage.

"Listen, why don't you just give her a key, say: 'food's in the fridge, the bus goes by up the street every thirty minutes, have a nice stay, then you can spend the weekend with me."

Xiene lifted her head. "Yeah, that's a good idea. I'll just avoid the problem altogether, and let her take care of herself. I mean, I didn't invite her here."

"Exactly."

Xiene turned around and kissed Allen. "Thanks, babe."

Did I give her the wrong advice? When she started nibbling on his stomach, he stopped worrying about it.

Allen saw Xiene once during the week. They had dinner at the Upper Crust, a pizza parlor near Lennox Mall. Afterward, Xiene had a spare key made for Verna. Allen made a spare key of his apartment for Xiene, to replace the one she lost slam dancing at the Acid Pit.

That Friday, Allen waited for Xiene to get dressed so they could pick up Verna. She came out wearing a mild, pink shirt, plain blue jeans, and a pair of white canvas shoes. Her hair had been pulled back and braided. She wore small pearl earrings and no makeup.

"Holy shit, you look like a yuppie," Allen said, looking her up and down.

Xiene punched him in the stomach. "I told you I'm not entertaining her! I'm trying to look as plain as possible!"

Allen caught his breath. She grabbed her keys and walked out. She stopped at the door. "Wait a minute, I can't pick her up in my van. It has all that hippy shit painted on the sides!"

Hippie shit?

"I know, we'll pick her up on the subway!"

"What?" Come on, Xiene, don't you think you're going a little too far? I mean, when she stays at the apartment, there are enough crazy things around here to entertain her for years."

Xiene looked around. "Shit. You're right. Okay, we'll take the van, but by god, I'm going to try my best to bore the hell out of her! By the time she goes back to South Carolina, Atlanta will seem like Hicksville!"

In the airport terminal, Allen told Xiene about watching a female employee pop a zit on the chin of another female employee."

"Why didn't they do that in private?" a confused Xiene asked.

"I don't know. I wondered if it was a woman thing."

Xiene smacked the back of Allen's head. "Woman thing?"

"Ow! Why did you do that? You've been hitting me all day. One more whack, and I'm going to—"

The passengers appeared in the terminal, interrupting Allen's threat. Xiene and Allen walked over to the gate and watched the parade of terrified passengers depart the plane. Women with handkerchiefs and men holding their heads or stomachs were among the sights.

"Must have been a rough flight," Allen commented to Xiene, who was busy looking at the businessman down a handful of laxatives. Allen saw a woman stop at the gate and turn around. "Jimmy! Billy!" she called down the tiny hall. Two little boys, ages ten and eleven, came running up to her, one yelling, "She's coming!

She's coming!" the woman grabbed the two boys by the hands and scurried away.

Xiene turned to Allen. "What the hell happened to these people?"

"Christine!" A very loud yell roared from down the hall.

Xiene and Allen turned their heads. "Holy shit!" they said simultaneously.

Even in her most bizarre outfit, Xiene was no match for Verna. Her hair, which, if laid flat, would reach down to her butt, had been spiked in a purple mohawk, which almost touched the ceiling. Her ears had at least twelve earrings in each one—everything, from crucifixes to miniature fetuses in the collection. Earrings were attached to her nose ring in her right nostril via a double chain. On her left eye, she had a fiery tattoo that ran from her eye to her hairline. It had the appearance that her left eye was on fire. She wore shiny black vinyl on her entire body. Chains, stud patches, and spikes could be seen everywhere. Underneath her black vinyl jacket, she wore nothing but a black bra, which showed off the Kama Sutra tattoo on her right breast. On her stomach, you could see a few scars. *Self-inflicted?* Her vinyl pants and hip-hugger boots caused a squeaky noise as she walked. She kept in rhythm with the squeaking by using a switchblade expanding and retracting in her right hand.

How did she get that on the plane? Allen backed up and got behind Xiene. Xiene dropped her purse.

The creature walked up to her. "Christine? Holy shit! Is that you? You look like a fucking yuppie!"

Xiene stood with mouth open, not sure what to say.

Verna looked at Allen. "Who the hell are you?"

"I'm Allen, a friend of Xiene's."

"Oh, gee, I guess I can't kill you, then." She started laughing insanely.

Allen shook Xiene to snap her out of her shock.

"Verna? Is that you?"

"Yep. In the flesh." She opened her jacket, revealing her bra and multiple tattoos to the world.

"What happened to you?" Xiene asked.

"What happened to me? What happened to you? The last photo Mary sent to me of you, you had all this cool leather shit and your hair was white and black and all stuck up in every direction. But now…" she gestured at Xiene's appearance, "you look like shit."

"I think she looks fine," Allen said, defending Xiene.

"Who the fuck asked your opinion, dick breath?"

"Dick breath?"

"Verna," Xiene interrupted," how can you dress like this where you come from?"

"Are you kidding? I'm the fashion hero back in Goose Creek!"

Goose Creek?

'I've never been so popular since I started dressing like this." She walked over and put her arm around Xiene. "And I owe it all to you."

"Me? What did I do?"

"You, my sweetie, are the ultimate rebel in the family! Do you think all the things you got up to down here go unmentioned at family get-togethers? Grandma Hillman said if she ever saw you again, she would put you in an insane asylum."

"That grandma, what a card," Xiene said with a sneer.

"Yep. Anyway, I used you as my mentor to change from boring old Verna Hillman," she stepped onto a bench, "to the popular rebel I am now."

Allen felt like hitting Verna with a suitcase.

"Verna," Xiene seemed confused, "Verna, I'm not the wild, crazy nutcase you think I am. I mean, I do some crazy things, but there's nothing legendary about it.

Allen raised one eyebrow.

"Bullshit! I heard about your adventures. Hell, you could write a Novel about that shit!"

"Verna, I—"

Xiene was interrupted by Verna running past her. She had spotted one of the motorized golf carts used for taking elderly passengers up and down the terminal. She ran up and pushed the driver off, causing him to fall to the floor.

"Holy shit?" Allen yelled.

Verna got in the driver's seat and floored the cart, making skid marks on the carpet. The old woman in the back seat rolled off and was caught by a stewardess, causing both of them to fall on the ground.

Xiene and Allen looked at each other, then at the cart heading down the terminal.

"Your cousin?" Allen said as they started running after the cart.

People dodged and fell out of Verna's way. A porter pushed his luggage rack out of her way, causing it to plummet down the escalator. Two businessmen jumped out of the way one landed on the escalator's midsection, causing him to shoot down it like a sliding board. Allen and Xiene saw the cart round a corner, then a very loud crash.

They made it around the corner, saw the cart sticking out of a window, and Verna was nowhere in site.

"Your cousin?" Allen repeated.

The police and security guards checked everyone who left the terminals. Xiene and Allen headed for her van.

"I say we leave that crazy bitch! She can steal another golf cart for transportation!"

"We can't leave her. She's my cousin."

"To hell with her! Let's get out of here before the cops make a connection to us!"

"No, we're going to drive around the parking lot until we find her."

They hopped in the van and started searching.

"What was this girl like when you last saw her?"

"Very country, very quiet."

"Is this something that runs in your family? Weren't you quiet and shy before you came to Atlanta?"

"Yeah," Xiene said, rounding a corner. "But when I rebelled, I was never like this."

Allen raised an eyebrow in disbelief. "My eyebrows are starting to hurt."

"What?"

"Nothing."

They stopped the van to let some people with suitcases walk in front of them. Allen looked to the right and spotted something. It was Verna, hiding between a stack of trunks. She looked at Allen and before he could say, 'Let's go home. I don't see her anywhere,' she sprinted to the van, opened the door, and jumped in. Xiene turned and looked at Verna, who started laughing.

"Boy, that was fucking wonderful!"

"You crazy—"

Verna interrupted Xiene's insult. "Hey, I bet you do things like that all the time."

"No, I don't! Who the hell do you think I am? The Terminator?"

"Gee whiz, Christine, I didn't know you were a socialite now."

"Socialite?" yelled Xiene.

"Xiene, let's get out of here!" Allen said, noticing a policeman walking around the van.

Xiene floored the van, causing Verna to tumble and hit the back door. As they moved onto I-20 towards downtown Atlanta, Xiene continued yelling at Verna.

"…Stupid, dangerous things I've ever seen!"

"Oh, like you've never done anything like that!"

"I haven't!" Allen looked over at Xiene. She looked back. "Shut up!"

They drove the rest of the trip in silence. Xiene got out of her car with a slam of the door and started walking towards her apartment. Allen turned to Vera.

"I just remembered—where is your luggage?"

"Didn't bring any."

"Why?"

"If I'm going to start a new life, I'm gonna have to start from scratch."

Xiene dropped her keys and turned around. "What?"

"Yeah, you think I came down here to go to some stupid tractor pull? I'm running away, man!"

Xiene put her hand on her head. "I need an aspirin."

Inside the apartment, Xiene laid down on her couch on Allen's lap with a wet towel on her head. Meanwhile, Verna continued exploring the apartment.

"Oh, cool!" She picked up a necklace. "Oh, wow!" She picked up a cow skull.

"I'm going to kill her," Xiene mumbled.

"Shhh. Quiet down. You need to relax."

"Hey, Christine, how much is your rent?"

"Too much for you to live here!" Xiene answered between clenched teeth.

"Fuck you! I didn't say I wanted to live with you! I'm gonna find my own place."

"Good. The sooner, the better!" Xiene mumbled.

Verna went into Xiene's bedroom. Xiene removed the towel from her head. "Did she just go in my bedroom?"

"Er, ah," Allen waffled. Is Xiene going to beat Verna up now?

"Verna!" Xiene yelled, "Get out of there!"

"Oh, cool," Verna said, coming out of the bedroom holding a red piece of paper. "Where is the GGG Club?"

The lights in the apartment went out, then cut on again. Xiene and Allen looked at each other.

"Says here, tonight is ladies' night. I can get in free!"

"Not at your age," Allen suggested.

"Hey, do I look under twenty-one?" Verna spread out her arms. *I wonder if she would make it inside? After all, she's tall, developed, and in all that makeup she could be a ninety-year-old lady.*

"Verna, you're not going to that club!"

"Oh, sorry, Mom!" Verna said in a snippy voice.

"Verna! Damn it! that place is dangerous! If you want to go to a club, I know a lot of places for all ages nights."

"Oh, god! Kiddie shit! I want to party, not drink Kool-aid and dance like some teeny-bopper!"

"You are a teeny-bopper." Allen interrupted.

"Hey, eat me, four-eyes!"

Xiene's head popped onto the couch as Allen hopped up, preparing to trash Verna. Xiene grabbed his belt buckle. Verna had her switchblade out and ready.

"Better leash your dog, Christine."

"Get out of here!" Xiene yelled.

"What?" said Verna.

"I said get the hell out of my apartment! You stupid shit!"

Allen turned to Xiene, who seemed more upset than angry. Verna picked her jacket up off the floor and left with a slam of the front door. Allen turned to Xiene.

"You didn't give her your key, did you?"

"No," Xiene said, putting the towel back on her face.

"Good. At least you don't have to worry about her coming back and robbing you."

"Shh. Please be quiet," Xiene said, trying to relieve her headache.

As Xiene slept on the couch, Allen checked the apartment to see if Verna had stolen anything. He searched the kitchen and found some spaghetti in the refrigerator. When he finished reheating it, Xiene came trudging in, rubbing her eyes.

"What time is it?"

Allen checked the cuckoo clock on the wall.

8:30 pm

"Shit. I've been asleep for two hours. Has Verna called yet?"

"Why should she? You kicked her out."

"Damn it! That's right. That was stupid of me."

"What? She asked for it. The girl's a psychopath," Allen said, putting some spaghetti into a bowl for Xiene.

"Oh, and I'm not?"

"You're what I call…logically-crazy. You do crazy things, as long as the innocent don't get physically hurt. Verna seems to want to hurt anyone that gets in her way of fun."

Xiene held some spaghetti on her fork and blew on it. "I don't know, Allen, she still reminds me of when I first came here. I mean, I did some pretty stupid things."

"True, you still have your vandalistic tendencies, but at least you don't endanger—well, you do endanger people's lives, but you're not malicious about it."

They started eating their meal. After a moment of thinking, Xiene crossed her arms and leaned back in her chair. "I fucked up."

"What?"

"I lost my temper and now my cousin is loose on the streets of Atlanta getting robbed and raped."

"Or doing it herself," Allen interrupted.

"I'm serious. There's no difference between us. She just needs to calm down a little and get the idea out of her head that you can do whatever you want in this world."

"Gee whiz, Xiene, you sound almost like your mother." She kicked him in the shin. "Ow! Okay, you're not like her!"

Xiene started unbraiding her hair. "You're damn right I'm not like her, and that's why I think I was wrong to kick Verna out. It sounds like what my mother would have done!" Xiene stood and started undressing.

"What are you doing?"

"I'm taking this shit off. I'm not a yuppie!"

Allen laughed. "You see what's happening? Verna is scaring you into thinking you're some sort of unhip square socialite now."

"Maybe she's right." Xiene walked out of the kitchen in her undergarments.

"Xiene, being a responsible adult does not make you a square!" he yelled.

"No, but judging people and considering yourself better than them makes you one!" she yelled from the bedroom.

Allen finished eating his meal and walked into the living room. Xiene came out of her bedroom wearing a black T-shirt with white fish skeletons all over it. Her jeans appeared to have been torn apart and sewn back together with electrical wires of different colors. She walked to the closet and put on a pair of combat boots and a black leather jacket with a painting of Elvis on the back resembling velvet art. She put her diamond nose ring in, reached up, and started messing up her hair. "There. Now who's a yuppie?" she asked.

"Not you, but why did you get your jacket?"

"Because we're going out."

"Why?"

"To look for Verna."

"Are you nuts? Do you want that monster spending the weekend with you?"

"Allen, she's my cousin! Now you and your family may not be that close, but mine are."

"Oh, I'm sure that's why you moved down here, to be closer to your family."

"I moved down here to be independent because my parents wanted to take care of me and tell me how to run my life!"

Allen started pacing. "I still don't see why you feel obligated to babysit Verna!"

"Because if she gets hurt, I have no one to blame but myself!"

"No way! She can take care of herself!"

Xiene put on an amethyst necklace. "She's only sixteen, remember? She has nowhere to stay and she knows no one! Sounds like prime meat for scumbags. If I can at least get her to stop thinking that being a rebel without a cause is cool, then I'll be satisfied."

"Let's see, what are your chances of talking sense into Verna's head." Allen began counting on his fingers. "I think one in three thousand."

"It's not zero. That sounds like good odds to me," she said before grabbing Allen's hand and heading out the door.

12:30 am

Allen checked his watch.

Xiene finished describing Verna to the cashier at Plaza Drugs.

"If I had seen someone who looked like that, then I would definitely would have remembered," he told her.

Xiene walked away from the counter and came up from behind Allen. He turned around and comforted her.

"Whelp, where to next?"

"I don't know," she said in a tired voice. "We've been to every hip conceivable place in North Atlanta.

Allen thought for a moment. "All except one place."

"Where?"

"Dare I say it?"

She lifted her head. "You mean the GGG Club?"

"Stick 'em up!" yelled the man holding a gun at the cashier. The man turned his gun towards Xiene and Allen. "You two, get the fuck out of here!"

Xiene and Allen raised their hands and hastily walked out. A few minutes later the thief ran out with a paper sack. He hopped into a brown Monte Carlo and screeched away. A moment later the cashier came out, holding a 38 revolver, and fired a couple of shots at the car.

Xiene had to stick around to help with the police report. By the they finished their investigation, the time read:

1:48 am

"Shit. If she was at—"

Xiene slapped her fingers on Allen's mouth. "Don't say it! What the fuck just happened?"

"Anyway," he said, removing her fingers, "if she was still <u>there</u>, she probably left by now."

"We still have to try!"

"You have anything we can use for protection?"

"Sure. I have my diaphragm," Xiene joked.

They started walking to the van, Allen looked around for a stick or metal rod to use as a weapon.

A bottle smashed behind Xiene's van as they rounded the corner on Stewart Avenue. This let them know they were close to the club. Two hookers were strangling each other on the right side of the road; on the left, a man opened his coat and exposed himself to Xiene. Xiene pointed and laughed, causing the man to run away like a dog with its tail between its legs. Xiene stopped at a red light. Six men from both sides of the road started converging on the van. Some yelled, 'Can I borrow a quarter?'. The VW screeched away, running the red light and avoiding the burning shopping cart in the middle of the road.

"Is that it?" Xiene asked, slowing down.

Allen didn't see what she was pointing at because he was too busy looking at the two large women rolling around in the street fighting. He turned to see what Xiene was pointing at.

If you took the house of the Adam's Family put 'GGG' on it and added 50 motorcycles outside, you would have the GGG club. Allen expected to see bats flying around the roof, but the smell in the air probably scared them off. They pulled up to the entrance gate. A mannequin smashed out of a top-floor window and landed three feet in front of them. A drunken biker came up to Xiene's door, smelling of salami and beer.

"Hey, what's the password!" he yelled at Xiene.

"What?"

"Password! No one gets in here without one!"

Xiene took a piece of paper and a pen out of the glove compartment. After scribbling on it, she handed it to the biker.

"What's this? I can't read this!"

"It's the password."

"That doesn't look like 'Harley Davison' to me!"

"Oh, sorry," Xiene said, grabbing the paper. She scribbled the correct password and gave it back to the man.

"Okay, that's better. Drive on."

Xiene began looking for a parking space. They found one next to an old gutted school bus with screaming kids painted on the sides. As they got out, Xiene kept looking inside her van to see if anything valuable worth breaking inside could be seen through the window.

Allen looked around the ground for a weapon. He ignored two switchblades because he didn't want his fingerprints on them. Xiene grabbed his left hand and dug her nails into his palm.

"Ouch! Not so hard."

"Sorry, I'm a little tense right now."

"I couldn't guess why."

"Shut up! You've been whining all day! Cut it out or I'll send you home on that bus!"

Allen put his hand up to his mouth and made a zipper-being-shut gesture. They walked up to the front entrance. Some bikers hung around, leaning on their choppers. Two very large, rough types stood at the entrance. One had a shotgun. Allen and Xiene walked up to them. They didn't move out of the way.

"Hello, can we get through?" Allen asked nervously.

The two guards still glared without speaking. Xiene leaned over and whispered in Allen's ear.

"I think they want money."

"Oh, yeah."

Allen ruffled through his pockets for money. He pulled out a $10 bill. "Is this enough?"

The guards ignored him.

"Must not be enough," Xiene said, searching her back pocket. She pulled out a ten. "How's this?"

Still no word from the guards.

"I got it," Allen said. "How's this: GGG Club!"

Just when he said that a crashing sound and glass breaking were heard behind their backs.

"My bike! He ran over my bike!" the guard on the left yelled. The two ran past Xiene and Allen to beat up the guy in the pickup truck who backed over the guard's chopper.

Xiene and Allen rushed in before they got back.

"Why wouldn't they let us in?" Xiene asked.

"I don't know. Maybe we pay with ammo or drugs here."

They made their way through what must have been a living room. A few sofas were taken up by beer-bellied bikers and their ugly girlfriends. Some of the women had their tops off, showing their various tattoos. An old chandelier overhead had surprisingly been taken good care of. The tiny fake diamonds on chains sparkled and illuminated the volcano model in the middle of the room. Allen watched as a skinny biker with bifocals and a greasy beard walked over to the volcano, put a glass at the bottom of a trench running down the side, pressed a button, and with a rumbling noise and glowing lights, the volcano dispersed beer and foam out of the top, down the side, and filled up his glass.

They left the living room and made their way down a tiny hall towards some music playing a Grateful Dead song. Xiene looked at the photos on the wall. Pictures of various bikers and their so-called mammas were in most shots. All seemed to have been taken at conventions or cookouts of some sort. One shot that caught Xiene's attention had a nude woman in bed with nude men and the words 'Thanks for the memories' written along the bottom.

They walked into the room on the right. Allen spotted a picture of George Bush on the left wall. This distracted his view of the four men and women rolling around on the large couch against the window. They left the room and entered the next. This room appeared more like a bar than the others, with a bar overlooked by a moose head with a broken antler and a beer can in its mouth, and pool tables. It appeared to be the heart of the entire house. Bikers, mamas, and assorted insane types filled the room. Several bikers playing pool stared at Xiene and Allen as they entered and looked around the room. Xiene walked away from Allen to the bar. Allen looked at the shirtless redneck type leaning against the wall glaring at him. Allen looked at Xiene asking the bartender about Verna. A woman in a black tank top walked up to Xiene. Allen walked over to prevent the woman from attacking her.

"Hey, I know who you're talking about," she told Xiene.

"Really? Is she here?" asked Xiene.

"No, she left with Spider about an hour ago," the woman said, scratching her armpit.

"Where's this Spider?" Allen asked.

"He lives up the street in that old mannequin warehouse. You can't miss it."

"Thanks," said Xiene. She turned and grabbed Allen's arm. "Let's get the hell out of here."

They walked towards the exit. Suddenly someone grabbed Xiene's shoulders.

"Hey, baby, the party hasn't started yet," said the smelly Grizzly Adams clone.

"Hands off, scumbag!" Xiene wrested her shoulders away, only to be grabbed by another man.

"Hey, don't be so frigid, baby."

Allen walked over, fist clenched, ready to get a broken nose. Someone grabbed his shoulders.

"Hey, partner, don't be so uptight. We just gonna have some fun," he said to Allen with sardine breath.

Xiene elbowed the guy on the left in the stomach. He heaved over, backed away, and threw up off to the side. The other biker grabbed Xiene in a Full Nelson. She tried to kick his shins, but he had thick leather books on. Allen wiggled away from Sardine Breath and ran towards Xiene. Someone stuck their foot out, causing Allen to trip and plummet to the ground. Laugher all around. Allen tried to get up, but a boot on his back prevented him.

"God, I hate the GGG Club," he said.

A gun went off. Everyone turned to the bar to see the bartender holding a shotgun.

"Alright, that's enough. Leave them alone," he said.

The men released Xiene and Allen. Both slowly backed out. When they made it to the exit, they began running to Xiene's van. The two guards they had snuck past started running after them, one yelling, "Hey! You owe us one hundred bucks!"

So that's how much admission was.

They hopped in the van and Xiene floored it. With a loud thump. She backed into one of the guards and then burned dirt out of the parking lot. Allen looked behind to see the run-over biker getting up and holding his shoulder.

"He alive?" Xiene asked.

"Yeah."

"Shit!!"

They rode up the street looking for the mannequin warehouse. After an hour of searching, they concluded that the story of a guy named Spider and a mannequin warehouse had been false.

"Let's check the answering machine for messages," Allen suggested.

Xiene pulled the van into a liquor store parking lot. She got out and went to use the pay phone. Allen looked at the ten or twelve vagrants hanging around, most drinking. Xiene punched in her message relay code on the pay phone. She failed to notice the three vagrants making their way over to her.

"What's with this fucking neighborhood?" Allen mumbled, getting out of the van.

He walked over and stood next to Xiene. The three vagrants turned around and went back to join the others.

"Oh, shit," Xiene said, hanging up.

"What?"

"I got a message from the police department. Verna got arrested."

"On what charge?"

"Homicide."

Allen almost fainted.

"Come on, let's go!"

As they left, Xiene cursed under her breath and beat the steering wheel. By the time the van rounded Grady Hospital and came within one block of the police station, Xiene was cursing out loud.

"Stupid bitch! Comes down here and makes my life a living hell! Dumb, son-of-a-bitch! White trash piece of shit!"

Allen realized something and debated telling Xiene in her tempered mood.

"Don't," Xiene said.

"What?" Allen had been caught off guard.

"I said, 'Don't I give people the benefit of the doubt?"

"What are you talking about?" Allen asked.

"Goddamnit, you weren't listening!"

"I was thinking."

"About what? How fucked up my family is?"

"No, just the fact, why would a policeman call your home to tell you Verna had been arrested? Don't people make their own call when they're arrested?"

Xiene slammed on the brakes, causing the van to run up on the sidewalk in front of the police department.

"Damn it to hell!" Xiene yelled. Two policemen walked over to the van. "That stupid little shit! It was some sort of practical joke!"

Allen looked at the policemen looking in.

"She all right?" asked the Black one with the mustache.

"Fucking son of a bitch!" Xiene yelled.

The policemen's expressions showed shock and confusion.

"It's that time of the month," Allen lied.

"Okay. But get this thing off of the sidewalk."

"Oh, Xiene, honey, can we go, please?"

Xiene reversed the van while mumbling something about murdering Verna.

"And get some Midol!" yelled the policeman as the van sped off.

"Fuck you and your Midol!" Xiene yelled.

They got on I-20 and the van reached 70mph before Allen spoke.

"Er, Xiene, could you, like, conduct your light-speed experiments on your own relative time?"

"What? Oh, sorry!" she said.

"So, where to?" he asked, looking over at Xiene biting her nails on her right hand.

"The sun's coming up, we might as well go have breakfast."

The House of Pancakes on North Avenue had its regular crowd. Xiene rested her head on the table. *Is she sleeping or thinking?* The coffee pot had been placed next to her. She lifted her head, poured coffee into a cup, and handed it to Allen.

"Want me to test it for poison?"

"No, I don't want to stay awake. I just want to go home, sleep, and forget I ever had a cousin."

Allen held up the coffee cup. "So, I guess you're giving up the search?"

"Fuck her! She can take care of herself!"

Allen took a sip of coffee.

Xiene searched her left pocket. She pulled out a pack of cigarettes and searched her right pocket for her Godzilla lighter. "Shit. I left my lighter at home!"

"Amen," Allen praised.

"Ha! I'll just get a light from someone else." Xiene turned around to the girl in the black vinyl jacket and very high mohawk. "Excuse mee–eea_hholy shit!" Xiene replied.

Verna turned around and looked at her. "Oh, shit!" Verna yelled before getting up and running towards the door.

Xiene and Allen jumped up and ran after her.

"Verna, come back here!" yelled Allen.

Verna shoved past a yuppie in a grey suit and his girlfriend. Xiene and Allen pushed them into a newspaper rack, causing a stack of brochures to fall to the ground. Vera ran down the hill, towards the Rio Shopping Center, laughing the entire time, Xiene and Allen close behind.

Xiene hit a crack in the sidewalk, causing her to fall and tumble in front of the Turkey King concession stand. Allen helped her up while Verna ran across the street towards Rio. By the time they made it across, Verna had disappeared. They checked everywhere in the eclectic mall: the soup and salad bar, the Buppie seafood shop, the record store, the bookstore, and some planted bamboo trees. Xiene put her hand in the pond surrounding the midsection of the mall, decorated with 100 large golden frog sculptures on top of the water, all pointing to a huge geosphere made of scaffolding. Sometimes the scaffolding would spray water, producing a mazy mist around it and watering the grass below and more golden frogs surrounding the base. Allen checked the midsection again near the giant video monitor made up of television sets, all displaying a different section of an image. It sometimes worked at night, playing disco music and showing rock videos to the outside eaters and drinkers from the small bar, also located on the island.

"Holy shit!" yelled Xiene, followed by Verna's echoed laughter. Allen ran around the island towards the geosphere. He spotted Xiene looking up at it, along with the golden frogs. He wondered if she had lost her mind and now worshiped the sphere like the frogs.

"What is it?" Allen looked at Xiene, who just pointed. Looking up, Allen spotted Verna standing on top of the sphere, arms out.

"Hey, you assholes, look at me!" she yelled.

"Why?" Allen asked. How did she get up there?

"Verna, come down! The game's over! Let's go home!"

"No way, man! It's only Saturday. I got two more days!"

"Wait…I thought you were running away." Allen asked.

"You little shit! You were putting us on!" Xiene yelled. "You did come down here to go to the tractor pull."

"Hell, no! I came down here because my mom and dad got sick of looking after me, so they sent me away!"

"I can see why," Allen added.

"Allen, shush!" Xiene yelled.

"Hey, fuck you, dick breath!" Verna yelled.

"That's it! Let's go home! She can be the Frog Goddess for the rest of her miserable life!" Allen grabbed Xiene's hand, but she wouldn't budge.

"Verna, come down! Now!" Xiene yelled.

"Oh, I'm soooo scared!" Verna yelled "Coming from a yuppie like you!

"Get your ass down here or I'm gonna come get you!"

"Ha-ha! Right!" Verna laughed.

Xiene took off her jacket and handed it to Allen.

"Hey, wait! No! Don't go up there! This rickety thing may collapse!"

"Don't worry, I'll be fine."

Xiene began climbing up. Verna started walking on a rod like a tightrope walker.

"Hey!" a security guard yelled from across the street. By the time he ran over, Xiene was at the midpoint.

Verna squatted down and started impersonating a frog. "Ribbit! Ribbit! Worship me, my frog friends!" she called to the many staring golden frogs below.

Allen looked at Xiene on the scaffolding. He gripped her jacket and chipped some paint on Elvis' ear.

"Come down from there!" yelled the security guard, standing next to Allen.

"She's trying to get the girl on top to come down," Allen explained, hoping the guard wouldn't call the cops.

"Oh, oh, she's getting close!" Verna said in a child's voice. She took off her vinyl jacket and began swatting at Xiene's fingers.

"Stop that!" yelled Allen.

"Hey, cut it out and come down. Now!" yelled the security guard.

Xiene continued climbing. Verna's jacket sleeve hit her on the right side of her head. Xiene slipped and almost fell. She let go of her hands and swung into the inside of the sphere, holding on with her legs and hanging upside down. Xiene rubbed the side of her head.

Verna started walking towards Xiene, wrapping her jacket around her right hand. Allen, afraid she was going in for the kill, picked a cobblestone off the ground and threw it at Verna. It hit her left shoulder.

"You bastard!" she yelled. She reached into her jacket and pulled out her switchblade. After activating it, she threw it at Allen and the security guard. They scampered down the hill towards the water.

Xiene swung back into the climbing position. Verna placed her boot on her back.

"Hey, bow down to the Frog Queen!" she yelled.

Xiene grabbed Verna's leg, causing her to fall onto her back.

Allen and the security guard waded out of the knee-high water and slogged back up the hill.

"That's it! Enough shit! Verna! Let's go home!" Xiene yelled, holding onto Verna's leg.

"I can't go home! I don't have one!" Verna kicked Xiene in the jaw, causing her to slide down the side of the sphere. Before she completely started to fall, she grabbed onto a rod.

"You crazy bitch, leave her alone!" yelled Allen.

"I'm calling for backup!" the security guard yelled while running.

Allen started throwing more stones at Verna. One hit the left side of her head.

"You little shit!" she yelled, feeling her head.

Xiene seemed to be hurt as she held on for dear life.

"Verna, it's over! You have to calm down!" Xiene yelled.

"Calm down? Calm down like you? Shit, no! I'm never going to stop partying! I don't want to end a socialite square like you! I mean, look at you! Just because you get old doesn't mean you have to give up fun!"

"I didn't give up fun, you little shit1 I have fun, but that doesn't mean you have to hurt people to do it!"

"Bullshit!" yelled Verna. "If I had a list of all the fights I've heard you've been in—"

"Verna, I defend myself! I don't attack people!" Xiene looked down at Allen. "Shut up!" she yelled at him before he could correct her.

"You were my hero! Now you're shit." Verna started making her way towards Xiene. "Now, get the fuck off my ball! I'm the only one who—"

Verna slipped between the holes and dangled. Xiene started making her way over to Verna. Allen looked around for the security guard.

Verna kicked at Xiene. "Stay away from me! I don't need your—or anyone's fucking help! Never have, never will!"

"Verna, climb back up, and let's get off this thing!"

"You were my idol! Now you're scared as hell and I'm the strong one!" Vera said, pointing to Xiene. "But you're nothing! Just like everyone else! Afraid of dying! Afraid of living! You're shit, Christine!"

The rod Verna was holding onto gave way. Xiene reached out but to no avail. Allen never saw Verna hit the ground because he averted his eyes at the last minute, but he did hear the sound of cobblestones, steel, and a thump. He opened his eyes to see the body of Verna in the center of the sphere.

He looked up at Xiene reaching her hand out. He began walking towards Verna. The sight of blood on the white scaffolding turned his stomach and prevented him from walking any farther. He looked up at Xiene, still holding out her hand. "Stay there! Don't make a move! Don't look at Verna!"

Xiene didn't listen and continued staring.

Allen ran to get a ladder. By the time he gave up looking the security guard and a policeman were inside the sphere looking down at Verna. Allen ran back towards them.

"You got to help her down!" Allen said, pointing at Xiene.

They all looked up at Xiene, who appeared to be in shock

"Hey, little lady, you take it easy, now! Help is on the way!"

"Who is she?" he asked Allen.

"Her name's Xiene!"

"Xiene?"

"Yeah, like Magazine."

"Okay. Hello, Xiene? You just stay put, honey! Don't worry, fire truck is coming!" He turned to Allen. "Why the hell were you guys climbing around on this thing?"

"We were trying to get her cousin down, but she slipped."

"What was she doing up there?"

Allen thought for a minute. "Trying to be better than her." Allen pointed at Xiene.

The policeman's walkie-talkie blurted out something. He took it off his belt. "Yeah, we have a 10-109. Girl on top of the ball at Rio. And we have a body inside it. Send an ambulance. Code 10."

Allen sat down to prevent fainting. It was 6 am, and he hadn't slept all night. Now he had just witnessed someone die. He sat down on the cobblestones and tried to sort out his emotions.

The sound of a firetruck woke Allen up.

How could I sleep at a time like this? Allen got off the ground and watched the fire truck pull the net to the curb. A local news crew was already there, in addition to five police cars and two ambulances. Allen ignored the paramedics working on Verna and looked up at Xiene, still in shock.

A fireman made his way up the sphere while others held a safety net below.

"She's gone," a paramedic said to the policeman.

"Tell me, what is your involvement in this accident?" asked the news reporter.

Allen ignored them and walked away to witness the fireman rescuing Xiene. The fireman picked her up and threw her over his shoulder like a rag doll.

A policeman started asking Allen a lot of questions about himself, Vera, and Xiene. Allen finished giving the policeman information about the earlier events. A paramedic gave Xiene some oxygen.

Allen pushed through the crowd of firemen towards her she stood up on the curb, still using the oxygen, and reached out her hand. A paramedic removed the oxygen mask. Xiene ran over to Allen, grabbed him, and began crying on his shoulder.

"Okay, you two need to come downtown and make out a full report," a policeman stated.

Xiene and Allen got into a police car. Allen looked back at Verna's body, now covered up. Xiene curled up in a ball and appeared to absorb herself. Allen held her tight and tried to block the bloodstained sheets out of his mind.

Allen and Xiene both took time off from work the next week. Xiene would not accept any phone calls. Allen had to be the source of information for her family members. Dealing with members of Verna's family was the worst calls of all. There was lots of crying and cursing.

By the fourth day, Allen stopped answering the phone. He stayed in his bedroom all day. At night, Brandon brought his food to him and tried to cheer him up.

The next day, Allen assumed Xiene must be in worse shape than himself. The thought of her starving from her depression forced him to get out of bed and visit. He tried to call first, but still got her answering machine.

He took the bus over to her apartment. The white curtains were all closed. He climbed the entrance stairs and spotted a note on her door. Allen removed it and read: "Christine, I'm going to go to Verna's funeral on Saturday. Be ready to leave Friday at noon, Mary."

He wondered if Xiene had already left with her sister. Allen knocked on the door. No answer. After a minute of kicking, he used his key. Even in his worst anti-cleaning moods, Allen couldn't trash an apartment like Xiene did. He smelled pot. Clothes, records, empty food wrappers, newspapers, and an unraveled roll of toilet paper littered the living room. He stepped over a half-full bag of potato chips. A song by Vangelis skipped on the record player. He walked over and stopped it.

Xiene came out of the bedroom. Her hair was unintentionally messy. She wore a long blue Mickey Mouse T-shirt. No pants or footwear. In her left hand, she held a chocolate cupcake. Some of the icing smeared on her right cheek. She stopped at her bedroom door and stared at Allen with a freaked expression. She held her arms out. "Hi," she said with a half smile.

While making his way over, Allen stepped on a record and some clothing.

"Hey! My Misfits record," she complained.

"I'll buy you the disk." Allen kicked a box of Stay Free Maxi Pads out of his way.

They hugged. Xiene dropped the cupcake. The icing smeared the back of Allen's shirt. After what felt like an hour, Allen pulled back.

"How are you?" *Dare I ask?*

"Fine. Hungry as hell, as you might have guessed." She laughed.

"I saw a note from Mary on your door."

"Yeah, I already called her. I'm not going to the funeral."

"Really? Why? Not up to it?"

"That, and the fact I never knew Verna. I think you shouldn't go to funerals or weddings just because you're family members."

"How does her family feel about you not coming?"

"Fuck them. If I died they wouldn't come to my funeral." Xiene let go of Allen and walked over to a stack of dirty laundry.

"Did they blame you for her death?" Allen asked

Xiene squatted down and started picking up clothes. Her pink panties let Allen know she was wearing something underneath. "Oh, of course. My aunt Frida said if she wouldn't have idolized me, she wouldn't have been so wild."

"What did you say?"

"I told her to eat me!"

"Wow."

"Yeah, I mean, Verna came down here because they got sick of watching after her, and the reason she idolized me so much has to do with the fact no one in her family paid any attention to her. So the only person she could idolize was me. Her family always talked about me and how weird I was, so she thought she could get some attention or love by acting like a simplified version of me. So fuck them. They never liked me, and going to Verna's funeral and being attacked by them won't bring her back to…" Xiene paused, almost cried, then continued, "…back to life."

"How are you…really?" Allen started walking towards her.

"I'm okay. I'm just waiting for the nightmares to come."

"That's funny, I haven't had any nightmares either. Maybe we're both okay…or suppressing her death…low in our subconscious," Allen said in a mock German accent.

"Well, the hell with it. I'm gonna clean up this place and get on with my life." Xiene started picking up objects.

Allen started organizing a scattered stack of newspapers. He felt two emotions: one, of happiness that Xiene had handled the Verna problem, and the second, sadness that she didn't need his help. He bent over and picked up the Misfits album he had stepped on earlier. Xiene's arms came around his waist and she hugged him from behind and she began to wail in anguish.

BUSTED PIPES!

Allen sat in the food court at Lennox Mall watching the social parade walk in front of him while being watched by look-gooders and yuppies. He checked his watch:

7:30 pm

Xiene was late. Some businessmen passed in front of him. He noticed each had expensive-looking watch bands and expensive glittery watches. A crowd of Black male teenagers passed by him and headed towards the video arcade. *What could be going through the heads of two White women in mink coats sitting near Chick-fil-A? I tell you, Margo, this used to be such a safe mall until those undesirable elements took over,* Allen pictured them saying. He found it strange that Black people get such strange reactions when they are in groups. *Why didn't anyone look at the White yuppie businessmen in a group and think, My, looks like a corporate gang to me? Bet they stole those rings!* Allen looked to the left at the windowed red elevator rising to the third floor, and to the right to see the yuppie crowd eating at the California Pizza Kitchen. A Phil Collins song blaring from its speakers echoing around the open mall space turned Allen's stomach. He heard a whistle from behind.

He turned around. Xiene was coming down the escalator. *I wonder what reaction she's gonna get in her white fishnet shirt and black bra underneath.* A security rent-a-cop came out of the men's room near the bottom of the escalator. He turned around, spotted Xiene, and walked to the bottom of the escalator to wait for her.

Allen walked over.

The guard grabbed her right arm. Xiene quickly turned out of his grip. They started talking back and forth. Allen couldn't hear what they were saying, but he could tell by Xiene's expression, and the guard's finger-pointing, that they were not discussing the weather.

"I don't care! You can't walk around here dressed like that!"

"If I were Madonna you wouldn't be hassling me!" Xiene argued back.

"Hey, you just take yourself back home and don't come back in here, unless you're dressed decently!" He stated, pointing at her bra."

"Hey, Rent-a-pig! Kiss my ass!" Xiene yelled. "Not my fault you sexualize women!"

"You want me to run you in? Because I'll do it if that's what you want!" he yelled back.

Allen grabbed Xiene's left arm. "Let's go," he said, pulling her up the escalator.

"Here! Pig! Pig! Pig!" Xiene yelled. "Sooowee! Rent-a Pig!" all of the shoppers stared at him and Xiene." Allen felt embarrassed, but he also felt like laughing.

"God, I hate security guards! Why do they always have to be so fascist?" she said, opening the exit door.

"I don't know. Maybe they're upset because they aren't tough enough to be nuns."

Xiene laughed. She spotted one of the white Bronco security vehicles, its lights flashing at all times. The car was empty and no security guard was in sight. Xiene looked around and walked around to the driver's side. Allen dropped his bags, preventing him from stopping her potential attack on the vehicle. Xiene reached in, turned the Bronco off, pulled out the key, and threw it into a garbage can.

"Not as bad as what I thought she was going to do," he said to himself.

Xiene started skipping towards her van, mixed in with the hundreds of other vehicles underneath the parking deck. By the time they pulled off, Allen spotted the security guards looking around the Bronco for the keys. One guard, the same from inside the mall, kept beating the hood and yelling, "We gotta find it. It's going to be my ass! We gotta find it!" Allen looked over at Xiene.

"Bwa-ha-ha, revenge is so sweet sometimes." she cackled.

He pictured her with sharp teeth.

She put a Nitzer Ebb tape in her player. The Euro-industrial beat rattled the van windows. Xiene kept in rhythm with the songs by moving her head forward and backward, causing her white hair to swish back and forth.

On Lennox Road, they stopped at a red light. Two men in a grey convertible Mercedes on the left looked over at Xiene. She looked back. She turned to Allen. "Hey, look at that!"

Allen leaned over to look out her window. Xiene pointed at the Mercedes' back tire, then turned to Allen. "Looks bad, doesn't it?" Allen looked at the tire it looked fine. Xiene kept pointing and making distressed expressions. The man on the rider's side tried to look at the tire, but it was out of sight. The light turned green and Xiene drove on, still pointing at the Mercedes.

Out of the rearview mirror, Xiene saw the car pull over and the two guys got out and started searching for the invisible car damage. "Ha-ha! That's two so far," Xiene chortled.

"What is this, National Evil Day?" Allen yelled over the electronic drum beat.

"Yes. Have you abused someone today?" she asked.

"Okay," Allen said. He reached over and poked her under her armpit.

She shrieked. "Stop!"

"Ha-ha!," Allen said in a sinister voice. He continued poking her ticklish weak spots. She shrieked and slapped his hand. Allen stopped when she started swerving the van from lane to lane, yelling, "I'll crash this fucker!

Would she trash her van just to get even with me? Scared to tempt her, he put his hands on his lap and behaved the rest of the trip to his apartment.

"How was work?" Allen asked as they got out of the van.

"Shitty, as usual," she replied. "We lost some computer records and I had to write down the names and code numbers of 250 CDs. I tell you, it made me want to quit. Again."

"No, don't do that. I don't think they'll ask you to come back twice."

Allen walked to the front door and started searching for his key. Xiene already had the spare out. She opened the door. Allen checked the mailbox. "Bill, junk mail, bill, junk mail," Allen stated while flinging the mail onto the rocking chair near the door. Xiene rewound the answering machine. "Got a message?" he asked.

"Yep." Xiene turned the knob to play. After two hang-ups, a message. "Very funny, Allen," the voice said, referring to Allen's recording saying, 'This machine cost $15. Please use it.' The message continued. "This is Beverly. I'm going up to Watermill tomorrow and I was wondering if you and Xiene would like to join me. Okay, call me, bye."

"Where's Watermill?" Allen asked.

"It's up north, near Dahlonega and Helen in the mountains," she answered.

"You want to go?" he asked.

"Sure. I love the mountains, the fresh air, the trees—"

"The Klan towns you pass through to get there," Allen interrupted.

"Hey, if we drive fast enough, the Confederate flags will look like blurs."

Allen bowed down, walked over to Xiene, and picked her up in a fireman's carry position.

"Hey! Put me down!" she screamed. Allen started turning around. She beat him on the back. "Stop! I'm going to throw up!" Allen continued spinning. Xiene hit him between the shoulder blades with her fist. He put her down.

"Ow! Jesus! That hurt!"

"Good! I said let go! I was getting sick!"

"Sorry, I thought you were kidding!" Allen sat down on the couch against the front window feeling between his shoulder blades. "I think you broke something," he whined.

"Ah, poor baby," she whined back while heading into the kitchen. Allen flipped her a bird. "I saw that!" she said, entering the kitchen.

"Bitch," Allen said under his breath."

I heard that!" She leaned her head out of the kitchen. "If you're going to call me a bitch, you better do it to my face!"

Allen felt embarrassed and angry. She went back into the kitchen. He lay down and stared at the large plants near the left wall window. He crossed his arms and fumed in anger.

Xiene came out of the kitchen with a soda in her right hand. She sat on the little couch facing the television cabinet. She looked at Allen. "You mad at me?"

"No, I always have this expression on my face," he snapped.

"Oh, maybe I should go." She put the soda on the floor and started walking towards the door. Allen wanted to stop her, but his pride refused to give in. Xiene opened their door. "You going tomorrow?"

"Yes!" Allen yelled.

"Good. See you."

Xiene left, slowly closing the door. Allen heard her boots click on the concrete steps. *Get up, stupid!*

"Fuck you," he told his conscience. "God, why am I dating that girl? I mean, all she does is get me into trouble and beat me up." *Well, there is the great sex, his other side explained.* "Ha! You can get great sex from a $100 escort service!" *You love her.* "I love chocolate mousse cake too." *She loves you.* "She also loves horseback riding. *It's the longest you've ever dated.* "I've been wearing my glasses since I was ten. Does that make them a good thing?" *Yes. It does*

Tired of arguing with himself, Allen fell asleep. Brandon came in, followed a few seconds later by Oswald and Monroe.

"Awaken," Brandon said, holding his hand out like a wizard.

"Look what I got," Oswald said, holding up a new CD.

Allen rubbed his eyes and read: Stockhausen. "Ew. I thought you hated this album."

"I do, but this was marked down from $30 to 20."

Allen raised an eyebrow. Monroe accidentally kicked over Xiene's soda near the loveseat.

"Whoops! Sorry," he said, picking it up.

"Not mine. Xiene's."

"Where is she?"

"She left. That reminds me, I have to call Beverly." Allen got up and walked over to the phone next to the kitchen entrance. He dialed Beverly's number while Brandon offered Allen some corn chips. It seems the threesome had picked up some videos and planned a night of movie-watching and junk food eating.

"Hello?" Maggie answered.

"Hi, Mag, it's Al."

"Hold on, Al. Hey, Bev, it's Al," she yelled. They said something to each other. Allen couldn't hear, but both could be heard laughing.

Beverly answered the phone. "This is Bev."

"Argh! Enough already," Allen answered, getting irritated.

Beverly laughed. "Okay, what's up?"

"You wanted me to call you."

"Oh, yeah. Right. You want to go?"

"Sure. What's the occasion?"

"There's an arts and crafts fair up there, and Maggie's friend has some stuff on display."

"What kind of stuff? Pictures and statues of naked, embracing women and anything else mountain folk would find offensive?"

"Pots, glassware. You know, country things," Beverly answered.

"What time will you be leaving?"

Beverly yelled the question at Maggie. Maggie yelled something back. "Be ready at nine," Maggie yelled something else. Beverly laughed. "Maggie says don't you just love our intercom?"

Allen laughed.

Allen put his shirt on just when someone knocked at the front door. He opened it and was briefly blinded by the golden morning sunlight.

"Hi," said Xiene.

Allen turned and walked to the loveseat to put on his tennis shoes. Xiene came in and took off her green John Lennon glasses. Her outfit jingled from all of the tiny bells, charms, and other knickknacks she had on top of her Native American hippy-looking attire.

"You still mad?" she asked.

Allen put his finger inside his left tennis shoe heel to pry it on. "What do you think?" he mumbled.

"I don't know. Do you want me to stay home?"

"You're already here, you might as well go along," Allen mumbled.

Xiene crossed her arms and looked down at her blue suede boots. "I'm not mad at you, even if you are being a baby."

"Shut up, please," Allen said, putting on his other shoe. Xiene turned on her heel and hastily walked out the door. He followed. He spotted Xiene walking down the concrete stairs towards Maggie's cream-colored Volvo station wagon. Beverly leaned on the right side of the car holding a video camera.

"Hey, wave!" she yelled at Xiene. Xiene flipped her a bird.

"Maybe I can edit that part out."

Allen locked the door and followed Xiene. He watched her as she spread out her arms and started dancing for Beverly's video camera.

"Yeah, that's better. Now do a cha-cha," Beverly instructed. Xiene did it. "Now a scene from Swan Lake."

Allen made it to the bottom of the stairs. "Allen, you join in," Beverly said, waving him over to join Xiene in her amateur fifth-position ballet pose.

"No, thanks. Allen walked around the car and got in.

"Hi, pumpkin," said Maggie, showing her chubby cheeks and smile.

"Hello," Allen said in a drab voice.

"What's wrong?" she asked, her face showing true concern.

"Nothing, just tired. I've been so tired lately."

"Oh, you and Xiene doing too much wild thang, huh?" Maggie started doing rapper hand gestures.

Beverly got in the car. Xiene hopped in next to Allen.

"'Walk Like an Egyptian?'" Beverly asked, referring to Maggie's hand movements.

"No, 'Wild Thang'," she replied.

Allen looked out of his window, then glanced at Xiene. She was mad. *I guess we're equal now. This should be a fun trip.*

"Are we ready, kids?" Beverly asked, looking back. She looked at Allen and Xiene. "Boy, what a couple of sourpusses back there." She tapped Maggie on the shoulder. "Look at that."

Maggie turned around. "Such sad faces on a beautiful Saturday morning."

"Yeah, now cheer up or I'll kick both your butts," said Beverly like Mr. T.

Allen and Xiene smirked.

After an hour of traveling, the Volvo pulled into a rest stop off I-75. Beverly got out to use the bathroom. Xiene searched her bag for a cigarette. Maggie adjusted her rearview mirror to look at Xiene and Allen. He looked at the mirror and saw her eyes spying on them. He looked away, out of his window, at the cars and trucks passing by down the hill. Xiene got out of the car with her Godzilla lighter and cigarettes. Allen looked back at the mirror. Maggie still stared.

"What?" he asked.

"You guys have been pretty silent back there. What happened?"

"Nothing. Just your typical fight."

"Really? Over what?"

"I don't know. She's just getting on my nerves. She thinks she's such hot shit."

"What do you mean?"

"You know how Xiene is, always treating me like a kid. Beating on me when I piss her off. Acting like she's never wrong. I mean, in the time I've known her, I can't remember her-—"

Maggie and Allen noticed Xiene had leaned against the car. Scared Xiene would overhear the conversation, Maggie cut it short. "I'll talk to you later."

"Okay," Allen said, looking at Xiene's back against the window. He heard her cough, and then her hand rested on top of the roof. Next, she started drumming her nails on the top, giving the sound of pebbles or raindrops. Allen felt like punching the roof and yelling stop. He crossed his arms, looked back towards the highway, and sighed.

Beverly came from the restroom and walked up to Xiene. Allen heard them talking about something. After a while, Beverly moved next to Xiene. Allen turned to see Beverly hug her. They got into the Volvo, Xiene saying, "I guess not," then laughed. Beverly also laughed.

The Volvo pulled off and merged back onto the I-75. Allen lay back and slept.

He woke to the sound of the Cramps 'Stay Sick album. He looked around to see what was going on.

"No, none of that," said Beverly. She reached for the cassette player and ejected the tape. "What else do you have?"

Allen looked at Xiene, ruffling through her cassette box.

"How about this?" she handed Beverly the tape.

Beverly read it. "Butthole Surfers? Don't you have anything that doesn't require slam dancing?" asked Maggie.

"Okay, okay, let me see." Xiene reached in and got another tape. "There." She handed it to Beverly.

"Jethro Tull?"

"Yeah," Maggie praised.

Beverly put the tape in and then looked back at Allen. "Hey, sleepyhead, you missed some great sights."

"I assume you videotaped them?" Allen asked.

Beverly lifted the video camera over the seat. "But of course. I got fifteen hours of cow footage."

"And we've only been on the road for two hours," Maggie added.

The red light on the video camera cut on, indicating it was recording. "Hey, Allen, lean over and give Xiene a big, wet, smooch." Beverly zoomed in on Allen.

"No, thanks," Allen said, crossing his arms and looking out the window.

Beverly pointed the camera at Xiene. "Okay, Xiene, plant a sloppy one on Allen." Xiene bit her bottom lip, giving her the appearance of a rabbit, looked towards the camera, and acted as if she were punching it. "Hey, no pictures, Geraldo!" she yelled.

Beverly laughed. "And this, ladies and gentlemen, is my lover Maggie." Maggie put her hand between the camera and herself. "My god, my career is ruined! Please don't tell my husband." She faked crying.

Beverly put the camera down. "How is C.J.?" she asked.

"Fine. He and his wife are going to be passing through Atlanta sometime next month."

"They bringing Tommy?"

"Are you kidding?" Maggie answered. "Hi, son, you remember your lesbian mother," Maggie said in a deep voice.

Beverly put her left hand behind Maggie's neck. She leaned over and kissed her.

Allen thought how, before he met these two, and learned to accept people for who they were, their actions would have turned his religiously raised stomach. He moved his hand to the middle of the seat. He wondered if Xiene would take it and they could end their altercation. She looked at Allen and then crossed her arms and looked out of the window at a mountain miles away, seen over some trees. Allen crossed his arms and looked out of his window at the grey, broken-down barn surrounded by unattended land.

Thirty minutes later, the Volvo pulled off to the side of the road next to a fruit stand. The two farmers got off the tailgate of an old pickup truck to greet the foursome. *Did Maggie stop to buy fruit or look at the mountain scenery?* She walked over to the farmer's peach baskets. Beverly and Xiene got out of the car and started walking towards the guard rail to get a better look at the mountains. Allen followed a minute later. By the time he made it to the rail, Beverly had started panning the scenery with her camera. Xiene leaned against the rail, looking down at her right boot kicking a grass-covered rock.

Allen looked off in the distance at the blue mountain of trees. The occasional wind made him wonder if he could hang glide in this area. A hawk flew into sight. Allen tapped Beverly's shoulder. "Look." He pointed. She moved the camera to record the bird.

"Ohh, look, Xiene." Beverly pointed.

Xiene peered up at the bird. It never flapped its wings once. It circled in one spot for a minute, then would move into the next. Allen looked down at the tiny trees. He spotted a farmhouse. It appeared the size of a sugar cube. He closed one eye and put his fingers in front of his eyes. Using pincer movements, he imagined crushing the farmhouse between his thumb and forefinger.

Allen looked over at Xiene. She still stared at the hawk. She looked at him. He turned to Maggie, busy putting some peaches into a brown paper bag. An elderly farmer pointed at some and mumbled something to her in a mountain accent too deep for Allen to understand. He wondered if Maggie understood or if she just smiled and nodded out of politeness. The other farmer, who looked like Ed from those Bartles & Jaymes commercials, sat on the tailgate in his blue overalls and hat staring at Beverly videotaping.

A grave sound averted Allen's eyes to the white minivan pulling up next to the Volvo. Two shorts-wearing, sun-glassed yuppies got out, followed by their two kids. The parents moved next to Beverly.

"Yeah, you see that patch of trees near that lake?" the man said, pointing.

The woman lifted a pair of binoculars to her eyes. "Er, yeah."

"That's where we're going to put the tennis court, and over there," he pointed to a different area, "that's for the golf course."

Allen looked at Beverly. She put her camera down.

"Let's go," she said with a look of disgust. Allen turned to Xiene, who had a pissed-off expression.

"Maggie, you ready?" yelled Beverly.

Maggie handed the farmer five dollars and picked up her sack. "Yeah."

"Timber!" yelled one of the kids.

Allen looked at the blond-haired boy as he stepped on a five-foot-tall tree near the guard rail. After a couple of stomps, the tree gave way and fell. Allen looked at the little girl. A couple of ants were eating out the potato chip bag she'd dropped. She looked down at them and then started stomping wildly, killing a few and sending the rest scattering.

Xiene stood against the guardrail, fist clenched, mouth tightly closed viewing the kids' actions.

"Allen, you ready?" yelled Maggie.

Allen turned around and walked to the car. Xiene remained still, almost shaking. He wanted to go get her, but he didn't know if they were still mad at each other.

"Xiene!" called Maggie.

Xiene walked over to the little boy. Allen expected her to pick him up and throw him into the valley. She knelt. The little boy shuffled around nervously, then walked away. Xiene got up and went over to the little girl. She knelt and talked to her. The little girl bent down and picked up the potato chip bag. Xiene smiled. The mother walked over and grabbed the little girl's hand and yanked her away from Xiene. She glared at Xiene with an angry expression. The little girl turned around and waved bye to Xiene. She smiled and walked back.

"What did you tell them?" asked Maggie as Xiene got into the car.

"I told the little boy that the Teenage Mutant Ninja Turtles or Robocop would never hurt trees. And I told the little girl that Barbie hates little girls that litter.

Allen had been amazed that Xiene had used child psychology instead of violence or foul language. He realized this was one of the qualities that kept him from leaving her. He felt like telling her he was sorry. *No, you asshole! Hold your ground. You're always apologizing! But look at her.'* Allen did. *'She's so beautiful. How can anyone with eyes that green be a complete bitch?'* Allen's other side explained. *Fuck her! Plenty of* mass-murdering, *rapists were considered good-looking! She loves you. If she does, why doesn't she apologize? For what?*

Tired of the debate in his head, Allen lay back and closed his eyes.

The sound of gravel and dirt under the tires woke Allen up. He opened his eyes and spotted a park ranger directing traffic up to the dirt road parking spaces in the woods. The Volvo followed behind a white jeep spewing a cloud of dry orange dirt onto Maggie's car.

"My poor, freshly washed car!" she protested, driving around a couple walking on the side of the road. The Volvo passed by at least thirty filled parking spaces off to the side, all near huge pine trees. A large white banner hung between two totem poles and read, 'Watermill Arts and Crafts Fest' in black and red letters.

There's one," Beverly said, pointing to the left. Maggie squeezed the Volvo between a Volkswagen and a minivan. A feeling came over Allen, one he always gets when visiting Disneyland or a national monument for the first time—an anxiety attack, complete with butterflies in the stomach. He never figured out why he felt this way at these times.

The foursome stepped out of the car onto the brown pine needles Beverly grabbed her video camera bag. Maggie checked the film in her disk camera. Xiene loaded her 35mm SLR with a large zoom lens attachment. Allen felt naked for not bringing a camera.

"What, are you gonna do, take pictures of the moon?" He asked Xiene before he realized he had broken his vow of silence.

She looked over at him and then continued adjusting her camera.

You see? She's not going to speak to you. It's over, man, hang it up! Shut up! Allen told his inner voice.

"Hey, Allen, where's your camera?" Maggie asked, setting up a shot of Allen leaning on the car.

Allen pointed to his head. "Up here."

Maggie took a picture of him touching his forehead.

"Oh, great shot," Allen said sarcastically. "It's going to look like I'm saying, 'Duh, look, I got brains.'"

Maggie laughed. Allen turned to Xiene. She was pointing her lens at him.

Look, she's taking your picture. You see? She's not mad at you.

"Maggie, will you please tell him to get out of the way?" Xiene said.

Maggie looked at Xiene and then at Allen. She had a confused look on her face. Allen walked away, looked to the right, and spotted the van parked next to the Volkswagen. Painted on the side of the van was a painting by Pablo Picasso, The Three Musicians. Allen walked around the back of the van to see if another part was as interesting. On the back was another painting by Picasso, Girl Before a Mirror. Allen glanced on the left side, showing Picasso's Seated Woman. He expected something else with three in it. The driver got out of the van. A tall man, between the ages of 21 and 23, with long blond hair, no shirt, and cut-off blue jeans with peace signs painted on them.

"Nice van," Allen said to him.

He looked at Allen, then reached into his van and pulled out a guitar case. He closed the door, then walked past Allen without speaking. *Well, okay then.*

"Neat paintings," Xiene said to him as he rounded the back of the van.

"Thanks. I painted it, myself," he bragged.

"Really? You're an artist?"

"Yeah, I'm also in a band called Radical Vasectomy. You heard of us?"

"Er, no,"

"Oh well, you will when we become big."

Allen watched as the guy continued talking to Xiene. She laughed at something he said. Allen turned around and walked towards the front of the van. He spotted something inside and craned his neck to see what it was. Five pairs of lady's panties hung on the rearview mirror. A pair of red high heel shoes were on the floor. Allen guessed he was either a playboy or a cross-dresser. He looked towards the back. The sight of leopard-skin wall decorations and a bed with red satin sheets didn't surprise him.

Xiene laughed again. Allen left the van and hiked towards the woods, ignoring Beverly calling his name. "Stupid! She is so stupid!" he said to himself. "Why do I bother with her? She's nothing but pure abuse!" Allen kicked a pine cone out of his way. "This is it! I refuse to be dumped by her! If any dumping gets done, I'm going to do it! She won't mind, anyway, she has Blond Jesus back there! She's always had her pick of men! Boy, if I had a list of all of the guys that hit on her when we go out…*And yet, she stays with me. Why? 'Because she loves you, stupid. Go back and tell her you're sorry. Fuck you! She's with Blondie! It's over! 'Shut up, she's just talking to him. If she wanted to leave you, believe me, she would have done it a long time ago.' Hey, I've already tried to apologize. She ignored me! 'Saying 'what are you gonna do, take pictures of the moon?' is not an apology!'*

Allen couldn't debate the other side anymore, so he stopped walking and looked around. A warm breeze rustled the tall pine trees and caused the sunlight to pale among the leaves. The trees swayed, and pine cones thumped onto the needle-covered ground. He realized at this moment he was lost. *Okay, the smartest thing to do now is turn around and head back in the opposite direction.* He did a 180° turn and walked into a tree.

"Shit! Where did this come from? Okay, wrong way. I'll try this path." He turned slightly and continued walking. A few minutes later he almost walked into a stream. "Damn it! This wasn't here!"

After an hour of walking, Allen sat down next to an oak tree. He put his hand down and felt something slimy. Looking down, he discovered he had put his hand on the fly-ridden fur of a dead raccoon. After impersonating Curley of the Three Stooges, he ran for five seconds before tripping into a deep ditch. He slammed against the side and plummeted into knee-high water. Ignoring the cut on his leg, he struggled to climb out. The muddy, slippery walls prevented him from climbing up. He started walking along the ditch looking for an easier place to climb up.

After thirty minutes of walking in the muddy brown water, sweaty, and bleeding, he finally came to a shallower part of the wall. He climbed out and studied his surroundings. He was on top of a steep grassy hill. Looking at the bottom, he saw the site of the arts and crafts fest.

"How the hell did I get way up here?"

He started walking down the large grassy hill towards the bottom. He noticed, that with each step, he was walking faster and faster. After a while his feet barely touched the ground as he ran uncontrollably at breakneck speed. His screaming and waving caught the attention of two little girls next to a flower booth. They looked up and spotted him waving his arms around, running and screaming. The little girls pointed and shrieked at Allen. This caught the attention of some tourists looking at a woodcarving exhibit. The two women in the foursome grabbed onto their husbands' and pointed at Allen, the Whirling Maniac, and screamed. By the time he heard the four females screaming, he crashed into the flower booth, sending roses, mountain coral, and tulips in every direction.

A crowd gathered around Allen, wondering if he had broken his now pain-ridden arm. A big guy in German lederhosen helped Allen up.

Allen started to clean up his mess

"Don't worry about it, nothing was broken." the guy said, putting his hand on Allen's shoulder. But, are you alright?"

"I don't know. I think I'm fine. Just banged up.

"Allen!" someone yelled.

He looked over the staring heads and spotted Beverly and Maggie running towards him. The twosome pushed through the crowd.

"God, what the hell happened to you? We've been looking all over for you," Beverly asked.

"I got lost."

"Why did you walk off by yourself? We were worried sick about you."

"Okay, Mom," Allen said sarcastically while pushing through the crowd.

Beverly had a pissed expression on her face. "Well, excuse the shit out of us for worrying about you!"

Allen continued walking towards a public bathroom. Before he went in, he heard Beverly ask Maggie 'What's wrong with him?' Allen entered the men's room just when a tourist in a white fishing hat was zipping up his fly. The smell of deodorizers filled his nostrils. He looked around the small, wooden green building. The high windows with screens on them made him wonder if a peeping Tom could look in by climbing the tree seen over the third stall. He walked to the sink. Looking in the mirror, he saw what kind of mess he had become: clothes muddy and torn in some places fit the permanent angry expression on his face.

He took his clothes off and began washing his shirt and pants in the sink. He examined the cut on his leg, which was not as bad as he thought. But its continued bleeding would have to be tended to. He walked over to a toilet stall. All of the doors had been taken off. He reached for the toilet paper cased in a 1990s model toilet paper dispenser. Its white casing and brown-tinted plastic window made Allen wonder what was wrong with the bar on the wall. He reached under the device to pinch out the paper. The tissue was too far inside the box to be reached. He struggled and stretched to get to the roll but to no avail. Two of his fingers nipped a small piece of the roll. He tried to pull the rest of the paper down using his two fingers. All he got were pieces too small to wipe a rat's butt. Allen looked around the box and spotted a large opening between the box and the wall. If he can get behind the device, he could grab the entire roll and pull it out. He slipped his fingers behind the box. He cut his index finger. When he quickly pulled his hand back, he cut his forefinger. The metal box had unexpectedly sharp edges.

He looked at his two bleeding fingers, grabbed the box, and ripped it off the wall. He turned around and noticed the two little boys watching this man in his underwear vandalizing the bathroom. He handed the box to the blond one. "Here!"

The boy took it and tried to figure out what it was. The brown-haired boy watched Allen walk back to the sink.

✖

An hour later, Allen finished drying his jeans as much as he could under the hand dryer. He slipped them on and felt the hot button's snaps burn his stomach. He combed his hair and walked out. Beverly and Maggie sat on the wooden porch outside. They had their backs to him and stared at passers-by. Allen thought about sneaking away but figured he would have to confront them eventually. He walked over and sat down next to Maggie.

"Oh. So nice of you to join us," said Maggie.

I knew she was going to say that.

"Allen, what the fuck is wrong with you? Where the hell did you go?" said Beverly, very pissed.

"I went walking. I got lost. I fell off a mountain. The end!"

"Warn us the next time you go wandering off!"

"I notice someone wasn't crazy worried about me," he said with one eyebrow raised.

"Xiene?' Maggie asked. "Is that what this is all about?"

"What else?" Beverly said, putting her chin on her kneecap. "God, Allen, you guys. I mean—sometimes I wonder why you two stay together. I mean, all you do is fight and make up over and over"

This was not what he expected Beverly to say. *What the hell has Xiene and Beverly been talking about?* "Are you saying we should break up?"Allen felt his stomach drop. The thought of breaking up with Xiene gave him an anxiety attack

"No…Well—I mean you both seem a little stressed lately after Verna's death. Don't break up, but at least step away from each other and clear the air." Beverly said.

"That's a terrible idea." Maggie said. "I don't think you should do that. You need to talk it out. Find out what you want."

"Where is she?" Allen asked.

"She's watching the blond guy perform over in the courtyard." Maggie pointed.

Allen hopped up and walked to the courtyard. He avoided the group of beer-drinking tourists and looked around for the blond guy.

"Allen?"

He heard a stranger call his name. He looked down and saw a woman sitting at an arts and crafts booth, stocked with hand-blown glass sculptures and wicker baskets.

"Pardon me?" he asked.

The woman in her late twenties had a banana peasant dress on and flowers in her hair. Her black, curly hair accented her smooth, creamy skin, her rosy cheeks shone as she smiled at him. "Are you Allen?"

"Er, yes."

"I'm Angie I'm a friend of Maggie. They're looking for you, you know."

"Yeah, I found them. How did you know what I looked like?"

"Maggie showed me a picture."

"Not the one of me at Christmas?"

"That's the one."

Allen thought about the shot of him with the Christmas lights, balls, and tinsel surrounding him. "I look even better as a human than a tree," he joked.

She giggled. "Ahh, I thought you looked cute," she joked.

Allen smiled, then looked down at a small glass elephant. "You did this?"

"I did all of this," she gestured around.

"Wow. Where do you work?"

"In my home."

"You have glass-blowing stuff in your house?"

"It's a warehouse. I also have a ceramic kennel to do these." She held up a beautifully crafted swan.

Allen studied it. *This person is a pro!* "Do you do this for a living?"

"Half and half. My other income comes from working at the crystal shop in Little Five Points.

Allen never saw her there, but realized he is usually in Little Five Points on weekends.

"You an artist?" she asked.

"Yeah, sort of."

"Sort of?"

"I'm a T-shirt designer."

"Really? Wow, I've always wanted to get into that!"

"Really? How strange. I've always wanted to get into ceramics. The only chance I had was back in high school, and, let's face it, everyone's too busy making bongs and beer mugs to do any serious artwork."

She laughed. Do you live in Atlanta, too?

"Yeah, originally from Charlotte."

"You're from Charlotte?" she screamed. "Me, too!" she shook his hand. "I never met anyone from there.

They began discussing Charlotte and how each one came to Atlanta. Both had been to art school: he the Art Institute of Atlanta, she the Neopolitan Art Academy. Both had worked at the art supply stores and Allen's biggest surprise, she liked the kind of music he listened to.

Allen picked up a glass unicorn. "Angie, I'm going to have to buy something from you now! Not many people like my music." Allen reached into his pocket and paid her ten dollars.

"Thank you Allen, and take this." She reached into a mahogany box and pulled out a business card. Allen studied the ink drawing of a glass cat and the words 'Angie Faith's ceramics, sculptures and crystals', followed by her phone number and address.

"Faith?"

"It's Indian. I'm part Cherokee, Italian, and part African, Irish."

Allen looked at her to find the African and Cherokee but couldn't.

"Tell you what, if you are ever in my part of town, look me up. Or, if you're in Little Five Points, I work these hours." She took the card and wrote on the back.

Allen took the card and studied the handwriting. High ascending that were sharp indicating an extremely extroverted person with lots of confidence. He kept his handwriting analysis to himself.

"See you later." She reached out her hand. Her delicate fingers with unpainted nails had two crystal rings on her index and forefinger. One was an amethyst, the other a jade stone. Allen shook her hand. She gave him a firm handshake. Allen always hated weak, limp-fish handshakes. They meant 'I'm not interested in knowing you'. He smiled.

"Okay. I'll see you. Bye."

He walked away. He turned and noticed her looking at him. She waved. He waved back and continued walking.

Allen spotted the blond guy playing his guitar. He sat, legs crossed on some grass near a white tent that sold flutes. In front of him an old cowboy hat filled with money. He played and sang Greensleeves and occasionally would look at Xiene, seated on his right. She smiled and moved her hair out of her face.

A small crowd would form and disband occasionally as he played. He finished his song. Everyone clapped and some people put money in his hat. Xiene clapped enthusiastically

"I love that song."

Of course. Every moron with a guitar can play it!

"Thanks, the guy said to Xiene.

"Do you know Scarborough Fair?"

"Okay." He picked up the guitar and began playing again. This time Xiene sang. Allen could never figure out how someone so hard rock could have such a soft voice. His only guess is that she was just a good imitator. After all, she could impersonate voices very well. She always killed him with her Marge Simpson impersonation she could do with a blue towel on her head.

A crowd gathered around the twosome. Xiene spotted Allen for the first time. Her smile left her, but she continued singing. The crowd started putting money in the hat even before they finished their song.

Allen looked up and noticed the darkening sky. He hoped it would rain at that moment and drench the happy musicians. No luck. The song ended, and the crowd applauded and gave more money. *Not once did Blondie say thank you! What an asshole!*

The guy took a handful of money and put it on Xiene's dress. "Here's your share," he said

"No! I couldn't take this!" she said.

"What the hell, I'm just gonna give my share to charity. I never keep any of the money. I just like to play."

"Ahh," Xiene said. Allen expected her to lean over and kiss him. He wondered what kind of running start he would need to successfully kick Blondie's head off. Allen gave a mean expression to Xiene. She returned it then reached over and put her hand on Blondie's bare back.

Allen looked up to see if the rain had started yet. A strong wind knocked something over behind Allen.

Xiene stood up. "Looks like rain. We better get inside."

"Hold on," he said, picking up his stuff.

"Greg!" someone called. Blondie turned around. Allen spotted Angie running towards them.

Blondie, now known as Greg, answered, "What?"

The wind picked up and the sky darkened more. A tent blew over, spilling wooden flutes everywhere. Xiene helped Greg pick up his blanket.

Angie ran over. "Hi, Allen!"

"Hi." Allen smiled and waved his fingers.

"Greg, my stuff is blowing away and I need your help." Angie pleaded.

"Er, okay. He turned to Xiene. "Oh, Xiene, this is my girlfriend, Angie."

"Hi, Xiene." Angie waved.

The expressions on Xiene's and Allen's faces could have been compared to opening a Christmas present only to find a turd inside. She looked at Allen and realized he had been with Angie as she had been with Greg.

Greg and Angie ran to her tent. A drop hit Allen on the forehead. He and Xiene stood paralyzed, not sure what to do or say. More and more raindrops. "Xiene, Allen, let's go!" Beverly and Maggie called out.

They looked at each other and then began running to Maggie's car. Halfway there, the rain hit full level, joined by an occasional thunder-and-lightning show. The now drenched twosome made it to Maggie's car and hopped into the back.

"Shit, I hate this weather!" Beverly complained.

"How's your camera?" Maggie asked.

"It looks okay to me."

"Test it."

She held it up in Allen's direction.

"You film me, and that is the last shot your camera will take," he said.

Beverly saw that it was serious. "I'll just film Xiene then." Xiene reached under the camera, gripped the lens cap, and put it on the front, blocking Beverly's vision. "Oh-oh, looks like a news blackout."

"God, another joke," Allen mumbled.

"What?" Beverly asked.

"Don't you ever stop making jokes?" Allen bitched.

"Shut up," Xiene told Allen.

"What?"

"I said 'Shut up'. There's nothing wrong with her making jokes. They're a lot better than the ones you make," she hissed.

"Xiene, that's enough," Maggie intercepted.

"Who asked you? Maggie, you're always sticking your nose into everyone's business." Xiene said.

"Hey!" yelled Beverly. "Lay off!"

"Oh, shut up! Who the hell died and made you boss?" Allen snapped.

"Who the hell do you think you are? She can talk if she wants to," Xiene jabbed.

"Oh, shut the fuck up! Who asked your damn opinion?" Allen answered.

"Fuck you, you two-timing piece of shit!" Xiene yelled in his face.

"Me? How about you, you dumb, butt-kissing canary bitch!"

Xiene brought her hand back for a slap. Allen brought his hand up to block.

Beverly's arms reached from the front seat and separated the two. "That is enough, you two! Jesus fucking Christ! What the hell is wrong with your two? You're acting like a couple of assholes! Xiene! This corner!" She pointed to the right side of the car. "Allen! This corner!" She pointed to the left.

They scooted to their sides.

"I don't want you two to touch each other I don't want you to talk to each other as long as you both shall live!"

"Amen!" Maggie added.

"No problem!" Allen said.

"Me, neither!" Xiene added.

"Shut up!" Beverly screamed, her voice getting hoarse. Beverly turned around and mumbled to herself. Maggie put her arm around her.

Allen looked out of the window. The rain calmed down a little. The Volvo made it to the main road before the dirt one completely turned into an impossible mud trail. They trudged down the wet, foggy, rainy highway, through the stop-and-go traffic towards Atlanta. The foursome sat without speaking. The sound of the squeaky windshield wipers, the wet tires on the road, and the engine rumble were all that could be heard. An hour went by. Allen looked over.

Before he could speak, Maggie broke the silence. "I remember when C.J. and I used to fight. He would start something like, 'You don't respect me', and I would say, 'Why should I? You don't respect me.' 'Bullshit! I respect you more than you respect me.' 'Prove it,' I would say. But he couldn't. I mean, how could he? If you have in your mind that someone doesn't respect you, there's nothing they can do to prove it to you."

"Some people think that respect means obeying someone's orders," Beverly said.

I didn't want that. I wanted someone who loved me and did things for me for that reason.

"Some people think that respect is an offshoot of fear. It's not. It comes from love and, overall, trust. If you don't have at least trust in another person, then you don't love them. You just fear losing them."

Beverly laid her head on Maggie's shoulder. Maggie put her arm around her and kissed her forehead.

"Sometimes I wonder if hadn't discovered that I was a lesbian, and C.J. had cleaned up his act, how things would have turned out."

"You two would have divorced anyway," Beverly mumbled.

"You think so?"

"Of course. You two went past the final mark. You know, there are certain points where you can forgive a person, but once you cross over that final point, there is no turning back. Even if you stay married, nothing will ever be the same. That's what I think decides if a relationship is to survive. If you are willing to hold yourself from that line."

"You think there's no turning back?" Maggie asked.

"Do you think you and C.J. could get back together?"

"Hell, no! Why would I want to get back together?"

"Right. Do you think you'll ever let things get as out-of-control with me as they did with C.J.?"

"I can't picture it."

"Right, and you know why?"

"Why?"

"Because we get things off our chest. We argue and don't hold it in like you and C.J. It's like a steam valve. If you slowly release steam, you will get rid of it. But if you let it build up, it will burst the pipes, and then it's too late to fix."

Allen thought for a moment. When was the last time he and Xiene had discussed things that bothered each other? He couldn't remember. Ever since Verna's death, they had both been trying to take it easy on each other. But, without mentioning things that bothered them, everything had built up and as Beverly said, the confrontation back home had caused the pipes to burst. He had been blowing at least two months of steam at her. But why did she get mad at him? *All I did was tell her to shut up.* He thought for a moment. *The words 'shut up', to Xiene, mean 'I no longer want to see or hear you! If you tell little kids to shut up when they are crying, it will cause them to grow up abused. Xiene hates those words. That's why she liked to express her opinion so much and talk things out. Telling me I was acting like a baby is not cause enough to tell her to shut up.*

He heard a sigh. He looked over at Xiene. She leaned back in her chair. Her right hand gripped the door handle. She ran her thumbnail up and down the textured light brown vinyl.

"Speaking of pips," Beverly said, "what about that leak under the sink?"

"The repairman won't be in until Monday, so what I did was, I took some wax and melted it around the leak," Maggie answered

"It works?"

"Of course, my dear. I'm an expert."

Maggie and Beverly giggled.

How interesting. She said you couldn't fix a busted pipe and yet a simple act fixed the leak until a permanent repair job can be made. Allen felt someone staring at him. He knew it was Xiene. He wanted to look over, but couldn't. He didn't feel like talking in a stuffy Volvo about his and her entire future life. *When?* He asked himself. *Do I call her at home? Will she answer the phone? Do I visit in person? Will it be too late?*

Allen closed his eyes to think. He wished Xiene would say something but realized she was waiting for him. He pictured the many roads in his mind: one, where he doesn't say anything, they break up, everyone is miserable, they break up, he steals Angie away from Greg they live happily ever after, says something, they make up and go off into the sunset together, or she says 'fuck you, I'm going to steal Greg away from Angie'. It was all too much to think about. He fell asleep.

"Allentown! Allentown!" repeated Beverly, impersonating a train conductor. Allen awakened and realized they had made it to his apartment. The rain had gotten heavier.

"Damn, I should have brought my umbrella," complained Maggie.

"Looks like you'll have to make a run for it," said Beverly.

"No problem," Allen said, reaching for the door handle. "I'll see you guys later…" He patted Maggie and Beverly on their shoulders. He looked at Xiene. She looked at him. "…Bye."

"Bye," she answered. He opened the door and jumped out. The rain drenched him. He ran around the back of the Volvo, made his way to the right side of the car, and then started walking up the sidewalk towards his apartment.

Allen thought about his past relationships and imagined multiple pipes bursting over and over again. He heard the Volvo preparing to leave the curb.

"No!" he yelled. Allen turned around. Maggie had left the curb and the car stopped at an angle. The threesome looked at Allen getting drenched and standing still he reached out his right hand towards the car. Xiene pulled down her window.

"What?" she asked.

"Take my hand," he yelled.

"Why?" she yelled back.

"Because Maggie's wrong! Sometimes you can repair a busted pipe! You replace the old ones and start over!"

"But what will keep them from bursting in the future?"

"I'll install a reverse valve."

Xiene smiled, then got out of the car. She walked up the hill towards Allen, her white hair turning golden and straight from the rain, her outfit getting ruined. Allen felt his tennis shoes full of water. His glasses spattered with droplets. Xiene reached him and stood a foot away.

"What now?" she asked.

"I don't know. Will an 'I'm sorry' be good enough?"

"I don't know. Will that be good for me?" she asked back.

"Can I have a hug?" he asked.

"No," Xiene said.

Allen was startled. She leaned her head forward and kissed him on the cheek. Allen reached his hands out for her. She held her hands up. "Hey, whoa, you're going too fast. We're supposed to be starting over, remember? I hardly know you well enough for that yet."

Allen giggled. "Tell you what, Mrs. Richards, do you care to join me inside for dinner?"

"No."

"What?"

"I'd rather go for a walk. It's such a lovely day."

Allen looked up at the grey sky, the swaying trees, and the raindrops. He looked down at the streams running down the sewer, the muddy grass, and the spattering sound of droplets on the concrete. He looked back at Xiene.

"You're right. It's a beautiful day."

She smiled at him. They turned and started walking he heard the Volvo toot its horn before pulling off. He pictured Maggie telling Beverly, 'You see? My plan worked perfectly.'

He looked at Xiene. She smiled back.

"Mrs. Richards?"

"Yes?"

"Would it be too pushy in this stage of our relationship if we were to hold hands?"

"Oh, I can live with that."

Allen stretched out his hand and she grabbed it with a firm grip.

XIENE IN HELL!

Xiene came into the apartment carrying a bag of charcoal and some lighter fluid.

"It's about time," said Oswald, sitting on the couch massaging Mi Cha's legs.

"Hey, I got a fucking ticket!"

"What?" said Allen, sitting criss-cross apple sauce on the carpet.

"Yeah, I ran a red light up by Lennox and got pulled over by the Buckhead Fuckheads!

"What were you doing in Buckhead? You usually come by 85," asked Mi Cha.

"I had to pick up my last paycheck from Tower."

"You got fired?" Allen shouted.

"Oh well, there go my record discounts," mumbled Oswald. Mi Cha slapped the back of his head.

"Oh, honey," Allen moaned, reaching his hands out to Xiene, "first you got fired, then a ticket."

Xiene dropped the groceries, sat on the floor, and curled up on Allen's legs in a fetal position. He started stroking her dyed black hair.

"Why did they fire you?"

"Because I told them to stop acting like cooley-snob non-conformist conformists and start helping customers."

"What's wrong with that?" asked Mi Cha.

"Nothing, until one of them said, 'Fuck you, you're not the manager', so I threw a copy of Milli Vanilli's album at his head."

"Ouch. I bet that hurt!"

"No, I missed him and the record hit this styrofoam display of Madonna grabbing her crotch. It fell over right when the manager came around the corner."

"And he fired you."

"No, he fired me because I refused to work on Sundays and holidays."

Allen and Oswald looked at each other.

"Poor baby." Allen bent his neck and kissed Xiene's head. "What about the ticket?" He removed a dyed black hair from his tongue.

"I don't want to talk about it."

"Okay. Ahh, what a shitty day you've had."

"Yeah, reminds me of what happened at work yesterday," Oswald said.

While he told his story of computer failure and inadequate access to efficient roadways in his work area, Allen got up to start the charcoals and to get the blood flowing back into his legs.

Brandon and Monroe came from the back door on the porch. Behind them a sorry excuse for a barbecue caused by the lack of supplies.

"Hey," waved Monroe to Xiene. She didn't reach up her hands for hugs.

"What's wrong?" asked Brandon.

While Xiene retold her story, this time with more embellishment, Allen took the charcoal and fluid to the back. He dreaded missing the new version of Xiene's story, but he figured the next time she told it, that version would be even more entertaining. He liked that about her. Talking to Xiene is an action flick, each sequel more exciting and sometimes more violent than the previous. He added more charcoal and lighter fluid to the grill and brought it up to the official cookout standard.

Laughter came from the living room. *Xiene's embellishment.* Thirty minutes and five seconds later, Xiene came outside to join Allen. She still seemed down.

"Still feeling bad?"

"Yeah," she said, slumping.

Allen put his arm around her. "Poor, sweet baby," he said, before kissing her on the nose.

"Thanks, Snoopy," she mumbled with a half smile.

"Oh, cheer up." He began rubbing her back. "You'll find another job."

"What about the ticket? I'm completely broke."

"What happened to all that money you got on your birthday?"

"I used it for rent."

"What? Why? Haven't you been…" Allen stopped himself from nagging her for spending money on frivolous things. "…Your paycheck should cover the ticket."

"Ha-ha! It's going to go for my utilities."

"Shit. I could lend you the money."

"Hell, no! You know how I feel about borrowing money from you! Taking money from someone you have sex with is weird!"

"What else can you do?"

"I don't know." She slumped her head onto her knees. Allen got behind her and began a neck massage. Time passed. The heat on Allen's back told him the fire was ready.

"Brandon, it's ready!" he yelled.

This startled Xiene, who had fallen asleep. Brandon came out carrying a tray of carnivores mixed with vegetarian hot dogs. Xiene got up and stretched. She began walking along the grass behind the apartment. Allen joined her.

"You want to go lie down?"

"No," she said quietly. "I just want to…." She paused. "I don't know what I want to do."

Allen put his arm around her. She seemed tired and drained. "I think you should lie down."

"Yeah, I guess." She turned around. As they walked to the house, they heard a crash around the other side of the apartment. Brandon, Allen, and Xiene ran around the apartment. Oswald, Mi Cha, and Monroe appeared from the front door. Along with some neighbors, they looked down the hill and spotted a white Nova pulling away from Xiene's van and speeding down the street.

"Goddamn it!" yelled Xiene. She ran towards her van, followed by the gang. Allen looked to see where the car went. It disappeared. Xiene looked at the left side of her van. It was completely demolished.

"Jesus Christ!" someone said.

"Goddamn it!" Xiene yelled. "Son of a bitch! You get his license?" she yelled at Allen.

"No."

"Maybe we can catch up with him!" yelled Mi Cha.

"No, that fucker's miles from here!" yelled Xiene. She grabbed her hair as if she were going to tear it out. "Shit! Shit! Shit! I have to pay a ticket for a car I don't have!"

"We should call the police," said Monroe.

"I don't see why! Those assholes won't do anything!"

"We'll still have to report it," said Allen, afraid of the backlash from Xiene.

Xiene let go of her hair and turned around. Her fist clenched. Oswald and Mi Cha looked at the damage. Allen slowly approached Xiene, who was standing in the middle of the street. A car approached. Allen was about to warn Xiene to get out of the way, but the car had already come to a slow crawl. Xiene didn't move. The car stopped. The driver, an overweight Black woman, tapped her horn. Xiene looked at the car.

"Excuse me," the woman said.

Allen walked to Xiene, put his hand on her back, and nudged her to the other side. Xiene swung her hand back, knocking his arm away.

"You need to calm down."

"Calm down? Calm down?" she yelled.

"Yes."

"You're right! Don't worry, be fucking happy!" She danced a little. I just had the worst day of my fucking life and you say 'calm down'?" her voice got louder.

Allen started walking towards a creek near the road surrounded by trees and a few stone benches and tables near it. He gestured with his hand for Xiene to follow. She stomped after him. Allen and Xiene sat in the faux park in silence. Allen looked at Xiene to see if the scrawl on her face had gone away, and then he looked at the wreck site to see if the police had shown up. Monroe and Brandon checked under the hood. Allen's eyes panned up the hill to the apartment, to the backyard, and to the burning hot dogs.

"Brandon, hot dogs!"

Brandon looked at Allen. He gestured to the smoke. Brandon ran up the hill. Xiene smiled at the sight.

Allen reached over and grabbed her hand. She held tight, almost painfully.

"I don't believe this is happening!" she said in a weak voice."

"This kind of shit happens to me every day," Allen said.

Xiene looked at him and gave a 'don't try to outdo me' look."

"Sorry," Allen muttered.

They sat for forty minutes before the lone policeman showed up. Allen shushed Xiene, who mumbled 'About fucking time'.

The policeman made out his report.

"What are the chances of catching him?" asked Xiene.

"Not very good. You didn't get a license plate or a physical description.

"Great," she snapped.

"We'll see what turns up," the policeman said, returning to his car. "Your insurance should take care of this if you have a collision."

Xiene's face seemed to fall on the sidewalk.

"Oh-oh, no collision?" the policeman asked.

Xiene put her hands on her head.

"What about his liability?"

"That's only if we catch him."

"And you can't do that without a description," she added.

"Sorry," he said before getting into the patrol car. "I'll let you know if something comes up."

"If he says that again, I think I'll kill him," Xiene mumbled.

The policeman pulled off.

"Let's see how it runs," Oswald suggested.

Xiene took her keys out and handed them to Monroe. Every time, the engine refused to turn over. Xiene's expression got worse on the last try she turned around and headed towards the apartment.

"It's dead, Jim," Oswald joked.

Allen walked after Xiene. She sat on the porch and lit a cigarette. She didn't smoke it. She held it and ran her fingers through her hair.

"You're gonna get ashes in your hair," Allen said before realizing what a dumb thing to say. Xiene didn't respond. He grabbed onto a decorative porch support and tried to figure out what to say. Silence was the best option.

The sun went down. The group went in. Allen and Xiene stayed outside. Xiene let the cigarette burn down to her fingers without taking a puff. Allen took the cigarette from her and stamped it out.

"How long have you had that van?"

"Five years."

"Gads! You took good care of it."

"Yeah, lot of good that did, huh?" Xiene scraped the heel of her boot on the sidewalk. She reached down and whacked a mosquito on her thigh. "Thanks. That's just what I needed."

"Gee whiz, Xiene, did you make a pact with Satan or something?"

"I'm starting to wonder."

After a while of deep thought, Xiene stood up and headed into the apartment. Allen walked down to the van. While feeling over the dents, he heard voices. Looking from behind the van, he spotted some kids returning from the swimming pool. Their loud chattering, gleeful screeching, and towel-popping passed by.

"God, I hate kids," Allen sneered. He went inside. The group was already eating. Allen followed the phone cord from the living room into the kitchen. Xiene was engaged in a long-distance call with her mother. He was going to complain about her making the call, but he figured she couldn't afford it on her phone bill.

"That your mom?"

Xiene waved him to shut up. "No…yeah…did you check under Mary's bed? Shit! I'm sorry," Xiene quickly apologized.

Allen went into the dining room and ate. A while later Xiene came in.

"Oh well, you can fuck collision insurance."

"What? Why?" asked Brandon, swallowing his tofu hotdog.

"My mom found my insurance papers and I'm not covered."

"Wait, aren't you supposed to carry that stuff in your car?" Mi Cha asked.

That stuff got stolen along with my radio."

"When did this happen?"

"Last week. Someone broke into my van at the Acid Pit.

"You never told me that," Allen said, wondering how something like that could slip her mind.

"Why would someone want to steal your insurance papers?"

"I don't know. Maybe they're stealing my car one part at a time. First the radio, then the papers. Next, the tires!" Xiene's voice got louder with every statement. "I guess now it doesn't fucking matter! There's nothing left to steal!" She raised her arms.

The neighbors next door turned up their TV set. Allen patterned Xiene on the back.

"God, I need a back rub! I need a new life!" she moaned.

"Let's try the back rub first."

✖

Xiene took off her shirt and lay on Allen's bed. Allen started from the top and began massaging her back. Her muscles were very tense. Allen felt as if he were massaging a bodybuilder. "Relax."

"Ha!" she responded.

"Okay, what we need to do is put your problems in order and try to solve them one step at a time." Allen moved her hair to massage her neck. He noticed a pimple on her back. Dare I say? he thought. He didn't. She moaned. Her muscles began to relax. She reached her arm back.

"Could you massage this spot?" She moved her fingers along the pimple. "What the? What's that?" she rustled around trying to reach it.

"It's just a pimple."

"Jesus Freaking Christ!" She lifted off the bed, throwing Allen off of her. "That's just what I fucking need!" She dashed out of the room past Oswald, whose only view of what was happening was Xiene yelling, then running out of the room with her shirt off.

Allen didn't feel like explaining. He followed Xiene into the bathroom. In a strange, chicken-like position, she moved her body to see her back in the mirror. Allen pointed to it to prevent her from breaking her arms. "It's there."

"Shit! Goddamn it!"

"It's no big deal."

"Yes, it is! This is the icing on the cake! Jesus, who did I offend? I've been good, I give 5% to charity!" Allen raised an eyebrow. "I do!" She yelled.

"Okay. Don't yell."

"I have to! This is bullshit! Is there a curse on me?"

"I don't know. Maybe it's bad karma?"

"I've been good lately! I haven't vandalized public property in two months! I sent Mary a Christmas card! I didn't bitch at Richard for volunteering for Saudi Arabia!"

"He has to go, Xiene he's in the Air Force."

"So? Still, I supported him even if we are fighting for George Fucking Bush!"

How did we get into politics? "How is sending your sister a birthday card good karma?"

"Because she's such a bitch! I should have sent black roses and a year's subscription to Dog Shit Illustrated!"

Allen laughed, then grabbed onto Xiene. "I hate to tell you, but even the pope has a bad day."

"Oh, yeah? What's a bad day for him? 'Oh, my, I dropped the communion wafer on the floor'!" Allen hugged her and snickered. "I'm glad you're enjoying this!" she said while laughing and almost crying. She held onto him and began sobbing. They held each other for a while. Now and then the sound of footsteps would be heard coming up the stairs, then return to the living room. Finally the sound of people leaving through the front door.

"You want to spend the night?"

"I want to go home and curl up in my bed and die."

"How are you getting home? The subway stops running in…" Allen looked at his watch, "thirty minutes ago."

"Can't Brandon take me?"

"I don't know. It's one o'clock and he has to go to work tomorrow."

"Shit," she said silently. "Okay, let's go." She went back into the bedroom.

3:45 am

Allen felt a hand on his genitals. He hoped it was Xiene he felt her bare breast rub against his back. Confident that it was her, he allowed himself a hard-on. She began kissing her way from his belly button up to his head. They tried to minimize the moans so as not to disturb Brandon, who commented once about Xiene's orgasm shriek. Xiene ran her hair around Allen's chest. *Is this a bad idea? After all, having sex to ease stress can't be all smart—Shut up!* he told his conscience as Xiene put her tongue in his ear

5:30 am

Allen's alarm went off, giving him thirty minutes of sleep. Xiene cut it off. They both fell back asleep.

"Shit!" Allen said, waking up at ten. He looked at the clock. "Shit! Shit! Shit!" He hopped out of bed and put his underwear on. "I'm so late." He wrestled with his clothes.

"Why don't you call in sick?" said Xiene.

Allen stopped putting on his clothes. "Oh, yeah."

He sat down on the edge of the bed and called work. "Er, hi, Don. I'm sorry I couldn't call earlier. My girlfriend's car got totaled and I have to identify the car for a police report. It was a hit and run…the police haven't shown up yet…yeah, she's alright…I'll call you when the police leave."

"Not!" said Xiene when Allen hung up the phone. "You liar!"

"I didn't lie. I just told him what happened yesterday. I call it a 'time warp'."

""Time lie, more like it. He thinks I was in the car."

"So I withheld information."

"Damn, Allen, you should go into politics." She put her foot on his back and began making circles.

"So, I guess you're feeling better?"

"Ooh, yes," Xiene said in a sultry voice.

Allen lay back and placed his head on Xiene's stomach. She began playing with his hair. He closed his eyes. Suddenly, Xiene buckled and pushed him off of her. "What?"

He turned to see her jump out of bed. She opened the door and ran downstairs. Allen grabbed a sheet and wrapped it around himself in case the downstairs blinds were open. *At least the mailman would get only half a free show.*

Xiene rushed downstairs. Allen slowly followed. She opened her purse and dumped the contents onto the carpet.

"What's wrong?"

Xiene searched through her stuff and found a blue compact. "Oh, shit! Oh, god no!"

"What? What is it?"

"Jesus, no!"

"What?" Allen said, walking over.

"It's my birth control pills! I forgot to take one."

Allen's stomach fell into his feet. "Don't worry about it. You can be late. It takes a while for you to be fertile again, right?" The shaking nervousness of his voice didn't calm her.

"Yeah, but with my luck, you know I'm gonna be pregnant!"

Allen's heart joined his stomach in his feet. "Don't p-p-panic. You're just paranoid."

"Oh, Christ! What if I am pregnant?"

He walked over and knelt beside her. "Come on, you can't get pregnant every time you have sex, otherwise women would have eleven hundred kids."

"Oh, God, I was on top! Isn't that a fertility position?" Xiene said, grabbing her head.

"No. And calm down. Jesus! Xiene! As soon as you get your period you'll how stupid this is.

Days later, at work, Allen finished folding a Stealth Fighter model out of black construction paper. He flung it across the room and then turned back towards the digital watch thumbtacked to the wall.

3:30 pm

"Shit, thirty minutes more."

His boss knocked on the glass separating his office from theirs. This meant 'telephone call'. Allen picked up the phone.

"Hello."

It was Xiene. Her voice indicated she had been crying. Allen picked the phone up and stretched it into his office. He closed the door to keep Pat, the world's nosiest woman, from eavesdropping on his conversation. "What's wrong?"

"I'm pregnant."

Allen's skull split open, the heart and stomach in his feet leaped out into the carpet, and his knees turned to Jell-O. "What? Are you sure?"

"Yeah, my period is late."

"Have you tried an EPT test?"

"No."

Allen's heart and stomach went back into his feet. "Well, lots of women have late periods."

"Yeah, well, they haven't been having a shitty life like I have!" Xiene's voice got louder.

"Xiene, why don't you take the ETP test and I'll see you after work."

"How can I drive over without a fucking car?"

"Xiene, I can take a bus to you!"

"Okay, but hurry!"

Allen got on the bus at Cumberland Mall located next to the police station. He guesses they put the stop there to keep the undesirable elements away from Cobb County. He found it silly that the people in Cobb County rejected public transportation because they thought Black people would come into the haven and rob them. For Allen to get to work, he had to catch a bus to the subway station, ride to downtown Atlanta, catch another bus from Atlanta to Cobb County twenty minutes away, transfer to another bus, and then walk half a mile to work. He couldn't picture doing all this while carrying a television and an abductee.

Two men sat on either side of him. One was a common sight or smell on the back of the bus—a man who smelled so much that his clothes and breath reeked of 300-year-old cigarettes. Allen compared the smell to sticking old cigarette butts up your nostrils and making a sandwich out of an ashtray with pepper. Allen would hold his breath as long as he could until someone would get off the bus, sending a fresh breeze into the bus. At this point, he would inhale, hold his breath, and wait for more oxygen.

At Art Center Station downtown, Allen took the subway to Midtown. He never could figure out how she could afford a $500 apartment, but figured if he didn't have those stupid student loan payments and a desire for art supplies, CDs, and props for the Great Science Fiction movie he would make one day, he could afford it too. He liked his $400 apartment in North Atlanta and his roommate beat the hell out of the drug dealer, psychopath, and compulsive liars Allen had roomed with before.

Allen realized he had been rambling on about apartments in his head and remembered he could find out he was about to be a father. *A father? Me?* He never wanted to have kids under these circumstances. *What if Xiene is pregnant? Abortion? She's not religious, and she is a feminist in some ways. No, she probably won't do it. Xiene loves to experience life, and she'll probably keep the baby just to see what it's like. What a good reason: 'Son, I had you just for the thrill of it!' he pictured Xiene saying. And what about my role? I'll have to get a better job and help pay child support. Damnit! Why did I ever stop using condoms? Because Xiene wanted to feel me.* He remembered Xiene saying, "Gads, what if one of us has AIDS?" He thought about his minuscule sexual history. Except for the horrible thing that happened to her in high school, she never really talked about her sexual history. *I think something would have shown up by now. Yeah, right, but still, a rubber would have guaranteed no pregnancy!*

He caught the bus from Midtown Station to North Highland. Being rush hour, the bus took an extra fifteen minutes to get there. Allen pictured the kid he and Xiene would have, a boy named David named after Xiene's father or David Lynch after Xiene's favorite director. A girl—Electra, after the complex, or Siouxie, after Siouxie and the Banshees rock group. Then he thought about names he would pick: 'Charles Allen', after his dad and himself. 'Christine' after Xiene's real name.

Allen walked up the sidewalk to the apartment. He felt more relaxed now, even though his life might go belly up with one sentence. He knocked on the door and ignored the Christmas wreath still up from seven months ago. Xiene opened the door. The stereo was playing an Enya song very loud. Allen tried to figure out if this was a celebration song or a 'throw yourself in front of a steam roller' song.

He walked up and hugged her. Her body was limp. *Oh, oh.* He pulled away, walked to the stereo, and turned it down. The record was Claanad's 'Non-de Difference'. Xiene had a letter in her hand.

"What's that?"

"My eviction notice."

"What?" He yelled.

"Yeah. These apartments are going condo."

"Oh, fuck!" Allen wanted to hug her but didn't know if it would do any good. He sidetracked. "What about the EPT test?"

She calmly and quickly turned around as if she would break something if she moved fast. "I have five more minutes to tell." She looked at the clock on the wall. Allen walked over and took the letter from her. Xiene sat on her black beanbag sofa.

"The letter says you can stay at the apartments once they go condo for the higher rent or you can leave and still receive your deposit even if you break the lease. Well, at least you get your deposit back." Xiene twirled her index finger in the air. "You can just put that towards your next apartment."

"What next apartment? I don't have a fucking job!"

"Xiene—"

"I don't have a car!"

"Xiene, if—"

"I don't have a place to live!"

"Xiene—"

"And I'm pregnant!"

"Xiene, you don't know that!" Allen yelled.

"Boy, when my shit hits the fan, there's an elephant in front of it, taking a circus-sized dump!"

Allen sat down and put his arm around the limp rag doll Xiene. "Hmm, let's see. Ain't got no money, ain't got no home, ain't got plenty of nothing," Allen said, almost singing a verse from the musical: Porgy and Bess. Xiene dug her nails into his leg. "Ow!" Oh, well, anger is always better than depression." He rubbed his leg.

"What am I going to do?"

"Tell you what, you can come to stay with Brandon and me."

"No way! You have your art and music shit and I have my photo equipment. How the hell could I fit in there?"

"Simple. We'll turn the third bedroom into a storage area. We'll move your bed into my room since it's bigger, and then we'll move my bed and all unwanted stuff to the curb, or have a yard sale.

"Yeah…I guess that would work." She seemed to cheer up a little.

"Meanwhile, you'll look for another job and when you get back on your feet, you can find another apartment, buy a car, and return to your normal lifestyle."

"What if I'm pregnant?"

"We'll burn that bridge when we come to it."

"Huh?"

"Something like that."

Time passed. Allen looked at the clock. The test had one minute left.

"Why don't you, Brandon, and I just stay together instead of me moving in and then moving out?" Xiene asked.

Allen dreaded this question but he felt it coming. "Because we only have one bathroom." *Good answer!*

"Why don't we move into a bigger apartment?"

Think, Allen! "Because I'll drive you insane." Good job! Turn the reason on yourself!

"No, you won't. I can be around you all day, I love you."

Shit! She returned my volley! "The test is ready!"

Xiene hopped up and ran into the bathroom. Allen tried to follow, but she slammed the door. He heard her moving bottles around. Something fell and shattered on the ground.

"You alright?"

"Yeah, just some perfume."

"Don't cut yourself."

Silence followed, then a loud "Yesowe!"

"What? Is that a 'yes' or a 'no'?"

Xiene opened the door. She limped out. "I'm not pregnant."

"Alright!" Allen yelled.

"But I stepped on some glass." She hopped over to the black metal rocking chair. Allen went into the bathroom and looked for a Band-Aid. Xiene had already opened a box and spilled the contents into the puddle of perfume stinking up the bathroom. He grabbed a towel and tried to clean up the mess while in the other room, Xiene performed surgery on her foot.

"Damn it to fucking hell!"

"Your bad luck seems to be working in shifts."

"Tell me about it."

Allen cleaned up the glass and went over to join Xiene. "You poor kid."

"If I hear the word 'poor' one more time…"

"Okay, okay, you pathetic fool, you."

"That's more like it." She moved the rocking chair forward picked up a pink sock and put it on the injured foot. When she leaned back the rocking chair's back leg rolled over Allen's foot.

"Ow, ow, ow!" He pushed the chair forward, sending Xiene to the floor. "I'm sorry."

Xiene looked at him as if he had just murdered her entire family. "What did I do to deserve that?"

"Nothing. You rocked onto my foot." Allen massaged his foot.

Xiene laid on her back. "Just let me die here, Lord."

"Shut up! It's just a freak month for you."

Xiene blew a raspberry. Allen sat in the rocking chair and stared at the down and out Xiene. She was in such a pathetic state that he wished he could say just the right thing and she would hop up and be the go-getting, ass-kicking, fuck-life-let's-dance girl he loves so much. But he couldn't think of anything. 'Don't worry, be happy' would get him a kick in the balls. Hard! 'Life's a bitch' will get him a slap. 'Cheer up' will make him kill himself for saying something so stupid. Physical contact may result in sex and pregnancy scare again.

Xiene fell asleep. Allen got up and went into her bedroom. He cut on the television. Some CNN reporter was talking about an Air Force pilot that went down in Bagdad. Allen was burned out on the war coverage. Every day the most minuscule things were reported on. It was the same fleet as Xiene's brother. *Oh, shit! Should I? No, she's resting. She needs to rest. Plus, they don't know who it is*—the name of the pilot is going to be withheld until notification of the family. *Great. No phone calls from home so far. That's a good sign.*

Xiene came in rubbing her eyes. She looked at the TV. Allen changed the channel to the Beverly Hillbillies. She sat down on the bed and put her head on his lap. They watched the rerun in the dark room with just the eerie glow blue light of the TV. A news message scrolled on the bottom of the screen while Jethro complained about Ellie-May.

"Stupid Jethro," Allen said, grabbing the remote control. He changed the channel just when the words 'Air Force pilot shot down' scrolled into view.

"Wait! What was that?" Xiene protested.

"I don't know and I don't care."

"Well, I do!" Xiene grabbed the remote just when further details scrolled off the screen. "Shit! We missed it."

"It was probably nothing."

"Yeah, right. It may have been about a peace conference."

"I doubt that. Sadam keeps talking about the 'mother of all battles'."

"Maybe if they keep bombing him there won't be a ground battle.

"Are you new to war? Let's change the channel."

Bea Arthur walked onto the set and said a smart-aleck comment to the actress in the wig who plays her mother even though she's younger than the entire Golden Girls cast. "I still say she's a man."

"She is not," said Xiene. "No Adam's apple."

"So? If you have enough neck fat, you don't show one."

A message scrolled onto the screen, the same one. *Shit, is it following me?* He grabbed the remote and flipped the channel.

"No!" Xiene grabbed it back and returned to the channel. Allen reached for it but she slapped his hands. "What? Air Force?" Xiene read.

Allen grabbed her T-shirt and raised it over her head. "Let's make out!"

Xiene struggled with the T-shirt. "You asshole! Stop!" She put her hand on his chest and pushed him back. Allen reached up and undid her bra. "Stop! Goddamn it!" She threw her shirt at his face and held him down. "My god!"

The letters continued scrolling while a laugh track howled at a cheap sexual innuendo.

"Christ, Richard!"

"Is that his fighter's group?"

"I don't know." Xiene ran to the phone and frantically dialed while trying to put the other half of her bra back on. She looked confused and then dialed again. "Shit!"

"What?"

"My phone's been cut off!"

"Didn't you pay the bill?"

"Yes. The check must have bounced!"

"Don't you have any money in the bank?"

"No, I live check to check! You know that!"

"Oh, Xiene, Xiene, Xiene."

"Allen, don't you fucking lecture me! I'm not in the fucking mood!"

"Okay. Okay, why don't we go over to Beverly's and Maggie's?"

"Why?"

Allen put his thumb on his ear and his pinky next to his mouth. "Phone."

"Oh, yeah."

It took forever to walk to Beverly and Maggie's. Allen looked around for any sign of danger as they neared Piedmont Park. Xiene seemed to be sleepwalking, oblivious to the world.

"It may not be him." Allen broke the long silence. She didn't respond. A car Allen had seen earlier passed by them. "Fucking Techies," he mumbled, picturing the four boys in it as fraternity jocks from Georgia Tech. The car came around the block again. A blond jock-type leaned out of the window.

"Hey, baby, how much?" he yelled. The others smiled with their $200 dentist bill teeth. Xiene ignored them.

Strange. No 'fuck you's'?

"Hey, hey!" One of the guys held a green bottle of yuppie beer out of the car window. He shook it and it squirted into the air, simulating masturbation. A bit of the spray got on Xiene. She kept walking.

"Hey! How much for the slut?" One of them yelled.

"Fuck you, asshole!" blurted from Allen's mouth before his brain could say 'Ignore them and they'll go away'.

"What? What did you say?"

Allen tried to ignore them, but it was too late. One of them got out of the car and began walking across the street. A police car came between him and the twosome.

"What seems to be the problem here?" The cop asked.

"No problem," the guy said, walking backward."

The policeman looked at Xiene and Allen. "Everything alright?"

"It is now," Allen commented.

"Alright."

The cars drove on in their opposite directions. Xiene and Allen turned onto Myrtle Street and made it to Beverly and Maggie's ho*use.*

Such a big house. The last time he was in here was when he helped Beverly and Maggie move into it. From what he could tell, it had four bedrooms, two baths, a basement, and an attic. Xiene could move in here easily. He wished he could suggest it, but couldn't figure out how to say, 'Xiene, why don't you move in here? There's more room and you won't drive them nuts. What an evil thing to say about someone you love, that they drive you nuts sometimes. Then again, I drive her completely bat-shit at times. Two perfect reasons not to live together. But what if we got married? Then we'll be forced to deal with each other's idiosyncrasies.

Xiene rang the doorbell. Some folk music was being played inside.

"Just a minute," Beverly's voice said.

Allen looked at Xiene, still in her drab state. Beverly opened the door holding an Eskimo pie in her right hand. Her grey sweat suit hinted at not expecting visitors.

"Hi, guys."

"Hi, we need to use your phone," Allen spoke for Xiene.

"You came all the way here to use my phone?"

"Oh, and to see you, of course." Allen went up and hugged Beverly while Xiene made a beeline for the phone.

"What's wrong with her?"

"God, you wouldn't believe her luck today."

"Really? Let's hear it.

Allen sat down and looked around the makeshift decorated living room, complete with cinder block shelves, a 9,000-year-old stereo with an 8-track, a sofa fished out of the garbage, and a

50x50" poster of Molly Yard over an inactive fireplace. *If Xiene did move in, at least we'd get for-real furniture.*

While Xiene sat on the metal foldaway chair in the next room in a crouched-over position, talking on the phone, Allen finished Xiene's tales of terror: "...and then a cop showed up and chased them off. And that happened an hour ago."

"Jesus!" Beverly said. She rubbed the head of an orange cat. "I see what you mean about a curse."

"I've never seen anything like it. Except...I have bad luck, but it's usually spread out over torturous months."

Beverly put the cat down and walked over to the cinderblock shelves. Xiene rocked back and forth while talking to her mother. A black and white cat came up to her leg and began rubbing against her. She stopped rocking and reached down and picked the cat up.

Beverly came back with a tin box. She opened it up to reveal five joints. She took one out and lit it.

God, I hate that smell!

She tried to hand it to Allen. "No, thanks."

"Let's see: Xiene has no job, no car, no phone, no apartment, a speeding ticket, and a brother in Saudi Arabia." She took a drag on the joint.

The record stopped playing the folk music. Beverly got up to change the record. Allen got up to see if Xiene wanted anything and to get away from the smell of dope. With the cat in her lap, she was a lot calmer. She smiled. "I love you, too. Let me speak to Dad."

Allen walked over and kissed her forehead. She grabbed his hand.

She kissed Allen's hand and then let go when her dad answered the phone.

In the next room, a Jethro Tull song started up. Allen went to the refrigerator and looked at the photographs plastered on its door. Lots of women he had never seen. Beverly and Maggie at an N.O.W. protest. Beverly's newspaper clipping of her getting dragged away by the cops at a pro-abortion rally. Xiene and Allen at Christmas time, her in a black leather outfit and Santa Claus hat, him wearing Christmas lights strung around his body like a human Christmas tree.

"I can? Great! Thanks, Daddy," said Xiene.

Allen looked into the living room. Beverly sat either in deep thought or a hallucination state. Allen opened the back door and stepped out onto the screened-in back porch. The crickets chirped all around. The streetlight nearby shined dimly on the loads of objects stored in the area. He made his way to what he could best figure out in the dark to be a wicker chair. Xiene was heard faintly on the phone inside, from where the yellow kitchen light shone through. She laughed.

I guess her brother's okay.

Beverly came onto the porch. "Hey, Doodle Bug, what are you doing out here?"

"I don't know."

Beverly sat down on what appeared to be a washing machine. "What's wrong?"

"I'm okay, just…, I just feel so…useless."

"Why?" Beverly began bumping her heels on the washing machine.

"Xiene is having all of this bad luck and there's nothing I can do. I mean, I can let her stay with me and Brandon, but you know that will only be a temporary solution. And the car—I can't get a car for myself. Her brother, Richard. I didn't vote for George Bush. The phone bill. Why have a phone without an apartment?"

"What's your point?"

"What?"

"Sounds like you have everything figured out."

"Yeah. If you think about it, there's really nothing you can do, except let her stay with you, which can be a first step for her to get back on her feet, even though the thought of Brandon living with Xiene doesn't make a pretty sight."

"Brandon likes her."

"So? I love you, but that doesn't mean we could live together."

Allen pictured himself surrounded by cats and pot smokers. "Yeah, I guess. But that means I can't even give her a place to stay."

"She can stay here!"

Yes!

"We have a spare bedroom."

"What about Maggie?"

"We'll see when she gets home."

"Where is she?"

"She's at Grady doing volunteer work."

Xiene peeked her head in. "Hello?"

Beverly hopped off the washer and headed out. Allen followed as she walked Xiene from the kitchen to the living room. Xiene revealed the contents of her phone call.

"Richard is still in Saudi Arabia. My mom got a letter from him Tuesday saying he's being used only as a backup."

"That's good," said Beverly.

My dad is going to let me borrow his old car and my mom is going to lend me money for the ticket."

"Now, if I can move in with Allen and find a job, I'll be set."

Allen walked behind the two feeling like a fifth wheel

"Hon," said Beverly, I think instead of moving in with Allen you should stay here with me and Maggie."

"Why?"

"Because there's more room, and it's closer to Little Five Points."

Xiene thought. Allen was glad she mentioned Little Five Points, Xiene's mecca for hip clothes stores, shops, and her favorite record store.

"Okay, but what about Maggie?"

At that moment Maggie came in. "Speak of the devil." Beverly walked over and kissed Maggie. She seemed depressed. "What's wrong?"

"God, what a day!" Maggie groaned.

"What happened?"

"That guy I told you about."

"The musician?"

"Yeah, he died today."

"Oh, no." Beverly hugged Maggie.

"What did he die of?" Allen asked.

"AIDS."

A dead silence filled the room.

"How awful," said Xiene. "Were you friends?"

"Yeah, sort of. I got to know him towards the end. He even gave me his record." Maggie walked over to the record rack and searched through it. She pulled out a small, white-sleeved generic-looking single.

"Who put that out?" Allen asked.

"He did. It's his first, and, I guess, last…" Maggie gestured with a backhand swing motion, "Album."

"So he was undiscovered?"

"Yup. Sad, huh?" She put the record on.

Allen sat in a yard sale Laz-e-boy chair. Xiene sat on the arm. Beverly and Maggie sat on the couch. The record started. It was folk music. The man's voice reminded Allen of James Taylor. Not Allen's favorite kind of music, but on a technical level the guy was just as good. Maggie teared up and Beverly comforted her. Xiene was mesmerized. Allen stared at the unlit fireplace. He wondered what it looked like when it was going. How peaceful it would be with the music playing.

Beverly comforted Maggie. Allen looked at Xiene, who wiped her cheek. *Gosh, this is a bummer. I wish I were home. I wish Xiene and Maggie were happy.* He put his hand on Xiene's back. She reached her left hand back and held onto his fingers.

The song finished. The record static continued for a while until the auto-stop activated. The room remained silent for a few minutes. Allen looked at this watch. 1*:45. Shit! No subway home.*

"Can you still catch MARTA?" Beverly asked.

"No."

"Why are you catching MARTA? Didn't Xiene drive you over?" Asked Maggie.

"No."

Allen was about to explain. "My car got trashed," Xiene interrupted.

"The bottom worst is, that Xiene is also getting evicted."

"What?"

"Yeah, her apartment is going condo."

"That's awful."

Xiene slumped in silence.

"Why don't you come stay with us?" Maggie suggested.

Xiene looked up.

"I already asked her," Beverly said.

"Okay, okay. Xiene?"

"Sure. But I don't have a job, so I can't pay you rent for a while."

"So what? I'll help you find one. Matter of fact, Angie, my friend who works at the crystal shop, needs someone. I'll talk to her tomorrow."

"Wait, from the Arts festival? Allen asked.

"No! Thanks!" Xiene and Allen said together.

"I mean, thanks," Xiene said cheerfully. She still seemed depressed.

"Alright, Xiene. There's hope yet." Beverly smiled.

The three women began discussing moving-in plans while Allen flipped through a Greenpeace magazine. After a while, he heard Xiene say, "Allen is pregnant!"

"What?" he asked.

Xiene was just trying to get his attention after numerous unsuccessful attempts. "What?"

"I said, do you want a ride home?"

"Yeah, but in what?"

"Maggie's Volo."

"Oh, yeah. Sure. At least I'll get," he looked at his watch—2:30, "three hours of sleep.

"Oh, poor baby," she said, rubbing his head. "I've been keeping him up lately.

Beverly and Maggie laughed.

"Not in that way," Allen said in a sarcastic tone.

Xiene and Allen said goodbye to Beverly and Maggie.

"Don't you wreck their car!" Allen joked, half serious.

"Yeah, yeah, yeah," said Xiene. "Like I'm going to do doughnuts in this old heap."

"Hey, it may be a heap, but it's my heap," Maggie responded.

Allen and Xiene got into the Volvo station wagon. "

The two women waved while holding hands at the front porch.

The Volvo pulled off. Xiene rounded a corner while fiddling with the radio station.

"Er, Xiene, I don't remember them saying, 'While turning a corner, please turn the dials of your radio station' in driver's ed."

Xiene took her hand off the radio. "I remember them saying, 'While turning a corner, tickle your boyfriend'." She began poking Allen under the armpit. He shrieked and laughed. She giggled.

"Well, you're suddenly in a good mood."

"Yeah."

A song by Depeche Mode played on the college radio station Xiene selected.

"I'm sorry I wasn't able to help."

"What?" she said before turning the radio down. "You helped me."

"How?"

"Support. You kept me from going apeshit."

"Big deal. That didn't solve your problems."

"So? It's not your job to solve my problems. I'm responsible for them. Except for the pregnancy one."

"If I wore rubbers or got a vasectomy, we wouldn't have to worry."

"It's not entirely your fault. I'm the one who suggested no rubbers and you can't get a vasectomy. We may want to have kids one day."

Allen felt shocked. *This is the first time Xiene mentioned having kids with me.* "Light's green." Allen pointed to the traffic light. They moved on.

"You also didn't panic."

"What?"

"When I told you I was pregnant, you didn't head for the hills like some guys do."

"Of course not. You know I'll stay with you no matter what."

She grabbed his hand. They rode in silence.

"Xiene?"

"Yeah?"

"Don't you feel bad about asking your mom and dad for help? After all, you always hated receiving help from them."

She thought for a few seconds. Allen dreaded bringing up the subject.

"No. And you know why?"

"Why?"

"My mom and dad have really changed ever since Richard went to Saudi Arabia. They seem to appreciate me more, it's like they're afraid of losing us. They're the ones who suggested helping me, and it seemed like something they really wanted to do like therapy. You know what I mean?"

"Yeah, they need to be needed right now."

"Exactly. They sounded so down when I called, and when they found out I needed help, they, like, cheered up immediately."

"So did you."

Yeah, I guess. But you know what helped?"

"What?"

"That guy's record. I mean, I don't like that kind of music, but the fact that he had all of this talent and probably had his career opening up in front of him, then boom! AIDS! You're dead!" Silence followed. "Here I am complaining because I lost a stupid job. I ran a red light, my car got hit and if the cop had asked for my papers would have hauled me off to jail. I bounced a check off the phone company and was late with my birth control."

"What about those Techies and your eviction?"

"Fuck those Techies and fuck the apartment! I found another place to live in one day! It's so weird. I solved most of my problems in one day and that guy had no options. Me, I have you," she squeezed his hand, "and Beverly and Maggie to help me. His friends actually couldn't do anything for him, and now he's dead. Gads, life is weird."

"Later, they pulled up to the apartment. A note had been placed on the windshield of the van.

"What's that, another ticket?"

Allen got out and checked. "No, a warning that if you don't move the van, it will be towed.

"Good. Now I don't have to pay for it to get towed."

"You better get your valuables out then."

"What valuables? My radio's been stolen, there's nothing I want in there."

Allen walked to the passenger side of the Volvo. They kissed for a few minutes. Xiene rolled up the window, cranked up the stereo, and screeched the tires pulling away she blew the horn, waking up anyone within earshot.

The next week things were a little better for Xiene she didn't get nor want the job at the crystal shop, but did have a very good chance of getting a job as a bouncer at the Acid Pit.

"You, a bouncer?" Allen questioned her before she twisted his arm around and slammed him against the wall.

On Friday Allen, Monroe, Brandon, and Oswald helped Xiene move into Beverly and Maggie's. It took four trips, a lot of muscle, and 500 swear words, but they finally succeeded. Xiene flew home on Saturday to spend a week with her parents and drive her dad's car down. There was a rumor the plane before hers got into a crash, killing all on board. 'Ha they missed me,' she told Allen on the phone. The day before she was to come back, Allen phoned her.

"God, I'll be so glad when I get back!"

"What's wrong?"

"My parents are driving me insane! 'Change your hair color', "Wear more dresses', 'Date a Republican!' God! I can't take it! And to top it all off, I started my period yesterday!"

"That's great."

"Not when you're surrounded by control freaks!"

"Sounds like you feel better."

"Yeah, I guess. I just want to get out of here!" Mrs. Richard mumbled something in the background. "Mother! I'm on the phone!" Xiene yelled. "God, you see what I mean? I almost don't want their help!" Xiene continued complaining for another hour. Allen listened and tried to comfort her as best he could. After all, that's the best he could do for now.

DISCIPLINE!

Six guys tried to dance with Xiene in only three minutes. She ignored them by turning her back and continued dancing. Some were so relentless that she would have to cross the dance floor to escape. One jock yuppie kept following her.

"Yeah! Alright!" he would say holding onto his green bottled yuppie beer.

Meanwhile, Allen and Monroe were on the stage, dancing in front of the 15-foot screen showing Russ Myers' 'Mondo Topless'. Allen didn't see Xiene's trouble because he was too busy watching the 15-foot woman with the 40-inch breasts. He figured a 15-foot woman with 40-inch breasts would have 120-inch breasts.

The twenty or more speakers blared out more house music beat, making the three drag queens in suspended golden cages blow their whistles and throw confetti onto everyone's heads. Five shirtless men danced on top of the wrecked cars with the headlights flashing on and off. Allen realized that one was a woman with small breasts.

He tried to figure out where Xiene was. He heard, "Yeah! Alright!", the yuppie jock mating call. Xiene was thrashing, hoping her violent movement would keep him at a distance. He instead tried to imitate her and did a sorry version of thrashing.

Monroe jumped off the stage and went over to Xiene. She spotted him and grabbed onto his arm. They began to spin around, faster and faster, creating a force field of potential collision for anyone who got near them. The yuppie got the hint and took off. Xiene and Monroe stopped. She hugged him thanks, then pointed to the screen behind Allen. He turned around and spotted the closeup of the 120-inch breast. He reached up his hands, like a man trying to paw the 50-foot woman. Xiene laughed. She then pulled her sweaty tank top forward, looked down her shirt, and looked at Allen with a sad, pouty expression.

Allen laughed, then jumped off the stage. "Feeling inadequate?" he yelled to her over the music.

She laughed, grabbed him around the neck, and pushed his head between her breasts. Allen imitated suffocation. She laughed, pulled his head back, and kissed him.

The threesome danced for another hour Allen and Monroe would take 10-minute drink breaks at the bar, while Xiene would drink a cup of water bought to her by Allen while she continued to dance. Allen and Monroe felt like old men compared to Xiene as she continued her weekly dance-a-thon. Allen hated sitting down and resting because at these moments guys would try to move in on Xiene like wolves on a sheep. *It's not that I'm completely jealous, I just hate seeing her get that 'leave me alone' face over and over.*

A few girls, obviously under twenty-one, went up to Xiene. She recognized them and started dancing slowly so she could speak to them. The three of them headed off in a hurry.

"Where are they going?" Allen yelled at Monroe.

"I don't know, LFO," said Monroe.

"What?"

"Let's find out," he yelled.

They followed Xiene to the bar near the exit. Lying on the floor was a guy with spiked hair, also under twenty-one, wearing leather and chains. Xiene leaned over him.

"Rollo! Hey, Rollo, get up, man!"

He moved his head back and forth.

"Come on, now! You're blocking the aisle!"

"Fuck you! Leave me alone!" he yelled.

"You need help?" Allen asked Xiene.

"No! I got it!"

"Hey! Rollo! You can do this in two ways. You can get up and let Vera and Sandy take you home, or if don't, I'm gonna get Chauncey to stick your head in a toilet."

Allen wondered who Chauncey was until a Black guy yelled, "Oh, yeah, honey! Let me at 'em! It's baptism time!"

The guy got up off the ground mumbling, "Don't you fuck'n touch me!"

Xiene led him to the exit. Allen slowly followed in case violence broke out, he could break the Rollo's fist with Allen's nose.

Xiene took him into a hallway and quietly talked to him. Not what Allen expected.

The guy began crying. "I know she ain't ever coming back!"

"You have to get over it, Rollo!"

Xiene spotted Allen and waved him away. Allen returned to the main area. A bouncer that reminded Allen of Santa Claus approached him.

"Where did that guy go?"

"Xiene got him up. She's talking to him."

"Shit, that's not what I would have done," he complained. "Baptism time!"

"Yeah, thank god he saw her first."

The guy chuckled. "You're Allen, aren't you?"

"Yeah," Allen said, wondering how many other employees of the Acid Pit knew who he was.

"I'm Bear." He held out his multi-tattooed arm for a handshake. "Xiene's doing a good job here. First time I've ever seen a female bouncer, at least one as small as her."

"Yeah, but she can take care of herself."

"Yeah, I'll say. Did she ever tell you what happened last Thursday?"

"Briefly," Allen responded, remembering Xiene had just told him she had a bad day at work and never went into detail.

"Yeah, it was Mohawk Night, and these two guys were slamming in the dance area. You know, you're supposed to slam only inside that area." He pointed to a separate area near the stage, fenced off by a 10-foot fence and barbed wire on top. "Xiene tried to get them to cut the shit out and one of the bastards pushed her down. So she hops up and slapped the shit out of the guy and the other one is just standing there like, 'Duh, what should I do?', so Xiene grabs the two motherfuckers by their hair and just dragged them out the door. It was funnier than shit!" the man chuckled.

Allen laughed nervously, thinking of Xiene in a fight with two guys. Someone poked Allen under the armpits. He shrieked. The guy laughed Xiene walked around him.

"I was just telling Allen what happened last week."

"Oh, yeah, those two assholes."

"Yeah, you better watch out for her, Allen, she's a scrappy one."

"Tell me about it."

Xiene looked at her Jesus watch. "Oh-oh, I have to go watch the parking lot."

The guy looked at her watch. "What does it say?"

"Jesus time!" Xiene answered.

"Sort of like Hammer time," Allen commented.

"No. I got it at a yard sale. It's so hilarious when it's 9:15!" Xiene stretched her arms out, signifying crucifixion. The bouncer laughed.

Allen looked for Monroe. He was on the dance floor with the topless woman with small breasts. Now and then she would try and rub her body against his, but Monroe would pull back.

"Gotta go. See you later, sweetie." Xiene kissed Allen on the cheek.

"Want me to come with you and keep you company?"

"No, I got it."

Xiene slipped away. Allen went and sat inside one of the wrecked cars, decorated with fuzzy dice, Christmas tree lights, leopard-skin upholstery, and St. Christophers on the dashboard. He looked at the movie screen on the stage, and after all of the times he has been to the Acid Pit, realized what the cars represented. If you sit in them, you feel like you're at a drive-in movie.

1:30 am

The Acid Pit became packed with late-shift people getting off work. Allen sat in the car and watched as the strobe-lit shapes moved around the car. Monroe came up to the car covered in sweat.

"You ready to go?" he asked Allen.

"No."

"Then why aren't you dancing?"

"I'm resting," Allen lied.

"Okay," Monroe yelled over a loud remix.

"What happened to that topless woman?"

"That wasn't a woman."

"Oh. I was wondering why you didn't go for it."

"Yeah, they had a bigger bulge than mine." Monroe put his hand on his crotch.

Allen laughed. He spotted someone on a trapeze near the slam dance pit. He pointed. "Look, an acrobat."

Monroe and Allen watched the acrobat do twirls, hang by her legs then hang by her teeth.

"Must be Circus Night."

Allen thought about the drag queens in cages wearing animal prints. "Could be."

"I'm going back to dance."

"Okay, see ya."

Monroe maneuvered through the bustling crowd, while Allen waited patiently in the car for Xiene to arrive. He cherished their moments together more than ever, especially as her demanding schedule began to take a toll on their time together. Xiene worked from 9 PM to 4 AM, six nights a week, and her schedule was packed: Sleep from 5 AM to 2 PM, followed by a quick brunch and a flurry of chores and errands. If everything went smoothly, she might squeeze in a dinner or sex with Allen—though there was never enough time for both. By 8 PM, she had to start preparing for work again.

To Allen, sex on this schedule turned it into a job instead of pleasure. Gone were what Xiene used to call 'the weekend fuck-a-thons: spending an entire weekend in bed trying to break their old records. Now they were reduced to dreary rainy Mondays or quickies, making Allen feel like an actor in an Italian sex movie, where the woman would completely remove her clothes and the man would just undo his fly. This never happened, but the cheapness was still there. Then the unthinkable happened: Xiene and Allen went two weeks without sex.

Allen decided the only way he could spend more time with her was to come see her at work. Thus far, this was unsuccessful. She was moved from station to station every two hours, and they couldn't exactly make out while she was working. The 30 minutes he and Monroe spent dancing with her was the most they'd ever seen her all evening.

Allen went outside to talk to her. She was talking to another employee. They both had flashlights and cut them on whenever a car came into the main gate. He would check the front seat and she would shine it in the back seat. Allen couldn't figure out whatever happened to make them check cars out in this way. Someone in the back seat of the car said something, which caused Xiene to howl with laughter. When the car pulled off, Xiene told the other employee something.

"You're fucking crazy!" he yelled before they both burst into uncontrollable laughter.

Gads, she's having such a good time working here. Everyone likes her and she's finally making lots of money.

Xiene spotted Allen and waved. "Hey, sugar bumps!" she yelled.

"Sugar bumps?" the guy questioned.

Xiene whacked him on the shoulder.

"Ow!" he said, rubbing his shoulder.

"I love you!" she yelled.

"I love you, too!" Allen yelled back.

Xiene resumed talking to the guy. Allen turned around and went back into the club. At 4 am, the club closed its doors to the public. Monroe was engaged in a lengthy conversation about Medieval poetry with Melonie, a female bartender. Allen finished his beer, sat on the edge of the stage, and watched the television sets in the warehouse window. Window by window, they stopped showing images and just broadcast static snow.

The closing doors and sounds of cleaning up echoed all around. Xiene came up to Allen, her many bracelets jingling, her boots clacking on the concrete floor. She stopped, lit up a cigarette, then continued towards him. She puckered her lips in his direction and he leaned forward to kiss her. She blew smoke into his face and laughed at her little prank.

"Ha-ha, cough-cough, ha-ha," Allen laughed sarcastically.

"Ahh," she apologized, then kissed him.

"We have to talk," he said quietly.

"Yeah, I know." She bit her bottom lip.

"Xiene!" someone yelled.

"Yeah?" She walked towards a pony-tailed balding guy in a suit. Next to him, was an overweight Asian guy in black. Allen recognized him as Buddha, Xiene's supervisor.

Monroe walked over to Allen. "Boy, she's nice, real fun to talk to."

"Who?"

"Melonie."

"Oh, yeah, she is nice."

Allen looked down at his hiking boots. His left shoe was untied. He left it that way. Xiene finished her conversation and happily skipped back over.

"Hey, guess what?"

"Chicken butt!" Monroe responded.

"No!" Xiene elbowed him. "I'm a supervisor!"

"In only two months?" Allen questioned.

"Yeah."

"That's great!" Monroe hugged her.

Allen reached out his arms. "Come here."

Xiene danced like Steve Martin towards him.

"Xiene!" Buddha called.

She turned and ran towards him. Allen felt he had been blown off. The guy handed her something.

Monroe shuffled around and began kicking a bottle cap on the ground. He kicked it towards Allen. He kicked it back. Monroe returned the volley. They began playing a bottle cap soccer game, kicking it towards a specific goal.

Xiene finished talking to Buddha and ran over to the athletes. She kicked the cap from Allen and started kicking it towards the bar. Monroe tried to intercept, but she pushed him out of the way. Allen caught up with her and managed to stop the cap. She kicked him in the shin.

"Ow!"

"Oh shit! I'm sorry!" A look of fright filled her face.

"Jesus Christ!" Allen stumbled over to a chair.

"I'm sorry!"

"Damnit, Xiene!"

"I said I was sorry!"

"Fine! Just keep those combat boots away from me!"

"Okay, fine." She turned to Monroe. "Look what I got!" she pulled out a key with a skull-face keyring.

"What's that?"

"The Acid Pit Key."

"What, is that, like the key to the executive washroom?" Allen asked while rubbing his ankle.

"No, I get to open up!"

"That's good. That means they trust you," Monroe said.

"What time do you have to be here?"

"8:00."

"Christ! That means…" Allen added up in his head, "we'll only have like one or two hours together during the week."

"I know," Xiene said, her eyebrows showing concern but not regret."

"Oh, well," Allen stood up. "I guess celibacy ain't so bad."

Monroe looked confused. "You still have your weekends off?" he said.

"So? That still only gives us a few hours till she has to go to work.

"A few hours? Allen I have until 8:00. That's pretty much a full day together on weekends when you're off."

"Yeah, but you know I like to spend the night with you on weekends. We can't do that anymore."

"Oh, stop whining. It could be worse."

"How?"

"I could work from five to twelve. Then we wouldn't have a few hours at all."

Is this next? I can see it now: the Acid Pit starts serving dinner, and Xiene gets on a 24-hour schedule. 'Sorry, Allen, I can't see you. The Acid Pit is now the Acid Barbecue Pit!', she would say.

"Fine, let's just get out of here."

The threesome piled into Xiene's father's green Lincoln town car. Before getting in, Xiene would recite her ritual, "God, I hate this car!" This time, Monroe and Allen were ready for her and all three recited it at once.

"With the money you're making, it should be a matter of time before you get your new car.

"Ha!" she responded to Allen's statement. "Not until I get that drum set."

Allen rolled his eyes at Xiene's financial priorities. "How do Maggie and Beverly feel about you getting drums?"

"Fine, as long as I keep them in the basement." Xiene whipped the car around a corner, causing Allen and Monroe to lean against the door from inertia. She then pulled around a Volkswagen while cutting on the radio and scratching her armpits.

"You need to shave your pits," Allen commented.

"I like hairy armpits on women," Monroe commented.

Xiene turned around. "Thank you, Monroe. See? Monroe likes my hairy pits."

"I didn't say you have hairy pits, they're just a little stubbly." Allen reached over and rubbed her right armpit. She shrieked, then wandered into the opposite lane in the path of an oncoming truck. The three screamed as the Peterbilt truck came close to releasing their souls from their bodies. At the last minute, Allen grabbed the wheel and yanked the car in the opposite direction, sending it into a construction site. Screams all around. Allen's life passed before his eyes on fast forward. Xiene jerked the wheel and avoided a tractor. Unfortunately, this sent the car over a huge pile of dirt. Someone yelled "Shit!". The car quickly came down in a small, freshly dug pit. The engine idled in a high rev. No one moved.

Realizing they were alive, Allen looked around. Monroe was no longer in the back seat. Allen checked behind the seat. Monroe was on the floor trying to see if the bottle that spilled on him was water or blood. Xiene had turned rigor mortis and had the look of a zombie queen. Allen reached over and turned off the engine. A long pause. Monroe got off the floor, examining his shirt under the glow of a nearby street light. Xiene had relaxed, and instead of the scared-to-death expression, had changed to an 'I'm going to kill you, Allen!' look.

Allen decided to get a head start. He slowly opened the door and crawled out, just when her hands grabbed at him, nails extended, he took off. He heard her running close behind. She paused, picked up a metal pole five feet long, and continued chasing him.

"Hey, put that down!"

"Sure, I'll put it down—in your skull!"

She chased him around a bulldozer. Allen tried to double back and fool her. She instead ran around in the opposite direction and intercepted him. He screamed in surprise.

"You ruined my dad's car!"

"Did not!"

"If you hadn't tickled me I wouldn't have wrecked!"

"Yeah, true, but I didn't know you would freak out so easily!"

"Well, I did! Now my dad's going to kill me!"

"No, he won't! I didn't see any damage!"

"Ha!" she said before swinging in his direction. The iron rod connected with the bulldozer's headlight, smashing it into bits.

"Oh, shit!"

Xiene's expression turned to panic. Allen realized she was just threatening and wouldn't have creamed him. She threw the rod down and slowly walked towards Allen with her hands in a choking position.

When she was a foot away, he tried a last resort. "I love you, Xiene?"

She stopped and lowered her hands. "Cheap shot, Allen."

"Come on, you know it was an accident."

Xiene reached into her pants.

"Shoot, you do jokes like that on me all the time."

"Ha! Where are my damn cigarettes?

"They're probably still in the car."

"Shit." Xiene kicked at some dirt clods.

"Come on, let's go have a look at it."

Allen put his hand on her back. She turned around and growled at him like an angry dog. "Down, Fido." She grabbed his hand and bit. "Ow! Stop! That kind of hurt!"

"Good. It's just half of what you're going to get!"

"Oh, boy, S&M." Xiene snarled. "Oh—" Xiene glared at him and prevented him from saying, 'Oh, cheer up'. "Okay, okay, let's go."

When the two approached the car, Monroe was already trying to back it out of the pit. Except for dirt covering it, it appeared to have no external damage. Monroe revved the engine. The tires spun in place, sending a cloud of light brown into the air.

"Hold on!" Allen ran in front of the car. Xiene joined him. "Okay."

Monroe revved it again. They pushed. The car got farther but then rolled back into its dug-in position. Xiene hit the hood.

"Shit! Son of a bitch!"

"Well, at least it's not wrecked."

"No, but it's stuck!"

"Let's try again."

Allen and Xiene pushed again. Monroe gave it more gas. For a second, it seemed they might succeed, but the car rolled back forward. Allen, afraid Monroe might run over him, backed up over a dirt mound and fell on his back. Monroe cut the car off. Xiene howled with laughter.

"Ha-ha, har-hardy-har-har," Allen said with obvious sarcasm.

"It doesn't look like we can drive it out of here," Monroe said, getting out of the car.

"Why don't we call a tow truck?" Allen stood up and brushed himself off. "Where's the nearest phone?"

Xiene stopped laughing enough to answer. "A 24-hour grocery store is that way." She pointed towards the right.

"You have insurance that tows?" Allen asked.

Xiene gave him a 'yeah, right' look.

"You really have shitty car insurance. Oh, well, we'll just have to look up a tow service in the phone book."

The three climbed the hill and began walking south.

"What time is it?" Allen asked Xiene.

"Five."

"Hmm, the sun should be coming up soon."

"Fucking great! I won't get to bed by at least eight which means as soon as I wake up, I'll have to go to work." Xiene complained.

"Which reminds me of something I have to talk to you about."

"Guys, I think I should bail out," Monroe said.

Is this a ploy by Monroe to get me and Xiene to talk alone? "There's no reason for me to hang around. I mean, how many people do you need to make a phone call?"

"Oh, come on, where's your sense of adventure." Xiene went over and got arm-in-arm with Monroe. "Let's go. We're all in this together." She began pulling him down the street. Monroe looked back at Allen. Allen shrugged his shoulders as if to say: 'Oh, well, you tried'.

The group walked through some neighborhoods with newly renovated houses. Xiene pointed out which ones she would buy if she were rich. Some, Allen couldn't figure out why. Xiene let go of Monroe's arm and started staring at an old burnt-out house. She seemed hypnotized. She walked up to a 'Caution Do Not Cross' ribbon. She took out her pocket knife and cut it away.

Now what? "Xiene!" Allen yelled. A dog next door started barking.

"See what you did? Keep it down," she shushed.

Allen looked at Monroe. "Should we follow?"

"Why not?"

They joined Xiene. "Don't you—"

She shushed Allen.

"What?"

"Shut up!" she seemed to be listening. She slowly crept up the stairs. Allen tried to hear, but the loudspeakers from earlier still caused his ears to ring. The burnt-out, wet wood smell filled their nostrils. Xiene walked along the porch like a predator looking for a snack. Monroe walked over to a porch swing. Allen looked through the smokey front door window decorated with etched flowers. The whole back part of the house was gone. Xiene peeked around the right side of the house. Allen resisted the temptation to get her under the armpits.

Suddenly a loud crash on the porch. Xiene and Allen spazzed out for a split second.

Monroe held a chain in his hand connected to a fallen porch swing. "Whoops."

Allen grabbed his stopped heart. Xiene whispered 'Jesus Christ', then continued sneaking around the side of the house. She paused and put her hands on her hips as if she couldn't hear anything anymore.

Monroe jumped off the side of the house, right behind Allen, giving him another shot of adrenalin. He turned around to choke him.

"Shush!" Xiene said. She picked up a rock the size of a baseball.

"What's that for?"

"Will you be quiet?" she whispered.

They continued walking towards the burnt-out back of the house. Allen ran probable explanations for what was going on. Not one had a logical reason.

Xiene knelt next to a tiny basement window.

"Allen, how do you spell 'orangutan'?" she asked.

"What?"

"Orangutan."

"I don't know. Why do you ask?"

"No reason. I just wanted to confuse you more."

Monroe laughed.

Xiene put the rock down. "Monroe, turn around," she asked.

Monroe turned around.

Xiene took off her tank top, exposing her breasts to the world.

"What are you—" Allen stopped before Xiene glared at him. She wrapped the rock in her tank top. *She's completely lost her mind!*

She hit the window with the rock, cracking it slightly. A second blow completely broke the window out with relatively little noise.

A break-in?

Xiene undid the rock and put her dirty top back on. She reached through the hole and unlatched the window.

"Xiene, we don't have time for this!" Allen whispered loudly.

Just then, something the size of a small dog ran out of the open window, between Allen's legs and up a large oak tree behind them. Allen's thought process went as follows: *something, something big, something grey, grey rat, big rat, big rat running between legs—choices: faint, die, scream, proceed to scream.*

And he did.

So did Xiene. Monroe tripped over a water hose trying to run away. Xiene watched the object go up a tree.

"It's a cat. It's a cat!"

They turned around and looked up at the tree. A small grey cat peered down at them with glowing green eyes set off by the early morning light.

"A cat? How in the world did you hear a cat from the street?"

"My bionic ears, do-do-do-do-do." She impersonated the sound effect of super-hearing from The Bionic Woman.

"Well, why don't you do a bionic jump, Jamie Sommers, and get the cat down?"

"Okay." She went over to the tree and began climbing. Her boot slipped on the bark for a second, but she caught herself.

"Wait, stop! Don't climb that tree! That cat's going to come down eventually!"

"No, he won't. The poor dear will starve to death!"

"Have you ever seen a cat skeleton in a tree?" Allen asked.

At that moment the cat meowed.

Xiene laughed. "We can't just let him stay in this old house. We have to find him a home."

"Like it's our job," Monroe said.

Xiene grimaced.

"Let's go to the grocery store," Allen insisted.

Xiene turned around and continued climbing.

"Wait! Stop!" Allen went over and pulled her down by the waist. She landed on his foot. "Yeow! For crying out loud! Why don't you just take an ax and cut this foot off?"

"Sorry."

Before grabbing onto the bark, Allen made monster-like gestures at Xiene. "Okay, I got better shoes on, so let me try to scare him down."

"Be careful," Xiene said then whacked him on the butt as he began his climb.

Higher and higher he went, getting closer to the spooked cat. Xiene put her knuckles on her mouth and seemed authentically worried. The dog next door, now identified by Allen as a brown pit bull with a spiked collar, went barking crazy as Allen the Snack hovered overhead.

"Ah, shut up!" he said.

"I didn't say anything," Xiene said.

"Not you, Cujo over here." Allen pointed.

Xiene peeked over the wooden picket fence. "Holy shit!" Xiene began to whistle. "Here, boy, here boy!"

The dog ran up to the fence and tried to bite Xiene's face off. She jumped back in the nick of time. "Hey, shhh!" she said before laughing.

Allen shimmied on the branch towards the grey cat. *What am I doing here?* Looped in his brain. He heard a rattling noise below. Xiene was running along the fence rubbing it with a stick. The dog followed the sound back and forth and Xiene and he seemed to be dancing. Xiene was laughing her head off.

"Will you please stop that?" Allen pleaded, thinking of the meaner the dog gets, the worse he'll get ripped to shreds if he falls. The grey cat backed up with every inch Allen came towards him.

Xiene began singing in rhythm to her dancing pit bull. "I'm just wild about Harry," she'd run the other direction," and he's just wild about me." Reverse.

Allen almost reached the cat. Suddenly it ran over his head, down his back, down the tree, and under a nearby parked car. Allen paused. Xiene and Monroe ran over to the parked car and tried to coax the cat out, forgetting about Allen up the tree. The dog returned his attention to Allen. Allen turned his attention to the breaking branch.

"Guys."

The branch broke more.

"Hey, er, guys?"

Monroe was crawling under the car. Xiene was smelling her armpit.

"Hey, er, guys?" the branch slowly bent to the ground, closer to bite height. The dog went crazy, like feeding time at the Wolverine cage. Allen kicked at him. The dog nipped his shoe.

"Allen?" Xiene called.

The branch gave way and Allen crashed to the ground. The dog ran out of the falling branches way. Allen got up quickly, unaware of any injuries due to the adrenalin telling him to get up fast and move out. The dog charged at him.

"Heel! Sit! Stay! Stop!" yelled Xiene.

The dog stopped its angry attack and became motionless. Xiene leaned over the fence and held out her hand. "Come on, before he attacks!"

On the word 'attack', the dog lunged again.

"Heel! Sit! Stay! Stop!" Allen yelled. The dog stopped again. "Don't say that word again."

"What word? 'A-tom?" she joked. Allen's heart stopped. "'Atlanta?'"

"Will you stop?"

Xiene and Monroe laughed in the face of someone else's danger. Allen slowly crept over to Xiene. The dog stayed put. He reached the fence and grabbed Xiene's hands. At that split second the dog started growling. Allen let go. The dog stopped growling. He grabbed the hands again, and the dog growled. He let go. The dog stopped. This went on for a minute.

"One more time," Xiene said.

Allen held out his hands. Xiene touched his hands and let go in a rap scratch record rhythm, causing the dog to growl musically. Xiene and Monroe cracked up laughing.

"I wonder if he takes requests," Xiene said between chuckles.

Allen fumed in anger. If looks could kill, Xiene and Monroe would be on fire right now.

"Ha! Okay, okay. Ha-ha," Xiene said, catching her breath. "Monroe and I are gonna yank you over the fence."

"Yeah, right, impaling my guts on the top, right?"

They laughed again.

"No, no, ha-ha." She held her stomach trying not to laugh. "Monroe, give me that rug."

Monroe bent down and picked up an old, wet pink bathroom rug covered in leaves. Xiene took it and draped it on the fence.

"Ha-ha! There. We'll pull you over this."

"That nasty old thing?"

"Like you have a choice," Monroe suggested.

"Okay, let's go. Allen, hold out your hands." Xiene positioned herself. "Okay, Monroe, get ready to pull."

"Wait a minute." Monroe bent down and picked up a stick.

"What's that for? You gonna cream him?" Allen asked.

"No, for distraction. I'm gonna throw it over his head. Once he looks at it, we'll pull you over."

"Sounds logical. I wonder what's going to go wrong?"

"Oh, Allen, don't be so negative!" Xiene said.

Allen mumbled, "I'll show you negative!"

"Okay, get ready," Monroe said, ready to toss the stick. "Now, when he watches the stick fly over, we grab Allen, okay?"

"Check."

"Whatever," Allen responded.

"Ready?"

"Yes," they said simultaneously tired of waiting.

"Here goes." Monroe threw the stick.

Even if he tried ten times, there's no way he could have clobbered the dog on the skull like he did on one throw. The dog yapped and fell back. The three looked in shock and a little bit of admiration at Monroe's marksmanship. Allen's only wish was for Monroe to have thrown hard enough to knock the dog out. Instead, it shook off the blow and charged.

This time heel/sit/stay didn't work.

Allen hopped onto the rug. Monroe and Xiene grabbed his arms and pulled. He almost made it over the fence but the dog grabbed his jeans and pulled back. Monroe and Xiene heaved back, causing the dog to lift in the air as he hung on to Allen's pants leg. The dog's wiggling and tugging caused Allen to fall in his direction. Monroe and Xiene pulled back, sending the dog in the air. This see-saw tug-of-war went back and forth until the rug began to slip in the dog's direction.

"Er, guys?"

"Oh, shit!" Xiene yelled.

"Oh, shit is right! Help!" Allen pleaded.

Inch by inch, they lost to the dog until an idea struck Xiene. "Wait! I got it!" she let go of Allen, giving the dog even more leverage.

"What the hell are you doing?"

"Hold on!" She grabbed an old license plate and started running along the fence again, singing *I'm Just Wild About Harry.* The dog let go of Allen and began chasing the noise again. Allen flew over the fence and landed on Monroe.

Xiene ran back to them. "You alright?"

"Which one? Monroe is squashed and I have dog drool running up my leg."

They got off the ground and checked for damage. The worst thing they found were holes in the bottom of Allen's jeans.

"Gads, I'll never, ever do anything like that for you again!" he complained.

"Oh, sure you will," responded Xiene before giving a peck on the lips.

The journey continued. The sun appeared. Monroe and Allen, not used to the Xiene work hours, felt catatonic.

Xiene jumped and skipped like a rabbit. "Oh, perk up, guys, it's a beautiful Sunday morning."

"Shut up!" Allen and Monroe said simultaneously.

They made it to Food Land. The three telephones up front were the best things Allen had ever seen. Xiene picked up the 20-ton phone books on the moveable racks. She tried to hold the book up and flip the pages at the same time. "I hate these things. As if some jackass is gonna steal a fucking phone book!" She found the two service pages. She took out her knife and cut out the three pages. "Ha! Bet they didn't expect that!" she said with a vengeance.

Monroe and Allen sat on a bench in front and tried to rest. Monroe fell asleep. Allen tried to stay awake but sleep grabbed him and pulled him down. Allen woke up maybe thirty minutes later. Xiene was gone. "What the? Xiene?" he called out. He nudged Monroe. "Where's Xiene?"

"Wha-what? I don't know."

"God, what if something happened to her?" Allen hopped up. "Come on, let's go!"

"Who are you, Batman?"

"Yes! Now get the hell up, Robin!"

They searched around the parking lot and then returned to the entrance. They went inside and spotted her immediately. She was riding on one of the mini forklifts around the frozen food section. Allen looked around for the obligatory authority figure who usually squashes all fun and illegal activity. None in sight. They ran after her. She rounded a corner and knocked over a stack of toilet paper.

"Damn it to hell!" Allen said under his breath.

"Come on, get on!" she yelled.

Monroe laughed, ran over, and hopped on, which pissed Allen off, who warned him not to encourage her little pranks.

“Choo-choo!” she went like a train. Monroe turned around to Allen and waved him to come on.

“No, thanks. I know as soon as I jump on, the authority figure is going to come out of nowhere.”

“Wee-ha!” she yelled as the lift rounded the cereal section. A second later a loud crash.

“Oh, shit!” Allen ran around in the other direction. Even in a mathematician’s dream, there’s no way he can calculate Xiene and Monroe running head-on into another forklift with the manager on it.

“What the hell do you think you’re doing? Get off that thing!” yelled the balding manager. Was *he goofing off on that forklift?*

Monroe jumped off. Xiene remained.

“Hey! I said get off! You don’t belong on one of these things!”

“Hey! You didn’t say please!”

“I’ll give you please!” He jumped down. Xiene backed up, knocking over a towering pyramid of stacked 2-liter Coke bottles. The manager tried to grab Monroe, who wiggled his hand away and ran over to the checkout counter.

Where is everyone?

Xiene reversed the forklift into the dog food.

“Stop that!” yelled the manager, avoiding the cans rolling towards him.

“I advise getting off that thing!”Allen yelled at Xiene.

“Why?” she asked, knocking over a rack full of Alpo dog food.

“Because it’s not very fast!”

The moment the manager grabbed her belt, she switched the forklift into reverse, causing the man to lose his grip, fall forward, and roll onto the ground. Xiene jumped off the forklift and ran towards the door. The manager stood, brushed himself off, looked at Xiene and Monroe running out the front door laughing, then turned his attention to Allen.

Shit! Allen was in his direct aisle. He switched aisles. The manager switched also. He switched to another. The manager did the same.

Gee, how come he didn't move this fast when he was after Xiene? Allen ran to another aisle, reversed, and started running up the previous lane. It worked. The manager was in the other aisle. This would give him at least a second to escape. Just when he made it to the end of the aisle he got grabbed.

"Got you!"

"Let me go! I'm not with the other two!"

"Yeah, right! We'll just see about that!"

Allen was just about to punch the man's arm when he heard a pop and a fizz. Something brown sprayed on them.

The manager looked at the brown liquid on his hand. Allen wiped it off his head and tasted it. *Soda?* The popping and fizzing continued.

"Oh no!" The Manager yelled. Looking with a shocked expression at the continuously exploding and spraying soda bottle pyramid, Xiene had run over earlier. "Oh God! No!" The man let go of Alex and ran towards the tower to somehow prevent the oozing brown lake of goo from expanding. Allen ran between the checkout counter. He failed to notice the chain stretched across. He tripped and fell. At that moment Xiene and Monroe came into the automatic door. They grabbed Allen by the shoulders and dragged him out of the store. The three ran around the side of the store. Monroe and Xiene helping Allen along. He felt like Peggy Lipton in the Mod Squad introduction.

"Let me go. I can walk." He shook them off.

They ran around to the back and stopped. Xiene laughed.

Allen fumed. "Of all—"

"Yeah, I know: Of all the stupid idiot things blah, blah, blah. I've heard it before, Allen."

"Good. Then I don't have to repeat myself. What the hell were you trying to do?"

"Ah, just a little fun." She put her hands behind her back, pouted, and twisted back and forth.

"It ain't going to work. Don't you realize they have cameras in grocery stores? Our pictures are going to be on America's Most Wanted.

Monroe stopped laughing.

"Oh, bullshit. I used to work here. I know what I'm doing." She walked over to a box. She opened it and revealed some wires which had been cut. "See? I did this before I went in." She put her hands in the box and started reconnecting the wires. "These are the cameras. Without this, they can't work.

Allen stood in shock.

"There! Now they work again," she said when a little red light came on."

"I'll remember this when I want to rob this store," Monroe joked.

"You can't get in here with this on." She held up a padlock off the ground and put it back on the box. She took out her keyring selected a red key and relocked the box.

"Jesus Freaking Christ, why in the world did you have a key for that? And why did you disconnect those wires?"

"Just to fuck with the manager. That guy's a dick. I'm surprised he didn't remember me. He'd fire any girls that didn't want to sleep with him."

"So? That doesn't give you the right to trash this store!"

"Fuck this store! They're owned by anti-abortion, apartheid, Falwell supporters!"

"So?" This did make Allen feel better about trashing the store, but he didn't want to let on. "It's still an irresponsible thing to do! No one died and made you the people's vigilante!"

"Oh! but I am!" She put her arm up and covered her nose and mouth like Bella Lugosi. "I'm the Crazed Bitch Avenger!"

Allen didn't smile. "Oh, lighten up, Allen! You're just mad because you can't do things like that."

"Oh, yeah, like I'd want to."

"Yeah, right. Remember that bookstore that fired you? Or the art supply store you worked at that didn't hire you at the other store when they closed yours down after you worked the entire place by yourself for a year? Wouldn't you just love to drive a van full of rattlesnakes into those places?"

Rattlesnakes? "Yes, of course. But I have something called a superego that says; No! Allen! A van full of rattlesnakes would be wrong! And I suggest you start listening to yours once in a while. It's obviously on vacation." He turned around and started walking towards some railroad tracks up on a hill.

"Where are you going?"

"Home! I've had it!"

"You're going the wrong way.?

"So what? Maybe this way I can throw the cops off my trail!" Allen climbed the hill and started walking along the tracks.

Xiene and Monroe stayed behind. Monroe said something to Xiene. She reached over and hugged him. He went in the opposite direction. Xiene climbed the hill and started walking after Allen. Allen looked back. She walked behind him. He turned around and continued walking. They walked for five minutes in silence.

"What do you want?" Allen asked.

"Nothing. Just going for a walk."

"You won't meet your tow truck on these tracks."

"I told him where the car was. he said he would pick it up and take it to his garage."

"And where's that?"

"Oh, two miles in the opposite direction."

Allen turned around and headed in the other direction. He passed Xiene. She caught up and started walking beside him. She put her hands behind her back and hopped from railroad tie to railroad tie. Allen ignored her. She started singing 'I'm just wild about Allen!' Allen knew she was trying to get to him. She kept singing louder and louder. She got on his side and started shaking her breasts like a stripper. Allen looked over and smiled.

"Ah-ha! Got you !" She yelled.

"Yeah, very funny. Ha-ha," he said sarcastically, trying not to laugh.

"I know you enjoy my little pranks. Admit it!"

"Okay, sometimes they can be funny, but other times you do some shit that can land us in jail!"

"Oh, big deal, Allen. Haven't been caught yet."

"So, when you do get caught, then what?"

"Then I'll deal with it."

Allen sighed. He realized Xiene was pretty much set in her jokester ways and it was useless trying to change her. "All I wish is that you at least—at the very least—wouldn't involve me in your pranks. I mean, it's as if you were to murder someone, run around the corner, throw me the gun, and yell, 'Run, Allen!'"

Xiene laughed.

"Yeah, ha-ha. You can laugh now, but you know what it's like having some bastard grab you and say, 'I've got you!', and I'm going 'What the hell is going on'?" Xiene laughed. "I'm glad you're enjoying this." Allen started walking again. He raised his hands as if he had given up.

"Oh, Allen." Xiene ran up and jumped on his back.

"Ow!"

"You know you wouldn't have me any other way. No more than I want you to change."

Allen began carrying her along the tracks. "I'm so sure you like me just the way I am."

"I do." She kissed his neck."

"Stop that," Allen said, trying to hold on to his anger. Xiene giggled, then kissed him again. "I said stop! You're not getting out of this situation that easily."

She giggled, then began kissing his neck over and over, giggling periodically.

"Stop!" Allen repeated. He dropped her and started running away. Xiene ran close behind, tickling him whenever she reached him. "Stop!" He turned around.

Xiene slowly approached with her hands up, wiggling her fingers.

"No! Stop! Every time I scold you, you try to turn the conversation into sex! it's not going to work this time!" Xiene put her hands up his shirt. "I'm ignoring you!" She ran her tongue up his chest. "It's not going to work!" She reached her hands down the back of his jeans and put her crotch against his. "You might as give up!" didn't work due to Allen's hypocritical hard-on.

Oh, shit! It's over! He grabbed her butt. She moaned, arched her back, and bent over backward. *Jesus freaking Christ!* He ran his free hand up her tank top and cupped her breast. She quickly straightened up and gazed at him with a serious expression. Allen looked around. The railroad tracks were fairly isolated, but he could still see the main road about three blocks away.

"Er, I don't know. We may be seen?"

Xiene ran her nails up his back and started rubbing her crotch against his right leg.

Okay, I either adjust to the situation, find a better place around here, or cream my pants. He frantically searched around for a more out-of-the-way place. He spotted an old abandoned car on the side. "There!" He pointed.

Xiene put the bottom of his shirt in her teeth. She then walked backward and led him to the car. *I've never seen her like this! I mean, here we go without for two weeks, and now this?* She grabbed the car handle and pulled. It didn't open she tugged it. *Oh, no!*

She backed up. "Cover your eyes," she said with clenched teeth and the shirt in her mouth.

Allen held his hands up. Xiene growled and kicked the window in, reached in, and opened the door.

"Again, a break-in."

Allen helped clear the glass out. The inside of the car was a lot cleaner than Allen imagined, probably due to the locked doors and windows, keeping the dust and rain out.

When he brushed the last piece of glass off, he felt her hands on his shirt collars. She easily ripped it open. Sending some buttons into his face. "Oh shit!" he said.

Xiene's button-fly jeans made Allen feel like he had achieved the same effect. He grabbed her tank top and tried to do the same but to no avail.

"Wait!" she said. She took it off in the regular fashion.

They started having intercourse. Xiene ripped the window crank off. She looked surprisingly at it and then threw it in the back seat. Allen heard the train approaching. He ignored it until he realized it would pass right by them. He stopped momentarily then continued thrusting. He stopped again when he realized the driver might see them. He could see the train. It was coming and yes, the driver would see them when the train passed by.

"Why do keep stopping?" Xiene yelled.

"The train is coming!"

"So am I! Hurry! Keep going, damn it!"

Allen continued. The train arrived. The moment the engine passed by, the driver blew his horn. *Oh, well, we've been spotted. How embarrassing!*

Xiene ran her nails down his back and screamed. This made Allen forget the train. She put him in a scissor hold with her legs and convulsed, the driver stopped blowing his horn. The boxcars passed by. Allen realized he was keeping in rhythm with their clacking noise. A second engine came along, pushing the train. The engineer must have conveyed the Xiene and Allen sight to the brakeman because he was leaning out his window. The train blew its horn again. Xiene screamed and constricted her thighs causing Allen to finish up. When he finished, she screamed again and kicked the front window several times.

Allen collapsed on top of her. They both lay still, just breathing heavily, slowly calming down.

A few minutes later, Xiene spoke. "Get up, honey, my leg's asleep."

Allen got up and looked around in case a vagrant was standing around ready to applaud the show. Xiene stood and lifted her pants. She buttoned them and sat down on the car seat. Allen pulled his pants up, trying to come to grips with what had happened. He was going to talk to Xiene about not having sex for two weeks, how her schedule was ruining their sex life, and now this, perhaps the best sex he has ever had.

"Ohh!" Xiene yelled.

"What?"

"I thought I was going to come again."

"What?"

"Yeah…" She took a deep breath. "That was great." She took a drag on her cigarette. "I've never come that many times in my life."

"What?" Allen dared not ask how many times for the risk of sounding like a braggart. "Strange, I think that's the best I've had, too."

"Yeah, we should come down here more often."

"Hmm, I don't think so. Too hard to get an engineer to blow his horn on cue like that. Xiene laughed. Allen reached over, grabbed her cigarette, and took a drag. Xiene's eyes almost fell out of their sockets. He handed the cigarette back. She stared at him. "I needed that."

"God! You must have had a good time!"

He walked over, bent down, and kissed her. She stood up and they continued kissing.

Allen pulled back. "You know, this is what I meant to talk to you about."

"Yeah, I know. We can't see each other that much with my new job."

Yeah, I was going to tell you to lower your hours or quit or some bullshit like that, but now I realized that our relationship can survive any schedule change. I mean, it doesn't matter when we see each other, as long as we do. So, what were you going to say?"

"Oh, nothing new," Xiene said. "I was thinking of trying to get Sundays off. That way I can see you one full day per week."

"If you want."

"If I want?" she said in a deep voice. "Listen to you: Oh, Xiene, if you want?" She said in a deep voice.

They laughed.

"So, you're going to ask for next Sunday off ?" He asked.

"Next Sunday, shit—I'm going to ask for this Sunday!"

"What if they say no?"

"I'll quit."

"I thought you liked this job."

"I do, but only because they don't supervise me."

"Undisciplined to the end."

Xiene frowned, leaned forward, and bit his nose.

"Ouch!"

"You're damn right! And admit it!" She poked him in the chest. You...like...me...undisciplined!"

"No, I don't!"

"Yes, you do." She poked him under the armpits. He shrieked.

"No, I don't!"

She started chasing him down the tracks. "You like it!"

"No, I don't!" Allen saw another train coming. He jumped off the tracks and turned to Xiene. She stayed still.

"Get off the tracks."

"Tell me you like my undisciplined behavior!"

"What?"

"You heard me."

"Get off the tracks!"

"Tell me!"

"No!" Allen said, figuring she would jump off.

"Okay, then. Splatted Xiene coming up!"

The train got closer.

"Move!"

"Say it!"

"No way you're going to blackmail me!"

"Alright, then." She put her hands behind her back. Allen could see the train. It blew its horn. "I'm not going to ask you again!"

"Okay." She stood.

The train blew its horn again and got closer and closer. *She's trying my patience!* The train laid on its horn.

"Move it! Now!" Xiene smiled Allen looked back and forth between the train and Xiene. It was now in a dangerous proximity. "Okay, I like crazy antics!"

"And?"

"And what?"

"What about love?"

"What?"

The train blew its horn.

"Love!"

"What? Do I love you?"

"Yes."

"Of course I do!"

"Say it!"

"What?" the train blew its horn. "I love you."

"What? Couldn't hear you."

"I said I love you!"

The train came closer.

"What?"

"I love you, damn it! Now move!"

"You sure?"

Allen ran towards her to push her off the track. "Will you damn well move!"

He tried to push her. She stood still.

"Oh, no, my foot's caught."

"What?" Allen looked down. Her foot was not stuck. "No, it's not!"

Xiene jumped off the track, grabbed Allen's hands, and ran down the hill eight seconds before the train passed by. Allen tried to keep from hyperventilating. Xiene was laughing.

"You're fucking crazy!"

"Yeah, I know. And you…" she kissed him, "love…" she kissed him again, "…it!" They kissed until the train went by.

"What do you want to do for the rest of the day?"

"First I want to get my car. Then I'm going to find that abandoned cat."

"What? That little scumbag? He almost got me killed!"

"Hmm, Scumbag. I like that name."

The two got back on the tracks and started walking towards the garage. Allen realized he still hadn't gone to bed, the cops were looking for the the people that wrecked a grocery store, Xiene's car was probably still in the pit, and his shirt was ripped open.

She turned her rear towards him, pointed at it with her middle fingers, and farted. Allen forgot what he was thinking about.

SIX FLAGS OVER MY DEAD BODY!

Xiene brought the sword down on Allen's head. Allen got off the ground. She did it again.

"Will you stop that?" he yelled.

Xiene chuckled and tried to do it again. Allen moved out of her striking distance. Unfortunately, he was hit on the head by a huge bald giant.

"Oh, great, you see what you did?"

Xiene laughed.

"Oh, yeah?" He grabbed her joystick and forced her into a group of barbarians. She tried to wrestle her control back. Allen reached over and pinched her buttocks. This allowed time to kill off her character. As she did to him. The message 'insert coin to continue' scrolled onto the screen.

"Damnit! Give me a quarter!" she demanded.

"No way! You killed me off!"

"Of course! You got in my way!"

"Now you're dead! Ha-ha," he said tauntingly.

Xiene reached into his pockets and tried to dig out a quarter. She grabbed his testicles by mistake. Allen recoiled in pain.

"Oops! Sorry." She pulled out a quarter inserted it into the video game and continued the Adventures of Xiene the Merciless.

Allen inched away from the game. He spotted Tommy in a sit-down racing game with three screens. He went over to see how he was scoring. The small child had blond hair unlike his mother Maggie. Allen never heard his age but he guessed five or six. He could see a little bit of Maggie in his nose, but the other features were from CJ, Maggie's ex-husband. Allen looked inside the canopy. Tommy was in the 3rd round. His Grand Prix car zipped around the French countryside and billboards advertising other video games. Allen kind of wished the kid would wreck just so he could read some of the signs. No such luck—he finished in 2nd place. Not the winner, but still good enough to continue racing.

"Alright, good job!"

He looked at Allen, smiled, and then resumed racing. *It's good babysitting this kid. He's quiet and polite and we both like the same cartoons.* He was glad Maggie trusted him—and especially Xiene—to take care of him while she was at work on the night shift. If it weren't for the shortage of nurses at the hospital, Maggie would have taken the whole day off. But she had to have a damn beeper. Allen just hoped she would get to spend time with him on Tommy's last two days.

Tommy placed 4th in the next race. Game Over.

"Shoot!" He hit the wheel.

"Oh, well, you're still did pretty good. Better than I could."

Tommy crawled out of the machine and straightened his Teenage Mutant Ninja Turtles shirt.

"What do you want to do now?"

"I'm hungry."

"Okay, let's get Xiene and get some pizza."

Allen patted Tommy's back and they went over to yank Xiene away from the game She had made it to the final level and was fighting against an army of skeletons, barbarians, and a large guy with a Viking helmet. *The odds are even.*

"Your mama!" Xiene yelled, obliterating a skeleton. "Oh, yeah, you want some of this?" Hack! Slash! "Oh, the big guy's angry! Come and get it while it's hot, baby!"

Tommy laughed. The big Viking didn't stand a chance. Xiene had saved up all of her mage points just for this guy. With a press of a button, a gigantic dragon head appeared and burned him back to ROM land. Her character then freed the king and queen and they all lived happily ever after.

Xiene turned around with a cat-canary grin.

"You think you're so bad," Allen complained.

"Hey," she put on her sunglasses, "I know I'm bad."

Tommy laughed.

"Yeah, you see he knows it too." She leaned down and began tickling him. "You know I'm bad, don't you?" He chuckled as she continued taunting him.

A guy walked by in a mouse costume. Thank God Xiene didn't see that walking potential victim!

"Give me five!" She stuck out her hand. Tommy slapped it. She turned her hand over. "On the backside."

On the backside? We always said the Black side

Tommy slapped her hand again.

She held her hand lower. "Down low!" This time she moved her hand before Tommy could slap it. "Too slow!!" she yelled.

Tommy and Allen laughed.

"What are we doing now?" Xiene asked.

"Getting some pizza," Allen answered.

"Oh, boy, pizza! Totally awesome, dude!" Xiene said, picking Tommy up and putting him over her shoulder. He chuckled as she carried him into the dining area of the Chunky Charles pizza parlor. Now and then she would swat him on the bottom and sing 'Deep In the Heart of Texas!' This bizarre sight amused the other kids playing all around the theme pizza parlor. Some even walked away from the guy in the giant mouse/rat costume and started following Xiene. The guy in the costume put his hands on his hips.

"Pick me up, too, " some kids pleaded.

"What?"

"Pick me up!" Some kids raised their hands. One by one she would pick them up, spin them around, turn them upside-down, or play their bellies like a slap bass. The kids were having a ball.

Allen leaned against a support beam and enjoyed the show. *Gee, what kind of mother would Xiene be?* He pictured the future: Allen and Xiene's kid is in his room doing his homework. Suddenly you hear loud thrash music. The kid gets up and bangs on the wall. 'Mother! Will you keep it down, please?" Xiene comes into the room dressed in leather and lace, smoking a cigarette. 'Hey, son, you wanna go to the Acid Pit with me? It's Mohawk Night!' Xiene rips off a wig, displaying a greying mohawk.

Allen shook his head at the thought. He looked at Xiene's current hairstyle. It was dyed white, cut very short in the back, and left long towards the front with two long bangs that hung in her face. The only long hair in the back was tied into a ponytail that reached past her shoulder blades. After the thought of an old Xiene with a mohawk, he decided he loved her new hairstyle more than ever.

Some parents came and took their kids away from the Xiene Ride. Exhausted, she excused herself from the kid coral, joined Allen, and fanned herself.

"I tell you, kids!" she grabbed Tommy around the neck in a headlock, "you can't live with them!"

Allen and Tommy laughed.

They ordered their pizza and sat down in the dining area. Xiene found it weird that this kid's place served beer also. "I can see it now: 'Hi, kids, what time is it?' 'Miller time!'" She impersonated a kid show host. "Wonder if they check your I.D.? Xiene pushed the bangs out of her face and looked at the stage. "Hey, what's the stage for? We get a strip show, too?"

Allen laughed, then cleared his throat and gestured to Tommy.

"What's a 'trip show'," Tommy asked.

"Trip show?" Xiene laughed, then took out a cigarette. Allen glared at her. She glared back.

"So? Hey, Tommy, anyone in your family smoke?"

"No. Stepmom hates anyone to smoke in the house."

"Really? You have nice furniture."

"Yeah, I'm not even allowed to play in the living room."

"Really? That sucks."

"Ahem," Allen said.

"Er, I mean gosh golly gee Wiley cats! That's terrible," Xiene corrected.

"Is the rest of the house nice, Tommy?" Allen asked.

"Uh-huh. We have a swimming pool."

"Really? That's great."

"No, I can't swim in it because Stepmom hates algebra."

"Algebra?" Xiene asked.

"I think he means algae."

"Oh, yeah." Xiene lit the cigarette. "Don't you have someone who cleans your pool?"

"We did, but Stepmom fired him."

"Really, why?"

"She says he wanted to rob us."

"How did she know?"

"I don't know. She just knew."

Xiene looked at Allen. Allen mouthed the word; minority."

"Was your pool man a Black guy?"

"No. He was from Mexico."

Xiene sneered in disgust at Tommy's stepmother. "¡Esa mujer es una puta!

"Wait! You speak Spanish?" Allen asked.

"You don't?" she asked.

The lights on the stage came on. "All alright, bring on the band," Xiene yelled, clapping. The band wasn't exactly what Xiene had in mind. It consisted of a large gorilla in a leisure suit on drums a dog in a cheerleading outfit on lead vocals, another dog with one tooth in country garb on banjo, and a bird of some sort which would pop out of a barrel to sing backing vocals. Xiene sat flabbergasted. As the robots started into a set of early Beatles tunes, Allen, who had been to this place before, found Xiene's expressions more entertaining than the show.

"My god, this sucks!" She yelled.

"Ahem!" Allen said.

"I mean, golly gum drop whisker doodles!"

Tommy laughed.

The pizza they had ordered arrived. When the animals finished their first set and rotated back off stage, Xiene kept staring at the curtain.

"Don't even think about it!"

She grinned at Allen, then finished off her slice. "I'm going to the ladies' room." She looked over at Tommy. "May I be excused?"

"Yes, you may," he said with his mouth full.

She got up and headed in the direction of the bathrooms. She glanced around and cut into the employee-only area.

Allen raised an eyebrow. *Now what? I could chase after her, but Tommy may be abducted by some pervert.* Tommy had sauce on his chin. Allen grabbed a napkin. "Hold on, kid." He wiped it off. "This stuff tastes better <u>inside</u> the mouth."

They continued eating. Allen looked around for Xiene. He rattled his fingers on the table.

"What's wrong?" Tommy asked.

"Oh, I'm sure we'll find out soon enough."

Tommy looked confused.

"So, kid, you and your dad get along okay?"

"I guess so. He's not home that much."

"So you're home alone with your stepmom?"

"Yeah, her and April."

"Who?"

"My stepsister."

"She nice?"

"No. She hates me."

"How do know?"

"She said my real mom is a lesbian."

"Oh." *Well, I'm sure Maggie will explain one day. Hopefully, before Tommy's new family scarred him for life!*

Fifteen minutes later, Xiene put her hands on Allen's shoulders and kissed him on the cheek. Tommy giggled. She walked over and did the same thing to him, then began tickling him.

What dastardly deed has Xiene done? He spotted two dishwashers from the back suddenly appearing around the corner speaking Spanish and looking at the stage.

"Solo espera un minuto!" Xiene yelled to them.

They laughed, then looked back at the stage.

"Xiene? What the gosh golly gee Wiley cat whisker doodles is about to happen?" Allen asked.

His questioning was cut short. The lights dimmed and once again the curtain opened up. Everything appeared normal. Suddenly a rock song completely in Spanish started playing over the speakers.

Okay, that's pretty bad, but not as bad as I expected. Allen got a good look at the animatronics. The large gorilla on the drum now had the head of the bird creature. The cheerleader's head was now just a metal armature skull mouthing the words, the dog on banjo had his head on backward, and you would see the back of his head move when the robotic mouth and eyes moved around. Allen wondered where the female dog's head was. A short-lived question: When the Spanish song hit the chorus, "¿Que pasa?", her head would pop out of the barrel and return.

The Spanish guys broke out laughing. The family near Allen broke out laughing Xiene fell on the floor laughing Tommy chuckled away. Allen kept a straight face.

"Xiene, that was such an irresponsible thing to do…" he said.

The backward head dog skull continued mouthing some words.

"Irresponsible…"

The female dog's head popped out of the barrel but this time it didn't stop. If flew out of the barrel and bounced off the stage.

"Oh, god! That's the funniest thing I've ever seen!" Allen laughed.

They left the kiddie pizza parlor and started searching the parking lot for Xiene's new car. Allen carried Tommy piggyback. Xiene still giggled from the show.

"God, did you see that cheerleader? She looked like the Terminator. Ha-ha!" She laughed.

"I hope those dishwashers won't get in trouble for lending you their tape," Allen said.

"Naw."

Allen spotted Xiene's nightmare-mobile, a pink hearse.

"There's my baby now!" Xiene said with her hands on her cheeks.

Allen put Tommy down and once again came to grips with Xiene's purchase. "Why couldn't you have gotten a Pinto or a Gremlin or maybe a Pacer?"

"Because this car has 'Xiene' written all over it."

"Yeah, 'Death and Happiness."

"Exactly! Everybody in!"

The pink hearse zoomed down Interstate 85, back towards Atlanta. Tommy fell asleep and leaned against Xiene.

"Aw," she said, then put her arm around him.

Allen looked over at Xiene. She seemed deep in thought. "Tick, tick, tick," he quietly said.

"What?"

"Tick, tick, tick—your biological clock."

She blew him a raspberry.

I knew it! Maybe Xiene wouldn't be that bad of a mom. He remembered the pizza parlor joke, then forgot the whole thing.

Tommy woke up when they pulled up to the house.

"Everybody out! Last stop: Beverly, Maggie, and Xiene's bungalow."

She helped Tommy up. Allen went up to the porch. Xiene's cat, Scumbag, came up to him and started rubbing his leg.

"Yeah, right. As soon as you want something you're nice to me." He reached down and petted him.

Xiene carried Tommy onto the porch. "Get my keys, Hon."

Allen reached into her pocket. "I should get you back for what you did to me."

"Not unless you can squeeze my ovaries from the outside."

"Shhh!"

"What?"

Allen took out her keys and unlocked the door. Scumbag the cat ran between Allen's legs inside the house and jumped on the couch next to Maggie.

"Hey." She raised her arms.

Xiene let Tommy down. He ran over to hug her.

"Hey, Peeper! What did you do tonight?"

"We went to Chunky Pizza!"

"Really? Did you see the robot animals onstage?"

Xiene smirked, then headed into the kitchen. Allen sat down next to the inactive fireplace.

"Yeah, there was a gorilla with a bird head!"

"What?"

"Yeah! And a dog's head! They shot out of a barrel and flew! Whoosh!" He gestured with his hands.

"Bird-headed gorilla? Dog heads flying out of barrels? Who did this puppet show? Mark Pauline?"

Xiene burst out laughing. Everyone looked in the kitchen as she covered her mouth and went out of sight. Maggie looked at Allen.

"The puppet show's a little different now," he answered.

"Must be. Okay, Peeper, it's past your bedtime. You go up and brush your teeth, say your prayers, and I'll come up and read you a bedtime story. Alright?"

"I want Xiene to read me!" Tommy shuffled.

"Oh? You don't want Mommy to read you a story?"

"No. I want Xiene!"

Maggie seemed hurt. "Hmm. Okay, go on upstairs."

Tommy raced upstairs. Xiene came out of the kitchen holding a plate full of cookies. Her eyes were watery.

"You alright?" Maggie asked.

She started laughing. Allen thought about the puppets and then started laughing too."

"What? What is it?"

"Nothing." They answered.

Allen caught his breath. "Mark Pauline—Ha ha ha!"

Xiene sat down next to Maggie on the couch. "I wish you could have been there."

"Yeah," said Allen, reaching for a homemade cookie.

"But I got all day tomorrow."

"What are you gonna do?" Xiene asked.

"Tommy wants to go to Six Flags."

"Oh, that's cool. He can compare it to Busch Gardens." Allen said.

"Where's that?" asked Xiene.

"Tampa," Maggie answered. "I don't know if he's been there or not. It's not that close to Jacksonville."

Xiene propped her feet on the coffee table. "When's Beverly getting back?"

"Tuesday."

I wonder if Beverly's trip to Alabama to visit friends was a plan to get Mom's lesbian lover out of town while Tommy visits, and if so, who's plan?—Beverly's, Maggies, or a condition of the court thing?

"Tommy wants you to read a bedtime story," Maggie said to Xiene.

"Really?" She perked up.

"Yeah, just remember how old he is, so don't read anything weird," Allen suggested.

"Ah." She jumped off the couch and headed up the stairs. "I'll read him some Kerouac!"

"No!" Maggie yelled.

They heard Xiene saying: "My whole wretched life swam before my weary eyes, and I realized no matter what you do it's bound to be a waste of time in the end so you might as well go mad…' As she headed into her room.

"You don't think she'd read Kerouac, do you?" asked Maggie.

"I don't know. I wouldn't put it past her."

Allen and Maggie sat downstairs eating while Xiene read to Tommy. Periodically you could hear him laughing. Maggie stopped eating when he did.

"When did you get a divorce?" Allen asked.

"Four years ago."

"So you haven't seen him in four years?"

"I go down to Florida once in a while to visit him. This is just the first time he's been able to visit me. Thank God for female judges."

"What?"

"The judge was a woman this time. That's probably the reason I won new visitation rights."

"Oh, baloney. A man could have done the same thing."

"Uh, yeah, right," Maggie said sarcastically then picked up another cookie.

Allen leaned over and took the last one. "Who baked these?"

"Xiene."

"Our Xiene?"

Maggie nodded.

"Humph. Never baked me cookies," he pouted.

"Yeah, she can bake and make kids smile. She's a regular Betty Crocker."

Maggie's statement sounded kind of insulting. A long silence followed

"Al?" She asked

"Don't call me Al."

"Sorry. Allen?"

"What?"

Did Tommy mention anything about, you know…me and Bev?"

"He knows you're a lesbian, but he doesn't know what it is."

"Really? Who told him? His dad?"

"No, actually. His stepsister."

"April?"

"Yeah, I think she was teasing him with it. Ten-to-one she doesn't know what a lesbian is either."

"Hmm." Maggie went into deep thought.

"I think it's time I headed on home. I'm gonna say bye to Xiene." Allen walked by the sofa. When he did, he scratched Maggie's red-headed scalp. She waved to him behind his back.

Allen climbed the stairs. He approached Beverly's bedroom, now Tommy's. He could hear Xiene still reading.

"…and the giant killed them. And they all died. The end," Xiene said.

"What? What in the world kind of story are you telling up here?" Allen asked.

Tommy giggled.

Allen looked at her book. She was reading 'Alice in Wonderland'. "Oh, ha-ha, very funny.".

Xiene laughed. "Anyway, Tommy, "Alice picked up the cookie, the one that read, 'EAT ME!'." On that, she turned around and looked at Allen. Allen lowered his eyebrows. Xiene smiled. Tommy was confused.

"I'm heading out, Mrs Carroll."

"Okay. I'll see you out." She gave the book to Tommy. "Keep my place, kiddo."

Xiene walked Allen downstairs. Maggie had gone to bed, Allen guessed. When Xiene opened the door, Allen pinched her leg.

"Ow!"

"Eat me?"

She laughed.

"You said 'eat me' in front of a child?"

"Oh, god, Allen, he hasn't a clue. God, you're so protective."

They went outside and walked to the front gate.

"Yeah, and you're under-protective."

Xiene put Allen's nose between two fingers. She then slapped that hand sown with her other. "Oh, Allen, lighten up!"

Allen rubbed his nose. "God, now I know what kinds of parents we're going to be."

Xiene got deathly silent on that statement.

"What?"

"Nothing. So, you going with us to Six Flags Over My Dead Body?"

"Sure, as long as you promise not to waterski down the log ride or something like that."

"Who, me?" She pointed to herself.

"Yeah, you!" Allen leaned over and kissed her. They then hugged for a while.

"He's cute, isn't he?" Xiene finally said.

"Tick, tick, tick," Allen responded.

She punched him in the stomach. Allen recoiled in pain and slowly went through the gate. "See you tomorrow." She waved.

"Yeah, if I can recover in time."

Allen arrived early that Sunday morning. He could smell bacon as he approached the front door. *Must be Xiene's, he figured. Maggie's a vegetarian.*

Maggie opened the front door wearing an apron and holding a spatula.

"Maggie, you look so…so domestic."

She swatted him playfully on the head with the spatula and laughed. Allen laughed and checked for grease in his hair.

"Where's Xiene?"

He heard the sound of drums. "Never mind." Allen walked to the basement. Maggie returned to the kitchen. A loud drum sound filled Allen's ears when he walked down the stairs. Xiene had Tommy on her lap and was playing the drums with his hands. Allen crossed his arms and watched. She spotted him and kissed him in his direction.

"Okay, that was a double-stroke roll. Now do this…" She started Tommy playing a snare drum. She filled in with the rest of the beat. Allen recognized it as a reggae beat. Tommy smiled at his achievement.

"Ya, mon!" Xiene yelled. "That's it, mon! Mi feel Irie!"

Allen laughed at Xiene's bad Jamaican accent. Maggie yelled something. Allen waved Xiene and Tommy to shush. They stopped playing.

"What?" Allen yelled.

"Breakfast," she yelled down the stairs.

"Oh-oh," Xiene said. She put Tommy down. "Let's go eat!" She grabbed his hand, then walked over and kissed Allen on the cheek.

"Hey, Mom," he said"

She stepped on his foot on purpose.

They went up the stairs and made their way into the sunny kitchen. Maggie almost frantically put the breakfast smorgasbord together. Scumbag and Marie Curie purred at her feet. She moved them away with her foot. "Out, move it!' The cats walked off towards the screened-in back porch. Xiene and Tommy took their places at the table.

Allen grabbed a pitcher of orange juice. *Freshly squeezed?* "Gee, you went all out, didn't you?"

Maggie ignored Allen's statement and set the plates down. Tommy reached for a piece of bacon.

"Tommy!" Maggie yelled. Use this." She gave him some tongs.

Xiene looked as if she were about to grab the bacon like Tommy almost did.

They set their plates.

"What, no sugary cereal like in the commercials to complete this breakfast?"Allen joked.

"Yeah, really, Maggie, this meal can't be complete," Xiene held an imaginary box up to her head, "without a box of yummy Sugar High cereal. Yes, Sugar High! Your kids will love it! The cops, won't!"

Tommy and Allen laughed.

"Xiene!" Maggie yelled.

"What?"

"Watch your language."

"What? You mean 'high'?"

Maggie put her napkin down and sighed. Xiene looked at Allen. He shrugged. They continued eating. Tommy used his fingers for bacon, imitating Xiene."

"Tommy, use your fork," Maggie complained.

"Why?" Tommy asked.

"Because I said so."

"But Xiene doesn't use a fork."

"You're not her, now, are you?"

"Yeah, Tommy. If I jumped off the Empire State Building, would you follow me?" added Xiene.

"I don't know," he said, kicking the legs of his chair with his heels.

Xiene giggled. "Have you ever seen the Empire State Building?"

"No."

"Me, neither," said Allen.

"Believe me, you wouldn't want to jump from it."

"Sure. I could," said Tommy. "I'll do like Spiderman."

"Oh, really?"

"Yeah, I'll spin a web and 'whoosh!'," Tommy waved his arm and knocked over his orange juice.

"Oh, Jesus Christ!" Maggie yelled, getting up.

Xiene grabbed some napkins. Allen tried to keep the cats at bay by holding his leg in their way.

"I'm sorry," Tommy said.

"You have to be more careful!" Maggie yelled.

"He said he was sorry," said Xiene.

"I didn't ask you what he said!" she snapped.

Xiene pulled back and continued eating. Maggie finished cleaning up the juice and then resumed eating in silence. Xiene mumbled something. Allen tapped her foot with his. She looked at him. He put his index finger up to his lips.

The ride to Six Flags was delayed due to a traffic jam two miles from downtown Atlanta. The threat of rain didn't help, either.

"God, what's holding us up?" Xiene asked.

Maggie, the driver, didn't answer Xiene's question. Allen, riding a shotgun, craned his neck around. "I can't see anything. Probably some woman in a bathing suit changing a flat tire."

Xiene laughed.

"It looks like it's gonna rain," Tommy said, putting his nose in the window.

"Maybe not." Xiene thought for a few seconds. "Hey, I got it—why don't we do a lucky sun dance?"

"What?" Tommy said, turning around.

"Yeah, do what I do." Xiene put her hands up like moose antlers and started chanting gibberish. Tommy giggled and danced with her. "Yeah, that's it!" Xiene said as they rocked back and forth. Allen looked at Maggie. She looked like she was about to scream. She gripped the steering wheel tightly.

"I thought you were vegetarian?" Allen asked, trying to ease her tension.

"What?"

"You ate some bacon this morning."

"That wasn't bacon—it was fake."

"Really? Sort of like Love Burger?"

"Yeah, something like that."

Allen didn't tell her that he did figure out that the bacon was fake. After all, it's hard to fool the taste buds of a rabid carnivore."

"It's working!" yelled Tommy.

Sure enough, the sun peeked through the clouds.

"Alright, we did it!" Xiene yelled. "Give me a high five!" She held out her hand and moved it when he slapped at it. "Too slow!"

"It's about bloody well time!" Maggie said as the traffic suddenly cleared up.

Xiene continued teasing the kid. She held her hand out. He would try to slap it and she would move it. This game lasted the rest of the trip.

Later, they all walked towards the park entrance, Xiene and Tommy's sun dance worked too well. The temperature rose to 94°, a typical Atlanta summer.

"Well! Fiddle-de-dee," Xiene said like Scarlet O'Hara. "It's hot enough to cook a brain on drugs."

"Yeah, it'll probably storm later. It always does when it's this hot." Allen said.

"Oh, Allen, don't be such a killjoy." Xiene took off her Harley-Davidson cap and swatted him with it. Everyone in the entrance line glanced over at them. Maggie was in front, holding Tommy's hand. He would periodically look back to see if Xiene was doing anything interesting. Xiene started sticking her tongue out at him. He started doing it back and giggling. Allen intervened before they pissed off Maggie again. He took Xiene's cat-eye sunglasses off her face.

"Hey!"

"Where did you get these?"

She took Allen's glasses off. "Where did you get these?"

He put her glasses on. "How do I look?"

"Oh, Honey, two snaps up." She snapped her fingers.

He took them off. She put his glass on.

"Whoa!" She started wobbling back and forth like a drunk. "God, how do you see out of these things?"

"With great difficulty without. Now give those back."

She started to hand them back, then snatched them away. "Too slow!"

"Errr! I'll show you 'too slow!'"

He tried to reach for them. She moved them from place to place, always out of his reach. He tickled her under the arm. She contracted her arm, sending the glasses flying out of her hand and landing in a fountain.

"Great! Good job!"

Xiene laughed. Allen bent over and reached into the water to retrieve the spectacles. He forgot Xiene was behind him. Before he could say, 'Don't even try it!' She pushed him into the fountain. He was in up to his elbows, causing the front of his shirt to get drenched. He heard Tommy and some other kids laughing. His 'Prepare to die!' wasn't heard by Xiene, who disappeared into the crowd.

Allen got up and squeezed the front of his T-shirt. He scanned the crowd. He figured if Xiene made a run for it, most people would be looking at where she ran. Unfortunately, everyone faced forward, which meant she either ran inside Six Flags or told everyone in the crowd not to give her hideout away. He opted that she go through the gate, which seemed strange because he had the money for the tickets. He looked in and spotted Maggie and Tommy. They waved.

"Alright, Xiene where are you?" He scanned the crowd again. "Ok hide all you want. I'll just leave your ass out here." Allen bought his ticket and went inside. Still no Xiene in sight. He walked up to Maggie and Tommy. Tommy was giggling.

"What?"

Xiene jumped from behind Maggie. "Ta-da!"

Allen ran after her. She weaved between two families who didn't move as fast out of Allen's way. She ran into an arcade.

"Ah-ha! Cornered!" Allen said, rubbing his hands. He went in. She was next to one of the many Skee-ball games holding one of the wooden balls. "Got you!"

She lifted the ball over her head. "Get back, turkey, or I'll bean you."

"Turkey?"

She laughed. "It's all I could think of."

Allen pointed behind Xiene and yelled, "Oh, my god!" She turned around and looked, which gave him time to grab her arms. They began wrestling much to the pleasure of the thirty or so witnesses. Finally, Allen bent down and picked her up in a fireman's pull. She struggled and yelled. Allen started carrying her, hitting her butt, and singing 'Deep in the Heart of Texas'. They almost made it out of the arcade until Xiene yelled, "Help! Pervert!"

Allen stopped and put her down, but it was too late. A security guard of some sort had already responded to Xiene's cry.

"There something wrong? Are you alright?" he asked with his hands on his nightstick.

"Yes, this man is a masher! Have him locked up!"

Allen fumed.

"That true, you bothering this lady?"

"I've never seen her before in my life!"

"Oh, yeah? Don't listen to him. He's a sweaty pervert! Why, just look at his shirt!"

The guard looked at Allen's water-drenched shirt. "Okay, maybe you should come with me to a holding room." He began to grab Allen.

"Xiene! Tell him the truth!"

"Xiene? Who's Xiene? My name is Christine Richards. You want to see my license?"

"Okay then, Christine Charlotte Richards of 1128 Myrtle Street, Atlanta, 20210, who has a picture of me in your wallet kissing you on the cheek! Tell him the truth!" Allen responded.

The guard stopped trying to take Allen away and looked at Xiene. She looked embarrassed and shuffled around a bit.

"Okay, okay, he's my boyfriend, officer. I was just pulling your chain." She thought for a few seconds. "I just got back from the Persian Gulf and I'm a little shell-shocked."

Allen's eyes bulged out.

"Really? You were in Desert Storm?"

"Er, yeah," she continued. The guard went into a story of himself serving in Vietnam. It took 25 or so minutes of pure, unembellished drone narration for him to tell his story. By the end, Allen felt as if he was going to drool from boredom.

"…and that's why I'm working at Six Flags," he completed.

"What?" said Xiene, in a daze.

"Your story, what was Saudi Arabia like?"

"I don't like to talk about it." She said.

"Yeah," Allen interrupted, "She doesn't like to talk about it. The horror," he said like Marlon Brando.

"Yeah, the horror," Xiene added. "I have to go deal with it." She walked away.

"I have to help her deal with it." Allen joined her heading out the door.

"Okay, see you later, and hey, remember, go Airborne!" he yelled.

"Yeah, semper fi!" Xiene mumbled. "God, I never thought anyone could make Vietnam sound so boring,"

Allen bit his bottom lip and waited until they were far enough away from the arcade. He then grabbed Xiene's neck. "Saudi Arabia? 'Help? Pervert'? Pushing me in the fountain?" She was laughing. He put both hands on her neck. She put her hands on his neck.

"Hey, let's go," she laughed, leaning forward and got one inch from his face. He closed his eyes, ready for a kiss. Xiene put her left leg between both of his legs and pushed him over onto the ground. She then skipped off, towards Maggie and a laughing Tommy.

Allen got off the ground. *I'll get my revenge later!*

Xiene picked Tommy up.

"Where were you guys?" Maggie complained.

"Don't ask. Just remember to stay away from Xiene! I don't want you to get hurt when I kill her."

The group started on all of the low-impact rides for Tommy's sake—the chairlift, choo-choo train, and spin-and-puke, as Xiene called it, among the choices. The havoc didn't start until the Monster Plantation, a ride where the viewer rides in a little boat through a so-called flooded Southern mansion. Inside, soft furry puppets sing, move, and try to entertain you. Allen and Xiene were in the boat behind the other two. Xiene sneered at some of the insipid soft sculptures and fake-gagged the musical numbers. When they passed a creature with an incredibly large mouth, Xiene took out her gum and threw it right onto its tongue. Whenever it opened its mouth the long pink goop stretched, then contracted again, over and over.

"I can't take you anywhere," Allen complained.

"No, you can't." She placed some gum on the end of his nose.

They spotted the puppet sheriff monster robot waving his arms and saying "Go back! Don't go in here. Stay back." Beside him, a sign with 'The swamp—keep out!' on it.

"Oh, boy, now we're gonna see some action!" Xiene said, rubbing her hands. This overstatement by Xiene proved false, as glowing eyes, cricket noises and a giant dragon head blowing mist on the travelers were all the danger to be seen.

"What a gyp!"

"What did you expect, Xiene? Flamethrowers, and Jason with two chainsaws?"

"Yeah! That would be neat! You could call the ride the Duck or Die!"

"More like, 'The Whirling Lawsuit!"

Again, the monster sheriff puppet appeared, this time saying, "He-heh-heh, I see you made it out of the swamp. Have a nice day."

"God, how droll," Xiene said, yawning. "Wonder if I can turn his head backward?"

While Allen said 'No, you can't! and don't try it!' Xiene was already standing in the boat and reaching for the puppet's cowboy hat.

"Stop that!"

"Grab my belt!" she said, leaning forward.

Allen thought this would be the perfect opportunity for his revenge joke—all he had to do was let her lean forward, and then —splash!—he'd let go of her. Unfortunately, there was an island in front of her, so all that would happen would be she would land on the plastic fauna on the island, get up, get back in the boat, and kill him. *I'll wait!*

Xiene reached for the hat.

"More slack." She commanded.

"Why am I holding you?" Allen complained.

She grabbed the tip of the hat, and then let go. She grabbed again this time she got a good grip. She started turning the hat around along with the head attached. Xiene continued turning as the boat passed away farther and farther. Suddenly, one more twist removed the entire head.

"Hey, check it out!" Xiene said before laughing.

"Oh, Christ, put it back!"

Xiene tried but the rest of the body was too far away. "It's too far. Shit!"

"We'll get busted!"

"What do you want me to do?" She held the big-mouthed monster's head in front of hers. "Booga-booga!"

"Give me that!" Seconds before they exited into daylight, Allen snatched the head and threw it behind them, and it floated out of sight.

Xiene and Allen got off the ride, her with a smirk, him a 'one of these days' expression. Suddenly they heard screaming from the boat behind them. They and everyone in line looked. They spotted the floating head being pushed by a boatload of Girl Scouts. Xiene nearly tore Allen's shirt off as she laughed and clawed at the sight. Allen pushed her through the crowd, trying to prevent everyone from figuring out who was responsible.

"What's all the noise?" Maggie asked. Allen rolled his eyes at her.

"Oh."

Xiene wiped the tears off her cheek. "Now that's what I call a monster: 'The Floating Head of the Lake'," she said in a scary voice.

Allen didn't smile.

"What?"

"You! Boy, you've been on a destructo-kick lately!"

"Moi?"

"Oui! Vous!" Allen said, pointing to her nose

"It's tu, not vous!" She bit at his nose.

"See? Always destructive and violent."

"Ha! I'll show you. The next ride we go on, I won't do anything destructive."

"Wanna bet?"

"Alright, what?"

"Okay." Allen paced for a bit. "If you do anything destructive on the next ride, that I get to pick, then you must eat a liver and onions sandwich." He pointed at her.

"Oh, boy, liver and onions!" Xiene said, rubbing her tummy and licking her lips. "My favorite!"

"Yeah, right," said Allen, remembering Xiene saying she hated liver more than Wednesday night television.

"Okay, and if I win…" Allen held his breath, "you'll have to put on my black leather miniskirt, some makeup, and heels and I get to take your picture."

Allen felt a cold chill on his back.

"Now wait a minute, all you have to do is eat a stupid sandwich and I have to ruin my political career."

"Political career?" Maggie asked.

"You never know," he said, turning to her.

"What, are you? Chicken?" Xiene started making chicken noises, nudged Tommy, and they both began taunting Allen with chicken clucks.

"Okay, okay, it's a bet! But I still don't know how I'm gonna fit in your miniskirt."

"Allen, you're no Arnold Schwarzenegger," said Xiene, feeling his skinny arm.

"And you're no Jack Kennedy."

Maggie laughed at Allen's Betson, Quayle debate reference.

Tommy and Xiene didn't get it.

"Okay, pick your ride, sucker!"

Allen thought of the possibilities of a ride that reeked of a practical joke, something that was already set up to fool around on.

"Mommy, I wanna go on the bum-pa cars," Tommy said.

Xiene's face showed stress, as if she knew the bumper cars, a demolition derby of potential pranks, would do her in.

Tommy and Xiene got into their green car, and Allen got into a black one, making him feel like a villain. *I must think of a way to crack Xiene.* He looked around. He saw a goofy-looking high school-aged attendant fixing some little girl's lap belt. While waiting in line, Allen watched this guy move around the track, pushing people's cars away from the wall and getting in the way.

Hmm. He signaled to Xiene. She looked over. He pointed to the guy. She saw him, sneered, then looked back. Allen gave the hand gestures for running over someone. Xiene laughed, then showed a snobbishly straight face. *Yeah, I'm so sure you can resist.*

The power started up and sparks flew from the cars' metal rods touching the ceiling. Everyone moved except for Xiene. Something was wrong with her car. Maggie broadsided Allen.

"Hey!"

She laughed, then went right and creamed some teenage boy. Allen went straight for Xiene and Tommy. A little girl cut in front of him. He rammed her, backed up, and did it again. She wouldn't move.

"Move, or I'll destroy you!" he yelled, imagining himself in a miniskirt. She headed off.

Xiene and Tommy were rocking back and forth, trying to get the car going. Like clockwork, the goofy teenager avoided traffic and skipped over to them. Allen stood his ground to see what was going to happen. Someone rear-ended him. The little girl.

"Argh!" he yelled while reaching for her. She laughed, then drove off to get on someone else's nerves. The goofy boy searched around Xiene and Tommy's car. He tried to move it. He looked inside, then said something to Xiene. She looked inside. Their car suddenly wiped sideways. The teenager fell over the hood and rolled onto the ground. He quickly got up and limped off the track. Xiene and Tommy were howling with laughter. Allen pictured them with horns and sharp teeth.

"Liver sandwich! Yum-yum!" he yelled at them.

"No way! It was an accident!"

"I'm so sure!"

Someone rear-ended Allen—the little girl again.

"That does it!" He started to do a 180° turn with the car so he could obliterate her, and then the power cut off. She jumped out of her car and ran off the course, giggling.

Allen turned his attention back to Xiene and Tommy. They were leaving. "Hey, wait up, Ms. Liver!"

Xiene cringed. Maggie grabbed Tommy's hand. Xiene tried to duck behind a pole.

"I see you!"

She slowly came around the side with a sad, pouting expression.

"So, do you want your liver cooked?"

"Unfair!, Allen! It was an accident!"

"Oh, yeah, good timing for an accident."

"No way! It was a freak happening! The bet's off!"

"Oh, really? Hey, Tommy! When that man you ran over talked to Xiene, what did he say?"

"Hey, Tom! let's go get some ice cream!" Xiene said grabbing his hand and trying to drag him off. Allen and Maggie pulled on his other hand, creating a tug-of-war.

"Oh, no, you don't! What did he say?"

Tommy laughed as his feet left the ground. "He said you have to press on the gas pedal to make it go."

Xiene stopped pulling. She put her right index finger in her mouth.

"Gee, whiz, Speedy McXieney, Ms. Bumper Car champ '94, didn't know how to work her car? The old lure-him-into-your-car trick—shame!"

"You're really enjoying this, Allen, aren't you?"

He went over and put his arm around her. "More than life itself. Finally! I will get revenge for all those jokes you've played on me! With just one slimy meal of your most hated food! Bwa-Ha-ha!"

Xiene elbowed him. "Okay, but I get to fix it!"

"Au contraire, mon frère. I will fix it!"

"It's Sœur, not frère!"

"Whatever! Cook? Did you say, 'cook'? Hmm, liver tartar with raw, crunchy onions on plain, bleached 100-slices-to-a-pack white bread."

Xiene put her hands on her head and screamed.

This gave Allen an idea. "Hey, let's go on the roller coasters."

Tommy, because of his height, couldn't do the roller coaster circuit, and Maggie just plain hated roller coasters. Allen and Xiene first tried the Mind Bender, your typical upside-down, 65mph, no pregnant mothers or people with bad backs coaster. This ride succeeded in giving them headaches. Next, the Ghost Train, a train-in-the-mine-shaft-duck-or-you'll-lose-your-head kind of ride. Because they sat in the back, this ride succeeded in giving them back aches. By the time they made it to the Scream Machine, a Coney Island one-nail-falls-out-and-everyone-dies coaster, there were no more parts to ache, so they enjoyed this one the most of all.

"Boy, the old-fashioned ones are always the best," Xiene said on the exit ramp. Allen was too busy wondering how to cook liver. "Oh, gee, look. The clouds are forming again!"

Allen looked up and studied the approaching storm. "See, I told you, whenever it gets really hot, the storm always follows."

"Hey!" yelled Tommy on the end of the exit ramp.

Xiene ran the rest of the way. She picked him up and started spinning him around. He was laughing.

"Xiene, don't do that," Maggie said. Xiene continued spinning the giggling child. "Xiene, I said stop!" Maggie yelled. Xiene stopped and looked at Maggie with confusion.

"Why?"

Maggie put her hand on her head as if she were getting a headache. "Because I don't want him to get sick."

"Sick? After all those spinning rides we've been on? How could he get sick now?"

"Don't argue with me! Just don't spin him!" Maggie's voice got louder.

"Well—"

Allen walked in front of Xiene, interrupting her. He put his finger to his lips. Xiene almost spoke again, but Allen silently whispered 'Shhh'. She turned around, put her hands on her hips, and sighed. Allen turned to Maggie. She had her arms crossed and was looking left, at the roller coaster. Tommy was looking at Allen. Allen knelt.

"What ride would like to go on next?"

"I wanna go home!"

Maggie turned and looked at him. "Tommy, we've spent $12 per ticket on this place and we've barely rode $8 worth of rides."

"I still wanna go home!"

"Hey, Tommy, have you gone on the log ride?"

"No."

"You'll like it. It's like a big boat that goes down a water slide and splashes at the end and everyone gets completely soaked." Allen's suggestion cheered Tommy up.

"No, we won't," Maggie said.

"What? Why not?" Xiene asked.

"The last thing I need is for Tommy to get soaked. What if he catches a cold?"

"I don't think that's very likely," Allen said, confused at how protective Maggie was.

"I don't care! I don't want Tommy going back home with a cold. I can hear C.J.'s wife now: You see what happens when he visits Maggie?" she said in a snippy voice.

Xiene turned around. "Gads, Maggie, don't you think you're being a little too protective?"

"Why don't you try being a mother for once, and then you'll see what I mean!"

"I don't see—"

"Okay, we won't go on the water ride, okay? Just cool it," Allen interrupted, feeling like a referee.

Xiene turned back around and walked towards a bench.

"I wanna go on the log ride!" Tommy yelled.

"And I said no! You'll catch a cold!"

Tommy stomped.

"God, I'm getting a headache." Maggie put her hand on her head. "There any place to get an aspirin?"

"There's a souvenir shop up that hill." Allen pointed towards the shops and concession stands up the asphalt hill.

"Right. I'll be back. Watch Tommy for me." Maggie took off.

Tommy frowned.

"Let's go." Allen put his hand behind Tommy and led him to the bench. He jumped up on the bench and sat next to Xiene, who had lit up a cigarette. Allen sat on Tommy's other side. The three sulked in silence. Finally, Xiene threw down her cigarette and stamped it out.

"Come on, kid, we're going on the log ride!" She stood up and pulled Tommy off the bench.

"Yay!" he screamed.

They began walking towards the water ride.

Allen gave chase."Hold it right there! You heard what Maggie said!"

"So what? I think she's being overprotective!"

"So what if she is? Tommy is still her son!"

"Yeah, well Tommy also came to Atlanta to have fun and visit his mom! So far, Maggie's acting like I picture his stepmom is like, always telling him no to this, no to that! He probably never has any fun! God, what's childhood without fun?"

Allen thought for a minute. *Xiene's childhood was a bland, strict upbringing Her parents raised her in a conservative Baptist atmosphere.* He finally understood her childish behavior (or more than ever) since Tommy showed up. She was using him as an antenna for her repressed childhood.

"…can't have any fun!" Xiene said.

"What?" Allen asked, catching the end of her speech.

"You weren't listening!"

"Yes, I was!"

"What did I say?"

"You said Tommy comes from a sterile, anal-retentive home. He then comes to Atlanta and Maggie is giving him the same treatment and not letting him have any fun."

Xiene paused. "Lucky guess!"

He raised his eyebrows at his accuracy. Tommy tugged Allen's pants. He looked down. "What?"

"I wanna go on the log ride."

Allen rolled his eyes. "Okay, we'll go. But you," he pointed to Xiene, "take full responsibility for this trip!"

"I always do." She moved one of her bangs from her nose.

The line moved quickly on the log ride due to the relatively short ride. People got into a large boat with seats. It floated over to a ramp that takes you about five or so stories in the air. It does a U-turn and plunges down a hill into the water, soaking the passengers and sending a wall of water at the exit bridge that passes overhead. Those who weren't satisfied with just having the effect of a bucket of water dumped on their heads could have the effect of falling into a swimming, pool fully clothed when they walked over the bridge.

In line, Allen watched the boat hit the water over and over, soaking the passengers and poor victims who stood on the bridge watching. He read the sign overhead warning 'You will get wet'. He looked at Tommy. He was hugging Xiene's left leg and sitting on her foot. When she moved, it was like Frankenstein as she made monster noises. Tommy laughed and held on. Allen heard screams. On the bridge, fourteen people waddled off, some wringing their shirts. One woman in a white T-shirt wasn't wearing a bra.

Nice! "Bad theme park attire," he said.

"What?" Xiene asked, trying to pry Tommy off her leg.

"White T-shirt, no bra."

Xiene pulled her shirt forward and looked down. She pushed it back, then continued prying Tommy.

What was her discovery? I don't want my girlfriend to be a participant in the Six Flags wet T-shirt contest. Xiene turned around. Allen spotted her bra strap and sighed in relief.

He wondered what Maggie was doing at that point. Knowing her, she will immediately figure it out and will come running after them. He searched the entrance. *No sign of her.*

A tennis shoe brushed Allen's left ear. He turned around. Xiene was holding Tommy in the air and turning him in different directions. *God, maybe I should buy her a doll!*

Xiene walked over and handed Tommy over to Allen. He leaned over the wooden fence and held Tommy over the water. "Hey, Tom! baptism time!"

Some people behind Allen laughed.

"Xiene, help!" Tommy yelled.

Allen wondered if he was serious.

Xiene reached over and grabbed him back. "Shame, Allen! You don't want Tommy to get wet. At least, not yet!" She put him down.

Allen grabbed Xiene's hand. Xiene moved forward and hugged him. Tommy giggled.

Xiene looked at him. "Boy, you act as if you've never seen a couple be affectionate before."

"He probably hasn't," Allen said.

"Is that true, Tommy? Your dad and stepmom ever act like this?" She kissed Allen.

"No."

"Really?"

"They just yell a lot. And then Daddy leaves town. Then he comes back and they yell some more."

"God, how shitty—" Xiene covered her mouth. "Sorry! God you poor kid."

"Sounds like they're headed for Divorce-ville," Allen whispered.

"You don't suppose that's why Maggie got visitation rights—because his family's about to split up?"

Allen spotted a woman who looked like Maggie at the entrance. "Duck!" he said and gestured. The three stooped down.

Allen slowly raised his head, confusing the people standing behind the three. Some turned around to see what Allen was looking at. The woman picked up a baby. "Not her."

Xiene got up. "Gads, Allen, she looks nothing like her!"

"I just saw that curly red hair…"

"And a baby!"

Allen blew her a raspberry. Xiene blew him a harder one, sending a mist of spit in his face.

"Yuck! Gross!" He wiped his face. Hearing laughter all around, Allen looked over the fence to scoop up some of the water. Something told him to grip the fence. He did just as Xiene tried to push him in.

"Ah-hah!" he yelled, turning around. Xiene had a guilty grin on her face. "Thought you could get me again, eh?"

"Can't blame a girl for trying."

"That makes two I owe you!"

"Hey, I already have to eat a liver sandwich! It should be one."

"Oh, no, that's a bet, and thank you for reminding me.

"Shit," Xiene said while stomping.

They made it to the front. One more boat and it would be their turn. Xiene turned around to Allen. She started fingering his chest and talking in a sweet voice. "You know, Allen, I can only think of one way you could get me to enjoy eating liver." She batted her eyelashes.

"Good try, Marilyn, but it won't work. Plus," he lowered his voice so Tommy couldn't hear, "there's no way in hell I'm going to put liver on my dick."

Xiene punched him in the stomach and put her cap back on.

Allen grabbed the guardrail and tried to catch his breath.

The boat floated into the gate. Allen looked down at the straddle-style wooden bench seating. *Completely wet! Oh well, starting with a wet bottom.*

The passengers got down into the boat and took their positions one behind the other. Allen put his arms around Xiene, hers around Tommy. Allen liked this position. He wished cars were like this, but then figured no one would take taxis anymore. He dry-spitted Xiene's hair out of his mouth. She turned her head around and grinned at him. She then began rubbing the back of her head against his face.

"Will you stop that? Gads, you're so cruel today!"

"Hey, if you're gonna punish me later, I'm gonna get in all my licks now!"

Allen took her cap off of her head. He leaned over the side and scooped up some water.

"Hey! My cap!" she yelled.

"Here you go," he said, placing it back on her head.

She screamed. The people in the back of the boat laughed. *People are probably more entertained by us than* by *the ride.*

"You ba—" Xiene almost said 'bastard' "Bubblehead! Mad Dog gave me this cap for my birthday."

"I don't care what your mother gave you."

Xiene pushed against Allen's chest with her back—hard. He tried to get out of the situation in his usual way—ticking the armpits. She brought her elbows in tight against her body, preventing access to the pits. She continued to push, forcing the air out of him.

"Okay,…okay,…you win! Stop!" he wheezed.

"Say you're sorry!"

"Okay, I'm sorry!"

"And I don't have to eat that sandwich!"

My only revenge? Give it up? She must be nuts! "Okay, you will not have to eat a liver sandwich! Xiene stopped pushing. "A liver pie? No, a liver salad?" Allen continued thinking of other alternatives.

The boat climbed the ramp riding on a giant conveyor belt. Allen looked back towards the entrance. He spotted six women with red hair who could be Maggie. At the top of the hill, Xiene started up a chorus of Sid & Marty Krofft's Land of the Lost live-action show. "Marshall, Will, and Holly on a routine expedition…"

A few people joined her. Allen figured the reason she was doing this is because in the introduction to the show, the family is taking a rafting trip until an earthquake happens, sending them plummeting over a waterfall and they end up 100,000 years back in time. The key element of this scene is the sorry excuse of a scream the family gives going over the fall. Xiene timed the song just right and when the boat plummeted down the hill, she and the strangers gave a harmonious, lame scream.

The boat whisked down the watery ramp and leveled off on the bottom. Suddenly everything went white as the water splashed all around them, causing even Xiene to scream. The wave hit the bridge up ahead, causing a little girl to fall. The wave subsided and the boat slowed down and traveled under the bridge.

Allen looked at himself. His pants were wet but not soaked. His shirt had gotten wetter when Xiene pushed him into the fountain. He took his glasses off, cleaned them, and then looked at Xiene. She turned her head and spat some water over the side. Tommy had received the least of the blow—just his hair had gotten wet.

"How did you do that?" Xiene asked, wringing out her shirt.

"I ducked down."

Xiene started shaking her head like a St. Bernard, sending water into his face.

"That does it. When we get off, you better make a run for it!"

"Oh, come on, I know you like me wet!"

The people up front turned around.

Allen clenched his teeth. "I'll give you a five-second head start."

The boat pulled into the boathouse. Xiene jumped up and grabbed Tommy. "Come on, Tommy! We only have five seconds!" She ran on the exit plank.

Allen, true to his word, waited five seconds, then ran after her. She ran onto the bridge and stopped. Allen looked up and spotted a boat rounding the corner preparing to plummet down the hill.

"Hey get moving! You're gonna get soaked!"

"That's right, bwa-ha-ha. You have a choice: Get off the bridge, giving us more time to get away from you, or we'll all get soaked!"

Tommy was laughing.

"Xiene, you are completely sinister."

"Yes, dahling, I know!" she said in a fake Russian accent.

Okay, what to do? If I get off the bridge she'll make a run for it I'll have to wait until the boat passes underneath and she'll get lost in the crowd, and by the time I find her it'll be time to go home, and I won't get revenge.

I'm staying!" he said putting his hands on his hips.

"All alright, us too!" Xiene turned Tommy around in the direction of the upcoming wave.

"Xiene, you'll get Tommy soaked! Maggie's gonna kill you!"

"Yeah, but who wants to live forever?"

Allen started walking over to grab Tommy and get him off the bridge. Suddenly he heard screaming. He turned and saw the boatload of people hitting the water. As if in slow motion, a wave of water at least six feet higher than the bridge itself came towards them. Everything went silent. Allen closed his eyes and felt hundreds of water pellets on his face. The pellets increased until a solid force slapped his entire body, sending him backward a few feet. The pellets ceased. Allen opened his eyes. Everything was blurry. *My god, I'm blind!*

"Here you go," Tommy said.

Allen looked down at Tommy holding Allen's glasses that had been knocked off.

"Thanks."

He put them on and through speckled lenses examined himself dripping on the bridge like a mop. Xiene was laughing and wringing her shirt out. Allen looked at her with her wet T-shirt, soaked jeans, and her hair like white yarn. She took off her tennis shoes and poured water out of them. Allen began laughing too.

As they walked down the asphalt road to the exit, Allen and Xiene held Tommy's hands. He was very happy, even though he looked like a wet rag dog. Xiene looked over at Allen and smiled. He smiled back, then saw yet another redhead at the exit. This one was the real McCoy. He stopped smiling and silently said "Oh-oh".

Xiene's face also got serious. Tommy still smiled. Maggie had a stone-cold, angry expression.

Xiene took the initiative. "I know what you're going to say, and I don't blame you, but Tommy came—"

"Shut up, Xiene! Just shut up!" Maggie said, waving her hands. Maggie grabbed Tommy and walked away. Allen and Xiene followed.

"You have to remember he came here to have fun!" Xiene yelled.

Maggie turned around. "Oh? And who are you, the Commissioner of Fun?"

"No, but—"

"But nothing! You deliberately went against my orders and took him on that ride! And you," she pointed at Allen, "I don't believe you went along with her!"

"Maggie, Xiene has a point. You have been—"

"I knew you would take her side! No matter what she does, you go along with it!"

"What?" Allen said with a confused look.

Maggie turned and hurried towards the exit, dragging Tommy along.

Allen turned to Xiene. "What now?" he asked.

"I don't care!" She waved her arms up and down. "She's not going to listen to anything I have to say!"

"I say we follow her unless you want to walk home." Allen and Xiene gave chase.

In the parking lot, Tommy started whining. "I don't want to go home!"

"An hour ago you were begging to go home. Now you don't want to go!" Maggie yelled.

"But I wanna stay now!"

"Too late! Get in the car!"

"No!"

Maggie paused. "Get in the car!" She pointed.

"I don't wanna!"

Maggie began to walk around to Tommy.

"Tom, go ahead and get in," Xiene said.

He got in. Maggie turned around and looked up as if she had given up. Xiene got in the back seat. Allen waited until Maggie turned back around and walked towards the car before he got in.

On the highway the destined rain storm hit. Traffic came to a crawl. Everyone sat in the car in silence. Xiene was picking at the bottom of her tennis shoe. Her eyebrows were down.

Tommy sat up front, arms crossed. Maggie gripped the steering wheel and sighed periodically. Allen tried to figure out what to do. Of most of the fights he's had with Xiene, Maggie and Beverly had always helped him out. But this problem was different. He felt like Xiene didn't do anything bad, and Maggie was just being a protective mother, which is what some kids should have had. *Neutral ground,* he figured, would be his goal.

"So much for the sun dance," he said, expecting at least Xiene to respond. He looked over. She was digging in the bottom of her shoe with her knife. "See, Maggie? We would have gotten wet anyway."

Maggie ignored him.

Okay, I'll try Tommy "So, Tommy, except for leaving, did you enjoy the park?" He nodded his blond head. "Think you'll ever come back?" He shook his head. "Really? Why not?" *As if I didn't didn't know.*

After a long pause, Tommy said: "Everyone fighting."

"Yeah, I know how you feel, but it's not really anyone's fault. I mean, Xiene is just a big kid at heart, being herself." Xiene looked up at Allen. "And your mother is just trying to keep you out of trouble so you won't go back to Florida with a broken arm or something." Maggie looked in the rearview mirror. "And me? Well, I don't know what I did. I guess I could have been more forceful in telling Xiene not to do some of her silly stunts." Xiene scrawled at Allen. He smiled back, as if to say 'Please don't kill me—I'm working here'. "And I guess I should have told your mother that you're a human boy, which means you're going to get immune to most diseases in the world and sometimes you're going to try some stupid stuff, just like all the other boys, and maybe break your arm or leg and the only thing your mother can do is guide you in safely instead of yelling, and—"

"That's enough! Allen," Maggie interrupted.

The car once again became silent. Xiene continued with her shoe carving.

Allen, tired of trying to figure out what she was doing, leaned over to see. She was carving her name on the bottom. "You realize you carved it backward? When you leave a footprint, it will say 'ɘnɘiX'.

"What?" Xiene put her foot down and lifted it, looked at it, and then put it down again as if leaving a footprint. "No, It won't!"

She smiled and tried to slap his shoulder. Allen blocked her hand and said: "Too slow!" Xiene laughed and slapped his other shoulder, he didn't have time to block it.

"Too slow!" She said.

Tommy lifted and looked over the seat to see what was going on. Xiene was about to start playing with him but stopped. "Tommy, you better turn around. If we get into a car accident, you'll break your back in half,"she said.

Tommy turned around.

Allen patted Xiene's hand. She lifted his left arm placed it around her shoulders and leaned on his chest.

The traffic moved faster. They made it to downtown. Traffic slowed down again as the rain got worse.

Maggie broke the silence. "You really don't want to come back here?" she asked Tommy.

"No."

"Why?"

"You're always fighting."

"Don't they fight where you live?"

"All of the time."

"Hmm." Maggie thought for a few minutes.

Xiene fell asleep on Allen's chest. She was drooling. Allen looked around for something to prevent her from dripping on him. He put the Six Flags map between his chest and her mouth.

"The only reason I yell is because I don't want anything bad to happen to you," Maggie said.

Tommy got an angry expression.

Allen looked around for a handkerchief.

"Tommy, I love you."

"You don't act like it."

"How am I supposed to act?"

"I don't know."

Xiene's eyes opened when Allen started wiping her mouth with an old, used dry tissue he found in between the seats. She started dry-spitting. "What are you doing?"

"You were drooling."

"I was not!"

"You were too!"

"I was not! If I were drooling I would be doing this…" She leaned her head over Allen's lap and opened her mouth.

Allen hopped over to the other side of the car just when spit appeared out of her mouth.

"You are the grossest person I have ever met in my life!" he yelled.

Xiene wiped her mouth and laughed. Tommy joined her. Xiene leaned over the seat. "You see, Tommy, if you don't listen to your mom, you'll grow up to be a disgust-o just like me."

Maggie smiled.

Later, at the Mellow Mushroom Pizza Parlor, the group sat at the corner table near the neon sign. Xiene pushed a wadded napkin along the table by blowing through a straw. Allen blew it in a different direction. She blew it back, signifying the start of a game. Tommy joined in. Maggie watched. The paper went back and forth, sometimes landing on the floor only to be picked up and returned. It blew into Maggie's space. She looked down at it. Everyone went silent. She sighed, picked up a straw, removed the paper from the end, and blew the rest. The wrapper flew off and hit Xiene right between the eyes. She bent back in mock pain, screaming, "Argh! My third eye. I'm holistically blinded!"

Maggie almost fell over backward laughing.

✖

The next day Allen stopped by the house on his way home from work to see Tommy off, and to have dinner with Xiene before she headed off to work. When he approached the house he spotted Xiene in the front yard sitting on the porch, playing with Beverly's old 1950's bicycle. Her biking pants gave him the clue she had dragged the 500-pound monster down from the attic and had been running errands with it.

"My god, how did you get that thing down?"

Xiene looked up and continued tightening the wheel with a monkey wrench. "It wasn't easy. This thing is like a tank. It's a bitch getting up a hill."

"I can imagine. Where's Mag and the kid?"

"She's finger-painting with him."

"Oh? Sounds like she definitely loosened up a bit."

"Yeah."

Xiene's voice sounded down.

"What's wrong?"

"I don't know. I guess I'm feeling kind of left out."

"You know he came up here to spend time with Mags."

"Yeah, but you know, I guess…" Xiene paused for a while.

"You guess what?"

"I don't know."

"I know you like having a kid around."

"No!"

"Yes, you do. You have mother instinct, a biological clock."

Xiene squirted Allen's shirt with her oil can.

"That does it!" Allen gave chase. After riding all day, Xiene was too tired to get away. Allen grabbed her around the waist and tackled her onto the grass. He turned her over and pinned her. She tried to free herself but Allen finally got her in a helpless position.

"Ha-ha!" Now I've got you. What shall it be? Spit in your face?"

"No!" she screamed.

"No? Vomit." Allen fake-gagged. Xiene struggled to free herself but to no avail. "Ha-ha, a bit tired, aren't we?"

"Allen, you bastard! Let me up!"

"On one condition!"

"What?"

"Liver sandwich!"

"Again? What is with you and that damn sandwich? Is it a sexual fantasy of yours or something?"

"No, it's the food you hate the most!"

"What?… No, it's not!"

"Yes, it is. You told me threw up all night after eating liver!"

"Yeah, and I also drank a fifth of Jack Daniel's before that!"

Allen thought for a minute. She was right, he had forgotten that part. "Then, what do you hate?"

"I hate you! Now get off!" She struggled. Allen picked a blade of grass and began tickling her nose. "What food do you hate?"

"Stop!" she yelled and laughed. Allen continued brushing her nose hairs while a car pulled up. Allen paused.

Xiene looked back at the car. "Who's that?"

"I think it's CJ."

"Let me up!" Xiene wiggled away from Allen, stood up, and brushed the grass of her behind.

"Love that Spandex," Allen replied, watching the butt ripples travel down her legs.

C.J. got out of the car. He was tall and skinny, with brown hair and a mustache. He had a brown suit on. No tie. Allen stood up.

"Tommy here?" C.J. asked.

"He's inside with his mom," Xiene answered.

"I'll get him," Allen said, heading towards the house. He figured finding Tommy would be easier than holding one of those uncomfortable fake conversations you have with people you don't want to know. When Allen went inside he found Tommy and Maggie on the kitchen floor finger-painting. Maggie took some red and dabbed Tommy on the nose. He laughed and put some blue on her nose.

Allen felt like the grim reaper of bad news having to end their fun.

"C.J.'s here."

All fell silent. Maggie then began to gather up the mess. "Tommy, you go upstairs and wash up."

Tommy got up and walked to the stairwell. He left a blue handprint on the wall before he started climbing. Maggie looked over at the print and then smiled, almost crying. She muttered, "Damn artist."

Allen walked over to Maggie and tried to help her clean up.

"No, I'm alright. Allen, why don't you go outside and keep Xiene from attacking C.J.?"

"Good idea." Allen headed out, hearing Maggie sniffling behind him

Xiene had returned to the porch and resumed fixing the bike. C.J. sat on the hood of his Trans-Am, smoking a cigarette. D*id Xiene tell him not to come in the yard, or was it his choice?* Allen sat down next to Xiene. She struggled to get a rusted bolt off the back tire.

Allen looked at C.J. " I wonder what his wife looks like."

Xiene ignored Allen's question and continued struggling with the bolt. Her face was stressed.

"Where's the oil?" he asked.

"On your shirt."

He looked down at the brown stain on his T-shirt. "Oh, yeah, thanks, Xiene."

"Don't mention it."

A long pause. Xiene looked kind of pissed. "Alright I know this is a silly question, but what the hell did I do?" He asked.

"Nothing." She stripped the bolt.

"Well, you're mad at me."

"I am not!"

"Yes, you are."

C.J. looked over at Xiene and Allen. Xiene stripped the bolt again. "Goddamn it!" She threw the wrench down and put her head on her hands. Allen put his arm around her. She lifted her head.

"It's just…it's…"

"What?"

"When I'm with Tommy I find myself wanting to have kids."

"Yeah, so?"

"So, nothing. I don't want kids! Ever!"

Allen felt confused. She seemed to get along with kids so well. "Why not?"

"I don't want them to go through the things in life I've been through. I mean, you know how life is just a cesspool, one shitty thing after another."

Allen smirked. "Yeah, it is. So?"

"So how can a human being be so cruel as to curse a creature with the poison called life?"

"Gall-lee, Xiene, what brought this on?"

She turned her head. "I knew you wouldn't understand."

"What's there to understand? Life sucks and you die. They've been saying that since Biblical days. You know that. Why are you so surprised?"

"Because things got worse! Families don't stay together anymore. Drugs everywhere! Child molesters! Parents that treat you like shit!" Xiene gestured towards C.J." "It's so hopeless!"

Allen thought for a minute. "You know, someone once said ' Today's youth are undisciplined and the world will come to an end very soon.'"

"So? Sounds about right to me," Xiene said, putting her head on her knees.

"This was said during the Roman days."

Xiene turned her head and looked at Allen. "You're full of shit."

"Nope."

A long pause. Tommy came up behind them on the porch carrying a little suitcase. Xiene stretched up. "Okay, kid, you have everything?"

He nodded.

"Tommy!" C.J. called.

Tommy glanced at his dad, then back at Xiene. She squatted down. "Now, are you gonna behave yourself?" He nodded. "Don't do that. Give your dad and his wife hell." Allen bumped Xiene. "I'm just kidding—sorta. You behave yourself, and I'll see you the next time you come to Hotlanta."

"I don't wanna go."

"We don't want you to go, but life…life is unfair sometimes so you just have to enjoy what you have." Tommy still looked sad. "I'm sorry, I sound like a Hallmark card."

"What she means," Allen interrupted, "is we'll write you, and you make sure you write back."

"Yeah, Tommy, I write good letters. Right, Allen?"

"Allen thought of the letter she sent him cut into at least fifty pieces. It took him hours to assemble and read it. Hopefully, she will be more lenient with Tommy.

"So you make sure you write back, okay?" He nodded. "Give me a big kiss." Xiene gave him a peck on the lips and a big hug. Allen had to tap her shoulder to get her to stop

Tommy reached his hands up to Allen. Allen picked him up and hugged him. Xiene wiped her face. Allen carried Tommy to his dad.

Allen looked behind him at Maggie waving from the porch She then crossed her arms and looked up as if to keep her emotions intact. Xiene also had her arms crossed and was kicking at some leaves on the walkway.

"Hey, Tiger," C.J. said, reaching over for Tommy.

Allen handed him over. "Take care, kid."

C.J. took Tommy to the passenger side of the car. "Did they treat you okay?"

Allen felt like saying, 'Yeah, you can hardly see the bruises and whip marks'.

C.J. walked around to the driver's side. *Not much for long visits,* Allen thought. Tommy hopped in and put his hands against the window. C.J. said something to Tommy. He put his hands on his lap. Xiene slowly walked over to Allen. Maggie made her way down the porch steps. The car revved and then crept away, Tommy was staring at the threesome. They watched until the car went out of sight.

Xiene put her hands behind her head. Maggie wiped the tears off her cheeks.

"Goddamn it!" Xiene said.

"Gee whiz, Xiene, you guys act as if he's going to be murdered or something."

"Might as well!" She crossed her arms. Maggie put her arm around Xiene.

"Oh, don't worry. He'll be okay." She patted Xiene's back. Xiene turned and they hugged. "I'm sorry, Pumpkin," Maggie said.

"It's alright," Xiene said. They continued hugging.

Allen looked down the street at the setting sun. "What time do you have to be at work?"

Xiene checked her watch. "Shit! I have to get ready! She pulled from Maggie. "Love you."

"Love you, too," she responded. "Love you, too, Allen," Maggie said.

"And I love you, Maggie," Allen said in a Peewee Herman voice.

"Then why don't you marry her?" Xiene said in her best Peewee voice.

They all laughed. Xiene ran into the house.

"So, when's Bev getting back?"

Maggie became dead serious. "I don't know."

"What?"

"We had a fight before she left."

"About what?"

"Tommy. The judge thought it would be a good idea if Beverly wasn't around for his visit."

"What? That's stupid! They can't do that!"

"Well, they did."

"Why didn't you fight it?"

"Because I wanted to see my son."

Allen couldn't respond to that reason. "You're not breaking up, are you?"

"I don't know. We'll see when she comes back."

Allen breathed harder to settle the anxiety in his stomach. Maggie looked at Xiene running off the porch She had changed her shirt and now wore one with 'Fuck Censorship!' on it. She patted Maggie on the shoulder.

"See you later, Red."

"Okay, Blondie."

Xiene grabbed Allen's right hand with her and dragged him to her hearse. "I'll call you on my break."

"Alright. I'll be waiting patiently by the phone like a faithful dog." He said.

"Woof! Woof!" She slapped his butt.

Does she know that Maggie and Beverly had a fight? He decided he would discuss it tomorrow. This will give Beverly time to tell her.

"Later, Shithead!" Xiene kissed Allen.

"Alright, Liver Breath."

As Xiene got into her car, Allen swatted her behind. She scrawled. He looked back at the house.

Maggie was carrying the bike inside.

Xiene rolled down her window. "You better run, you bastard! I'm giving you a five-second head start!"

"Yeah, right."

Xiene screeched the hearse down the street, then weaved into a screeching 3-point turn. Not wanting to chance it, Allen speed-walked to the curb. Xiene headed right at him with an evil grin on her face. He jumped onto the bumper of a Volkswagen seconds before the hearse came within a foot of hitting him. Xiene screeched to avoid the Volkswagen and headed down the street. She tooted her horn three times before rounding the corner.

Allen put his hands on his hips. "She should <u>not</u> have kids."

THE RING!

It was a stupid thing to do. Perhaps the stupidest he has ever done. Allen reached into his wallet and pulled out $300. He checked the bills and then handed them to the saleswoman.

"Okay, out of $300?" She opened the register. "And your change." She handed him $11.80. "All alright, you want me to wrap it for you?"

"No, thanks. It comes in a little box," Allen said before realizing she already knew that. Allen put the box in his backpack.

"Okay. Have a good day. I hope she says yes."

"Thanks. Me, too."

The butterflies in Allen's stomach didn't stop his hands from shaking. He now had the task of getting the box home without being robbed. *Step one!*

Allen left Lennox Mall and headed towards the subway station. Periodically he would pat his backpack to feel the box. Everyone everywhere looked like potential criminals with x-ray vision. Allen panicked for a second. *The receipt!* He reached into his pants. He felt it next to his keys. He took it out and put it in his wallet. The thought of not being able to return the box after Xiene says no.

Allen had heard criminals can smell fear on victims like dogs. If this were true, he would have a sign on his back that says 'Rob me, please'. Whenever anyone looked at him longer than five seconds, he would walk away from them. A tourist almost caused Allen to jump onto the third rail when he came up from behind and asked how to get to Underground Atlanta. "I don't know," Allen lied to get him away.

As he rode the subway north, towards his neighborhood he thought about the current changes happening in his life: Monroe, Brandon, and Allen decided they would all get a house together, Beverly was spending more and more time away from Maggie and seemed to always be out of town for one protest or another, and Xiene's sister, Mary, had graduated from Tech and returned to Virginia. But despite all of the changes, Allen had but one thing on his mind: getting the box home.

Today was special. Perhaps the best day of his life. Xiene's and his third anniversary. Tonight, they would meet and have a candlelit dinner. Then, when the time was right, Allen would ask her, like he'd done once before, to marry him. The only difference, he would have ammo this time.

Allen looked around the subway. Only one other person on board, an old lady in the back. Figuring it was safe to open the box, he pulled it out of his backpack. He opened the little suede top and peeked at the $250 diamond ring. *Two* weeks' *paycheck and I still haven't bought* the *wine.* The subway door opened. He ran off the train before the warning bell went off.

What if she says no? She said no before, but I was sort of joking when I asked her. If she says no and I'm dead serious, I may kill myself on the spot. Would that be bad dinner etiquette?

He crossed the street and began the mile walk home. This is the stupidest thing I've ever done. Why would Xiene marry me? I'm poor, uninspiring, lazy. 'But you're funny, intelligent and honest.' Mean, perverted, sexist. 'Sweet, chivalrous, talented.' Allen argued with himself back and forth the rest of the walk.

He spotted Oswald's car behind Mi Cha's. Everyone enjoyed using Brandon's and Allen's apartment as a headquarters, as it is a midpoint between each of their homes. *If this apartment wasn't at this location would Oswald and Mi Cha stop seeing each other rather than drive the extra 15 minutes?*

The door was unlocked. Loud music was playing. The washing machine was on, and Brandon was vacuuming upstairs.

"Hi," Mi Cha said, sitting on the couch. "Did you get it?"

Allen reached into his bag and handed her the box.

"Oh, that's beautiful. How much?"

"What?"

"How much?" she asked, putting it on. It didn't fit. "Gosh, Xiene has big fingers."

"No, you have tiny fingers."

"How much?"

"Too much!"

"Really?" Mi Cha held her hand against the blue light of the dusk-lit window. "I like this. Can I have it?"

"Sure. But you have to marry me first."

"Okay!"

"Hey!" Oswald complained, coming out of the kitchen holding a pair of socks, "that's my whoa-man," he said in his best Tennessee accent.

"Oh well, you'll have to give the ring back."

"You got it?" Oswald asked.

"Yep."

Mi Cha took it off and handed it to Oswald."

"Oooh, a sparkly." He examined it and then tried to put it on. "Gosh, Xiene has tiny fingers."

Mi Cha laughed.

"So, when's the moment?"

"Tonight at ten, Oakland Cemetery."

"What? Why there?" Mi Cha asked.

"That's where we met."

"I've always said she was grave-robbing," Oswald inserted. "Maybe that's where she'll get his ring."

Allen reached into his backpack and pulled out one of Xiene's eyeball rings. Mi Cha took it.

"Where did you get this?"

"It's Xiene's. I swiped it to get her ring size."

"She's going to kill you for stealing her ring."

"Yeah, right. Here, Xiene have a diamond ring. Uh, and by the way, I borrowed the other ring that you hardly wear anymore," Allen said sarcastically.

The vacuum cleaner cut off upstairs and Brandon came down. "You got it?"

Oswald handed it to Brandon."

"Oh, pretty! How much?"

Allen half-masted his eyelids. "If someone asks me that one more time—"

"You never told us!" Mi Cha said.

"It's enough to piss me off if she says no."

Brandon put the ring on his pinky. "Hey, it fits. Now we're married!"

"Give me that!" Allen yelled, thinking of it getting stuck on Brandon's hand.

He tugged. "Oh, shit, it won't come off," Brandon half-jokingly said.

"It better, or I'm getting a hacksaw. And it's not for the ring."

Brandon pulled the ring off. "Golly, what a grumpus. I wouldn't marry you if you were the last man on Earth."

Everyone laughed.

Allen polished the ring while Oswald tried to tell him what CD was playing and how much he paid for it.

The phone rang. Brandon answered. "Oh, hi. How are you?" He took the phone into the kitchen.

Allen put the ring back in its box. "Gosh, what the hell am I going to wear?"

"To a cemetery?" Oswald asked.

"Wear all black," Mi Cha suggested.

"That's original. You know even yuppies are starting to wear all black. It's like the whole county's in mourning.

"Allen, telephone!" Brandon yelled. Allen walked into the kitchen. "Okay, I'll talk to you later. Bye-bye." Brandon handed Allen the phone and punched him on the arm.

Allen figured it must be Xiene by the 'you big lug' punch. "Hello?"

"Hi, sweetie," Xiene said slowly in a very happy voice.

"Hello, dahlink."

Xiene sighed. Allen sighed. He felt like a high school student in love for the first time.

"So, where were you? I called earlier.

"Playing video games at Lennox."

"Oh, you vid addict."

"That's me. They're less than drugs and I can't go to jail with a Gameboy in my back pocket."

Xiene giggled. "Did you get some wine?"

"No," Allen said in a whiney voice.

"Oh, that's too bad," she said in a whiney voice.

"I'll get some at the liquor store on my way to Oakland," he whined back.

"Okay, enough of that. What are you wearing?"

"I don't know...a polka dot shirt and a tutu."

Xiene laughed. "Boy, you're in a strange mood, Allen."

"Yeah, of course. Always."

"Anyway, you bring some candles, too. I'm bringing the grub and the utensils, and I'll see you at ten, okay?"

"Right, don't be late."

"Hey, speak for yourself."

"Hey, if I showed up on time it would be out of character," Allen added.

Xiene giggled. "Okay, sweetie, see you later."

"Right. Love you."

"Love you more."

"Ha! I doubt that."

"Ha! yourself."

Allen and Xiene then blew each other raspberries before hanging up. "Who says human speech never evolves?" he said to Brandon watching from the living room.

As Allen took a shower, he remembered all of the things he had to do. He forgot flowers and candy, the traditional courting gifts. He pictured himself looking like Jethro Bodine from the Beverly Hillbillies. 'Mrs. Xiene, I'd sure be mighty proud if you be my sweetie,' he would say, giving her the candy and flowers. He decided to get abnormal candy and flowers—maybe nightshade and Gummy Worms.

Allen dressed in Xiene's favorite outfit of his: black pants and boots, a white shirt with a pearl-studded bolo tie, his black coat, and a black fedora Xiene had given him on his birthday.

"Oooh, look at you, you look like a gangster," Mi Cha said as Allen descended the stairs.

"Thanks." Allen patted himself. "The ring! Where is it?"

"On the kitchen table," Mi Cha said, pointing.

Allen quickly rushed over and located it.

"We aren't nervous, are we?" Oswald said.

"Who, me? Ha! Nerves O'Steele they call me. Look, my hands aren't even shaking." Allen held out his right hand and made spastic shaking motions with it.

Because Allen was running behind schedule, Brandon drove him to a liquor store to pick up the wine, and then to an A&P for the candles.

In the A&P, they talked.

"What if she says no?" Brandon asked.

"It depends on why. If she gives a good reason, then I'll just put it off."

"Hmm." Brandon picked up a package of Goya black beans. "What if she says yes?"

"First of all, I'll faint." Allen paused. Then what? Do we go out and get hitched? Put it off? Who's going to pay for this?

"Where will you live? What about kids and a house?"

Butterflies flowed into his stomach. "I don't know what I'll do."

"Hmm. You sure you're ready for this?"

"Of course. But I don't know, I just have this feeling and I know she feels it too. Like we have reached that level." He gestured with his hand over his head. "That level where all of the bullshit is out of the way and you don't argue anymore—at least about anything big, and you just want to spend all day with that person. I mean, we call each other two times per day and spend all day Saturday and Sunday together. And the biggest thing of all: Whenever I mention things like our kids or long relationship goals like that, Xiene likes talking about it. She even brought up what she would wear if we got married." He picked up some white candles.

"What would she wear?"

"I don't know, something silly like wrapped in cellophane with nothing underneath.

Brandon raised an eyebrow. "Hmm."

"What?"

"Nothing." Brandon turned and looked at some birthday cards.

Brandon dropped Allen off at the subway station and he rode it to Martin Luther King Station.

"God, am I ready for this?"

Take the ring back, and get your money back.

"But what if she's looking forward to me asking her?"

Yeah, right. Then she can ask you.

"Ha! Big fat chance. Xiene may be a 90s kind of woman, but she still believes in some old-fashioned ideas."

Really? Name one.

"Shut up!" He told his conscience.

Forty minutes later, he arrived at the Martin Luther King Station.

He ran down the stairs and away from the station as fast as possible. He felt that Auburn Avenue and the Martin Luther King area were okay during the day, but at night you see some shady characters hanging around the station.

The cemetery was dark, the only sounds were the road near the cemetery and the crickets. The gate was closed, but the five-foot-tall wall was easy to get over. He hoped a security guard wouldn't show up, saying, 'Finally someone's breathing in here. I can now practice my kung fu!' *No guard in sight.*

The path was not well-lit. He wouldn't be able to see the undead Confederate soldiers lunging at him. At a jogging pace, he looked for Xiene. *If they kill me, they'll have to catch me!* he figured. He ran straight to the mausoleum where he had met her three years ago. No sign of her. He checked his watch against the moonlight. *Damn LED.* He tried to rock his wrist back and forth to read it. He figured it was either:

10:14 or 10:34 pm

He didn't know if being in a cemetery after hours was churning his bowels, or if it was the waiting for Xiene. He paced back and forth. *Where are you?* What must have been thirty minutes passed. He tried to check his watch again. A car's headlight peered over the wall from the nearby street. He lifted his arm to use the light. He walked around the tomb trying to get a better view. "10:45? 10:50? What the hell does this say?" Suddenly, he walked into someone.

"Ten forty-five," they said in a scary voice.

As He jumped back ten feet or more and said, "Goddamn! Son-of-a-bitch!" He recognized Xiene in mid-flight. By the time he landed, she was already howling with laughter. Allen tripped backward over a small tomb and landed on his back. He played as if he had been knocked out.

Xiene stopped laughing. "Allen? You alright?" Allen made sure he lay perfectly still. "Oh, god, what have I done? What can I do? Mouth to mouth?" He almost smiled but kept his control. "Mouth to dick?" He felt her hand on his zipper. This almost worked, but he still kept calm and showed no expression. "I know…"

He heard her get up and walk away. *What could she plan better* than mouth-to-dick*?* He heard her footsteps, then silence. Suddenly, wine splashed onto his face and up his nostrils.

This worked. He got up and choked, wheezed, gagged, and tried to get the wine out of his nose. Xiene corked the wine and again howled with laughter.

"You are completely insane!" he said, taking his glasses off and wiping his face with his coat sleeve.

"You're alive, Allen! I don't believe it!"

He cleared his nostrils. *Why in the world do I want to marry her?* He looked over at her. She was holding her stomach and laughing so hard tears were forming. Her white hair shining blue in the moonlight matched her 1960s dress with white pumps. To complete the match, two long formal white gloves and on one, a large tacky diamond ring matching her earrings.

Xiene caught her breath. "Oh, lord, I needed that." She took a Japanese fan out of her white purse and cooled herself.

"Good lord, what are you wearing?"

"You like it? I saw it in a wind-a and I just had to have it," she said like Scarlet O'Hara.

"Wait, give me your lighter."

She rummaged into her purse, pulled out her Godzilla lighter, and tossed it to Allen. He unwrapped a candle and lit it. The blue light on Xiene now shone a warm, orange glow. She looked like a romantic painting. "My god…"

She twirled around. Allen could tell she had gotten a professional makeover. Her hair was different, too: What had grown back from her previous experiment had now been cut on one half, the rest left long and covering up half of her face. The dress could now be seen to have little pearls on the bottom and top pushing her cleavage up in a 1700s style, Allen's favorite century for sexy women's clothes. He was speechless.

"Well?" She twirled back and forth. He wondered if she had on 17th-century underwear, another favorite of his. "Hello?" Xiene leaned forward and snapped her finger twice in his face.

"Xiene?"A long pause. *Ask her! Now! No, wrong time!* "You are the most beautiful thing I have ever seen in my life."

"Thing?" She questioned.

"Things, like a flower or a sky or—" Allen remembered the flowers. He reached into his A&P grocery bag and pulled them out.

"Oh, how sweet." She smelled them. "A&P, right?"

He smirked. "Welll, excxxcuse me!"

"Xiene laughed. "I'm just kidding. Thank you." She leaned forward and kissed him.

He felt like grabbing her and ravishing her on the spot, but the thought of the candle catching her on fire told him to pull away. "Oops!"

"Here, give it to me."

"Beg your pardon?"

"The candle, you goob!"

He gave her the candle. She held it down and let it melt into the marble slab of someone named Mary Dickey. They then stood the candle upwards in the hot wax.

"Aren't you kind of desecrating a grave doing that?"

"Hey! I'll clean it up! Now stop complaining and kiss me!"

He grabbed her waist and pulled her to him. They stared at each other. Xiene looked up at Allen's hat. She took it off and tossed it over her shoulder. It landed on the hand of an angel statue nearby.

"Good lord, how did you—"

Xiene kissed him before he finished his question. After five or so minutes of lip-locking, they pulled away. He concentrated on his heartbeat. His method of rapidly reducing a hard-on. Xiene bent down and started getting more items out of her environmental canvas shopping bag. He reached into his plastic biodegradable-but-only-if-the-bags-are-left-in-the-sun-unfortunately-garbage-is-usually-buried shopping bag and pulled out two glasses and three more candles.

After they had lit the other three candles, they sat down on a checked blanket. He could see even more of Xiene. She was wearing a black broach with a white heart on it.

"What's that?"

"Oh, this?" She bent her head down. "This belonged to my grandma, god rest her soul."

"She dead?"

"No, Allen, people usually say 'god rest her soul when you want them to fall down the stairs and break their hips."

"Well, excuse me. I didn't know. I never heard you say anything about god before."

"Hey, I believe in god despite my parents."

"Then why don't you ever go to church?"

"I didn't say I liked religion. I think it's all a bunch of bullshit used by the rich to control poor people and—"

He raised his hand. "Excuse me."

"What?"

"Can we switch subjects? Your face is getting kind of red."

Xiene giggled. "I'm sorry.

"Anyway, it belonged to your grandmother."

"Yeah, she gave it to me before she died. She was my inspiration, you know."

"Really?"

"Yeah, she wore pants before women's lib and smoked cigars."

"She a lesbian?"

Xiene searched for something on the ground to throw at Allen.

"I'm sorry! I'm sorry!" he pleaded.

Unable to find anything to kill Allen with, Xiene continued her story. "Anyway," she said loudly, "She was her own person, who did what she wanted."

"Who's mother is she?"

"My mother."

"What? Incroyable!" How cool, independent like Xiene's grandmother have such a stuffed shirt like Xiene's mother. "Why is your mother so tight?"

"I don't know. I think it's Child Rebel Syndrome. You know, whatever the parents are like, there must be a >5% chance the kids will think differently.

"Hmm. So if you had kids, they would be stuffed shirts?"

"Well, it depends—if you're the father, probably not."

"Why not?"

"Because you're already a stuffed shirt, so our kids have a 50/50 chance." He lowered his eyebrows, bugged out his eyes, and sighed in anger. "Oh, you're not that bad, but let's face it, you can be kind of conservative sometimes."

He raised his finger in the air. "I refuse to be cast in the same class with George Bush and David Duke."

Xiene laughed. "Chill out. I like the fact that you're more…shall I say, more reserved than me."

"That's better."

"But let's face it, Allen, you could loosen up sometimes."

"Just like you can tighten up sometimes."

"True, true." A long pause. "I guess that's why we need each other."

"I guess so." She leaned forward and they kissed for a few minutes.

Xiene held the wine up to her nose. "What year is this?"

"How would I know," He got the cheese and French bread out of Xiene's bag.

"Hmm, 1982. Is that a good year?"

"Yeah, I think so. That's the year the grapes were attacked by beetles and harsh winter weather."

Xiene stared at Allen, not sure if she wanted to drink the wine now.

"I'm just kidding."

She took a sip.

"See, I can be loose sometimes."

"I didn't say you couldn't joke, I just said you're a lot more reserved than me."

"Oh, really? Like what?"

"Can we change the subject?" she pleaded.

"No. What do you mean?"

She held her hand up and drank as if to say 'Hold on'. She put the glass down on Mary Dickey. "Okay, I'll give you an example. "Remember when we first met?"

"No, I don't. I have no idea why I'm here." He rolled his eyes.

Xiene put her hands on her hips and tilted her head. "Anyway, on our second date, I took you to my apartment and we were sitting on the couch and you didn't take advantage of me. We just sat there watching *Pink Flamingoes*."

"Oh, yeah, right. Here it is, the second time I meet this woman I found in a graveyard, and you expect me to jump your bones? I didn't even know your name was Christine at that point. I didn't know anything about you. You could have been the AIDS poster child as far as I'm concerned."

"You sure changed your mind on the third date."

"Being drunk did help."

"You weren't drunk!"

"I was, too! We went to The Point, and I had two beers."

Xiene raised an eyebrow. "Allen, you and I both know it takes a lot of wine or liquor to get you drunk. Two beers just make you buzzy."

"So, good enough. Still loosened me up."

"Not that much. God, you were almost to the point of being obnoxious."

"I don't think I've ever seen you drunk.

"You have, you just didn't notice."

"Hmm, good point. I guess you were right, I wasn't really drunk, just happy to be in your apartment.

I wasn't about to take advantage of a drunk guy. Especially after what happened to me in high school. That's why I waited so long before we had sex. I wanted to be the one to decide when we did it."

"I would have waited forever."

She smiled and gazed into his eyes. "I know. That's why I love you so much, Allen, more than anyone on this Earth. You're the best thing that's ever happened to me."

Give her the ring now, you idiot!

She put her thumb and forefinger in her mouth, and then, one by one, she extinguished the candles.

"Er, Xiene, this—"

She put her right hand right on his lips. He felt her left unzipping his fly. She then leaned him back flat on the marble slab. "Lay still." She undid his pants and went down on him.

Good lord, here I am playing dead in a cemetery while a woman goes down on me. Egads, I wonder if Xiene's a necromantic.

She pulled back for a second. "You can make noise if you want." She continued.

Oh, good, she's not that weird.

After Xiene had finished him off, he returned the favor. He was wrong—1990s underwear. Being under her dress was like being under a tent, except now and then the tent supports would scissor-lock his head and squeeze.

After Xiene's climax had caused enough noise to wake the dead, Allen pulled his head out of her skirt and searched around for a security guard. None in sight. Either *they're not around, or they're watching from a distance, waiting until we finish.*

"God, Mary Dickey is going to come back and haunt us," Xiene said, pulling up her underwear.

"No, just the GBI."

"What?"

"Sodomy is against the law."

"Gee, it's so stupid. This state is so ass-backward."

"Tell me about it."

"You know, sometimes I just want to move."

"Well, why don't you?" he said, hoping she would use him as an excuse for staying.

"Duh," she said, crossing her eyes. "I don't know, Allen, why don't I leave Atlanta? Could it be er, ah, that old Southern hospitality? And could it be the 1996 Olympics they mention every goddamn day? Or, could it be—SATAN!" she yelled.

"I opt for him," he stated.

"Yes, that's right, I'm here for our local community of devil worshipers. Yes, hail Satan!" Xiene said, raising her arms up and down.

He joined her. "Yes, hail Satan!"

They laughed. "God, we are so going to hell!" She laughed.

"I know. Can you imagine someone watching us, first go down on each other on someone's tomb, then going into a devil-worshiping chant?

They laughed again. Then she got dead serious and looked up to the sky. "We're just kidding, you know!"

"Hey, I think God has a sense of humor. Why else would he have given us penguins and platypuses?"

"And bananas," Xiene added. "And gourds."

"Oh, yeah, and…and emus and kiwis—and fuzzy kiwi fruit for that matter."

"Yes, and who else but a comedian would stick us together?"He wondered if that was a criticism. "But I'm sure glad he did."

"She."

"They?"

"That works. Thanks to them, you're in my life for another year."

Now! "I have something for you."

"Oh! Me, too!" She turned and looked around. She found her shoes, put them on, and walked around the other side of the mausoleum.

"What in the world?"

She came back holding something around 16"x 20", wrapped in brown paper.

"Ho-ho a gift, eh?"

"Yep. Here you go! Happy anniversary, sweetheart." She kissed him and handed the package to him.

He felt the outside. It was a decorated wooden frame. Painting? *Why would she buy me artwork? I'm an artist. If I see something I like, I copy it. A photograph? Xiene is a photographer,* but she hasn't developed pictures in a year. Could be starting over? But she wouldn't put a photograph in this kind of frame.

"Hmm, what could this be…could it be—SATAN?" She smiled. "Enough of that We're already going straight to Hell as it is."

"Okay," she said, patting him on the shoulder. "Hold on," She took her lighter and lit the candles to illuminate the scene.

"Thanks."

"Alright, rip away, mi amor."

Allen turned it over and opened it to view the whole thing at once when he turned it over. On the back, he realized it was a canvas inside a frame. "Ah, a painting, eh?"

"Yes, yes, now turn it over!" Xiene said with giddy nervousness, hopping up and down.

Allen turned it over. He was right—decorated frame, gold color with swirls and cherub heads in the corners. The painting he immediately recognized was of him, done impressionistically but in a style he tried to place. In the painting, he stood in a pose like someone from the 1800s wearing the same outfit he now had on. He studied the the brush strokes and the color choices and realized that the style reminded him of *Monet?—not the same, but still, a good copy of his style. Abstract, in a way, but also realistic. Where did she get this from and how much?* He stared at the signature: Crystal Richards. *Sister? Cousin?* He looked at Xiene.

She looked as if she were going to wet herself waiting for his reaction. "Well ?"

"I'm speechless. It's wonderful. Who did this? Who's Crystal Richards?"

Xiene blew her hands on her knuckles and then rubbed her nails on her shoulder.

"You?"

She smiled.

"You did this?"

"Yep."

He stared at the portrait. It might not be too professional, but for a non-artist, it's beyond A+. "You? He pointed at her. "You did this?"

"Yes," she said as if insulted.

"But how? You're not an artist."

"So? I sketch now and then."

"But you're a photographer!"

"And you're an artist, yet you take some neat photographs."

The same *part of the brain.* "My goodness…this is wonderful! Thank you!"

He placed the picture down and gave her a very long, tight hug.

"Why 'Crystal Richards'?"

"That used to be my painting name. I figure if people hate my work, they can't hunt Xiene or Christine down."

"When did you start doing portraits?"

"This is the first one I've done since… you know, before that day."

"Really? Did you take art classes in high school?"

"Not really. I was just friends with the art teacher. He was so cool. I'd even go over to his house and we would draw and paint. He taught me some of his techniques."

"Wait…he didn't take advantage of you too, right?"

"No! It wasn't just me, there. We had a mini-class at his house. But, unfortunately, some other teachers thought what you thought and he had to quit or be fired."

"That sucks."

"Tell me about it. After that…that boy… I didn't want anything to do with high school after that."

"So you stopped drawing?"

'Yeah."

"Why did you start up again?"

Xiene crossed her eyes again. "Duh, I don't know."

"Okay, okay, I get it," he said picking up the painting. "Incredible! You should have never stopped. Do you realize how good you would be now?

"You think it's that good?"

"Of course, it's not a Monet, but for a—pardon the expression—amateur, you're damned good."

"Really?"

"Yes. Look, you even painted inside the lines," he joked.

Xiene took the painting, looking back and forth at it and Allen. "I don't know, I guess it looks like you."

"What did you use for reference?"

"An old photograph. You remember when we went to Stone Mountain?"

"Which time?"

"The time you tried to carry me up."

"Oh, yeah, I remember. God, that was stupid. I missed work because of that backache."

"I told you I would walk."

He stared at the portrait. He liked it more than ever. It's one thing to give someone a gift, but a part of themselves is worth a thousandfold. "Incredible." He took a deep breath and reached into his pocket to pull out the ring. *Okay. Do I say marry me Miss Xiene or Lady Christine? or…*"Wait. Why the name 'Crystal'?"

That's what my old art teacher called me. He knew I hated to be called Christine, especially after that damned horror movie came out."

"Oh, yeah. I never made the connection."

"Yeah, after that asshole..." she gestured, "you know."

"Yeah."

"He started bragging to his friends about how we had sex and called me Christine, a Mean Driving Machine. Next thing you know, the whole goddamn school was saying that. Someone even painted that on the school rock."

"Geez...I really hated high school."

Allen studied the painting's brush strokes while she continued her story.

"I didn't hate high school up until then. I was pretty popular." Xiene sat down.

"You weren't a cheerleader, were you?"

She put her fist to her mouth and pretended to be giving a blowjob.

"Okay, I assume that's a no.! But you're pretty popular now. I mean I can't go anywhere without some goober saying, hey, you're Xiene's boyfriend, aren't you?"

Xiene giggled. "I'm sorry."

"It's okay. I feel kind of like royalty."

"Yeah, I just like to brag about you to my friends sometimes."

"Oh, really?"

"Of course. Don't you brag to your friends about me?"

"Only the cool ones. Everyone else just turns their head sideways."

"Like your family?" she asked.

"Hey, they like you."

"Your dad's wife doesn't seem to."

"Well, that's her. But everyone else likes you."

"I like your family. They're cool."

"Hmm. Everyone always says that about a family they didn't grow up in."

"Not mine."

"Hmm. Good point."

"You're the youngest, right?"

"Gee, Xiene, I'm glad you remembered."

"You don't talk very much about your family."

"So, what's there to say? We don't have gigantic events happening in my family like yours."

"Your cousins are having babies, that's a big event, and one of them went to Desert Storm, and your brother just graduated from UNC with a degree in marketing?"

"That's Paul."

"Yes. And your dad is an engineer."

"Right."

"And your mom is a school teacher working with 6th graders."

He felt flabbergasted. "Gee, whiz, what a memory. You know, I know people who still don't even know my last name."

"Marshmallow, right?"

"Ha-ha, very funny, Crystal Hamburgers."

Xiene threw the flowers at him. "Don't make fun of my name, A-lee-in!"

"Hey, Alien is at least close to my name."

"And Crystal and Christine share some letters, so there."

"Hmmm, Crystal…Crystal. I like that. I think I'll call you that when I get mad at you."

"Okay, Alien!"

He put his nose up to the painting. "Hmmm, oils?"

"Yeah."

"Gads, even I can't work in oils."

"I got a set with a book."

"Oh, god, not How to Paint by Rusty Sienna'?"

"Who?"

"You know, those TV shows that paint using a piece of toilet paper and you end up making an entire forest with a log cabin in one stroke."

"I like those shows. I always watch them when I'm sick."

"Sick is right. When I worked at the art supply store, those damn rich Dunwoody housewives would watch these shows and decide they wanted to be an artist, so they would come in buy a zillion dollar's worth of art supplies, and then bring them back."

Xiene laughed.

"Yeah, I hate those women! You know, the kind you can tell are in a big old mansion by themselves and their husbands are always off on business trips, wink-wink."

"Really?"

"And it's worse if they have kids. It's as if they take a leash off when they come in."

"Really? God, I hate kids."

"Really? I thought you liked kids. What about Tommy?

"He's great, but I can't picture myself going through nine months of bullshit."

"Well, it can't all be bad."

"Ha! Says the man! Then you can have our baby!"

'Our baby?' Yet another long-term statement. He grabbed the ring box in his pocket. Maybe I'll say: Okay here's a start, and as for having a baby, I don't care if you want to have a baby or not, and if you want to have a baby and don't want to carry it, we'll get a surrogate, even if we have to do like they did in that movie. What was that one where they used a cow? We'll get the baby and put it inside of a cow…" he said nervously. "Wait, did I say that out loud?

Xiene looked confused. Allen? What the fuck?"

"You know, like in the movie Beast Master."

"I didn't see it."

"Oh…I guess what I just said sounded insane…We'll rent it one day."

"Oh, god! Another one of your weird movies! They're so booger-head."

"Excuse me?

"You don't like movies unless someone's either fucking or killing!"

"Hey! I like foreign films!"

"Great! Fucking and killing in German, fucking and killing in French, fucking—"

"Okay, okay, so what? You only like movies that slide into the box off and slither out again!"

"Like what?'

Like those fantasy films or documentaries. Worse yet, Akira Kurosawa films."

"What's wrong with him?"

Allen made a rapid snoring sound effect.

Xiene got up and put her leg behind him and pushed him down, then straddled him. "I like art films!" she said.

"Ha! Fucking and killing in black and white!"

Xiene laughed, then began tickling him. He squirmed and wriggled as she tortured him. He tried saying 'stop!' in between laughs. She stopped when he laughed so hard that tears came out. She wiped them off his face and looked at her fingers.

"You know, I've never seen you cry."

"Sure you have. Just now."

"You know what I mean. Of all the bad things we've gone through I've never seen you cry."

"That's because I don't do it in front of you."

"Why not?"

"I don't know. Most of the time you're not there."

"Like when?" she said.

"Like the time you were in the hospital. I was so worried about you, I cried in the bathroom."

"Sure it wasn't the smell?"

"What smell?"

"The bathroom smell."

He half-masted his eyelids.

"Sorry, continue. What other time?"

"Er-ah, when Tommy left to go back to Florida. I cried on the walk to the subway station."

"And what about when we thought I was pregnant?"

"No, that was just plain panic."

"Oh really? I thought you wanted kids," Xiene mocked in a deep voice.

He blew her a raspberry, which was stupid because the spray of spit came down on his face.

"How about when Tawana Brown took over that strip joint?

"Those were definitely panic tears."

Xiene smiled then leaned down and licked the tear on his cheek.

"Hmmm, he said, getting another hard-on. He reached his hands up to put them into the bottom of her underwear.

Xiene stood up and took off her underwear. He pulled his pants down and looked around for gawkers. Xiene sat on his lap and used the dress to cover up any exposed flesh.

Fine time to be shy!

She started riding him while waving the fan under her dress to create a strange, cool sensation on their genitals. At one point she threw the fan at the candles and knocked them over.

"Good god! Bruce Lee!" he said, witnessing her lucky marksmanship once again.

Xiene increased her pace and thrashed her fist in the air between moans and groans.

"This place…I feel like I'm a vampire and you're my victim." Allen groaned.

Xiene reached down and bit him on the neck, instantly reversing the roles.

✖

Much later, Xiene and Allen lay side-by-side, on top of someone named G. Henderson, a loving father, and husband. They passed a glass of wine back and forth. Xiene took a sip, kissed him, and tried to pass it from her mouth to his. Being caught off-guard, most of it dribbled down his chin onto his shirt.

"Oops, sorry! I guess I should have warned you!" she said

"Oh no," he said, looking at his stained shirt. "I guess I look like a vampire now."

Xiene gulped down the rest of the glass.

Allen looked at the candles burning lower and lower. This reminded him of time, time slipping away. *I need to take some action with my life—right now.*

"What's this?" Xiene patted Allen's pants pocket with the ring.

"Er, nothing."

"Nothing, eh? Feels like something to me."

"It's nothing!" He got up off the ground and walked over to the candles.

Xiene followed. "C'mon, what is it? Is that my gift?"

"No, it's..."

"What?" Xiene seemed confused by Allen's shaky voice. "What is it? What's wrong?"

"N-nothing." He walked away from her.

"What did I do?"

"Nothing!" he said loudly.

"You sure are acting weird. Is there something you want to tell me?"

Allen turned and looked at her. Her hair was mussed. She had one side of her dress down, exposing her bra. And one shoe on.

He sighed and smiled.

"What?" she put her arms out, one holding the other shoe.

"Xiene," He breathed deeply. Why is this so hard? I asked her to marry me before, but that was after the Tawana Brown incident when we thought we were going to die. Now, things couldn't be better. He stared at the lights of the subway passing on the tracks five blocks away.

"What is it?"

"He sighed again. "Do you love me?"

Xiene almost did her crossed-eyes thing again but stopped herself. "Of course I do."

"How much?"

"What do you mean?"

"How much? You know, like degrees."

"This much." She spread her arms out.

"That's not very much."

"I have short arms. Is that what's wrong? You don't think I love you?" She walked over and gave him a bear hug. She pulled back with the box in her hand.

He searched himself. "You sneak!"

She laughed evilly, looking at it.

"Give that back!"

"No way! This is mine, isn't it?"

"Of course not! It's for my grandmother!"

"Your grandmother's dead, Allen."

"Whatever! Give that back."

She held up her arms and kept him at bay. "What is this? Earrings? A wedding ring?"

No! Of course not!"

"Nose ring? Nipple ring?" She put it against her nose, then her right tit.

"No!"

"Necklace? No, too small What is it? An engagement ring? God, I hope not! I wouldn't marry you if you were the last man on Earth." Xiene chuckled, then looked at the dead serious expression on Allen's face. Her face got just as serious. She bought the box down and slowly opened it. A silence lasted for what felt like years as Xiene stared into the box, her mouth, slightly opened.

Periodically, she looked at Allen, then the ring. She took it out of the box and then tried it on. *Perfect fit!* She put both of her hands to her nose and began crying. He walked over put his arms around her and comforted her. She continued to weep on his shoulder. He didn't know if this was good or bad.

Eventually, she pulled back and wiped her face. "I'm alright."

"You sure?"

She nodded. "Hand me my purse, sweetheart. He did. She pulled out her cigarettes. Allen had her lighter out and lit by the time she had the cigarette in her mouth. "Thank you." She studied the ring. "Is it real?"

"He rolled his eyes.

Xiene nervously laughed. "I'm sorry." She looked at it again. "Whew! No one's ever given me a diamond since my sweet sixteen."

"Really? I thought you get pearls on your sweet sixteen."

"Not if your family's loaded."

"Hmmm." Allen wished she would answer, but didn't want to push her. She was very nervous, more than he'd ever seen her. She was breathing hard and her left hand with the ring was shaking. She used her right to steady it.

"Gosh, would you look at me?" She waved her arms. "Why do I feel so spastic?"

It's not every day someone asks you to marry them."

"Marry." Xiene turned around." Marry," she said again. She began pacing "You want to marry me?"

"Yes."

She continued pacing. "Me?"

"Yes."

"Crazy, bleach-haired Xiene?"

"Yes her too."

Xiene bit her bottom lip and paced some more. "When did you want to marry me?'

"What?"

"You know, when did you seriously decide to go ahead with asking me?"

"I don't know. I guess a year ago."

"And you waited until now?'

"Yes."

She paced some more. "You're nuts. You know that? You know my mother, of all people, said you were going to ask me to marry you one day."

"Really?"

"Yeah, she said that when I got into the hospital. Did you talk to her about this?"

"Xiene, not to change the subject, but what are you getting at?"

"I don't know!" She waved her arms around. "My mind is just wandering back and forth!" She paced faster. He went over and grabbed her shoulders.

"Okay, now, take a deep breath."

She slowly breathed in and out.

"Okay, now are you calm?"

"Yes." She took a drag on her cigarette and threw it into the glass of wine." She sighed. "Can I have a hug?"

He held her and stroked her hair. He felt her heart slowly going back to 68 beats per minute. Xiene pulled away. "You alright?"

She nodded. "Yes."

He got down on one knee and held her hand. "Ms Richards, I'd be mighty proud if you'd be my woman. Xiene laughed and cried. He laughed. "Golly, I've never seen you like this!"

"I know I feel so stupid!" She wiped her face.

"Here." He stood up and led her to Mary Dickey. "Sit down and relax."

Xiene sat on the tomb. "Okay. I need to be alone."

"Okay. Take all the time you need. I'll be over there." Allen pointed towards the Jewish section of the cemetery. Xiene lay down on the tomb.

He walked over to the Jewish section. Its Stars of David pylons and tombstones were tightly packed together. Allen liked this section because it made him feel as if he was a giant walking through a gothic city. He sat down near Walter Steinberg's headstone. He strangely felt calmer than before. He figured his job was done. Now, it was up to Xiene.

If she says yes, then what? Okay, decide where to live, and get a better job.

Kids? House? What about no? *Hmmm, no. Ask her again three years from now. Break up?* The thought of breaking up because Xiene wouldn't marry him made his stomach nauseated. *What if she says: Allen, you're going to have to find someone else, someone who will marry you if that's what's important to you?* He felt like throwing up at such a thought. He closed his eyes and listened to the crickets, the slight rustle of the wind, and the subway train clicking on the tracks nearby. He wondered about any negative aspects if she said yes. *Would we get sick of living together?* Xiene's used tampons in an un-flushed toilet. This time He could taste vomit in his throat. Xiene in curlers, a bathrobe, and slippers with white goop on her face. He found this thought kind of sexy in a sick way. *Plus she doesn't wear that to bed now, why would she start?* Her pantyhose hanging on the shower curtain? *Doesn't bother me now, why should it* be *in the future?* Seeing Xiene every day of the year for the rest of his life? He wasn't sure if this would bother him or not. Having sex with the same woman forever. *Sex with Xiene could never get boring.* D-I-V-O-R-C-E? *Hmmm, could happen. We do fight sometimes. Who knows? What if she just flat-out says no, she doesn't want to commit to me?* This kind of angered Allen. Here he is laying out his commitment to her and she says she won't do the same!

He clenched his fists and then slowly relaxed them. He looked at the full moon he had ignored all night. He figured this was why he could see the cemetery so well. He craned his head around the tomb to spy on Xiene. She was sitting cross-legged on the tomb, examining the ring under the candlelight. She started filing her nails, signifying this was her real occupation. She then took some makeup out of a compact and started applying it to her face. *Is this a good sign?*

By the time she started brushing her hair, he had turned back around and resumed thinking. What about her smoking? Can I live with that? She's cut down a heck of a lot, and maybe she'll quit one day. Why am I acting as if I'm perfect? I'm not the cleanest person in the world. Face it, I usually clean my bedroom when I can't walk through it without slipping on something, I never wash dishes, my cooking skills could only fill a three-page cookbook, and boy, am I a grumpus in the morning!

He heard Xiene singing. He peeked around the tomb again. She was still doing her nails. He picked out a few song lyrics and recognized the song from his This Mortal Coil album. She played it whenever she came over depressed. *Bad sign!*

"Allen!" Xiene yelled.

He quickly got up and walked back very fast.

"Allen!" she yelled again, not realizing he was nearby.

"I'm here."

She jumped. "Oh, Jesus! You scared me!"

"Hmmm, that's a switch."

Xiene giggled and gestured to the other side of the tomb. "Sit down."

He sat. She reached over and grabbed his hands. He stared at her. She was smiling. She leaned forward and kissed him. When she pulled back, she then lifted his hands and kissed them both.

"Hmmm, what's that for?"

"For you being the kindest, sweetest person I've ever known."

Oh-oh, Dump City coming up!

"I mean, I've been thinking about marriage a lot before you brought it up, and I have something I want to say to you." Allen's stomach turned upside down. "First, I love you very much. You know that, right?." He nodded. "And I would love to spend the rest of my life with you."

"Is that a yes?"

"Hold on. Anyway, I wasn't going to say anything, but I think my parents are getting a divorce."

"Wait, What?" he said wondering how she got on this subject. "What makes you think that?"

"For one thing, my dad had an affair a couple of years back. My mother found out about it and made him break it off or she was gonna take my brother and sister and leave him."

"This was before you were born?"

"She was pregnant with me."

"Your dad had an affair while your mom was pregnant?"

"Yep. Pretty low, huh? He called it off. Or, so we thought."

"How did you know it started up again?"

"My mom told me. She's been so open ever since I was in the hospital."

"Wow! What about your dad? Did he talk to you about it?"

"No, of course not. But let me finish. About the time I was in high school, he started seeing that woman again, but, get this—she was married to our preacher and they had a kid. And guess who he was?

"Wait…Holy fucking shit!" He yelled. "Not that same guy that attacked you!"

"Yep, that's him."

"Holy shit! I'm so sorry!". "Wait! Did your dad know he did that to you?"

"Of course, I told my mom and dad, right after."

"And the cops? Didn't try to prosecute that bastard?

The cops didn't do shit. They acted like it was my fault

"You got blamed for that? That's bullshit!"

"That's right. Life for girls in a small southern town."

Oh, my god! She never really talked about this. I thought the guy was put in jail or something and it was all over! Xiene was smiling. "How can you smile?"

"Hey, what else can you do but smile?"

Allen was even more confused. *Am I dreaming?* "So wait your dad's lover's son rapes you? And your dad didn't believe you?"

"He took his lover's side."

"I'm surprised your mom didn't kill him!"

"The first time when she found out about the affair, she started hitting him on the head with our Christmas presents." Xiene started giggling.

"I'm glad you find this kind of funny."

"I do now." She laughed and cleared her throat. "Anyway, she woke us all up and we had to get in the car in our pajamas and she took us away to my aunt's house. You know, the one with cousin Verna and the zillion kids."

"Oh, yeah."

"Anyway, we spent a month there.

"How old were you?"

"Sixteen."

"Gads, some Christmas."

"Oh, yeah—ho-ho-ho." Xiene gulped the wine bottle. "So my dad showed up a month later saying he had found Jesus and was born again and begged my mother to come back.

"I wouldn't have."

"Me, neither but she did, figuring it was the best thing for the kids."

"Now, wait, your mother drags you out of the house and spends a month with your hick cousins and yet you don't know what was going on?"

"Hey," she held her arms out," I figured they were just fighting over nothing. You know how your parents fight sometimes."

"Boy, do I ever!"

"When they fight, you leave the room!" Allen and Xiene said at the same time.

"Exactly," she said. So you never know what's going on. Anyway, we came back home and everything was 'fine'," Xiene used her fingers to indicate quotation marks over the word 'fine'."

"Now, wait, didn't you tell me that boy's dad was a preacher?"

"Bingo!" she said, pointing. I was just getting to that."

"Oh, my god," he said, putting his hands on his face

"It's alright," she giggled, then removed his hands. Anyway, when I was going out with the Asshole, my family had become pretty religious, going to church and stuff."

"Even you?"

"Even me. I was even in the church choir."

"You? God, no way!"

Xiene nodded. "Way! Anyway, he was also in the choir and his mom conducted. I mean, I never could figure out what my mom had against them. I figured she hated him the same way most mothers hate their daughters' boyfriends. Probably why I went out with him, that Bad Boy thing.

"Ugh. How did his mom treat you?"

"She didn't like me. No notes I sang were ever good enough for that bitch."

"Hmmm, maybe that's why he dated you, too."

"No, I think it's because I'm cute."

"Also true."

Xiene chuckled.

"Okay, you were saying…"

"Yeah, so he and I would go out and he would try to fuck me and stuff, like guys do, but I was such a good girl," she put her hands together as if praying, "…that I fought him off with the power of the lord. But he got sick of it and one day he drove me to the back of a Dairy Hut, which I still can't go near, and he held me down in the back seat and, you know…" she gestured.

"Yeah, sorry."

"Anyway, I went home, my shirt all open, hair a mess, and my mom freaked. She was so…mad. My dad came home and she almost slapped the taste out of his mouth.

"This is so weird. Your parents seemed so happy together."

"Yeah, right. Have you ever seen them touch each other?'

"Hmm," no.

"All alright, then. We went to confront his parents. It was a waste of time. No one mentioned the affair, of course. Asshole's parents blasted me especially, his mom calling me a tramp and shit."

"I can't believe your parents allowed this?"

"Let me finish," Xiene said, between clenched teeth.

"Sorry."

"So, eventually my dad takes their view, obviously because he was having an affair with the boy's mom. He didn't want her to say they were sleeping together in front of the preacher, and especially my mom, who didn't know he was back at it."

"So your mom must have freaked again?"

"Oh, yeah. She stomped out of the church, yelling. I didn't know what the hell to do. Here I had my dad his lover and her husband calling me a tramp," Xiene teared up, "and my mom was leaving, so I left, too. And when I went up to her she yelled, 'Why did you have to see that boy in the first place?' which, to me, sounded like it was my fault! I think she wasn't thinking, or something. But I got so incredibly angry that I ran away from her. If I didn't, I would have slapped her and then burned down that fucking church."

"Where did you go?"

"Atlanta."

"Jesus Christ, that some run."

"Yeah, I hitchhiked all the way to Atlanta, and guess who picked me up at one point?"

"Who?"

"Beverly and Maggie."

"Holy shit, that's right! I knew that."

"Yep, they put me up in their apartment and I had the best time in Atlanta. This is when I met a lot of people I know. I was here all summer."

"Why did you go back?"

"Basically, I just wanted to finish my last year of high school, get the hell out of Richmond. When I returned, things were so different. My parents were so mad. They thought I was dead. Mary was pissed. She missed a quarter of school because I was gone."

"And Richard?"

"He was already in the Air Force, so my parents came down hard on me. You know, to keep me from running away. They became all strict: wouldn't let me date, go out—nothing. I went to school, home, church. And on weekends, I was at my grandma's."

"Wait, why were your mom and dad still together?"

"Mom still didn't know about the second affair remember? And my disappearance kind of united them with a common goal."

"Why in the world did you listen to them and follow?"

"I didn't want to make waves. I just wanted to finish high school and get the fuck out of there."

He gulped the bottle of wine. Xiene lit up another cigarette. She put it in her mouth, took a drag then looked left, at the row houses appearing over a wall around the cemetery.

"Is that Cabbage town?"

He looked. "I think so."

"Why do they call it Cabbage Town?"

"I think it's an Irish ethnic thing. You know, the smell of boiling cabbage coming from the houses."

Xiene nodded. "Anyway, where was I?"

"Got the fuck out of Dodge."

"Oh, yeah." She gulped the bottle. By the time I left high school, I didn't have one friend my senior year. I became such a recluse. I started wearing black. Everyone thought I was becoming a witch or something, so I started dressing even worse. I looked like a beatnik one day or Welsh witch the next."

"I bet your parents nipped that in the bud."

"No, they figured as long as they knew where I was and I was getting good grades, I could dress any way I wanted."

"You didn't have any friends? I mean, in high school, if any girls dressed like you, they would attract guys like me."

"Yeah, guys came onto me, I wouldn't go out with them. And girls thought I was a slut, thanks to the Asshole's story. But the only other place I could go was grandma's house."

"Pants-wearing, cigar grannie?"

"That's the one. She was the only one who believed my rape story." Xiene paused, looked down, and picked the locket up. She slowly opened it. He leaned forward. Inside, a tiny picture of her grandmother.

"No picture of your grandfather?"

"No, he died before I was born." She closed the broach and looked at the row houses again.

"So this is when you really started Xiene-ing out? When you hung around your grandma?"

"Oh, yeah. It was great." Xiene perked up. "She read poetry and taught me about witchcraft."

"She sounds so cool."

"She was great. I started smoking to be just like her." Xiene held up the cigarette. I know now her cigars are what killed her. That's why I'm trying to cut down." She mashed out the cigarette.

How did we get from 'Will you marry me' to her life story? And she still hadn't answered. "So, you were saying," he said, catching her staring at the houses again.

"Anyway, she was an artist and photographer, which is why I started taking pictures."

"Then why did you stop? It's what you went to school for. You haven't developed pictures in two years, right?"

"Guess who died two years ago? That's why I'm glad I did this painting. It's the first major art thing I've done in eons."

"You did a damn good job." He stared at the painting, leaning against a statue.

"She was the one that talked me into going to college and getting a degree, saying a woman without an education is a slave to men. That's when I applied to GSU."

"I'm surprised your parents let you come all the way down here."

"They had no choice, Allen. I was eighteen. They tried to stop me by not paying for college, but then this convenience store sign fell on my car and I sued them, or rather my insurance did, and instead of buying another car, I used that money to go to school."

"Your parents didn't take the money from you?

"How could they? It was mine."

"What happened to that money? You left college because you ran out, didn't you?"

"Do you know how much photography equipment costs? And lab fees and shit?"

In art school, art supplies would run at least $20 per week. Photography equipment must have been astronomical!

"I also lived alone, so I was paying rent and utilities and gas. I could only last three years.."

"Then you met me, right?"

"No, I didn't meet you until a year later."

"Why don't you finish school? You only have one year left."

"Because I still can't afford it. The Acid Pit only pays enough to survive. My parents have been trying to pay my last quarter, but I said, 'No way. I don't want anything from them!"

"Okay, what does all of this have to do with you marrying me?"

"Nothing. I just thought it was a neat story."

"What?"

"Just kidding! Let me finish! So, I worked here and there before I met you and that's when I started dressing weird and acting it, I guess. Every time I went home, I would spend most of my time over at grandma's. She loved my new styles. She believed in being yourself, dressing as you wish, and never let anyone take your individuality away."

Is this a hint for no?

"So, then I met you."

"Yay!" he said, raising his arms.

"Oh, and this is the weird part: I had just got back from Richmond and my grandma did my tarot and said I would meet someone very soon."

"Weird. One question, though."

"What?"

"When we met, Monroe was with us. Why not him?"

"Good question. I think it's because you seemed so confused by me, and terrified, and yet you also seemed fascinated and attracted to me. I wanted to find out how someone can be such a living contradiction. Even today, you contradict yourself constantly. Like, you're so liberal and yet conservative about it. It's so wild. You're like a yin-yang symbol." She moved her hands like a scale.

"That's what attracted you to me?"

"That and your sexual aura."

"Oh, really?"

"Oh, yeah. I wanted to nail you when we met." He cleared his throat. "But, you held off and I had to make the first move. See what I mean?" She gestured with her hands again. "Hmmm. Anyway, where was I?"

"Tarot cards."

"Oh, yeah, anyway, we got together blah, blah, blah." She waved her hand to signify time passed on, "And just when I'm getting closer to my parents again—my mom and everything seems okay, boom! My mom finds out my dad's been at it again."

"Geez, when did she find out?"

"Last week."

"Christ, you didn't mention it or seem upset."

"I was upset at first, but then I thought, hey, it's not my fault. It's my parents' problem. Let them work it out, and that was that."

"I guess your mom freaked again."

"Oh, not really. She was calm. I mean, she knew it was happening at least two years ago."

Suddenly Allen's stomach turned. "Uhh, I got to say something."

"What?"

He stood up. "I hope you won't be mad at me."

"What is it?"

He sighed. "God, I had forgotten all about this."

"What?" she yelled.

"When you were in the hospital, I heard your dad talking to the other woman over the phone." Xiene looked shocked. "I didn't say anything because I figured it was none of my business."

"Hmmm."Xiene moved her mouth to the side.

"I'm sorry. I should have told you, but you were, you know, sick. So I waited, then I forgot about it.

"Hmmm." Xiene was silent.

Oh, shit, I should have told her! I'm doomed. He turned around.

"Hey!" she called. He turned around. She gestured. "Come here!" He walked over and sat back on the slab. She leaned over and kissed him. "That's for being honest." She then put two fingers around his nose and slapped them down.

"Ow!"

"And that's for not telling me!"

"Hey, what could I do you were sick!"

"So? If I were on my deathbed, I would still want people to tell me the truth."

"Your parents looked happy, and I didn't want to ruin their relationship. Plus, I'm not sure if you would have believed me."

"Well, you know better now."

"I'll say." He rubbed his nose. "So what does this—"

"I'll get back to the proposal thing soon enough! Keep your shirt on!"

"Okay," he said, reaching for Xiene's top. He pulled it down. "You take yours off."

She slapped his hands. "Stop! Let me finish. Plenty of time for that later."

"So, how did your mom find out?"

"Get this: My parents were in church with Mary."

"The virgin mother? I'm pretty sure that's where she belongs."

"No! Mary! My sister, you dope!"

"I don't want to marry your sister."

Xiene pushed Allen onto the ground. She then poured the remainder of the wine on him. He quickly stood up and wiped himself off.

"You crazy woman, you!"

Xiene laughed.

He took off his coat and used it as a towel.

"So, they're in church…"

"And his mistress, the preacher's wife, goes up in front of the whole congregation and says, 'Everyone, I'd like to confess I've been having a non-stop affair with Donald Richards for the past twenty-six years, and I wanted to ask for you and God's forgiveness."

Allen laughed.

"What's so funny?"

"I'm sorry, I'm just picturing your dad's face."

Xiene smiled, then joined him laughing. "It's not funny," she finally said, punching his arm.

He straightened up. "You're right. But why did she do that?'

"I have no idea, guilt? But oh, man! My mom and dad have been banned from that church."

"Wait, wait, she gets up there and admits this affair, yet your parents get banned? Why?"

"Confession is good for the soul, I guess. Maybe they looked at her as a victim of lust or some shit."

"What about her preacher husband?"

"What about him?"

"He forgives her?"

"Who cares? I hope they all go to Hell."

"With Asshole, of course."

"Oh, tie him naked to the front of the train to Hell."

"What is he doing, by the way?"

"I don't know and I don't care."

"Your parents are finally getting a divorce. Is that your story? Do you think we'll be like that if we marry? I have interest in having an affair with a preacher's wife."

"Hold on, I have another thing to tell you."

"Oh, no," He groaned. "Not another story!" He turned around and laid his head between Xiene's crossed legs. She picked up her brush and hit his head. "Ow!

"Shut up and listen!" She started brushing his hair. "Beverly and Maggie are having some problems."

"Yeah, I know. It started when Tommy visited and Bev had to leave town, right?"

"Yeah, but it's gotten worse."

"What?" He sat up.

"Yeah, Allen, I think they're breaking up, too."

A dark cloud formed in Allen's mind. "No."

"That's right. Beverly's coming back to Atlanta. She's gonna get her stuff and move into a commune in Dalohnega with some friends."

"But, but why?"

"Maggie is gonna get custody of Tommy. His dad and stepmom are splitting up and the dad said he would hand Tommy over only if Beverly moves out."

"No way! That sucks."

"Way. And it does suck."

"Oh, Jesus! I can't believe it! They've known each other since the '70s—they're breaking up? That can't be. They seem so happy together! Why would Maggie do that?"

"All she kept saying was Tommy is her son, and she would do whatever she had to do to get him back."

"This sucks!" Allen yelled. He stood up and fumed in anger. He kicked a rock with his boot, stubbing his big toe. He ignored the pain and started pacing. "I can't believe it! I can't believe it!" He stared at the subway leaving the station.

Xiene got up, walked to him, and put her arms around his waist. "I know how you feel. I still can't accept it myself.

He turned around. "How long have you known about this?"

"About a week."

"Talk about me holding info. You didn't tell me! Why?"

"Ding-dong, ding-dong!" she yelled like a bell. "You have just hit reason number two."

"For what?"

"All alright, sit down."

They resumed in their old spot. She held his hand.

"Allen, I love you more than anyone I've ever known, but…" she sighed, "…but for now I really don't believe in marriage."

"But why? We're not them!"

"You weren't listening?"

"I was! Your mom and dad are nuts!"

Xiene got an angry expression. "What about Beverly and Maggie?"

"They're not married."

"No. But don't you see? Two committed couples, one with a lot of major problems and one with one major problem."

"I still don't see what they have to do with us! Big or little, we'll stick it out!."

Xiene sighed. "Let me put it this way: Do you love me?"

"Yes! Of course!"

"Do you promise to love and cherish me and to hold me forever and ever, until death do we part?"

"Yes!"

"Good. That's good enough for me."

"But it's not the same!" He stood up.

"What's the difference between what we just did and a marriage? With a marriage, if we get a divorce, I get all of your shit!"

"What shit?"

"I don't know. I Kinda like your computer."

"Ha! You can have it! But what does everyone fucking up their relationships, have to do with us?"

"Don't you see? On paper, my parents were a perfect couple, they're breaking up. Beverly and Maggie, the perfect Liberal Lesbian power couple, Splitsville!"

"Do you think we would break up?"

"I hope not. But you never know."

Allen sighed and grabbed her hands. "Xiene…I'll never cheat on you, or leave you."

"Thanks. But right now we're in love. I can't predict the future. What if I turn ugly and you and you turn into an angry dick? Then what?"

"I'd say, 'I love you, Ugly.'"

Right. And then I'd say, Thanks…" She pointed her finger at him like a gun. "Take that you dick!" Blam! Blam! Blam!"

"Why didn't you tell me about Maggie and Bev, and for that matter, your mother and father?"

"Ding-ding!"

"Again with the bell?"

"Right. You see, that's one of my points. I didn't tell you about Bev and Mag because I was waiting for the right moment. Just like <u>you</u> didn't tell me about my parent's affair!"

"What?"

"Don't you see? We still keep secrets from each other. How can you get married when we do that? My dad kept one big damn secret from my mom!"

"But that's different."

"Really? Remember when Kail tried to steal me away from you?"

"Yeah, of course."

"If we were married, what would you have done?"

"I don't know. Probably get mad, like I did."

"Yes, with one change. In marriage, not only are you living together, but you have this big secret weapon called divorce, which, by today's standards, is used more often than a middle finger."

"I wouldn't have divorced you."

"Yeah, right, Allen! You didn't speak to me for a whole week! A whole week! And that trip to Watermill? Can you imagine if we were in the same house together, and married? You would have put my stuff outside with the divorce papers!"

Allen walked away. He felt insulted. He sat on a tomb near the wall.

"You see, you're doing it right now!" Xiene yelled.

He got up and returned. "I don't see how you would think we wouldn't work it out!"

"I'm not saying that!" She sat him down and put her arm around him. "All I'm saying is I don't want to live the rest of my life with a middle finger in my back pocket!"

Allen thought. "What about living together?"

"Beverly and Maggie still split up."

"Then. What do you want to do?"

"I want to live! I want to breathe! I want to love!" she yelled.

"You can do all those things, married to me."

"I can also do all those things without being married to you."

"But," Allen held her hand, "What about commitment?"

She put her left hand on her heart and raised the right. "I, Christine Charlotte Richards hereby solemnly swear to have and to hold, for richer, for poorer, for better or worse, you Allen Montgomery."

A warm feeling filled Allen's stomach.

"How's that?"

"Til death do you part?"

"No. I hate that line. It's morbid."

"I guess that's okay."

"Isn't this better than a marriage ceremony?"

"No."

"Why?"

"No church, no organ or bridesmaids, best man, bachelor's party…"

"I think that's what you want—you don't want to get married, you just want to tell the whole world, 'Hey, look what I got' and then throw a party!"

"You know marriage is more than that. What about marriages that do work?"

"Zip-a-dee-doo-dah for that one out of four marriages!

Allen sighed. "I guess. Your parents really scared you off marriage, and Bev and Mag scared you off living together."

"I didn't say I was against living together."

"Yes, you did. You used Bev and Mag as an example."

"I meant that no matter how perfect the couple is, shit is going to happen. And if they were married, they'd be fighting over who gets the house and who gets the Volvo."

Allen leaned against Xiene. She stroked his head. At that moment he realized the sun was coming up. They had been talking all night. "Christ, what time is it?"

"5:45."

"Geez, I spent the night in a cemetery. So much for my college hazing ritual."

"Yep."

Xiene played with Allen's shirt buttons. They listened to the morning traffic and the rustling of leaves.

"God, I've been wanting to tell you about your dad for so long, but I was afraid."

"You can't marry someone you're afraid of."

"What if we had heart plugs, like in *Dune*, so if we screw up you just pull it?"

"Naw, I'd rather just press a button to make your balls explode."

"Ow!" Allen grabbed his crotch.

Xiene giggled. They heard a bird chirping. The wind blew some leaves around the tomb. Allen stared at the candles, now just red, waxy puddles.

"So, if I said, 'Would you move in?' Would you do it?"

"I don't know. Ask me."

Allen kneeled once again.

"Christine Richards, will you move in with me?"

"Oh, gosh, Mr. Montgomery, this is so sudden! I don't know what to do—where's my fan?" She searched around. Allen found it near his knee and handed it to her. She frantically fanned herself like a belle. "Whatever shall I do?"

"Marry him!" Allen said out of the corner of his mouth.

She swatted him on the head. "No. I won't marry him. But will move in with him."

Allen smiled. "Really?

She nodded and smiled.

He stood up and hugged her.

The sun peeked over the wall and shined in Allen's face. He moved his head and kissed her. She moved hers and kissed his neck. Allen got another hard-on. He pulled back. "Oh, no! No more fucking in a cemetery. I do my best work in bed."

"I don't know, you fuck better than anyone else here."

"Oh, ha-ha. Very funny.

Xiene swatted him on the butt. He swatted her back. She hit him again. They got into a butt-swatting fight. He chased her around the tomb. She then started running up an asphalt road, her heels clicking, holding her dress up with both hands.

Allen, far behind, in all black, his black coat flapping behind like a vampire cape. They passed the main office. Seconds later they heard someone go, "Hey! Hey! Hey!"

"What? What? What?" yelled Xiene just when Allen grabbed her around the waist.

"You're not allowed in the cemetery until nine," said the old Black man.

"But we live here," said Xiene.

"What?"

"Yeah, we live here."

"What? Where?"

Xiene started walking towards the man, her hands down in a claw motion. "We live here."

"You said, live where?"

"Here," she said, slowly walking towards him, her face in a spooked scare.

"Who are you?"

"We are the people that live here," said Allen in a deep voice.

The man noticed the red stains all over Allen's shirt and slowly backed into the office.

"We live here," Xiene said, getting closer.

Allen started walking towards the man.

"We are the people…" Xiene said.

"…Who lives here," Allen completed her sentence.

Suddenly, they started saying it together. The man turned around and ran into the office. Xiene and Allen started scraping the door with their claws. Allen looked through the window and saw the guy calling the cops. He patted Xiene.

"He's calling the cops!"

They ran back to their picnic spot and picked up their junk. Allen looked at Mary Dickey's tomb.

"Gee, I didn't get a chance to clean all that red wax off!"

"Forget it!" Xiene yelled. "Gives the guard something to talk about."

They gathered up their trash, and Allen took his hat off the angel statue. He realized when Xiene and he had met, this was the one she had sat on, breaking the arm off as he took her picture. "Hey!" Xiene looked over. "They glued the arms back on."

They could hear a police siren in the distance. “Let’s go!” She yelled.

In Xiene’s pink hearse, they headed towards Midtown and Xiene’s pad. Allen looked over at her. She still had his ring on. He wondered if she should keep it. *After all, she turned down my engagement and probably wasn’t going to wear it anyway.* At a red light, he reached over and rubbed it, to give her a slight hint about the ring. She looked at his hand and then grabbed it. *Oh well, she must think I wanted to hold her hand. Forget it, she’ll at least figure it out when she takes a shower.*

Xiene laughed.

“What’s so funny?”

“I don’t believe you did that.”

“Did what?”

“You actually participated in one of my jokes. I’ve never seen you do that!”

“You see? I’m not so conservative.”

She kissed his cheek. “Living contradiction?”

They drove on and stopped at Krispy Kreme for some doughnuts. Allen waited in the car and thought about all he had learned last night. He looked at Xiene inside the shop. People stared at her in the prom dress. She said something to a vagrant who commented on her appearance. She picked up the doughnuts, walked back over to the vagrant, and gave him a doughnut. Allen heard him speak when Xiene opened the exit.

“I knew you were a princess!” he yelled.

Xiene smiled and got in the car.

“Hey! Princess!”

She shoved a doughnut in Allen’s mouth. Allen took it out.

“One question.”

“What?”

“Do you want to go back to school?”

"Sure, but I can't afford it."

"Hmmm." Allen thought what Xiene's grandmother said about women without an education."

" Would you like to be able to afford it?"

"Sure. We gonna sell crack?"

"No, you silly woman. I was thinking: that Brandon and Monroe were going to get a house together. And right now, I'm sure you aren't in the mood to be around Maggie, considering she forced Beverly out."

"I'm not mad at her, Allen. I mean, she didn't have a choice to make, it's her son!"

"My point is, you're willing to move in with me, right?"

"Correct."

"You have one year left of school why don't you, Brandon, Monroe and me get a house together for about $700 or $800 bucks? Divided among four, you could save enough to go back to school, then, after a year, we will move out and get our own place."

Xiene thought for a minute. "But I can't. I have to work from 8 to 4. That means I would come home, go to sleep, get up, go to school, then go to work. Blech! I wouldn't have any free time to bum around—or eat, for that matter."

"Not if you quit."

Xiene thought again. "But I like my job."

"Yeah, right. You hate your job. All you do is complain about cleaning puke off the bathroom floor."

"Ugh. Yeah, but…"

"But what? Think about it, Xiene. Back in school again you could take the bullshit four-hour job and there would be enough to pay for rent and stuff."

Xiene stopped the car in front of her house. She stared straight ahead, sighed, then pulled her hair back and smiled. "I could go back to school I could take an art class, too! I could finally get my BA! She laughed and looked at Allen. "All alright, I'll do it."

✖

The plan didn't go exactly as scheduled. Brandon didn't like the idea of living with Xiene, probably because she was twice as messy as Allen, and had a drum set. So Xiene and Allen decided to move in with Monroe in his two-bedroom apartment. Allen and Xiene both had to get rid of some of their stuff to fit in the second bedroom. Allen trashed his ugly bookshelf made of milk crates. Xiene got rid of her glass-top coffee table that Allen would ram his shin into on his way to the bathroom in the dark, every single time. Xiene won the bed challenge—although Allen's twin was comfortable, Xiene's queen-size was a better fit for different sexual positions.

One Saturday morning, Xiene brought the last load over in her hearse. Monroe and Allen sat on the apartment stoop awaiting her arrival.

"Xiene find another job yet?" Monroe asked.

"No. She's still looking, though. God, I can't believe we're moving in together. Oh well, it's the next best thing to marriage."

"And with Xiene, you already have a teenage delinquent son."

Allen smirked.

Monroe smiled, then pointed.

"Hark! Hope approaches—Dame Xiene!"

She pulled around the corner and stopped. Monroe and Allen walked over to get the rocking chair and rollup desk. Xiene bent over, reaching for her car keys. To Allen, her black spandex top and pants, and even her Brave's baseball cap made her beautiful. He grabbed her butt.

She quickly stood up. "Oh, god! I thought that was Monroe!"

"Yeah, right! No chance of that," Monroe said carrying a rocking chair.

"Gee, thanks, Monroe!" She complained

"Don't mention it!"

“Hey, I still think you’re a babe,” Allen said. “Even if you do wear yuppie-asshole glasses.” He took off her Wayfarers. “That’s better.” He looked at the purple dye in her hair. “Hmmm, I like it.”

They kissed.

"It’s my new hairstyle for our new life together.”

Xiene put her hand on Allen’s cheek. He felt the coldness of the ring, still on her finger.

END OF BOOK ONE!

ABOUT THE AUTHOR!

Alexander G. J. grew up in Charlotte, North Carolina. He moved to Atlanta, Georgia to study commercial art, then to San Francisco, California, to bolster his writing and fine arts skills. He currently lives in Richmond, California.

Novels by Alexander G. J.

Mary & I: The Real Story of Miss Mary Mack
Mary & I: Black Blood
Mary & I: The First Witch (coming 2025)
Flaming Jackass: Sex, Drugs, and Pizza
Flaming Jackass: In Love
Flaming Jackass: Returns
Flaming Jackass: O.M.F.G. (coming 2026)
Why Did The Chicken Cross the Universe?
XIENE!
Life with XIENE! (Coming 2026)

Instagram: rabbookspublishing
Facebook: facebook.com/rabbitstudiosbigpush
Author's page: amazon.com/author/alexanderg.j
TikTok:@ alexscafe

www.ingramcontent.com/pod-product-compliance
Lightning Source LLC
Chambersburg PA
CBHW020648120726
47906CB00001B/171

* 9 7 8 0 9 9 8 2 4 7 4 5 8 *